Tales from
Beyond the
Grave

Tales from Beyond the Grave

Octopus Books Limited

First published 1982 by

Octopus Books Limited
59 Grosvenor Street
London W1

Illustrated by Lawrence Mynott

Copyright © 1982 selection, arrangement and illustrations

Octopus Books Limited

ISBN 0 7064 1798 4

Printed in Czechoslovakia

50 437

Contents

I could a tale unfold whose lightest word
Would harrow up thy soul, freeze thy young blood,
Make thy two eyes like stars start from their spheres,
Thy knotted and combinéd locks to part,
And each particular hair to stand on end,
Like quills upon the fretful porcupine.

Shakespeare: **Hamlet** I v 15–20

The Shout
ROBERT GRAVES

WHEN WE ARRIVED with our bags at the Asylum cricket ground, the chief medical officer, whom I had met at the house where I was staying, came up to shake hands. I told him that I was only scoring for the Lampton team today (I had broken a finger the week before, keeping wicket on a bumpy pitch). He said: 'Oh, then you'll have an interesting companion.'

'The other scoresman?' I asked.

'Crossley is the most intelligent man in the asylum,' answered the doctor, ' a wide reader, a first-class chess-player, and so on. He seems to have travelled all over the world. He's been sent here for delusions. His most serious delusion is that he's a murderer, and his story is that he killed two men and a woman at Sydney, Australia. The other delusion, which is more humorous, is that his soul is split in pieces – whatever that means. He edits our monthly magazine, he stage manages our Christmas theatricals, and he gave a most original conjuring performance the other day. You'll like him.'

He introduced me. Crossley, a big man of forty or fifty, had a queer, not unpleasant, face. But I felt a little uncomfortable, sitting next to him in the scoring box, his black-whiskered hands so close to mine. I had no fear of physical violence, only the sense of being in the presence of a man of unusual force, even perhaps, it somehow came to me, of occult powers.

It was hot in the scoring box in spite of the wide window. 'Thunderstorm weather,' said Crossley, who spoke in what country people call a 'college voice', though I could not identify the college. 'Thunderstorm weather makes us patients behave even more irregularly than usual.'

I asked whether any patients were playing.

'Two of them, this first wicket partnership. The tall one, B. C. Brown, played for Hants three years ago, and the other is a good player. Pat

Slingsby usually turns out for us too – the Australian fast bowler, you know – but we are dropping him today. In weather like this he is apt to bowl at the batsman's head. He is not insane in the usual sense, merely magnificently ill-tempered. The doctors can do nothing with him. He wants shooting really.' Crossley began talking about the doctor. 'A good-hearted fellow and, for a mental-hospital physician, technically well advanced. He actually studies morbid psychology and is fairly well-read, up to about the day before yesterday. I have a good deal of fun with him. He reads neither German nor French, so I keep a stage or two ahead in psychological fashions; he has to wait for the English translations. I invent significant dreams for him to interpret; I find he likes me to put in snakes and apple pies, so I usually do. He is convinced that my mental trouble is due to the good old "antipaternal fixation" – I wish it were as simple as that.'

Then Crossley asked me whether I could score and listen to a story at the same time. I said that I could. It was slow cricket.

'My story is true,' he said, 'every word of it. Or, when I say that my story is "true", I mean at least that I am telling it in a new way. It is always the same story, but I sometimes vary the climax and even recast the characters. Variation keeps it fresh and therefore true. If I were always to use the same formula, it would drag and become false. I am interested in keeping it alive, and it is a true story, every word of it. I know the people in it personally. They are Lampton people.'

We decided that I should keep score of the runs and extras and that he should keep the bowling analysis, and at the fall of every wicket we should copy from each other. This made story-telling possible.

Richard awoke one morning saying to Rachel: 'But what an unusual dream.'

'Tell me, my dear,' she said, 'and hurry, because I want to tell you mine.'

'I was having a conversation,' he said, 'with a person (or persons, because he changed his appearance so often) of great intelligence, and I can clearly remember the argument. Yet this is the first time I have ever been able to remember any argument that came to me in sleep. Usually my dreams are so different from waking that I can only describe them if I say: "It is as though I were living and thinking as a tree, or a bell, or middle C, or a five-pound note; as though I had never been human." Life there is sometimes rich for me and sometimes poor, but I repeat, in every case so different, that if I were to say: "I had a conversation," or "I was in love," or "I hear music," or "I was angry," it would be as far from the fact as if I tried to explain a problem of philosophy, as Rabelais's Panurge did to Thaumast, merely by grimacing with my eyes and lips.'

'It is much the same with me,' she said. 'I think that when I am asleep I become, perhaps, a stone with all the natural appetites and convictions of a stone. "Senseless as a stone" is a proverb, but there may be more sense in a stone, more sensibility, more sensitivity, more sentiment, more sensibleness, than in many men and women. And no less sensuality,' she added thoughtfully.

It was Sunday morning, so that they could lie in bed, their arms about each other, without troubling about the time; and they were childless, so breakfast could wait. He told her that in his dream he was walking in the sand hills with this person or persons, who said to him: 'These sand hills are a part neither of the sea before us nor of the grass links behind us, and are not related to the mountains beyond the links. They are of themselves. A man walking on the sand hills soon knows this by the tang of the air, and if he were to refrain from eating and drinking, from sleeping and speaking, from thinking and desiring, he could continue among them for ever without change. There is no life and no death in the sand hills. Anything might happen in the sand hills.'

Rachel said that this was nonsense, and asked: 'But what was the argument? Hurry up!'

He said it was about the whereabouts of the soul, but that now she had put it out of his head by hurrying him. All that he remembered was that the man was first a Japanese, then an Italian, and finally a kangaroo.

In return she eagerly told her dream, gabbling over the words. 'I was walking in the sand hills; there were rabbits there, too; how does that tally with what he said of life and death? I saw the man and you walking arm in arm towards me, and I ran from you both and I noticed that he had a black silk handkerchief; he ran after me and my shoe buckle came off and I could not wait to pick it up. I left it lying, and he stooped and put it in his pocket.'

'How do you know that it was the same man?' he asked.

'Because,' she said, laughing, 'he had a black face and wore a blue coat like that picture of Captain Cook. And because it was in the sand hills.'

He said, kissing her neck: 'We not only live together and talk together and sleep together, but it seems we now even dream together.'

So they laughed.

Then he got up and brought her breakfast.

At about half past eleven, she said: 'Go out now for a walk, my dear, and bring home something for me to think about: and be back in time for dinner at one o'clock.'

It was a hot morning in the middle of May, and he went out through the wood and struck the coast road, which after half a mile led into Lampton.

('Do you know Lampton well?' asked Crossley. 'No,' I said, 'I am only here for the holidays, staying with friends.')

He went a hundred yards along the coast road, but then turned off and went across the links, thinking of Rachel and watching the blue butterflies and looking at the heath roses and thyme, and thinking of her again, and how strange it was that they could be so near to each other; then taking a pinch of gorse flower and smelling it, and considering the smell and thinking, 'If she should die, what would become of me?' and taking a slate from the low wall and skimming it across the pond and thinking, 'I am a clumsy fellow to be her husband'; and walking towards the sand hills, and then edging away again, perhaps half in fear of meeting the person of their dream, and at last making a half circle towards the old church beyond Lampton, at the foot of the mountain.

The morning service was over and the people were out by the cromlechs behind the church, walking in twos and threes, as the custom was, on the smooth turf. The squire was talking in a loud voice about King Charles the Martyr: 'A great man, a very great man, but betrayed by those he loved best,' and the doctor was arguing about organ music with the rector. There was a group of children playing ball. 'Throw it here, Elsie! No, to me, Elsie, Elsie, Elsie!' Then the rector appeared and pocketed the ball and said that it was Sunday; they should have remembered. When he was gone they made faces after him.

Presently a stranger came up and asked permission to sit down beside Richard; they began to talk. The stranger had been to the church service and wished to discuss the sermon. The text had been the immortality of the soul: the last of a series of sermons that had begun at Easter. He said that he could not grant the preacher's premiss that *the soul is continually resident in the body*. Why should this be so? What duty did the soul perform in the daily routine task of the body? The soul was neither the brain, nor the lungs, nor the stomach, nor the heart, nor the mind, nor the imagination. Surely it was a thing apart? Was it not indeed less likely to be resident in the body than outside the body? He had no proof one way or the other, but he would say: Birth and death are so odd a mystery that the principle of life may well lie outside the body which is the visible evidence of living. 'We cannot,' he said, 'even tell to a nicety what are the moments of birth and death. Why, in Japan, where I have travelled, they reckon a man already one year old when he is born; and lately in Italy a dead man – but come and walk on the sand hills and let me tell you my conclusions. I find it easier to talk when I am walking.'

Richard was frightened to hear this, and to see the man wipe his forehead with a black silk handkerchief. He stuttered out something. At this moment the children, who had crept up behind the cromlech, suddenly, at an agreed signal, shouted loud in the ears of the two men; and stood laughing. The stranger was startled into anger; he opened his mouth as if he were about to curse them, and bared his teeth to the gums. Three of the children screamed and ran off. But the one whom they called Elsie fell down in her fright and lay sobbing. The doctor, who was near, tried to comfort her. 'He has a face like a devil,' they heard the child say.

The stranger smiled good-naturedly: 'And a devil I was not so very long ago. That was in Northern Australia, where I lived with the black fellows for twenty years. "Devil" is the nearest English word for the position that they gave me in their tribe; and they also gave me an eighteenth-century British naval uniform to wear as my ceremonial dress. Come and walk with me in the sand hills and let me tell you the whole story. I have a passion for walking in the sand hills: that is why I came to this town . . . My name is Charles.'

Richard said: 'Thank you, but I must hurry home to my dinner.'

'Nonsense,' said Charles, 'dinnèr can wait. Or, if you wish, I can come to dinner with you. By the way, I have had nothing to eat since Friday. I am without money.'

Richard felt uneasy. He was afraid of Charles, and did not wish to bring him home to dinner because of the dream and the sand hills and the handkerchief: yet on the other hand the man was intelligent and quiet and decently dressed and had eaten nothing since Friday; if Rachel knew that he had refused him a meal, she would renew her taunts. When Rachel was out of sorts, her favourite complaint was that he was over-careful about money; though when she was at peace with him, she owned that he was the most generous man she knew, and that she did not mean what she said; when she was angry with him again, out came the taunt of stinginess: 'Tenpence-halfpenny,' she would say, 'tenpence-halfpenny and threepence of that in stamps'; his ears would burn and he would want to hit her. So he said now: 'By all means come along to dinner, but that little girl is still sobbing for fear of you. You ought to do something about it.'

Charles beckoned her to him and said a single soft word; it was an Australian magic word, he afterwards told Richard, meaning *Milk*: immediately Elsie was comforted and came to sit on Charles' knee and played with the buttons of his waistcoat for awhile until Charles sent her away.

'You have strange powers, Mr. Charles,' Richard said.

Charles answered: 'I am fond of children, but the shout startled me; I am pleased that I did not do what, for a moment I was tempted to do.'

'What was that?' asked Richard.

'I might have shouted myself,' said Charles.

'Why,' said Richard, 'they would have liked that better. It would have been a great game for them. They probably expected it of you.'

'If I had shouted,' said Charles, 'my shout would have either killed them outright or sent them mad. Probably it would have killed them, for they were standing close.'

Richard smiled a little foolishly. He did not know whether or not he was expected to laugh, for Charles spoke so gravely and carefully. So he said: 'Indeed, what sort of shout would that be? Let me hear you shout.'

'It is not only children who would be hurt by my shout,' Charles said. 'Men can be sent raving mad by it; the strongest, even, would be flung

15

to the ground. It is a magic shout that I learned from the chief devil of the Northern Territory. I took eighteen years to perfect it, and yet I have used it, in all, no more than five times.'

Richard was so confused in his mind with the dream and the handkerchief and the word spoken to Elsie that he did not know what to say, so he muttered: 'I'll give you fifty pounds now to clear the cromlechs with a shout.'

'I see that you do not believe me,' Charles said. 'Perhaps you have never before heard of the terror shout?'

Richard considered and said: 'Well, I have read of the hero shout which the ancient Irish warriors used, that would drive armies backwards; and did not Hector, the Trojan, have a terrible shout? And there were sudden shouts in the woods of Greece. They were ascribed to the god Pan and would infect men with a madness of fear; from this legend indeed the word "panic" has come into the English language. And I remember another shout in the *Mabinogion*, in the story of Lludd and Llevelys. It was a shriek that was heard on every May Eve and went through all hearts and so scared them that the men lost their hue and their strength and the women their children, and the youths and maidens their senses, and the animals and trees, the earth and the waters were left barren. But it was caused by a dragon.'

'It must have been a British magician of the dragon clan,' said Charles. 'I belonged to the Kangaroos. Yes, that tallies. The effect is not exactly given, but near enough."

They reached the house at one o'clock, and Rachel was at the door, the dinner ready. 'Rachel,' said Richard, 'here is Mr. Charles to dinner; Mr. Charles is a great traveller.'

Rachel passed her hand over her eyes as if to dispel a cloud, but it may have been the sudden sunlight. Charles took her hand and kissed it, which surprised her. Rachel was graceful, small, with eyes unusually blue for the blackness of her hair, delicate in her movements, and with a voice rather low-pitched; she had a freakish sense of humour.

('You would like Rachel,' said Crossley, 'she visits me here sometimes.')

Of Charles it would be difficult to say one thing or another: he was of middle age, and tall; his hair grey; his face never still for a moment; his eyes large and bright, sometimes yellow, sometimes brown, sometimes grey; his voice changed its tone and accent with the subject; his hands were brown and hairy at the back, his nails well cared for. Of Richard it is enough to say that he was a musician, not a strong man but a lucky one. Luck was his strength.

After dinner Charles and Richard washed the dishes together, and Richard suddenly asked Charles if he would let him hear the shout: for he thought that he could not have peace of mind until he had heard it. So horrible a thing was, surely, worse to think about than to hear: for now he believed in the shout.

Charles stopped washing up; mop in hand. 'As you wish,' said he, 'but I have warned you what a shout it is. And if I shout it must be in a lonely place where nobody else can hear; and I shall not shout in the second degree, the degree which kills certainly, but in the first, which terrifies only, and when you want me to stop put your hands to your ears.'

'Agreed,' said Richard.

'I have never yet shouted to satisfy an idle curiosity,' said Charles, 'but only when in danger of my life from enemies, black or white, and once when I was alone in the desert without food or drink. Then I was forced to shout, for food.'

Richard thought: 'Well, at least I am a lucky man, and my luck will be good enough even for this.'

'I am not afraid,' he told Charles.

'We will walk out on the sand hills tomorrow early,' Charles said, 'when nobody is stirring; and I will shout. You say you are not afraid.'

But Richard was very much afraid, and what made his fear worse was that somehow he could not talk to Rachel and tell her of it: he knew that if he told her she would either forbid him to go or she would come with him. If she forbade him to go, the fear of the shout and the sense of cowardice would hang over him ever afterwards, but if she came with him, either the shout would be nothing and she would have a new taunt for his credulity and Charles would laugh with her, or if it were something, she might well be driven mad. So he said nothing.

Charles was invited to sleep at the cottage for the night, and they stayed up late talking.

Rachel told Richard when they were in bed that she liked Charles and that he certainly was a man who had seen many things, though a fool and a big baby. Then Rachel talked a great deal of nonsense, for she had had two glasses of wine, which she seldom drank, and she said: 'Oh my dearest, I forgot to tell you. When I put on my buckled shoes this morning while you were away I found a buckle missing. I must have noticed that it was lost before I went to sleep last night and yet not fixed the loss firmly in my mind, so that it came out as a discovery in my dream; but I have a feeling, in fact I am certain, that Mr Charles has the buckle in his pocket; and I am sure that he is the man whom we met in our dream. But I don't care, not I.'

Richard grew more and more afraid; and he dared not tell of the black silk handkerchief, or of Charles' invitations to him to walk in the sand hills. And what was worse, Charles had used only a white handkerchief while he was in the house, so that he could not be sure whether he had seen it after all. Turning his head away, he said lamely: 'Well, Charles knows a lot of things. I am going for a walk with him early tomorrow if you don't mind; an early walk is what I need.'

'Oh, I'll come too,' she said.

Richard could not think how to refuse her; he knew that he had made a mistake in telling her of the walk. But he said: 'Charles will be very glad. At six o'clock then.'

At six o'clock he got up, but Rachel after the wine was too sleepy to come with them. She kissed him goodbye and off he went with Charles.

Richard had had a bad night. In his dreams nothing was in human terms, but confused and fearful, and he had felt himself more distant from Rachel than he had ever felt since their marriage, and the fear of the shout was gnawing at him. He was also hungry and cold. There was a stiff wind blowing towards the sea from the mountains and a few splashes of rain. Charles spoke hardly a word, but chewed a stalk of grass and walked fast.

Richard felt giddy, and said to Charles: 'Wait a moment, I have a stitch in my side.' So they stopped, and Richard asked, gasping: 'What sort of shout is it? Is it loud, or shrill? How is it produced? How can it madden a man?'

Charles was silent, so Richard went on with a foolish smile: 'Sound, though, is a curious thing. I remember once, when I was at Cambridge, that a King's College man had his turn of reading the evening lesson. He had not spoken ten words before there was a groaning and ringing and creaking, and pieces of wood and dust fell from the roof; for his voice was exactly attuned to that of the building, so that he had to stop, else the roof might have fallen; as you can break a wine glass by playing its note on a violin.'

Charles consented to answer: 'My shout is not a matter of tone or vibration but something not to be explained. It is a shout of pure evil, and there is no fixed place for it on the scale. It may take any note. It is pure terror, and if it were not for a certain intention of mine, which I need not tell you, I would refuse to shout for you.'

Richard had a great gift of fear, and this new account of the shout disturbed him more and more; he wished himself at home in bed, and Charles two continents away. But he was fascinated. They were crossing the links now and going through the bent grass that pricked through his stockings and soaked them.

Now they were on the bare sand hills. From the highest of them Charles looked about him; he could see the beach stretched out for two miles and more. There was no one in sight. Then Richard saw Charles take something out of his pocket and begin carelessly to juggle with it as he stood, tossing it from finger tip to finger tip and spinning it up with finger and thumb to catch it on the back of his hand. It was Rachel's buckle.

Richard's breath came in gasps, his heart beat violently and he nearly vomited. He was shivering with cold, and yet sweating. Soon they came to an open place among the sand hills near the sea. There was a raised bank with sea holly growing on it and a little sickly grass; stones were strewn all around, brought there, it seemed, by the sea years before. Though the place lay behind the first rampart of sand hills, there was a gap in the line through which a a high tide might have broken, and the winds that continually swept through the gap kept them uncovered of sand. Richard had his hands in his trouser pockets for warmth and was nervously twisting a soft piece of wax around his right forefinger – a candle end that was in his pocket from the night before when he had gone downstairs to lock the door.

'Are you ready?' asked Charles.

Richard nodded.

A gull dipped over the crest of the sand hills and rose again screaming when it saw them. 'Stand by the sea holly,' said Richard, with a dry mouth, 'and I'll be here among the stones, not too near. When I raise my hand, shout! When I put my fingers to my ears, stop at once.'

So Charles walked twenty steps towards the holly. Richard saw his broad back and black silk handkerchief sticking from his pocket. He remembered the dream, and the shoe buckle and Elsie's fear. His resolution broke: he hurriedly pulled the piece of wax in two, and sealed his ears. Charles did not see him.

He turned, and Richard gave the signal with his hand.

Charles leaned forward oddly, his chin thrust out, his teeth bared, and never before had Richard seen such a look of fear on a man's face. He had not been prepared for that. Charles' face, that was usually soft and changing, uncertain as a cloud, now hardened to a rough stone mask, dead white at first, and then flushing outwards from the cheek bones red and redder, and at last as black, as if he were about to choke. His mouth then slowly opened to the full, and Richard fell on his face, his hands to his ears, in a faint.

When he came to himself he was lying alone among the stones. He sat up, wondering numbly whether he had been there long. He felt very weak and sick, with a chill on his heart that was worse than the chill of his body. He could not think. He put his hand down to lift himself up and it rested on a stone, a larger one than most of the others. He picked it up and felt its surface, absently. His mind wandered. He began to think about shoemaking, a trade of which he had known nothing, but now every trick was familiar to him. 'I must be a shoemaker,' he said aloud.

Then he corrected himself: 'No, I am a musician. Am I going mad?' He threw the stone from him; it struck against another and bounced off.

He asked himself: 'Now why did I say that I was a shoemaker? It seemed a moment ago that I knew all there was to be known about shoemaking and now I know nothing at all about it. I must get home to Rachel. Why did I ever come out?'

Then he saw Charles on a sand hill a hundred yards away, gazing out to sea. He remembered his fear and made sure that the wax was in his ears: he stumbled to his feet. He saw a flurry on the sand and there was a rabbit lying on its side, twitching in a convulsion. As Richard moved towards it, the flurry ended: the rabbit was dead. Richard crept behind a sand hill out of Charles' sight and then struck homeward, running awkwardly in the soft sand. He had not gone twenty paces before he came upon the gull. It was standing stupidly on the sand and did not rise at his approach, but fell over dead.

How Richard reached home he did not know, but there he was opening the back door and crawling upstairs on his hands and knees. He unsealed his ears.

Rachel was sitting up in bed, pale and trembling. 'Thank God you're back,' she said. 'I have had a nightmare, the worst of all my life. It was frightful. I was in my dream, in the deepest dream of all, like the one of which I told you. I was like a stone, and I was aware of you near me; you were you, quite plain, though I was a stone, and you were in great fear and I could do nothing to help you, and you were waiting for something and the terrible thing did not happen to you, but it happened to me. I can't tell you what it was, but it was as though all my nerves cried out in pain at once, and I was pierced through and through with a beam of some intense evil light and twisted inside out. I woke up and my heart was beating so fast that I had to gasp for breath. Do you think I had a heart attack and my heart missed a beat? They say it feels like that. Where have you been, dearest? Where is Mr. Charles?'

Richard sat on the bed and held her hand. 'I have had a bad experience too,' he said. 'I was out with Charles by the sea and as he went ahead to climb on the highest sand hill I felt very faint and fell down among a patch of stones, and when I came to myself I was in a desperate sweat of fear and had to hurry home. So I came back running alone. It happened perhaps half an hour ago,' he said.

He did not tell her more. He asked, could he come back to bed and would she get breakfast? That was a thing she had not done all the years they were married.

'I am as ill as you,' said she. It was understood between them always that when Rachel was ill, Richard must be well.

'You are not,' said he, and fainted again.

She helped him to bed ungraciously and dressed herself and went slowly downstairs. A smell of coffee and bacon rose to meet her and there was Charles, who had lit the fire, putting two breakfasts on a tray. She was so relieved at not having to get breakfast and so confused by her experience that she thanked him and called him a darling, and he kissed her hand gravely and pressed it. He had made the breakfast exactly to her liking: the coffee was strong and the eggs fried on both sides.

Rachel fell in love with Charles. She had often fallen in love with men before and since her marriage, but it was her habit to tell Richard when this happened, as he agreed to tell her when it happened to him: so that the suffocation of passion was given a vent and there was no jealousy, for she used to say (and he had the liberty of saying) 'Yes, I am *in love* with so-and-so, but I only *love* you.'

That was as far as it had ever gone. But this was different. Somehow, she did not know why, she could not own to being in love with Charles: for she no longer loved Richard. She hated him for being ill, and said that he was lazy, and a sham. So about noon he got up, but went groaning around the bedroom until she sent him back to bed to groan.

Charles helped her with the housework, doing all the cooking, but he did not go up to see Richard, since he had not been asked to do so. Rachel was ashamed, and apologized to Charles for Richard's rudeness in running away from him. But Charles said mildly that he took it as no insult; he had felt queer himself that morning; it was as though something evil was astir in the air as they reached the sand hills. She told him that she too had had the same queer feeling.

Later she found all Lampton talking of it. The doctor maintained that it was an earth tremor, but the country people said that it had been the Devil passing by. He had come to fetch the black soul of Solomon Jones, the gamekeeper, found dead that morning in his cottage by the sand hills.

When Richard could go downstairs and walk about a little without groaning, Rachel sent him to the cobbler's to get a new buckle for her shoe. She came with him to the bottom of the garden. The path ran beside a steep bank. Richard looked ill and groaned slightly as he walked, so Rachel, half in anger, half in fun, pushed him down the bank, where he fell sprawling among the nettles and old iron. Then she ran back into the house laughing loudly.

Richard sighed, tried to share the joke against himself with Rachel – but she had gone – heaved himself up, picked the shoes from among the nettles, and after a while walked slowly up the bank, out of the gate, and down the lane in the unaccustomed glare of the sun.

When he reached the cobbler's he sat down heavily. The cobbler was glad to talk to him. 'You are looking bad,' said the cobbler.

Richard said: 'Yes, on Friday morning I had a bit of a turn; I am only now recovering from it.'

'Good God,' burst out the cobbler, 'if you had a bit of a turn, what did I not have? It was as if someone handled me raw, without my skin. It was as if someone seized my very soul and juggled with it, as you might juggle with a stone, and hurled me away. I shall never forget last Friday morning.'

A strange notion came to Richard that it was the cobbler's soul which he had handled in the form of a stone. 'It may be,' he thought, 'that the souls of every man and woman and child in Lampton are lying there.' But he said nothing about this, asked for a buckle, and went home.

Rachel was ready with a kiss and a joke; he might have kept silent, for his silence always made Rachel ashamed. 'But,' he thought, 'why

21

make her ashamed? From shame she goes to self-justification and picks a quarrel over something else and it's ten times worse. I'll be cheerful and accept the joke.'

He was unhappy. And Charles was established in the house: gentle-voiced, hard-working, and continually taking Richard's part against Rachel's scoffing. This was galling, because Rachel did not resent it.

('The next part of the story,' said Crossley, 'is the comic relief, an account of how Richard went again to the sand hills, to the heap of stones, and identified the souls of the doctor and rector – the doctor's because it was shaped like a whiskey bottle and the rector's because it was as black as original sin – and how he proved to himself that the notion was not fanciful. But I will skip that and come to the point where Rachel two days later suddenly became affectionate and loved Richard, she said, more than ever before.')

The reason was that Charles had gone away, nobody knows where, and had relaxed the buckle magic for the time, because he was confident that he could renew it on his return. So in a day or two Richard was well again and everything was as it had been, until one afternoon the door opened, and there stood Charles.

He entered without a word of greeting and hung his hat upon a peg. He sat down by the fire and asked: 'When is supper ready?'

Richard looked at Rachel, his eyebrows raised, but Rachel seemed fascinated by the man.

She answered: 'Eight o'clock,' in her low voice, and stooping down drew off Charles' muddy boots and found him a pair of Richard's slippers.

Charles said: 'Good. It is now seven o'clock. In another hour, supper. At nine o'clock the boy will bring the evening paper. At ten o'clock, Rachel, you and I sleep together.'

Richard thought that Charles must have gone suddenly mad. But Rachel answered quietly: 'Why, of course, my dear.' Then she turned viciously to Richard: 'And you run away, little man!' she said, and slapped his cheek with all her strength.

Richard stood puzzled, nursing his cheek. Since he could not believe that Rachel and Charles had both gone mad together, he must be mad himself. At all events, Rachel knew her mind, and they had a secret compact that if either of them ever wished to break the marriage promise, the other should not stand in the way. They had made this compact because they wished to feel themselves bound by love rather than by ceremony. So he said as calmly as he could: 'Very well, Rachel. I shall leave you two together.'

Charles flung a boot at him, saying: 'If you put your nose inside the door between now and breakfast time, I'll shout the ears off your head.'

Richard went out this time not afraid, but cold inside and quite clear-headed. He went through the gate, down the lane, and across the links. It wanted three hours yet until sunset. He joked with the boys playing stump cricket on the school field. He skimmed stones. He thought of Rachel and tears started to his eyes. Then he sang to comfort himself. 'Oh, I'm certainly mad,' he said, 'and what in the world has happened to my luck?'

At last he came to the stones. 'Now,' he said, 'I shall find my soul in this heap and I shall crack it into a hundred pieces with this hammer – he had picked up the hammer in the coal shed as he came out.

Then he began looking for his soul. Now, one may recognize the soul of another man or woman, but one can never recognize one's own. Richard could not find his. But by chance he came upon Rachel's soul and recognized it (a slim green stone with glints of quartz in it) because she was estranged from him at the time. Against it lay another stone, an ugly misshapen flint of a mottled brown. He swore: 'I'll destroy this. It must be the soul of Charles.'

He kissed the soul of Rachel; it was like kissing her lips. Then he took the soul of Charles and poised his hammer. 'I'll knock you into fifty fragments!'

He paused. Richard had scruples. He knew that Rachel loved Charles better than himself, and he was bound to respect the compact. A third stone (his own, it must be) was lying the other side of Charles' stone; it was of smooth grey granite, about the size of a cricket ball. He said to himself: 'I will break my own soul in pieces and that will be the end of me.' The world grew black, his eyes ceased to focus, and he all but fainted. But he recovered himself, and with a great cry brought down the coal hammer crack, and crack again, on the grey stone.

It split in four pieces, exuding a smell like gunpowder: and when Richard found that he was still alive and whole, he began to laugh and laugh. Oh, he was mad, quite mad! He flung the hammer away, lay down exhausted, and fell asleep.

He awoke as the sun was setting. He went home in confusion, thinking: 'This is a very bad dream and Rachel will help me out of it.'

When he came to the edge of the town he found a group of men talking excitedly under a lamppost. One said: 'About eight o'clock it happened, didn't it?' The other said: 'Yes.' A third said: 'Ay, mad as a hatter. "Touch me," he says, "and I'll shout. I'll shout you into a fit, the whole blasted police force of you. I'll shout you mad." And the inspector says: "Now, Crossley, put your hands up, we've got you cornered at last." "One last chance," says he. "Go and leave me or I'll shout you stiff and dead." '

Richard had stopped to listen. 'And what happened to Crossley then?' he said. 'And what did the woman say?'

' "For Christ's sake," she said to the inspector, "go away or he'll kill you." '

'And did he shout?'

'He didn't shout. He screwed up his face for a moment and drew in his breath. A'mighty, I've never seen such a ghastly looking face in my life. I had to take three or four brandies afterwards. And the inspector he drops the revolver and it goes off; but nobody hit. Then suddenly a change comes over this man Crossley. He claps his hands to his side and again to his heart, and his face goes smooth and dead again. Then he begins to laugh and dance and cut capers. And the woman stares and can't believe her eyes and the police lead him off. If he was mad before, he was just harmless dotty now; and they had no trouble with him. He's been taken off in the ambulance to the Royal West County Asylum.'

So Richard went home to Rachel and told her everything and she told him everything, though there was not much to tell. She had not fallen in love with Charles, she said; she was only teasing Richard and she had never said anything or heard Charles say anything in the least like what he told her; it was part of his dream. She loved him always and only him, for all his faults; which she went through – his stinginess, his talkativeness, his untidiness. Charles and she had eaten a quiet supper, and she did think it had been bad of Richard to rush off without a word of explanation, and stay away for three hours like that. Charles might have murdered her. He did start pulling her about a bit, in fun, wanting her to dance with him, and then a knock came on the door, and the inspector shouted: 'Walter Charles Crossley, in the name of the King, I arrest you for the murder of George Grant, Harry Grant, and Ada Coleman at Sydney, Australia'. Then Charles had gone absolutely mad. He had pulled out a shoe buckle and said to it: 'Hold her for me.' And then he told the police to go away or he'd shout them dead. After that he made a dreadful face at them and went to pieces altogether. 'He was rather a nice man; I liked his face so much and feel so sorry for him.'

'Did you like that story?' asked Crossley.

'Yes,' said I, busy scoring, 'a Milesian tale of the best. Lucius Apuleius, I congratulate you.'

Crossley turned to me with a troubled face and hands clenched trembling. 'Every word of it is true,' he said. 'Crossley's soul was cracked in four pieces and I'm a madman. Oh, I don't blame Richard and Rachel. They are a pleasant, loving pair of fools and I've never wished them harm; they often visit me here. In any case, now that my soul lies broken in pieces, my powers are gone. Only one thing remains to me,' he said, 'and that is the shout.'

I had been so busy scoring and listening to the story at the same time that I had not noticed the immense bank of black cloud that swam up until it spread across the sun and darkened the whole sky. Warm drops of rain fell: a flash of lightning dazzled us and with it came a smashing clap of thunder.

In a moment all was confusion. Down came a drenching rain, the cricketers dashed for cover, the lunatics began to scream, bellow, and fight. One tall young man, the same B. C. Brown who had once played for Hants, pulled all his clothes off and ran about stark naked. Outside the scoring box an old man with a beard began to pray to the thunder: 'Bah! Bah! Bah!'

Crossley's eyes twitched proudly. 'Yes,' said he, pointing to the sky, 'that's the sort of shout it is; that's the effect it has; but I can do better than that.' Then his face fell suddenly and he became childishly unhappy and anxious. 'Oh dear God,' he said, 'he'll shout at me again, Crossley will. He'll freeze my marrow.'

The rain was rattling on the tin roof so that I could hardly hear him. Another flash, another clap of thunder even louder than the first. 'But that's only the second degree,' he shouted in my ear; 'it's the first that kills.'

'Oh,' he said. 'Don't you understand?' He smiled foolishly. 'I'm Richard now, and Crossley will kill me.'

The naked man was running about brandishing a cricket stump in either hand and screaming: an ugly sight. 'Bah! Bah! Bah!' prayed the old man, the rain spouting down his back from his uptilted hat.

'Nonsense,' said I, 'be a man, remember you're Crossley. You're a match for a dozen Richards. You played a game and lost because Richard had the luck; but you still have the shout.'

I was feeling rather mad myself. Then the Asylum doctor rushed into the scoring box, his flannels streaming wet, still wearing pads and batting gloves, his glasses gone; he had heard voices raised, and tore Crossley's hands from mine. 'To your dormitory at once, Crossley!' he ordered.

'I'll not go,' said Crossley, proud again, 'you miserable Snake and Apple Pie Man!'

The doctor seized him by his coat and tried to hustle him out.

Crossley flung him off, his eyes blazing with madness. 'Get out,' he said, 'and leave me alone here or I'll shout. Do you hear? I'll shout. I'll kill the whole damn lot of you. I'll shout the Asylum down. I'll wither the grass. I'll shout.' His face was distorted in terror. A red spot appeared on either cheekbone and spread over his face.

I put my fingers to my ears and ran out of the scoring box. I had run perhaps twenty yards, when an indescribable pang of fire spun me about and left me dazed and numbed. I escaped death somehow; I suppose that I am lucky, like the Richard of the story. But the lightning struck Crossley and the Doctor dead.

Crossley's body was found rigid, the doctor's was crouched in a corner, his hands to his ears. Nobody could understand this because death had been instantaneous, and the doctor was not a man to stop his ears against thunder.

It makes a rather unsatisfactory end to the story to state that Rachel and Richard were the friends with whom I was staying – Crossley had described them most accurately – but that when I told them that a man called Charles Crossley had been struck at the same time as their friend the doctor, they seemed to take Crossley's death casually by comparison with his. Richard looked blank; Rachel said: 'Crossley? I think that was the man who called himself the Australian Illusionist and gave that wonderful conjuring show the other day. He had practically no apparatus but a black silk handkerchief. I liked his face so much. Oh, and Richard didn't like it at all.'

'No, I couldn't stand the way he looked at you all the time,' Richard said.

The Man and The Snake

AMBROSE BIERCE

It is of veritabyll report, and attested of so many that there be nowe of wyse and learned none to gaynsaye it, that ye serpente hys eye hath a magnetick propertie that whosoe falleth into its svasion is drawn forwards in despyte of his wille, and perisheth miserabyll by ye creature hys byte.

STRETCHED AT EASE upon a sofa, in gown and slippers, Harker Brayton smiled as he read the foregoing sentence in old Morryster's 'Marvells of Science.' 'The only marvel in the matter,' he said to himself, 'is that the wise and learned in Morryster's day should have believed such nonsense as is rejected by most of even the ignorant in ours.'

A train of reflections followed – for Brayton was a man of thought – and he unconsciously lowered his book without altering the direction of his eyes. As soon as the volume had gone below the line of sight, something in an obscure corner of the room recalled his attention to his surroundings. What he saw, in the shadow under his bed, were two small points of light, apparently about an inch apart. They might have been reflections of the gas jet above him, in metal nail heads; he gave them but little thought and resumed his reading. A moment later something – some impulse which it did not occur to him to analyse – impelled him to lower the book again and seek for what he saw before. The points of light were still there. They seemed to have become brighter than before, shining with a greenish lustre which he had not at first observed. He thought, too, that they might have moved a trifle – were somewhat nearer. They were still too much in shadow, however, to reveal their nature and origin to an indolent attention, and he resumed his reading. Suddenly something in the text suggested a thought which made him start and drop the book for the third time to the side of the sofa, whence, escaping from his hand, it fell sprawling to the floor, back upward. Brayton, half risen, was staring intently into the obscurity beneath the bed, where the points of light shone with, it seemed to him, an added fire. His attention was now fully aroused, his gaze eager and imperative. It disclosed, almost directly beneath the foot-rail of the bed, the coils of a large serpent – the points of light were its eyes! Its horrible head, thrust flatly forth from the innermost coil and resting upon the outermost, was directed straight toward him, the definition of the wide, brutal jaw and the idiot-like forehead serving to show the direction of its malevolent gaze. The eyes were no longer merely luminous points; they looked into his own with a meaning, a malign significance.

A snake in a bedroom of a modern city dwelling of the better sort is, happily, not so common a phenomenon as to make explanation altogether needless. Harker Brayton, a bachelor of thirty-five, a scholar, idler, and something of an athlete, rich, popular, and of sound health, had returned to San Francisco from all manner of remote and unfamiliar countries. His tastes, always a trifle luxurious, had taken on an added exuberance from long privation; and the resources of even the Castle Hotel being inadequate to their perfect gratification, he had gladly accepted the hospitality of his friend, Dr. Druring, the distinguished scientist. Dr. Druring's house, a large, old-fashioned one in what was now an obscure quarter of the city, had an outer and visible aspect of proud reserve. It plainly would not associate with the contiguous elements of its altered environment, and appeared to have developed some of the eccentricities which come of isolation. One of these was a 'wing,' conspicuously irrelevant in point of architecture, and no less rebellious in the matter of purpose; for it was a combination of laboratory, menagerie, and museum. It was here that the doctor indulged the scientific side of his nature in the study of such forms of animal life as engaged his interest and comforted his taste – which, it must be confessed, ran rather to the lower forms. For one of the higher types nimbly and sweetly to recommend itself unto his gentle senses, it had at least to retain certain rudimentary characteristics allying it to such 'dragons of the prime' as toads and snakes. His scientific sympathies were distinctly reptilian; he loved nature's vulgarians and described himself as the Zola of zoology. His wife and daughters, not having the advantage to share his enlightened curiosity regarding the works and ways of our ill-starred fellow-creatures, were, with needless austerity, excluded from what he called the Snakery, and doomed to companionship with their own kind, though, to soften the rigours of their lot, he had permitted them, out of his great wealth, to outdo the reptiles in the gorgeousness of their surroundings and to shine with a superior slendour.

Architecturally, and in point of 'furnishing,' the Snakery had a severe simplicity befitting the humble circumstances of its occupants, many of whom, indeed, could not safely have been intrusted with the liberty which is necessary to the full enjoyment of luxury, for they had the troublesome peculiarity of being alive. In their own apartments, however, they were under as little personal restraint as was compatible with their protection from the baneful habit of swallowing one another; and, as Brayton had thoughtfully apprised, it was more than a tradition that some of them had at divers times been found in parts of the premises where it would have embarrassed them to explain their presence. Despite the Snakery and its uncanny associations – to which, indeed, he gave little attention – Brayton found life at the Druring mansion very much to his mind.

Beyond a smart shock of surprise and a shudder of mere loathing, Mr.Brayton was not greatly affected. His first thought was to ring the call-bell and bring a servant; but, although the bell-cord dangled within easy reach, he made no movement toward it; it had occurred to his mind that the act might subject him to the suspicion of fear, which he certainly did not feel. He was more keenly conscious of the incongruous nature of the situation than affected by its perils; it was revolting, but absurd.

The reptile was of a species with which Brayton was unfamiliar. Its length he could only conjecture; the body at the largest visible part seemed about as thick as his forearm. In what way was it dangerous, if in any way? Was it venomous? Was it a constrictor? His knowledge of nature's danger signals did not enable him to say; he had never deciphered the code.

If not dangerous, the creature was at least offensive. It was de trop – 'matter out of place' – an impertinence. The gem was unworthy of the setting. Even the barbarous taste of our time and country, which had loaded the walls of the room with pictures the floor with furniture and the furniture with bric-a-brac, had not quite fitted the place for this bit of the savage life of the jungle. Besides – insupportable thought! – the exhalations of its breath mingled with the atmosphere which he himself was breathing!

These thoughts shaped themselves with greater or less definition in Brayton's mind, and begot action. The process is what we call consideration and decision. It is thus that we are wise and unwise. It is thus that the withered leaf in an autumn breeze shows greater or less intelligence than its fellows, falling upon the land or upon the lake. The secret of human action is an open one: something contracts our muscles. Does it matter if we give to the preparatory molecular changes the name of will?

Brayton rose to his feet and prepared to back softly away from the snake, without disturbing it, if possible, and through the door. People retire so from the presence of the great, for greatness is power, and power is a menace. He knew that he could walk backward without obstruction,

29

and find the door without error. Should the monster follow, the taste which had plastered the walls with paintings had consistently supplied a rack of murderous Oriental weapons from which he could snatch one to suit the occasion. In the meantime the snake's eyes burned with a more pitiless malevolence than ever.

Brayton lifted his right foot free of the floor to step backward. That moment he felt a strong aversion to doing so.

'I am accounted brave,' he murmured; 'is bravery, then, no more than pride? Because there are none to witness the shame shall I retreat?'

He was steadying himself with his right hand upon the back of a chair, his foot suspended.

'Nonsense!' he said aloud; 'I am not so great a coward as to fear to seem to myself afraid.'

He lifted the foot a little higher by slightly bending the knee, and thrust it sharply to the floor – an inch in front of the other! He could not think how that had occurred. A trial with the left foot had the same result; it was again in advance of the right. The hand upon the chair-back was grasping it; the arm was straight, reaching somewhat backward. One might have seen that he was reluctant to lose his hold. The snake's malignant head was still thrust forth from the inner coil as before, the neck level. It had not moved, but its eyes were now electric sparks, radiating an infinity of luminous needles.

The man had an ashy pallor. Again he took a step forward, and another, partly dragging the chair, which, when finally released, fell upon the floor with a crash. The man groaned; the snake made neither sound nor motion, but its eyes were two dazzling suns. The reptile itself was wholly concealed by them. They gave off enlarging rings of rich and vivid colours, which at their greatest expansion successively vanished like soap bubbles; they seemed to approach his very face, and anon were an immeasurable distance away. He heard, somewhere, the continuous throbbing of a great drum, with desultory bursts of far music, inconceivably sweet, like the tones of an æolian harp. He knew it for the sunrise melody of Memnon's statue, and thought he stood in the Nileside reeds, hearing, with exalted sense, that immortal anthem through the silence of the centuries.

The music ceased; rather, it became by insensible degrees the distant roll of a retreating thunderstorm. A landscape, glittering with sun and rain, stretched before him, arched with a vivid rainbow, framing in its giant curve a hundred visible cities. In the middle distance a vast serpent, wearing a crown, reared its head out of voluminous convolutions and looked at him with his dead mother's eyes. Suddenly this enchanting landscape seemed to rise swiftly upward, like the drop-scene at a theatre, and vanished in a blank. Something struck him a hard blow upon the face and breast. He had fallen to the floor; the blood ran from his broken nose and his bruised lips. For a moment he was dazed and stunned, and lay with closed eyes, his face against the floor. In a few moments he had recovered, and then realised that his fall, by withdrawing his eyes, had broken the spell which held him. He felt that now, by keeping his gaze averted, he would be able to retreat. But the thought of the serpent within a few feet of his head, yet unseen – perhaps in the very act of springing upon him and throwing its coils about his throat – was too horrible. He lifted his head, stared again into those baleful eyes, and was again in bondage.

The snake had not moved, and appeared somewhat to have lost its power upon the imagination; the gorgeous illusions of a few moments before were not repeated. Beneath that flat and brainless brow its black, beady eyes simply glittered, as at first, with an expression unspeakably malignant. It was as if the creature, knowing its triumph assured, had determined to practise no more alluring wiles.

Now ensued a fearful scene. The man, prone upon the floor, within a yard of his enemy, raised the upper part of his body upon his elbows, his head thrown back, his legs extended to their full length. His face was white between its gouts of blood; his eyes were strained open to their uttermost expansion. There was froth upon his lips; it dropped off in flakes. Strong convulsions ran through his body, making almost serpentine undulations. He bent himself at the waist, shifting his legs from side to side. And every movement left him a little nearer to the snake. He thrust his hands forward to brace himself back, yet constantly advanced upon his elbows.

Dr. Druring and his wife sat in the library. The scientist was in rare good humour.

'I have just obtained, by exchange with another collector,' he said, 'a splendid specimen of the *ophiophagus*.'

'And what may that be?' the lady inquired with a somewhat languid interest.

'Why, bless my soul, what profound ignorance! My dear, a man who ascertains after marriage that his wife does not know Greek, is entitled to a divorce. The *ophiophagus* is a snake which eats other snakes.'

'I hope it will eat all yours,' she said, absently shifting the lamp. 'But how does it get the other snakes? By charming them, I suppose.'

'That is just like you, dear,' said the doctor, with an affection of petulance. 'You know how irritating to me is any allusion to that vulgar superstition about the snake's power of fascination.'

The conversation was interrupted by a mighty cry, which rang through the silent house like the voice of a demon shouting in a tomb! Again and yet again it sounded, with terrible distinctness. They sprang to their feet, the man confused, the lady pale and speechless with fright. Almost before the echoes of the last cry had died away, the doctor was out of the room, springing up the staircase two steps at a time. In the corridor, in front of Brayton's chamber, he met some servants who had come from the upper floor. Together they rushed at the door without knocking. It was unfastened and gave way. Brayton lay upon his stomach on the floor, dead. His head and arms were partly concealed under the foot-rail of the bed. They pulled the body away, turning it upon the back. The face was daubed with blood and froth, the eyes were wide open, staring – a dreadful sight!

'Died in a fit,' said the scientist, bending his knee and placing his hand upon the heart. While in that position, he happened to glance under the bed. 'Good God!' he added, 'how did this thing get in here?'

He reached under the bed, pulled out the snake, and flung it, still coiled, to the centre of the room, whence, with a harsh, shuffling sound, it slid across the polished floor till stopped by the wall, where it lay without motion. It was a stuffed snake; its eyes were two shoe buttons.

The Haunted Station
HUME NISBET

IT LOOKED AS IF A curse rested upon it, even under that glorious southern morn which transformed all that it touched into old oak and silver-bronze.

I use the term silver-bronze, because I can think of no other combination to express that peculiar bronzy tarnish, like silver that has lain covered for a time, which the moonlight in the tropics gives to the near objects upon which it falls – tarnished silver surfaces and deep sepia-tinted shadows.

I felt the weird influence of that curse even as I crawled into the gully that led to it; a shiver ran over me as one feels when they say some stranger is passing over your future grave; a chill gripped at my vitals as I glanced about me apprehensively, expectant of something ghoulish and unnatural to come upon me from the sepulchral gloom and mystery of the overhanging boulders under which I was dragging my wearied limbs. A deathly silence brooded within this rut-like and treeless gully that formed the only passage from the arid desert over which I had struggled, famishing and desperate; where it led to I neither knew nor cared, so that it did not end in a *cul-de-sac*.

At last I came to what I least expected to see in that part, a house of two storeys, with the double gables facing me, as it stood on a mound in front of a water-hole, the mellow full moon behind the shingly roof, and glittering whitely as it repeated itself in the still water against the inky blackness of the reflections cast by the denser masses of the house and vegetation about it.

It seemed to be a wooden erection, such as squatters first raise for their homesteads after they have decided to stay; the intermediate kind of station, which takes the place of the temporary shanty while the proprietor's bank account is rapidly swelling, and his children are being educated in the city boarding schools to know their own social importance. By and by, when he is out of the mortgagee's hands, he may discard this comfortable house, as he has done his shanty, and go in for stateliness and stone-work, but to the tramp or the bushranger, the present house is the most welcome sight, for it promises to the one shelter, and to the other a prospect of loot.

There was a verandah round the basement that stood clear above the earth on piles, with a broad ladder stair leading down to the garden walk which terminated at the edge of the pool or waterhole; under the iron roofing of the verandah I could make out the vague indications of French doors that led to the reception rooms, etc., while above them were bedroom windows, all dark with the exception of one of the upper windows, the second one from the end gable, through which a pale greenish light streamed faintly.

Behind the house, or rather from the centre of it, as I afterwards found out, projected a gigantic and lifeless gum tree, which spread its fantastic limbs and branches wildly over the roof, and behind that again a mass of chaotic and planted greenery, all softened and generalised in the thin silvery mist which emanated from the pool and hovered over the ground.

At the first glance it appeared to be the abode of a romantic owner, who had fixed upon a picturesque site, and afterwards devoted himself to making it comfortable as well as beautiful. He had planted creepers and trained them over the walls, passion-fruit and vines clung closely to the posts and trellis work and broke the square outlines of windows and angles, a wild tangle of shrubs and flowers covered the mound in front and trailed into the water without much order, so that it looked like the abode of an imaginative poet rather than the station of a practical, money-grabbing squatter.

As I quitted the desolate and rock-bound gully and entered upon this romantic domain, I could not help admiring the artful manner in which the owner had left Nature alone where he could do so; the gum trees which he had found there were still left as they must have been for ages, great trees shooting up hundreds of feet into the air, some of them gaunt and bald with time, others with their leafage still in a flourishing condition, while the more youthful trees were springing out of the fertile soil in all directions, giving the approach the appearance of an English park, particularly with the heavy night-dew that glistened over them.

But the chill was still upon me that had gripped me at the entrance of the gully, and the same lifeless silence brooded over the house, garden, pool and forest which had awed me amongst the boulders, so that as I paused at the edge of the water and regarded the house, I again shuddered as if spectres were round me, and murmured to myself, 'Yes, it looks like a place upon which has fallen a curse.'

Two years before this night, I had been tried and condemned to death for murder, the murder of the one I loved best on earth, but, through the energy of the press and the intercession of a number of influential friends, my sentence had been *mercifully* commuted to transportation for life in Western Australia.

The victim, whom I was proved by circumstantial evidence to have murdered, was my young wife, to whom I had been married only six months before; ours was a love match, and until I saw her lying stark before me, those six months had been an uninterrupted honeymoon, without a cloud to cross it, a brief term of heaven, which accentuated the after misery.

I was a medical practitioner in a small country village which I need not name, as my supposed crime rang through England. My practice was new but growing, so that, although not too well off, we were fairly comfortable as to position, and, as my wife was modest in her desires, we were more than contented with our lot.

I suppose the evidence was strong enough to place my guilt beyond a doubt to those who could not read my heart and the heart of the woman I loved more than life. She had not been very well of late, yet, as it was nothing serious, I attended her myself; then the end came with appalling suddenness, a post-mortem examination proved that she had been poisoned, and that the drug had been taken from my surgery, by whom or for what reason is still a mystery to me, for I do not think that I had an enemy in the world, nor do I think my poor darling had one either.

At the time of my sentence, I had only one wish, and that was to join the victim of this mysterious crime, so that I saw the judge put on the fatal black cap with a feeling of pleasure, but when afterwards I heard it was to be transportation instead, then I flung myself down in my cell and hurled imprecations on those officious friends who had given me slavery and misery instead of release. Where was the mercy in letting me have life, since all had been taken from it which made it worth holding? – the woman who had lain in my arms while together we built up glowing pictures of an impossible future, my good name lost, my place amongst men destroyed; henceforward I would be only recognised by a number, my companions the vilest, my days dragged out in chains, until the degradation of my lot encrusted over that previous memory of tenderness and fidelity, and I grew to be like the other numbered felons, a mindless and emotionless animal.

Fortunately, at this point of my sufferings, oblivion came in the form of delirium, so that the weeks passed in a dream, during which my lost wife lived once more with me as we had been in the past, and by the time the ship's doctor pronounced me recovered, we were within a few days of our dreary destination. Then my wife went from me to her own place, and I woke up to find that I had made some friends amongst my fellow-convicts, who had taken care of me during my insanity.

35

We landed at Fremantle, and began our life, road-making; that is, each morning we were driven out of the prison like cattle, chained together in groups, and kept in the open until sundown, when we were once more driven back to sleep.

For fourteen months this dull monotony of eating, working and sleeping went on without variation, and then the chance came that I had been hungering for all along; not that liberty was likely to do me much good, only that the hope of accomplishing it kept me alive.

Three of us made a run for it one afternoon, just before the gun sounded for our recall, while the rest of the gang, being in our confidence, covered our escape until we had got beyond gunshot distance. We had managed to file through the chain which linked us together, and we ran towards the bush with the broken pieces in our hands as weapons of defence.

My two comrades were desperate criminals, who, like myself, had been sentenced for life, and, as they confessed themselves, were ready to commit any atrocity rather than be caught and taken back.

That night and the next day we walked in a straight line about forty miles through the bush, and then, being hungry and tired, and considering ourselves fairly safe, we lay down to sleep without any thought of keeping watch.

But we had reckoned too confidently upon our escape, for about daybreak the next morning we were roused up by the sound of galloping horses, and, springing to our feet and climbing a gum tree, we saw a dozen of mounted police, led by two black trackers, coming straight in our direction. Under the circumstances there were but two things left for us to do, either to wait until they came and caught us, or run for it until we were beaten or shot down.

One of my companions decided to wait and be taken back, in spite of his bravado the night before; an empty stomach demoralises most men; the other one made up his mind, as I did, to run as long as we could. We started in different directions, leaving our mate sitting under the gum tree, he promising to keep them off our track as long as possible.

The fact of him being there when the police arrived gave us a good start. I put all my speed out, and dashed along until I had covered, I daresay, about a couple of miles, when all at once the scrub came to an end, and before me I saw an open space, with another stretch of bush about half a mile distant, and no shelter between me and it.

As I stood for a few minutes to recover my breath, I heard two or three shots fired to the right, the direction my companion had taken, and on looking that way I saw that he also had gained the open, and was followed by one of the trackers and a couple of the police. He was still running, but I could see that he was wounded from the way he went.

Another shot was sent after him, that went straight to its mark, for all at once he threw up his arms and fell prone upon his face, then, hearing the sounds of pursuit in my direction, I waited no longer, but bounded full into the morning sunlight, hoping, as I ran, that I might be as lucky as he had been, and get a bullet between my shoulders and so end my troubles.

I knew that they had seen me, and were after me almost as soon as I had left the cover, for I could hear them shouting for me to stop, as well as the clatter of their horses' hoofs on the hard soil, but still I kept to my course, waiting upon the shots to sound which would terminate my wretched existence, my back-nerves quivering in anticipation and my teeth meeting in my under-lip.

One!

Two!!

Two reports sounded in my ears; a second after the bullets had whistled past my head; and then, before the third and fourth reports came, something like hot iron touched me above my left elbow, while the other bullet whirred past me with a singing wail, cooling my cheek with the wind it raised, and then I saw it ricochet in front of me on the hill side, for I was going up a slight rise at the time.

I had no pain in my arm, although I knew that my humerus was splintered by that third last shot, but I put on a final spurt in order to tempt them to fire again.

What were they doing? I glanced over my shoulder as I rushed, and saw that they were spreading out, fan-like, and riding like fury, while they hurriedly reloaded. Once more they were taking aim at me, and then I looked again in front.

Before me yawned a gulf, the depth of which I could not estimate, yet in width it was over a hundred feet. My pursuers had seen this impediment also, for they were reining up their horses, while they shouted to me, more frantically than ever, to stop.

Why should I stop? flashed the thought across my mind as I neared the edge. Since their bullets had denied me the death I courted, why should I pause at the death spread out for me so opportunely?

As the question flashed through me, I answered it by making the leap, and as I went down I could hear the reports of the rifles above me.

Down into shadow from the sun-glare I dropped, the outer branches of a tree breaking with me as I fell through them. Another obstacle caught me a little lower, and gave way under my weight, and then with an awful wrench, that nearly stunned me, I felt myself hanging by the remnant of the chain which was still rivetted to my waist-band, about ten feet from the surface, and with a hundred and fifty feet of a drop below me before I could reach the bottom. The chain had somehow got entangled in a fork of the last tree through which I had broken.

Although that sudden wrench was excruciating, the exigency of my position compelled me to collect my faculties without loss of time. Perhaps my months of serfdom and intercourse with felons had blunted my sensibility, and rendered me more callous to danger and bodily pain than I had been in my former and happier days, or the excitement of that terrible chase was still surging within me, for without more than a second's pause, and an almost indifferent glance downwards to those distant boulders, I made a wild clutch with my unwounded arm at the branch which had caught me, and with an effort drew myself up to it, so that the next instant I was astride it, or rather crouching, where my loose chain had caught. Then, once more secure, I looked upwards to where I expected my hunters to appear.

When I think upon it now, it was a marvel how I ever got to be placed where I was, for I was under the shelving ledge from which I had leapt, that is, it spread over me like a roof, therefore I must conclude that the first tier of branches must have bent inwards, and so landed me on to the second tree at a slant. At least, this is the only way in which I can account for my position.

The tree on which I sat grew from a crevice on the side of the precipice, and from the top could not be seen by those above, neither could I see them, although they looked down after me, but I could hear them plainly enough and what they said.

'That fellow has gone right enough, Jack, although I don't see his remains below; shall we try to get down and make sure?' I heard one say, while another replied:

'What's the good of wasting time, he's as dead as the other chap, after that drop, and they will both be picked clean enough, so let us get back to Fremantle with the living one, and report the other two as wiped out; we have a long enough journey before us, sergeant.'

'Yes, I suppose so,' answered the sergeant. 'Well, boys, we may say that there are two promising bushrangers the less for this colony to support, so right about, home's the word.'

I heard their horses wheel round and go off at a canter after this final speech, and then I was left alone on my airy perch, to plan out how best I was to get down with my broken arm, for it was impossible to get up, and also what I was likely to do with my liberty in that desolate region.

Desperate men are not very particular about the risks they run, and I ran not a few before I finally reached the bottom of that gulch, risky drops from one ledge to another, frantic clutchings at branches and tree roots; sufficient that I did reach the level ground at last more nearly dead than alive, so that I was fain to lie under the shadow of a boulder for hours without making an effort to rise and continue my journey.

Then, as night was approaching, I dragged myself along until I came to some water, where, after drinking and bracing up my broken arm with a few gum-trunk shards, and binding them round with some native grasses, while I made my supper of the young leaves of the eucalyptus bushes, I went on.

On, on, on for weeks, until I had lost all count of time, I wandered, carrying my broken fetters with me, and my broken arm gradually mending of its own accord. Sometimes I killed a snake or an iguana during the day with the branch I used for a stick, or a 'possum or wild cat at night, which I devoured raw. Often I existed for days on grass roots or the leaves of the gum-tree, for anything was good enough to fill up the gap.

My convict garb was in tatters and my feet bootless by this time, and my hair and beard hung over my shoulders and chest, while often I went for days in a semi-conscious state, for the fierce sun seemed to wither up my blood and set fire to my brain.

Where I was going I could not tell, and still, with all the privation and misery, the love of life was once again stronger in me than it had been since I had lost my place amongst civilised men, for I was at liberty and alone to indulge in fancy.

And yet it did not seem altogether fancy that my lost wife was with me on that journey. At first she came only when I lay down to sleep, but after a time she walked with me hand in hand during the day as well as in my dreams.

Dora was her name, and soon I forgot that she had been dead, for she was as living and beautiful as ever as we went along together, day after day, speaking to each other like lovers as we used to speak, and she did not seem to mind my ragged, degraded costume, or my dirty, tangled beard, but caressed me with the same tenderness as of yore.

Through the bush, down lonely gullies, over bitter deserts and salt marshes, we passed as happy and affectionate as fond lovers could be who are newly married, and whom the world cannot part, my broken chain rattling as I staggered onwards while she smiled as if pleased with the music, because it was the chain which I was wearing for her dear sake.

Let me think for a moment – was she with me through that last desert before I came to that gloomy gully? I cannot be quite sure of that, but this I do know, that she was not with me after the chill shadows of the boulders drew me into them, and I was quite alone when I stood by the water-hole looking upon that strange and silent house.

It was singular that the house should be here at all in this far-off and as yet unnamed portion of Western Australia, for I naturally supposed that I had walked hundreds of miles since leaving the convict settlement, and as I had encountered no one, not even a single tribe of wandering blacks, it seemed impossible to believe that I was not the first white man who had penetrated so far, and yet there it loomed before me, substantial-looking in its masses, with painted weather-boards, shingles, iron sheeting, carved posts and trellis-work, French windows, and the signs of cultivation about it, although bearing the traces of late neglect.

Was it inhabited? I next asked myself as I looked steadily at that dimly-illumined window; seemingly it was, for as I mentally asked the question, a darkness blotted out the light for a few moments and then moved slowly aside, while the faint pallor once more shone out; it appeared to be from the distance a window with a pale green blind drawn down, behind which a lamp turned low was burning, possibly for some invalid who was restlessly walking about, while the rest of the household slept.

Would it be well to rouse them up at this hour of the night? I next queried as I paused, watching the chimney tops from which no wreath of smoke came, for although it did not seem late, judging from the height of the moon, yet it was only natural to suppose that in this isolated place the people would retire early. Perhaps it would be better to wait where I was till morning and see what they were like before I ventured to ask hospitality from them, in my ragged yet unmistakably convict dress. I would rather go on as I was than run the risk of being dragged back to prison.

How chilly the night vapours were which rose from this large pool, for it was more like the moat from some ancient ruin than an ordinary Australian water-hole. How ominous the shadows that gathered over this dwelling, and which even the great and lustrous moon, now clear of the gable end, seemed unable to dissipate, and what a dismal effect that dimly-burning lamp behind the pale green blind gave to it.

I turned my eyes from the window to the pond from which the ghostly vapours were steaming upwards in such strange shapes; they crossed the reflections like grey shadows and floated over the white glitter which the moon cast down, like spectres following each other in a stately procession, curling upwards interlaced, while the gaunt trees behind them altered their shapes and looked demoniac in their fantastic outlines, shadows passing along and sending back doleful sighs, which I tried with all my might to think was the night breeze but without succeeding.

Hush! was that a laugh that wafted from the house, a low, but blood-curdling cachinnation such as an exultant devil might utter who had witnessed his fell mischief accomplished, followed by the wail of a woman, intermixed with the cry of a child!

Ah! what a fool I was to forget the cry of the Australian king-fisher; of course that was it, of course, of course, but—

The shapes are thickening over that mirror-like pool, and as I look I see a woman with a chalk-white face and eyes distended in horror, with a child in her hands – a little girl – and beside them the form of a man whose face changes into two different men, one the face of death, and the other like that of a demon with glaring eyeballs, while he points from the woman and child to the sleeping pool.

What is the devil-spectre pointing at, as he laughs once more while the woman and child shrink with affright?

The face that he himself wore a moment ago, the face of the dead man whom I can see floating amongst that silver lustre.

I must have fainted at the weird visions of the night before, or else I may have fallen asleep and dreamt them, for when I opened my eyes again, the morning sun was pouring over the landscape and all appeared changed.

The pool was still there but it looked like a natural Australian water-hole which had been deepened and lengthened, and artificially arranged by a tasteful proprietor to beautify his estate; water-lilies grew round the edges and spread themselves in graceful patches about; it was only in the centre portion, where the moonlight had glinted and the other reflections cast themselves, that the water was clear of weeds, and there it still lay inky and dangerous-like in its depth.

Over the building itself clustered a perfect tangle of vegetable parasites, Star-of-Bethlehem, Maiden-blush roses, and Gloire-de-Dijon, passion-flowers and convolvulus, intermingling with a large grape-laden vine going to waste, and hanging about in half-wild, neglected festoons; a woman's hand had planted these tendrils, as well as the garden in front, for I could see that flowers predominated.

As for the house itself, it still stood silent and deserted-looking, the weather-boards had shrunk a good deal with the heat of many suns beating upon them, while the paint, once tasteful in its varied tints, was bleached into dry powder; the trellis-work also on the verandah had in many places been torn away by the weight of the clinging vines, and between the window-frames and the windows yawned wide fissures where they had shrunk from each other.

I looked round at the landscape, but could see no trace of sheep, cattle, nor humanity; it spread out a sun-lit solitude where Nature, for a little while trained to order, had once more asserted her independent lavishness.

A little of my former awe came upon me as I stood for a few moments hesitating to advance, but at the sight of those luscious-looking bunches of grapes, which seemed to promise some fare more substantial inside, the dormant cravings for food which I had so long subdued came upon me with tenfold force, and, without more than a slight tremor of superstitious dread, I hurriedly crushed my way through the tangle of vegetation, and made for the verandah and open door of the hall.

Delicious grapes they were, as I found when, after tearing off a huge bunch, and eating them greedily, I entered the silent hall and began my exploration.

The dust and fine sand of many 'brick-fielders', i.e., sand storms, lay thickly on every object inside, so that as I walked I left my footprints behind me as plainly as if I had been walking over snow. In the hall I found a handsome stand and carved table with chairs, a hat and riding-whip lay on the table, while on the rack I saw two or three coats and hats hanging, with sticks and umbrellas beneath, all white with dust. The dining-room door stood ajar, and as I entered I could see that it also had been undisturbed for months, if not for years. It had been handsomely furnished, with artistic hangings and stuffed leather chairs and couches, while on the elaborately carved chiffonier was a plentiful supply of spirit and wine decanters, with cut glasses standing ready for use. On the table stood a bottle of Three-star brandy, half-emptied, and by its side a water-filter and glass as they had been left by the last user.

I smelt the bottle, and found that the contents were mellow and good, and when, after dusting the top, I put it to my mouth, I discovered that the bouquet was delicious; then, invigorated by that sip, I continued my voyage of discovery.

The chiffonier was not locked, and inside I discovered rows of sealed bottles, which satisfied me that I was not likely to run short of refreshments in the liquid form at any rate, so, content with this pleasant prospect, I ventured into the other apartments.

The drawing-room was like the room I had left, a picture of comfort and elegance, when once the accumulation of dust and sand had been removed.

The library or study came next, which I found in perfect order, although I left the details for a more leisurely examination.

I next penetrated the kitchen, which I saw was comfortable, roomy and well-provided, although in more disorder than the other rooms; pans stood rusting in the fireplace, dishes lay dirty and in an accumulated pile on the table, as if the servants had left in a hurry and the owners had been forced to make what shifts they could during their absence.

Yet there was no lack of such provisions as an up-country station would be sure to lay in; the pantry I found stored like a provision shop, with flitches of bacon, hams sewn in canvas, tinned meats and soups of all kinds, with barrels and bags and boxes of flour, sugar, tea and other sundries, enough to keep me going for years if I was lucky enough to be in possession.

I next went upstairs to the bedrooms, up a thickly-carpeted staircase, with the white linen overcloth still upon it. In the first room I found the bed with the bedclothes tumbled about as if the sleeper had lately left it; the master of the house I supposed, as I examined the wardrobe and found it well stocked with male apparel. At last I could cast aside my degrading rags, and fit myself out like a free man, after I had visited the workshop and filed my fetters from me.

Another door attracted me on the opposite side of the lobby, and this I opened with some considerable trepidation because it led into the room which I had seen lighted up the night before.

It seemed untenanted, as I looked in cautiously, and like the other bedroom was in a tumble of confusion, a woman's room, for the dresses

42

and underclothing were lying about, a bedroom which had been occupied by a woman and a child, for a crib stood in one corner, and on a chair lay the frock and other articles belonging to a little girl of about five or six years of age.

I looked at the window, it had venetian blinds upon it, and they were drawn up, so that my surmise had been wrong about the pale green blind, but on the end side of the room was another window with the blinds also drawn up, and thus satisfied I walked in boldly; what I had thought to be a light, had only been the moonlight streaming from the one window to the other, while the momentary blackening of the light had been caused, doubtless, by the branches of the trees outside, moved forward by the night breeze. Yes, that must have been the cause, so that I had nothing to fear, the house was deserted, and my own property, for the time at least.

There was a strange and musty odour in this bedroom, which blended with the perfume that the owner had used, and made me for a moment almost giddy, so the first thing I did was to open both windows and let in the morning air, after which I looked over to the unmade bed, and then I staggered back with a cry of horror.

There amongst the tumble of bedclothes lay the skeletons of what had been two human beings, clad in embroidered nightdresses. One glance was enough to convince me, with my medical knowledge, that the gleaming bones were those of a woman and a child, the original wearers of those dresses which lay scattered about.

What awful tragedy had taken place in this richly furnished but accursed house? Recovering myself, I examined the remains more particularly, but could find no clue, they were lying reposefully enough, with arms interlacing as if they had died or been done to death in their sleep, while those tiny anatomists, the ants, had found their way in, and cleaned the bones completely, as they very soon do in this country.

With a sick sensation at my heart, I continued my investigations throughout the other portions of the station. In the servants' quarters I learnt the cause of the unwashed dishes; three skeletons lay on the floor in different positions as they had fallen, while their shattered skulls proved the cause of their end, even if the empty revolver that I picked up from the floor had not been evidence enough. Some one must have entered their rooms and woke them rudely from their sleep in the night time, for they lay also in their blood-stained nightdresses, and beside them, on the boards, were dried-up markings which were unmistakable.

The rest of the house was as it had been left by the murderer or murderers. Three domestics, with their mistress and child, had been slaughtered, and then the guilty wretches had fled without disturbing anything else.

It was once again night, and I was still in the house which my first impulse had been to leave with all haste after the gruesome discoveries that I had made.

But several potent reasons restrained me from yielding to that impulse. I had been wandering for months, and living like a wild beast, while here I had everything to my hand which I needed to recruit my exhausted system. My curiosity was roused, so that I wanted to penetrate the strange mystery if I could, by hunting after and reading all the letters and papers that I might be able to find, and to do this required leisure; thirdly, as a medical practitioner who had passed through the anatomical schools, the presence of five skeletons did not have much effect upon me, and lastly, before sun-down the weather had broken, and one of those fierce storms of rain, wind, thunder and lightning had come on, which utterly prevented any one who had the chance of a roof to shelter him from turning out to the dangers of the night.

These were some of my reasons for staying where I was, at least the reasons that I explained to myself, but there was another and a more subtle motive which I could not logically explain, and which yet influenced me more than any of the others. *I could not leave the house, now that I had taken possession of it*, or rather, if I may say it, now that *the house had taken possession of me.*

I had lifted the bucket from the kitchen, and found my way to the draw-well in the back-garden, with the uncomfortable feeling that some unseen force was compelling me to stay here. I discovered a large file and freed myself from my fetters, and then, throwing my rags from me with disgust, I clad myself in one of the suits that I found in the wardrobe upstairs. Then I set to work dusting and sweeping out the dining-room, after which I lit a fire, retrimmed the lamps, and cooked a substantial meal for myself. The storm coming on decided me, so that I spent the remainder of the afternoon making the place comfortable, and when darkness did come, I had drawn the blinds down and secured the shutters, and with a lighted lamp, a bottle of good wine, and a box of first-class cigars which I also found in the chiffonier, with a few volumes that I had taken from the book shelves at random, and an album of photographs that I picked up from the drawing-room table, I felt a different man from what I had been the night previous, particularly with that glowing log fire in the grate.

I left the half-emptied bottle of brandy where I had found it, on the table, with the used glass and water filter untouched, as I did also the chair that had been beside them. I had repugnance to those articles which I could not overcome; the murderer had used them last, possibly as a reviver after his crimes, for by this time I had reasoned out that one hand only had been at the work, and that man's the owner of the suit which I was then wearing and which fitted me so exactly, otherwise why should the house have been left in the condition that it was?

As I sat at the end of the table and smoked the cigar, I rebuilt the whole tragedy, although as yet the motive was not so clear, and as I thought the matter out, I turned over the leaves of the album and looked at the photographs.

Before me, on the walls, hung three oil portraits, enlargements they were, and as works of art vile things, yet doubtless they were faithful enough likenesses. In the album, I found three cabinet portraits from which the paintings had been enlarged.

They were the portraits of a woman of about twenty-six, a girl of five years, and a man of about thirty-two.

The woman was good-looking, with fresh colour, blue eyes and golden-brown hair. The girl – evidently her daughter – for the likeness was marked between the two, had one of those seraphic expressions which some delicate children have who are marked out for early death, that places them above the plane of grosser humanity. She looked, as she hung between the two portraits, with her glory of golden hair, like the guardian angel of the woman who was smiling so contentedly and consciously from her gilded frame.

The man was pallid-faced and dark, clean-shaven, all except the small black moustache, with lips which, except the artist had grossly exaggerated the colour, were excessively and disagreeably vivid. His eyes were deep set, and glowing as if with the glitter of a fever.

'These would be the likenesses of the woman and child whose skeletons lay unburied upstairs, and that pallid-faced, feverish-eyed ghoul, the fiend who had murdered them, his wife and child,' I murmured to myself as I watched the last portrait with morbid interest.

'Right and wrong, Doctor, as you medical men mostly are,' answered a deep voice from the other end of the table.

I started with amazement, and looked from the painting to the vacant chair beside the brandy bottle, which was now occupied by what appeared to be the original of the picture I had been looking at, face, hair, vivid scarlet lips were identical, and the same deep-set fiery eyes, which were fixed upon me intently and mockingly.

How had he entered without my observing him? By the window? No, for that I had firmly closed and secured myself, and as I glanced at it I saw that it still remained the same. By the door? Perhaps so, although he must have closed it again after he had entered without my hearing him, as he might easily have done during one of the claps of thunder which were now almost incessant, as were the vivid flashes of wild fire or lightning that darted about, while the rain lashed against the shutters outside.

He was dripping wet, as I could see, so that he must have come from that deluge, bare-headed and dripping, with his hair and moustache draggling over his glistening, ashy cheeks and bluish chin, as if he had been submerged in water, while weeds and slime hung about his saturated garments; a gruesome sight for a man who fancied himself alone to see start up all of a sudden, and no wonder that it paralysed me and prevented me from finding the words I wanted at the moment. Had he lain hidden somewhere watching me take possession of his premises, and being, as solitary men sometimes are, fond of dramatic effect, slipped in while my back was turned from the door to give me a surprise? If so he had succeeded, for I never before felt so craven-spirited or horror-stricken, my flesh was creeping and my hair bristling, while my blood grew to ice within me. The very lamp seemed to turn dim, and the fire smouldered down on the hearth, while the air was chill as a charnel vault, as I sat with shivering limbs and chattering teeth before this evil visitor.

Outside, the warring elements raged and fought, shaking the wooden walls, while the forked flames darted between us, lighting up his face with a ghastly effect. He must have seen my horror, for he once more laughed that low, malicious chuckle that I had heard the night before, as he again spoke.

'Make yourself at home, Doctor, and try some of this cognac instead of that washy stuff you are drinking. I am only sorry that I cannot join you in it, but I cannot *just yet.*'

I found words at last and asked him questions, which seemed impertinent in the extreme, considering where I was.

'Who are you? Where do you come from? What do you want?'

Again that hateful chuckle, as he fixed his burning eyes upon me with a regard which fascinated me in spite of myself.

'Who am I, do you ask? Well, before you took possession of this place I was its owner. Where do I come from? From out of *there* last.'

He pointed backwards towards the window, which burst open as he uttered the words, while through the driving rain a flash of lightning seemed to dart from his outstretched finger and disappear into the centre of the lake, then after that hurried glimpse, the shutters clashed together again and we were as before.

'What do I want? You, for lack of a better.'

'What do you want with me?' I gasped.

'To make you myself.'

'I do not understand you, what are you?'

'At present nothing, yet with your help, I shall be a man once more, while you shall be free and rich, for you shall have more gold than you ever could dream of.'

'What can I do for you?'

'Listen to my story and you will see. Ten years ago I was a successful gold finder, the trusting husband of that woman, and the fond father of that girl. I had likewise a friend whom I trusted, and took to live with me as a partner. We lived here together, my friend, myself, my wife and my daughter, for I was romantic and had raised this house to be close to the mine which I had discovered, and which I will show you if you consent to my terms.

'One night my friend murdered me and pitched my body into that water-hole, where the bones still lie. He did this because he coveted my wife and my share of the money.'

I was calm now, but watchful, for it appeared that I had to deal with a madman.

'In my lifetime I had been a trusting and guileless simpleton, but no sooner was my spirit set free than vengeance transformed its nature. I hovered about the place where all my affections had been centred, watching him beguile the woman who had been mine until he won her. She waited three years for me to return, and then she believed his story that I had been killed by the natives, and married him. They travelled to where you came from, to be married, and I followed them closely, for that was the chance I waited upon. The union of those two once accomplished he was in my power for ever, for this had established the link that was needed for me to take forcible possession of him.'

'And where was his spirit meantime?' I asked, to humour the maniac.

'In my grasp also, a spirit rendered impotent by murder and ingratitude; a spirit which I could do with as I pleased, so long as the wish I had was evil. I took possession of his body, the mirage of which you see now, and from that moment until the hour that our daughter rescued her from his clutches, he made the life of my former wife a hell on earth. I prompted his murder-embrued spirit to madness, leaving him only long enough to himself after I had braced him up to do the deed of vengeance.'

'How did the daughter save the mother?'

'By dying with her, and by her own purity tearing the freed spirit from my clutches. I did not intend the animal to do all that he did, for I wanted the mother only, but once the murder lust was on him, I found that he was beyond my influence. He slew the two by poison, as he had done me, then, frenzied, he murdered the servants, and finally exterminated himself by flinging himself into the pool. That was why I said that I came last from out of there, where both my own remains and his lie together.'

'Yes, and what is my share in this business?'

'To look on me passively for a few moments, as you are at present doing, that is all I require.'

I did not believe his story about his being only a mirage or spectre, for he appeared at this moment corporal enough to do me a considerable amount of bodily harm, and therefore to humour him, until I could plan a way to overpower him, I fixed my eyes upon his steadfastly, as he desired.

Was I falling asleep, or being mesmerised by this homicidal lunatic? As he glared at me with those fiery orbs and an evil contortion curling the blood-red lips, while the forked lightning played around him, I became helpless. He was creeping slowly towards me as a cat might steal upon a mouse, and I was unable to move, or take my eyes from his eyes

47

which seemed to be charming my life-blood from me, when suddenly I heard the distant sound of music, through a lull of the tempest, the rippling of a piano from the drawing-room with the mingling of a child's silvery voice as it sang its evening hymn, and at the sound his eyes shifted while he fell back a step or two, with an agonised spasm crossing his ghastly and dripping wet face.

Then the hurricane broke loose once more, with a resistless fury, while the door and window burst open, and the shutters were dashed into the room.

I leapt to my feet in a paroxysm of horror, and sprang towards the open door with that demon, or maniac, behind me.

Merciful heavens! the drawing-room was brilliantly lighted up, and there, seated at the open piano, was the woman whose bones I had seen bleaching upstairs, with the seraphic-faced child singing her hymn.

Out to the tempest I rushed madly, and heedless of where I went, so that I escaped from that accursed and haunted house, on, past the water-hole and into the glade, where I turned my head back instinctively, as I heard a wilder roar of thunder and the crash as if a tree had been struck.

What a flash that was which lighted up the scene and showed me the house collapsing as an erection of cards. It went down like an avalanche before that zig-zag flame, which seemed to lick round it for a moment, and then disappear into the earth.

Next instant I was thrown off my feet by the earthquake that shook the ground under me, while, as I still looked on where the house had been, I saw that the ruin had caught fire, and was blazing up in spite of the torrents that still poured down, and as it burned, I saw the mound sink slowly out of sight, while the reddened smoke eddied about in the same strange shapes which the vapours had assumed the night before, scarlet ghosts of the demon and his victims.

Two months after this, I woke up to find myself in a Queensland back-country station. They had found me wandering in a delirious condition over one of their distant runs six weeks before my return to consciousness, and as they could not believe that a pedestrian, without provisions, could get over that unknown stretch of country from Fremantle, they paid no attention to my ravings about being an escaped convict, particularly as the rags I had on could never have been prison made. Learning, however, that I had medical knowledge, by the simple method of putting it to the test, my good rescuers set me up in my old profession, where I still remain – a Queensland back-country doctor.

Mrs. Amworth

E. F. BENSON

THE VILLAGE OF Maxley, where last summer and autumn, these strange
events took place, lies on a heathery and pine-clad upland of Sussex. In
all England you could not find a sweeter and saner situation. Should the
wind blow from the south, it comes laden with the spices of the sea; to
the east high downs protect it from the inclemencies of March; and from
the west and north the breezes which reach it travel over miles of aromatic
forest and heather. The village itself is insignificant enough in point of
population, but rich in amenities and beauty. Half-way down the single
street, with its broad road and spacious areas of grass on each side, stands
the little Norman Church and the antique graveyard long disused: for
the rest there are a dozen small, sedate Georgian houses, red-bricked and
long-windowed, each with a square of flower garden in front, and an
ampler strip behind; a score of shops, and a couple of score of thatched
cottages belonging to labourers on neighbouring estates, complete the
entire cluster of its peaceful habitations. The general peace, however, is
sadly broken on Saturdays and Sundays, for we lie on one of the main
roads between London and Brighton and our quiet street becomes a
race-course for flying motor-cars and bicycles. A notice just outside the
village begging them to go slowly only seems to encourage them to
accelerate their speed, for the road lies open and straight, and there is
really no reason why they should do otherwise. By way of protest,
therefore, the ladies of Maxley cover their noses and mouths with their
handkerchiefs as they see a motor-car approaching, though, as the street
is asphalted, they need not really take these precautions against dust. But
late on Sunday night the horde of scorchers has passed, and we settle
down again to five days of cheerful and leisurely seclusion. Railway

strikes which agitate the country so much leave us undisturbed because most of the inhabitants of Maxley never leave it at all.

I am the fortunate possessor of one of these small Georgian houses, and consider myself no less fortunate in having so interesting and stimulating a neighbour as Francis Urcombe, who, the most confirmed of Maxleyites, has not slept away from his house, which stands just opposite to mine in the village street, for nearly two years, at which date, though still in middle life he resigned his Physiological Professorship at Cambridge University, and devoted himself to the study of those occult and curious phenomena which seem equally to concern the physical and psychical sides of human nature. Indeed his retirement was not unconnected with his passion for the strange uncharted places that lie on the confines and borders of science, the existence of which is so stoutly denied by the more materialistic minds, for he advocated that all medical students should be obliged to pass some sort of examination in mesmerism, and that one of the tripos papers should be designed to test their knowledge in such subjects as appearances at time of death, haunted houses, vampirism, automatic writing, and possession.

'Of course they wouldn't listen to me,' ran his account of the matter, 'for there is nothing that these seats of learning are so frightened of as knowledge, and the road to knowledge lies in the study of things like these. The functions of the human frame are, broadly speaking, known. They are a country, anyhow, that has been charted and mapped out. But outside that lie huge tracts of undiscovered country, which certainly exist, and the real pioneers of knowledge are those who, at the cost of being derided as credulous and superstitious, want to push on into those misty and probably perilous places. I felt that I could be of more use by setting out without compass or knapsack into the mists than by sitting in a cage like a canary and chirping about what was known. Besides, teaching is very very bad for a man who knows himself only to be a learner: you only need to be a self conceited ass to teach.'

Here, then, in Francis Urcombe, was a delightful neighbour to one who, like myself, has an uneasy and burning curiosity about what he called the 'misty and perilious places' and this last spring we had a further and most welcome addition to our pleasant little community, in the person of Mrs. Amworth, widow of an Indian civil servant. Her husband had been a judge in the North-West Provinces, and after his death at Peshawar she came back to England, and after a year in London found herself starving for the ampler air and sunshine of the country to take the place of the fogs and griminess of town. She had, too, a special reason for settling in Maxley, since her ancestors up till a hundred years ago had long been native to the place, and in the old churchyard, now disused, are many gravestones bearing her maiden name of Chaston. Big and energetic, her vigorous and genial personality speedily woke Maxley up to a higher degree of sociality than it ever had known. Most of us were bachelors or spinsters or elderly folk not much inclined to exert ourselves in the expense and effort of hospitality and hitherto the gaiety of a small tea party, with bridge afterwards and galoshes (when it was wet) to trip home in again for a solitary dinner, was about the climax of our festivities. But Mrs. Amworth showed us a more gregarious way, and set an example of luncheon parties and little dinners, which we began to follow. On other nights when no such hospitality was on foot, a lone man like myself found it pleasant to know that a call on the telephone to Mrs. Amworth's house not a hundred yards off, and an inquiry as to whether I might come over after dinner for a game of piquet before bedtime, would probably evoke a response of welcome. There she would be, with comrade-like eagerness for companionship, and there was a glass of port and a cup of coffee and a cigarette and a game of piquet. She played the piano, too, in a free and exuberant manner, and had a charming voice and sang to her own accompaniment; and as the days grew long and the light lingered late, we played our game in her garden, which in the course of a few months she had turned from being a nursery for slugs and snails into a glowing patch of luxuriant blossomings. She was always cheery and jolly; she was interested in everything; and in music, in gardening, in games of all sorts was a competent performer. Everybody (with one exception) liked her, everybody felt her to bring with her the tonic of a sunny day. That one exception was Francis Urcombe; he, though he confessed he did not like her, acknowledged that he was vastly interested in her. This always seemed strange to me, for pleasant and jovial as she was, I could see nothing in her that could call forth conjecture or intrigued surmise, so healthy and unmysterious a figure did she present. But of the genuineness of Urcombe's interest there could be no doubt; one could see him watching and scrutinising her. In matter of age, she frankly volunteered the information that she was forty-five; but her briskness, her activity, her unravaged skin, her coal-black hair, made it difficult to believe that she was not adopting an unusual device and adding ten years on to her age instead of subtracting them.

Often, also, as our quite unsentimental friendship ripened, Mrs. Amworth would ring me up and propose her advent. If I was busy writing, I was to give her, so we definitely bargained, a frank negative, and in answer I could hear her jolly laugh and her wishes for a successful evening of work. Sometimes, before her proposal arrived, Urcombe would already have stepped across from his house opposite for a smoke and a chat, and he, hearing who my intended visitor was, always urged me to beg her to come. She and I should play our piquet, said he, and he would look on, if we did not object and learn something of the game. But I doubt whether he paid much attention to it, for nothing could be clearer than that, under that penthouse of forehead and thick eyebrows, his attention was fixed not on the cards, but on one of the players. But he seemed to enjoy an hour spent thus, and often, until one particular evening in July, he would watch her with the air of a man who has some deep problem in front of him. She, enthusiastically keen about our game, seemed not to notice his scrutiny. Then came that evening when, as I see in the light of subsequent events, began the first twitching of the veil that hid the secret horror from my eyes. I did not know it then, though I noticed that there after, if she rang up to propose coming round, she always asked not only if I was at leisure, but whether Mr. Urcombe was with me. If so, she said, she would not spoil the chat of two old bachelors, and laughingly wished me good-night. Urcombe, on this occasion, had been with me for some half-hour before Mrs. Amworth's appearance, and had been talking to me about the medieval beliefs concerning vampirism, one of those border-land subjects which he declared had not been sufficiently studied before it had been consigned by the medical profession to the dustheap of exploded superstitions. There he sat, grim and eager, tracing with that pellucid clearness which had made him in his Cambridge days so admirable a lecturer, the history of those mysterious visitations. In them all there was the same general features; one of those ghoulish spirits took up its abode in a living man or woman, conferring supernatural powers of bat-like flight and glutting itself with nocturnal blood-feasts. When its host died it continued to dwell in the corpse, which remained undecayed. By day it rested, by night it left the grave and went on its awful errands. No European country in the Middle Ages seemed to have escaped them; earlier yet, parallels were to be found in Roman and Greek and in Jewish history.

'It's a large order to set all that evidence aside as being moonshine,' he said. 'Hundreds of totally independent witnesses in many ages have testified to the occurrence of these phenomena, and there's no explanation known to me which covers all the facts. And if you feel inclined to say "Why, then, if these are facts, do we not come across them now?" there are two answers I can make you. One is that there were diseases known in the Middle Ages, such as the black death, which were certainly existent then and which have become extinct since, but for that reason we do not assert that such diseases never existed. Just as the black death visited England and decimated the population of Norfolk, so here in this very district about three hundred years ago there was certainly an outbreak of vampirism, and Maxley was the centre of it. My second answer is even more convincing, for I tell you that vampirism is by no means extinct now. An outbreak of it certainly occurred in India a year or two ago.'

At that moment I heard my knocker plied in the cheerful and peremptory manner in which Mrs. Amworth is accustomed to announce her arrival, and I went to the door to open it.

'Come in at once,' I said, 'and save me from having my blood curdled. Mr. Urcombe has been trying to alarm me.'

Instantly her vital, voluminous presence seemed to fill the room.

'Ah, but how lovely!' she said. 'I delight in having my blood curdled. Go on with your ghost story, Mr. Urcombe. I adore ghost stories.'

I saw that, as his habit was, he was intently observing her.

'It wasn't a ghost story exactly,' said he. 'I was only telling our host how vampirism was not extinct yet. I was saying that there was an outbreak of it in India only a few years ago.'

There was a more than perceptible pause, and I saw that, if Urcombe was observing her, she on her side was observing him with fixed eye and parted mouth. Then her jolly laugh invaded that rather tense silence.

'Oh, what a shame!' she said. 'You're not going to curdle my blood at all. Where did you pick up such a tale, Mr. Urcombe? I have lived for years in India and never heard a rumour of such a thing. Some storyteller in the bazaars must have invented it; they are famous at that.'

I could see that Urcombe was on the point of saying something further, but checked himself.

'Ah! very likely that was it,' he said.

But something had disturbed our usual peaceful sociability that night, and something had dampened Mrs. Amworth's usual high spirits. She had no gusto for her piquet, and left after a couple of games. Urcombe had been silent too, indeed he hardly spoke again till she departed.

'That was unfortunate,' he said, 'for the outbreak of – of a very mysterious disease, let us call it, took place at Peshawar where she and her husband were. And—'

'Well?' I asked.

'He was one of the victims of it,' said he. 'Naturally I had quite forgotten that when I spoke.'

The summer was unreasonably hot and rainless, and Maxley suffered much from drought, and also from a plague of big black night-flying gnats, the bite of which was very irritating and virulent. They came sailing in of an evening, settling on one's skin so quietly that one perceived nothing till the sharp stab announced that one had been bitten. They did not bite the hands or face, but chose always the neck and throat for their feeding-ground, and most of us, as the poison spread, assumed a temporary goitre. Then about the middle of August appeared the first of those mysterious cases of illness which our local doctor attributed to the long-continued heat coupled with the bite of these venomous insects. The patient was a boy of sixteen or seventeen, the son of Mrs. Amworth's gardener, and the symptoms were an anaemic pallor and a languid prostration, accompanied by great drowsiness and an abnormal appetite. He had, too, on his throat two small punctures where, so Dr. Ross conjectured, one of these great gnats had bitten him. But the odd thing was that there was no swelling or inflammation round the place where he had been bitten. The heat at this time had begun to abate, but the cooler weather failed to restore him, and the boy, in spite of the quantity of food which he so ravenously swallowed, wasted away to a skinclad skeleton.

I met Dr. Ross in the street one afternoon about this time, and in answer to my inquiries about his patient he said that he was afraid the boy was dying. The case, he confessed, completely puzzled him: some obscure form of pernicious anaemia was all he could suggest. But he wondered whether Mr. Urcombe would consent to see the boy, on the chance of his being able to throw some new light on the case, and since Urcombe was dining with me that night, I proposed to Dr. Ross to join us. He could not do this, but said he would look in later. When he came, Urcombe at once consented to put his skill at the other's disposal, and together they went off at once. Being thus shorn of my sociable evening, I telephoned to Mrs. Amworth to know if I might inflict myself on her for an hour. Her answer was a welcoming affirmative, and between piquet and music the hour lengthened itself into two. She spoke of the boy who was lying so desperately and mysteriously ill, and told me that she had often been to see him, taking him nourishing and delicate food. But today – and her kind eyes moistened as she spoke – she was afraid she had paid her last visit. Knowing the antipathy between her and Urcombe, I did not tell her that he had been called into consultation; and when I returned home she accompanied me to the door, for the sake of a breath of night air, and in order to borrow a magazine which contained an article on gardening which she wished to read.

'Ah, this delicious night air,' she said, luxuriously sniffing in the coolness. 'Night air and gardening are the great tonics. There is nothing so stimulating as bare contact with rich mother earth. You are never so fresh as when you have been grubbing in the soil – black hands, black nails, and boots covered with mud.' She gave her great jovial laugh.

'I'm a glutton for air and earth,' she said. 'Positively I look forward to death, for then I shall be buried and have the kind earth all round me. No leaden caskets for me – I have given explicit directions. But what shall I do about air? Well, I suppose one can't have everything. The magazine? A thousand thanks, I will faithfully return it. Good-night: garden and keep your windows open, and you won't have anaemia.'

'I always sleep with my windows open,' said I.

I went straight up to my bedroom, of which one of the windows looks out over the street, and as I undressed I thought I heard voices talking outside not far away. But I paid no particular attention, put out my lights, and falling asleep plunged into the depths of a most horrible dream, distortedly suggested, no doubt, by my last words with Mrs. Amworth. I dreamed that I woke, and found that both my bedroom windows were shut. Half-suffocating, I dreamed that I sprang out of bed, and went across to open them. The blind over the first one was drawn down, and pulling it up I saw, with the indescribable horror of incipient nightmare, Mrs. Amworth's face suspended close to the pane in the darkness outside, nodding and smiling at me. Pulling down the blind again to keep that terror out, I rushed to the second window on the other side of the room, and there again was Mrs. Amworth's face. Then the panic came upon me in full blast; here was I suffocating in the airless room, and whichever window I opened Mrs. Amworth's face would float in, like those noiseless black gnats that bit before one was aware. The nightmare rose to screaming point, and with strangled yells I awoke to find my room cool and quiet with both windows open and blinds up and a half-moon high in its course, casting an oblong of tranquil light on the floor. But even when I was awake the horror persisted, and I lay tossing and turning. I must have slept long before the nightmare seized me, for now it was nearly day, and soon in the east the drowsy eyelids of morning began to lift.

I was scarcely downstairs next morning – for after the dawn I slept late – when Urcombe rang up to know if he might see me immediately. He came in, grim and preoccupied, and I noticed that he was pulling on a pipe that was not even filled.

'I want your help,' he said, 'and so I must tell you first of all what happened last night. I went round with the little doctor to see his patient, and found him just alive, but scarcely more. I instantly diagnosed in my own mind what this anaemia, unaccountable by any other explanation meant. The boy is the prey of a vampire.'

He put his empty pipe on the breakfast table, by which I had just sat down, and folded his arms, looking at me steadily from under his overhanging brows.

'Now about last night,' he said. 'I insisted that he should be moved from his father's cottage into my house. As we were carrying him on a stretcher, whom should we meet but Mrs. Amworth? She expressed shocked surprise that we were moving him. Now why do you think she did that?'

With a start of horror, as I remembered my dream that night before, I felt an idea come into my mind so preposterous and unthinkable that I instantly turned it out again.

'I haven't the smallest idea,' I said.

'Then listen, while I tell you about what happened later. I put out all light in the room where the boy lay, and watched. One window was a little open, for I had forgotten to close it, and about midnight I heard something outside, trying apparently to push it farther open. I guessed who it was – yes, it was full twenty feet from the ground – and I peeped round the corner of the blind. Just outside was the face of Mrs. Amworth and her hand was on the frame of the window. Very softly I crept close, and then banged the window down, and I think I just caught the tip of one of her fingers.'

'But it's impossible,' I cried. 'How could she be floating in the air like that? And what had she come for? Don't tell me such—'

Once more, with closer grip, the remembrance of my nightmare seized me.

'I am telling you what I saw,' said he. 'And all night long, until it was nearly day, she was fluttering outside like some terrible bat, trying to gain admittance. Now put together various things I have told you.'

He began checking them off on his fingers.

'Number one,' he said: 'there was an outbreak of disease similar to that which this boy is suffering from at Peshawar, and her husband died of it. Number two: Mrs. Amworth protested against my moving the boy to my house. Number three: she, or the demon that inhabits her body, a creature powerful and deadly, tries to gain admittance. And add this, too: in medieval times there was an epidemic of vampirism here at Maxley. The vampire, so the accounts run, was found to be Elizabeth Chaston. . . . I see you remember Mrs. Amworth's maiden name. Finally, the boy is stronger this morning. He would certainly not have been alive if he had been visited again. And what do you make of it?'

There was a long silence, during which I found this incredible horror assuming the hues of reality.

'I have something to add,' I said, 'which may or may not bear on it. You say that the – spectre went away shortly before dawn?'

'Yes.'

I told him of my dream, and he smiled grimly.

'Yes, you did well to awake,' he said. 'That warning came from your subconscious self, which never wholly slumbers, and cried out to you of deadly danger. For two reasons, then you must help me: one to save others, the second to save yourself.'

'What do you want me to do?' I asked.

'I want you first of all to help me in watching this boy, and ensuring that she does not come near him. Eventually I want you to help me in tracking the thing down, in exposing and destroying it. It is not human: it is an incarnate fiend. What steps we shall have to take I don't know.'

It was now eleven of the forenoon, and presently I went across to his house for a twelve-hour vigil while he slept, to come on duty again that night, so that for the next twenty-four hours either Urcombe or myself was always in the room where the boy, now getting stronger every hour, was lying. The day following was Saturday and a morning of brilliant pellucid weather, and already when I went across to his house to resume my duty the stream of motors down to Brighton had begun. Simultaneously I saw Urcombe with a cheerful face, which boded good news of his patient, coming out of his house, and Mrs. Amworth, with a gesture of salutation to me, and a basket in her hand, walking up the broad strip of grass which bordered the road. There we all three met, I noticed (and saw that Urcombe noticed it too) that one finger on her left hand was bandaged.

'Good morning to you both,' said she. 'And I hear your patient is doing well, Mr. Urcombe. I have come to bring him a bowl of jelly, and to sit with him for an hour. He and I are great friends. I am overjoyed at his recovery.'

Urcombe paused a moment, as if making up his mind, and then shot out a pointing finger at her.

'I forbid that,' he said. 'You shall not sit with him or see him. And you know the reason as well as I do.'

I have never seen so horrible a change pass over a human face as that which now blanched hers to the colour of grey mist. She put up her hand as if to shield herself from the pointing finger, which drew the sign of the cross in the air, and shrank back cowering on the road. There was a wild hoot from a horn, a grinding of brakes, a shout – too late – from a passing car, and one long scream suddenly cut short. Her body rebounded from the roadway after the first wheel had gone over it, and the second followed it. It lay there, quivering and twitching and was still.

She was buried three days afterwards in the cemetery outside Maxley, in accordance with the wishes she had told me that she had devised about her internment, and the shock which her sudden and awful death had caused to the little community began by degrees to pass off. To two people only, Urcombe and myself, the horror of it was mitigated from the first by the nature of the relief that her death brought; but, naturally enough, we kept our own counsel, and no hint of what greater horror had been thus averted was ever let slip. But, oddly enough, so it seemed to me, he was still not satisfied about something in connnection with her, and would give no answer to my questions on the subject. Then as the days of a tranquil mellow September and the October that followed began to drop away like the leaves of the yellowing trees, his uneasiness relaxed. But before the entry of November the seeming tranquillity broke into hurricane.

I had been dining one night at the far end of the village, and about eleven o'clock was walking home again. The moon was of an unusual brilliance, rendering all that it shone on as distinct as in some etching. I had just come opposite the house which Mrs. Amworth had occupied, where there was a board up telling that it was to let, when I heard the click of her front gate, and next moment I saw, with a sudden chill and quaking of my very spirit, that she stood there. Her profile vividly illuminated, was turned to me, and I could not be mistaken in my identification of her. She appeared not to see me (indeed the shadow of the yew hedge in front of her graden enveloped me in its blackness) and she went swiftly across the road, and entered the gate of the house directly opposite. There I lost sight of her completely.

My breath was coming in short pants as if I had been running – and now indeed I ran, with fearful backward glances, along the hundred yards that separated me from my house and Urcombe's. It was to his that my flying steps took me, and next minute I was within.

'What have you come to tell me?' he asked. 'Or shall I guess?'

'You can't guess,' said I.

'No; it's no guess. She has come back and you have seen her. Tell me about it.'

I gave my story.

'That's Major Pearsall's house,' he said. 'Come back with me there at once.'

'But what can we do?' I asked.

'I've no idea. That's what we have got to find out.'

A minute later, we were opposite the house. When I had passed it before, it was all dark; now lights gleamed from a couple of windows upstairs. Even as we faced it, the front door opened, and next moment Major Pearsall emerged from the gate. He saw us and stopped.

I'm on my way to Dr. Ross,' he said quickly. 'My wife has been taken suddenly ill. She had been in bed an hour when I came upstairs, and found her white as a ghost and utterly exhausted. She had been to sleep, it seemed—But you will excuse me.'

'One moment, Major,' said Urcombe. 'Was there any mark on her throat?'

'How did you guess that?' said he. 'There was; one of those beastly gnats must have bitten her twice there. She was streaming with blood.'

'And there's someone with her?' asked Urcombe.

'Yes, I roused her maid.'

He went off, and Urcombe turned to me. 'I know now what we have to do,' he said. 'Change your clothes, and I'll join you at your house.'

'What is it?' I asked.

'I'll tell you on our way. We're going to the cemetery.'

He carried a pick, a shovel, and a screwdriver when he rejoined me, and wore round his shoulders a long coil of rope. As we walked, he gave me the outlines of the ghastly hour that lay before us.

'What I have to tell you,' he said, 'will seem to you now too fantastic for credence, but before dawn we shall see whether it outstrips reality. By a most fortunate happening, you saw the spectre, the astral body, whatever you choose to call it, of Mrs. Amworth going on its grisly business, and therefore, beyound doubt, the vampire spirit which abode in her during life animates her again in death. That is not exceptional – indeed, all these weeks since her death I have been expecting it. If I am right, we shall find her body undecayed and untouched by corruption.'

'But she has been dead nearly two months,' said I.

'If she had been dead two years it would still be so, if the vampire has possession of her. So remember: whatever you see done, it will be done not to her, who in the natural course would now be feeding the grasses above her grave, but to a spirit of untold evil and malignancy, which gives a phantom life to her body.'

'But what shall I see done?' said I.

'I will tell you. We know that now, at this moment, the vampire clad in her mortal semblance is out; dining out. But it must get back before dawn, and it will pass into the material form that lies in her grave. We must wait for that, and then with your help I shall dig up her body. If I am right, you will look on her as she was in life, with the full vigour of the dreadful nutriment she has received pulsing in her veins. And then, when dawn has come, and the vampire cannot leave the lair of her body, I shall strike her with this' – and he pointed to his pick – 'through the heart, and she, who comes to life again only with the animation the fiend gives her, she and her hellish partner will be dead indeed. Then we must bury her again, delivered at last.'

We had come to the cemetery, and in the brightness of the moonshine there was no difficulty in identifying her grave. It lay some twenty yards from the small chapel, in the porch of which, obscured by shadow, we concealed ourselves. From there we had a clear and open sight of the grave, and now we must wait till its infernal visitor returned home. The night was warm and windless, yet even if a freezing wind had been raging I think I should have felt nothing of it, so intense was my preoccupation as to what the night and dawn would bring. There was a bell in the turret of the chapel that struck the quarters of the hour, and it amazed me to find how swiftly the chimes succeeded one another.

The moon had long set, but a twilight of starts shone in a clear sky, when five o'clock of the morning sounded from the turret. A few minutes more passed, and then I felt Urcombe's hand softly nudging me; and looking out in the direction of his pointing finger, I saw that the form of a woman, tall, and large in build, was approaching from the right. Noiselessly, with a motion more of gliding and floating than walking, she moved across the cemetery to the grave which was the centre of our observation. She moved round as if to be certain of its identity, and for a moment stood directly facing us. In the greyness to which now my eyes had grown accustomed, I could easily see her face, and recognise its features.

She drew her hand across her mouth as if wiping it, and broke into a chuckle of such laughter as made my hair stir on my head. Then she leaped onto the grave, holding her hands high above her head, and inch by inch disappeared into the earth. Urcombe's hand was laid on my arm, in an injunction to keep still, but now he removed it.

'Come,' he said.

With pick and shovel and rope we went to the grave. The earth was light and sandy, and soon after six struck we had delved down to the coffin lid. With his pick he loosened the earth around it, and, adjusting the rope through the handles by which it had been lowered, we tried to raise it. This was a long and laborious business, and the light had begun to herald day in the east before we had it out, and lying by the side of the grave. With his screwdriver he loosened the fastenings of the lid, and slid it aside, and standing there we looked on the face of Mrs. Amworth. The eyes, once closed in death, were open, the cheeks were flushed with colour, the red, full-lipped mouth seemed to smile.

'One blow and it is all over,' he said. 'You need not look.'

Even as he spoke he took up the pick again, and laying the point of it on her left breast, measured his distance. And though I knew what was coming I could not look away . . .

He grasped the pick in both hands, raised it an inch or two for the taking of his aim, and then with full force brought it down on her breast. A fountain of blood, though she had been dead so long, spouted high in the air, falling with the thud of a heavy splash over the shroud, and simultaneously from those red lips came one long, appalling cry, swelling up like some hooting siren, and dying away again, With that, instantaneous as a lightning flash, came the touch of corruption on her face, the colour of it faded to ash, the plump cheeks fell in, the mouth dropped.

'Thank God, that's over,' said he, and without pause slipped the coffin lid back into its place.

Day was coming fast now, and, working like men possessed, we lowered the coffin into its place again, and shovelled the earth over it . . . The birds were busy with their earliest pipings as we went back to Maxley.

The Night the Ghost Got In
JAMES THURBER

THE GHOST THAT GOT into our house on the night of November 17, 1915, raised such a hullabaloo of misunderstandings that I am sorry I didn't just let it keep on walking, and go to bed. Its advent caused my mother to throw a shoe through a window of the house next door and ended up with my grandfather shooting a patrolman. I am sorry, therefore, as I have said, that I ever paid any attention to the footsteps.

They began about a quarter past one o'clock in the morning, a rhythmic, quick-cadenced walking around the dining-room table. My mother was asleep in one room upstairs, my brother Herman in another; grandfather was in the attic, in the old walnut bed which, as you will remember, once fell on my father. I had just stepped out of the bathtub and was busily rubbing myself with a towel when I heard the steps. They were the steps of a man walking rapidly around the dining-room table downstairs. The light from the bathroom shone down the back steps, which dropped directly into the dining-room; I could see the faint shine of plates on the plate-rail; I couldn't see the table. The steps kept going round and round the table; at regular intervals a board creaked, when it was trod upon. I supposed at first that it was my father or my brother Roy, who had gone to Indianapolis but were expected home at any time. I suspected next that it was a burglar. It did not enter my mind until later that it was a ghost.

After the walking had gone on for perhaps three minutes, I tiptoed to Herman's room. 'Psst!' I hissed, in the dark, shaking him. 'Awp,' he said, in the low, hopeless tone of a despondent beagle—he always half suspected that something would 'get him' in the night. I told him who I was. 'There's something downstairs!' I said. He got up and followed me to the head of the back staircase. We listened together. There was no sound. The steps had ceased. Herman looked at me in some alarm: I had only the bath towel around my waist. He wanted to go back to bed, but I gripped his arm. 'There's something down there!' I said. Instantly the steps began again, circled the dining-room table like a man running, and started up the stairs toward us, heavily, two at a time. The light still shone palely down the stairs; we saw nothing coming; we only heard the steps. Herman rushed to his room and slammed the door. I slammed shut the door at the stairs top and held my knee against it. After a long minute, I slowly opened it again. There was nothing there. There was no sound. None of us ever heard the ghost again.

The slamming of the doors had aroused mother: she peered out of her room. 'What on earth are you boys doing?' she demanded. Herman ventured out of his room. 'Nothing,' he said, gruffly, but he was, in colour, a light green. 'What was all that running around downstairs?', said mother. So she had heard the steps, too! We just looked at her. 'Burglars!' she shouted, intuitively. I tried to quiet her by starting lightly downstairs.

'Come on, Herman,' I said.

'I'll stay with mother,' he said. 'She's all excited.'

I stepped back onto the landing.

'Don't either of you go a step,' said mother. 'We'll call the police.' Since the phone was downstairs, I didn't see how we were going to call the police – nor did I want the police – but mother made one of her quick, incomparable decisions. She flung up a window of her bedroom which faced the bedroom windows of the house of a neighbour, picked up a shoe, and whammed it through a pane of glass across the narrow space that separated the two houses. Glass tinkled into the bedroom occupied by a retired engraver named Bodwell and his wife. Bodwell had been for some years in rather a bad way and was subject to mild 'attacks'. Most everybody we knew or lived near had *some* kind of attacks.

It was now about two o'clock of a moonless night; clouds hung black and low. Bodwell was at the window in a minute, shouting, frothing a little, shaking his fist. 'We'll sell the house and go back to Peoria,' we could hear Mrs. Bodwell saying. It was some time before Mother 'got through' to Bodwell. 'Burglars!' she shouted. 'Burglars in the house!' Herman and I hadn't dared to tell her that it was not burglars but ghosts, for she was even more afraid of ghosts than of burglars. Bodwell at first thought that she meant there were burglars in his house, but finally he quieted down and called the police for us over an extension phone by his bed. After he had disappeared from the window, mother suddenly made as if to throw another shoe, not because there was further need of it but, as she later explained, because the thrill of heaving a shoe through a window glass had enormously taken her fancy. I prevented her.

The police were on hand in a commendably short time: a Ford sedan full of them, two on motorcycles, and a patrol wagon with about eight in it and a few reporters. They began banging at our front door. Flashlights shot streaks of gleam up and down the walls, across the yard, down the walk between our house and Bodwell's. 'Open up!' cried a hoarse voice. 'We're men from Headquarters!' I wanted to go down and let them in, since there they were, but mother wouldn't hear of it. 'You haven't a stitch on,' she pointed out. 'You'd catch your death.' I wound the towel around me again. Finally the cops put their shoulders to our big heavy front door with its thick bevelled glass and broke it in: I could hear a rending of wood and splash of glass on the floor of the hall. Their lights played all over the living-room and crisscrossed nervously in the .dining-room, stabbed into hall-ways, shot up the front stairs and finally up the back. They caught me standing in my towel at the top. A heavy policeman bounded up the steps. 'Who are you?' he demanded. 'I live here,' I said. 'Well, whattsa matta, ya hot?' he asked. It was, as a matter of fact, cold; I went to my room and pulled on some trousers. On my way out, a cop stuck a gun into my ribs. 'Whatta you doin' here?' he demanded. 'I live here,' I said.

The officer in charge, reported to mother. 'No sign of nobody, lady,' he said. 'Musta got away – what'd he look like?' 'There were two or three of them,' mother said, 'whooping and carrying on and slamming doors.' 'Funny,' said the cop. 'all ya windows and doors was locked on the inside tight as a tick.'

Downstairs, we could hear the tramping of the other police. Police were all over the place; doors were yanked open, drawers were yanked open, windows were shot up and pulled down, furniture fell with dull thumps. A half-dozen policemen emerged out of the darkness of the front hallway upstairs. They began to ransack the floor: pulled beds away from the walls, tore clothes off hooks in the closets, pulled suitcases and boxes off shelves. One of them found an old zither that Roy had won in a pool tournament. 'Looky here, Joe,' he said, strumming it with a big paw. The cop named Joe took it and turned it over. 'What is it?' he asked me. 'It's an old zither our guinea pig used to sleep on,' I said. It was true that a pet guinea pig we once had would never sleep anywhere except on the zither, but I should never have said so. Joe and the other cop looked at me a long time. They put the zither back on a shelf.

'No sign o' nuthin,' said the cop who had first spoken to mother. 'This guy,' he explained to the others, jerking a thumb at me, 'was nekked. The lady seems historical.' They all nodded, but said nothing; just looked at me. In the small silence we all heard a creaking in the attic. Grandfather was turning over in bed. 'What's 'at?', snapped Joe. Five or six cops sprang for the attic door before I could intervene or explain. I realized that it would be bad if they burst in on grandfather unannounced, or even announced. He was going through a phase in which he believed that General Meade's men, under steady hammering by Stonewall Jackson, were beginning to retreat and even desert.

When I got to the attic, things were pretty confused. Grandfather had evidently jumped to the conclusion that the police were deserters from Meade's army, trying to hide away in his attic. He bounded out of bed wearing a long flannel nightgown over long woollen underwear, a nightcap, and a leather jacket around his chest. The cops must have realized at once that the indignant white-haired old man belonged in the house, but they had no chance to say so. 'Back, ye cowardly dogs!' roared grandfather. 'Back t' the lines, ye god-dam lily-livered cattle!' With that, he fetched the officer who found the zither a flat-handed smack alongside his head that sent him sprawling. The others beat a retreat, but not fast enough; grandfather grabbed Zither's gun from its holster and let fly. The report seemed to crack the rafters; smoke filled the attic. A cop cursed and shot his hand to his shoulder. Somehow, we all finally got down-stairs again and locked the door against the old gentleman. He fired once or twice more in the darkness and then went back to bed. 'That was grandfather,' I explained to Joe, out of breath. 'He thinks you're deserters.' 'I'll say he does,' said Joe.

The cops were reluctant to leave without getting their hands on somebody besides grandfather; the night had been distinctly a defeat for them. Furthermore, they obviously didn't like the 'layout'; something looked – and I can see their viewpoint – phony. They began to poke into things again. A reporter, a thin-faced wispy man, came up to me. I had put on one of mother's blouses, not being able to find anything else. The reporter looked at me with mingled suspicion and interest. 'Just what the hell is the real lowdown here, Bud?' he asked. I decided to be frank with him. 'We had ghosts,' I said. He gazed at me a long time as if I were a slot machine into which he had, without results, dropped a nickel. Then he walked away. The cops followed him, the one grandfather shot holding his now-bandaged arm, cursing and blaspheming. 'I'm gonna get my gun back from that old bird,' said the zither-cop. 'Yeh,' said Joe. 'You – and who else?' I told them I would bring it to the station house the next day.

'What was the matter with that one policeman?' mother asked, after they had gone 'Grandfather shot him,' I said. 'What for?' she demanded. I told her he was a deserter. 'Of all things!' said mother. 'He was such a nice-looking young man.'

Grandfather was as fresh as a daisy and full of jokes at breakfast next morning. We thought at first he had forgotten all about what had happened, but he hadn't. Over his third cup of coffee, he glared at Herman and me. 'What was the idee of all them cops tarryhootin' round the house last night?' he demanded. He had us there.

The Horla

GUY DE MAUPASSANT

MAY 8. WHAT A LOVELY day! I have spent all the morning lying in the grass in front of my house, under the enormous plane tree that shades the whole of it. I like this part of the country and I like to live here because I am attached to it by old associations, by those deep and delicate roots which attach a man to the soil on which his ancestors were born and died, which attach him to the ideas and usages of the place as well as to the food, to local expressions, to the peculiar twang of the peasants, to the smell of the soil, of the villages, and of the atmosphere itself.

I love my house in which I grew up. From my windows I can see the Seine which flows alongside my garden, on the other side of the high road, almost through my grounds, the great and wide Seine, which goes to Rouen and Le Havre, and is covered with boats passing to and fro.

On the left, down yonder, lies Rouen, that large town, with its blue roofs, under its pointed Gothic towers. These are innumerable, slender or broad, dominated by the spire of the cathedral, and full of bells which sound through the blue air on fine mornings, sending their sweet and distant iron clang even as far as my home; that song of the metal, which the breeze wafts in my direction, now stronger and now weaker, according as the wind is stronger or lighter.

What a delicious morning it was!

About eleven o'clock, a long line of boats drawn by a steam tug as big as a fly, and which scarcely puffed while emitting its thick smoke, passed my gate.

After two English schooners, whose red flag fluttered in space, there came a magnificent Brazilian three-master; she was perfectly white, and wonderfully clean and shining. I saluted her, I hardly knew why, except that the sight of the vessel gave me great pleasure.

May 12. I have had a slight feverish attack for the last few days, and I feel ill, or rather I feel low-spirited.

Whence come those mysterious influences which change our happiness into discouragement, and our self-confidence into diffidence? One might almost say that the air, the invisible air, is full of unknowable Powers whose mysterious presence we have to endure. I wake up in the best spirits, with an inclination to sing. Why? I go down to the edge of the water, and suddenly, after walking a short distance, I return home wretched, as if some misfortune were awaiting me there. Why? Is it a cold shiver which, passing over my skin, has upset my nerves and given me low spirits? Is it the form of the clouds, the colour of the sky, or the colour of the surrounding objects, which is so changeable, that has troubled my thoughts as they passed before my eyes? Who can tell? Everything that surrounds us, everything that we see, without looking at it, everything that we touch, without knowing it, everything that we handle, without feeling it, all that we meet, without clearly distinguishing it, has a rapid, surprising and inexplicable effect upon us and upon our senses, and through them, on our ideas and on our heart itself.

How profound that mystery of the Invisible is! We cannot fathom it with our miserable senses, with our eyes which are unable to perceive what is either too small or too great, too near to us, or too far from us – neither the inhabitants of a star nor of a drop of water; nor with our ears that deceive us, for they transmit to us the vibrations of the air in sonorous notes. They are fairies who work the miracle of changing these vibrations into sound, and by that metamorphosis give birth to music, which makes the silent motion of nature musical ... with our sense of smell which is less keen than that of a dog ... with our sense of taste which can scarcely distinguish the age of a wine!

Oh! If we only had other organs which would work other miracles in our favour, what a number of fresh things we might discover around us!

May 16. I am ill, decidedly! I was so well last month! I am feverish, horribly feverish, or rather I am in a state of feverish enervation, which makes my mind suffer as much as my body. I have, continually, that horrible sensation of some impending danger, that apprehension of some coming misfortune, or of approaching death; that presentiment which is, no doubt, an attack of some illness which is still unknown, which germinates in the flesh and in the blood.

May 17. I have just come from consulting my physician, for I could no longer get any sleep. He said my pulse was rapid, my eyes dilated, my nerves highly strung, but there were no alarming symptoms. I must take a course of shower baths and of bromide of potassium.

May 25. No change! My condition is really very peculiar. As the evening comes on, an incomprehensible feeling of disquietude seizes me, just as if night concealed some threatening disaster. I dine hurriedly, and then try to read, but I do not understand the words, and can scarcely distinguish the letters. Then I walk up and down my drawing-room, oppressed by a feeling of confused and irresistible fear, the fear of sleep and fear of my bed.

About ten o'clock I go up to my room. As soon as I enter it I double-lock and bolt the door; I am afraid – of what? Up to the present time I have been afraid of nothing. . . . I open my cupboards, and look under my bed; I listen – to what? How strange it is that a simple feeling of discomfort, impeded or heightened circulation, perhaps the irritation of a nerve filament, a slight congestion, a small disturbance in the imperfect delicate functioning of our living machinery, may turn the most lighthearted of men into a melancholy one, and make a coward of the bravest? Then I go to bed, and wait for sleep as a man might wait for the executioner. I wait for its coming with dread, and my heart beats and my legs tremble, while my whole body shivers beneath the warmth of the bedclothes, until all at once I fall asleep, as though one should plunge into a pool of stagnant water in order to drown. I do not feel it coming on as I did formerly, this perfidious sleep which is close to me and watching me, which is going to seize me by the head, to close my eyes and annihilate me.

I sleep – a long time – two or three hours perhaps – then a dream – no – a nightmare lays hold on me. I feel that I am in bed and asleep . . . I feel it, and I know it . . . and I feel also that somebody is coming close to me, is looking at me, touching me, is getting on to my bed, is kneeling on my chest, is taking my neck between his hands and squeezing it . . . squeezing it with all his might in order to strangle me.

I struggle, bound by that terrible sense of powerlessness which paralyses us in our dreams; I try to cry out – but I cannot; I want to move – I cannot do so; I try, with the most violent efforts and breathing hard, to turn over and throw off this being who is crushing and suffocating me – I cannot!

And then, suddenly, I wake up, trembling and bathed in perspiration; I light a candle and find that I am alone, and after that crisis, which occurs every night, I at length fall asleep and slumber tranquilly till morning.

June 2. My condition has grown worse. What is the matter with me? The bromide does me no good, and the shower baths have no effect. Sometimes, in order to tire myself thoroughly, though I am fatigued enough already, I go for a walk in the forest of Roumare. I used to think at first that the fresh light and soft air, impregnated with the odour of herbs and leaves, would instill new blood into my veins and impart fresh energy to my heart. I turned into a broad hunting road, and then turned towards La Bouille, through a narrow path, between two rows of exceedingly tall trees, which placed a thick green, almost black, roof between the sky and me.

A sudden shiver ran through me, not a cold shiver, but a strange shiver of agony, and I hastened my steps, uneasy at being alone in the forest, afraid, stupidly and without reason, of the profound solitude. Suddenly it seemed to me as if I were being followed, as if somebody were walking at my heels, close, quite close to me, near enough to touch me.

I turned round suddenly, but I was alone. I saw nothing behind me except the straight, broad path, empty and bordered by high trees, horribly empty; before me it also extended until it was lost in the distance, and looked just the same – terrible.

I closed my eyes. Why? And then I began to turn round on one heel very quickly, just like a top. I nearly fell down, and opened my eyes; the trees were dancing round me and the earth heaved; I was obliged to sit down. Then, ah! I no longer remembered how I had come! What a strange idea! What a strange, strange idea! I did not in the least know. I started off to the right, and got back into the avenue which had led me into the middle of the forest.

June 3. I have had a terrible night. I shall go away for a few weeks, for no doubt a journey will set me up again.

July 2. I have come back, quite cured, and have had a most delightful trip into the bargain. I have been to Mont Saint-Michel, which I had not seen before.

What a sight, when one arrives as I did, at Avranches towards the end of the day! The town stands on a hill, and I was taken into the public garden at the extremity of the town. I uttered a cry of astonishment. An extraordinarily large bay lay extended before me, as far as my eyes could reach, between two hills which were lost to sight in the mist; and in the middle of this immense yellow bay, under a clear, golden sky, a peculiar hill rose up, sombre and pointed in the mist of the sand. The sun had just disappeared, and under the still flaming sky appeared the outline of that fantastic rock which bears on its summit a fantastic monument.

At daybreak I went out to it. The tide was low, as it had been the night before, and I saw that wonderful abbey rise up before me as I approached it. After several hours' walking, I reached the enormous mass of rocks which supports the little town, dominated by the great church. Having climbed the steep and narrow street, I entered the most wonderful Gothic building that has ever been built to God on earth, as large as a town, full of low rooms which seem buried beneath vaulted roofs, and lofty galleries supported by delicate columns.

I entered this gigantic granite gem, which is as light as a bit of lace, covered with towers, with slender belfries with spiral staircases, which raise their strange heads that bristle with chimeras, with devils, with fantastic animals, with monstrous flowers, to the blue sky by day, and to the black sky by night, and are connected by finely carved arches.

When I had reached the summit I said to the monk who accompanied me: 'Father, how happy you must be here!' And he replied: 'It is very windy here, monsieur'; and so we began to talk while watching the rising tide, which ran over the sand and covered it as with a steel cuirass.

And then the monk told me stories, all the old stories belonging to the place, legends, nothing but legends.

One of them struck me forcibly. The country people, those belonging to the Mount, declare that at night one can hear voies talking on the sands, and that one then hears two goats bleating, one with a strong, the other with a weak voice. Incredulous people declare that it is nothing but the cry of the sea birds, which occasionally resembles bleatings, and occasionally, human lamentations; but belated fishermen swear that they have met an old shepherd wandering between tides on the sands around the litle town. His head is completely concealed by his cloak and he is followed by a billy goat with a man's face, and a nanny goat with a woman's face, both having long, white hair, and talking incessantly and quarrelling in an unknown tongue. Then suddenly they cease and begin to bleat with all their might.

'Do you believe it?' I asked the monk. 'I scarcely know,' he replied, and I continued: 'If there are other beings besides ourselves on this earth, how comes it that we have not known it long since, or why have *you* not seen them? How is it that *I* have not seen them?' He replied: 'Do we see the hundred-thousandth part of what exists? Look here; there is the wind, which is the strongest force in nature, which knocks down men, and blows down buildings, uproots trees, raises the sea into mountains of water, destroys cliffs and casts great ships on the rocks; the wind which kills, which whistles, which sighs, which roars – have you ever seen it, and can you see it? It exists for all that, however.'

I was silent before this simple reasoning. That man was a philosopher, or perhaps a fool; I could not say which exactly, so I held my tongue. What he had said had often been in my own thoughts.

July 3. I have slept badly - certainly there is some feverish influence here, for my coachman is suffering in the same way as I am. When I went back home yesterday, I noticed his singular paleness, and I asked him: 'What is the matter with you, Jean?' 'The matter is that I never get any rest, and my nights devour my days. Since your departure, monsieur, there has been a spell over me.'

However, the other servants are all well, but I am very much afraid of having another attack myself.

July 4. I am decidedly ill again; for my old nightmares have returned. Last night I felt sombody leaning on me and sucking my life from between my lips. Yes, he was sucking it out of my throat, like a leech. Then he got up, satiated, and I woke up, so exhausted, crushed and weak that I could not move. If this continues for a few days, I shall certainly go away again.

July 5. Have I lost my reason? What happened last night is so strange that my head wanders when I think of it!

I had locked my door, as I do now every evening, and then, being thirsty, I drank half a glass of water, and accidentally noticed that the water bottle was full up to the cut-glass stopper.

Then I went to bed and fell into one of my terrible sleeps, from which I was aroused in about two hours by a still more frightful shock.

Picture to yourself a sleeping man who is being murdered and who wakes up with a knife in his lung, and whose breath rattles, who is covered with blood, and who can no longer breathe and is about to die, and does not understand – there you have it.

Having recovered my senses, I was thirsty again, so I lit a candle and went to the table on which stood my water bottle. I lifted it up and tilted it over my glass, but nothing came out. It was empty! It was completely empty! At first I could not understand it at all, and then suddenly I was seized by such a terrible feeling that I had to sit down, or rather I fell into a chair! Then I sprang up suddenly to look about me; then I sat down again, overcome by astonishment and fear, in front of the transparent glass bottle! I looked at it with fixed eyes, trying to conjecture, and my hands trembled! Somebody had drunk the water, but who? I? I, without any doubt. It could surely only be I. In that case I was a somnambulist; I lived, without knowing it, that mysterious double life which makes us doubt whether there are not two beings in us, or whether a strange, unknowable and invisible being does not at such moments, when our soul is in a state of torpor, animate our captive body, which obeys this other being, as it obeys us, and more than it obeys ourselves.

Oh! Who will understand my horrible agony? Who will understand the emotion of a man who is sound in mind, wide awake, full of common sense, who looks in horror through the glass of a water bottle for a little water that disappeared while he was asleep? I remained thus until it was daylight, without venturing to go to bed again.

July 6. I am going mad. Again all the contents of my water bottle have been drunk during the night – or rather, I have drunk it!

But is it I? Is it I? Who could it be? Who? Oh, God! Am I going mad? Who will save me?

July 10. I have just been through some surprising ordeals. Decidedly I am mad! And yet! . . .

On 6th July, before going to bed, I put some wine, milk, water, bread and strawberries on my table. Somebody drank – I drank – all the water and a little of the milk, but neither the wine, bread, nor the strawberriies were touched.

On the seventh of July I renewed the same experiment, with the same results, and on 8th July, I left out the water and the milk, and nothing was touched.

Lastly, on 9th July I put only water and milk on my table, taking care to wrap up the bottles in white muslin and to tie down the stoppers.

Then I rubbed my lips, my beard and my hands with pencil lead, and went to bed.

Irresistible sleep seized me, which was soon followed by a terrible awakening. I had not moved, and there was no mark of lead on the sheets. I rushed to the table. The muslin round the bottles remained intact; I undid the string, trembling with fear. All the water had been drunk, and so had the milk! Ah! Great God! . . .

I must start for Paris immediately.

July 12. Paris. I must have lost my head during the last few days! I must be the plaything of my enervated imagination, unless I am really a somnambulist, or perhaps I have been under the power of one of those hitherto unexplained influences which are called suggestions. In any case, my mental state bordered on madness, and twenty-four hours of Paris sufficed to restore my equilibrium.

Yesterday, after doing some business and paying some visits which instilled fresh and invigorating air into my soul, I wound up the evening at the *Théâtre-Français*. A play by Alexandre Dumas the younger was being acted, and his active and powerful imagination completed my cure. Certainly solitude is dangerous for active minds. We require around us men who can think and talk. When we are alone for a long time, we people space with phantoms.

I returned along the boulevards to my hotel in excellent spirits. Amid the jostling of the crowd I thought, not without irony, of my terrors and surmises of the previous week, because I had believed – yes, I had believed – that an invisible being lived beneath my roof. How weak our brains are, and how quickly they are terrified and led into error by a small incomprehensible fact.

Instead of saying simply: 'I do not understand because I do not know the cause,' we immediately imagine terrible mysteries and supernatural powers.

July 14. Fête of the Republic. I walked through the streets, amused as a child at the firecrackers and flags. Still it is very foolish to be merry on a fixed date, by Government decree. The populace is an imbecile flock of sheep, now stupidly patient, and now in ferocious revolt. Say to it: 'Amuse yourself,' and it amuses itself. Say to it: 'Go and fight with your neighbour,' and it goes and fights. Say to it: 'Vote for the Emperor,' and it votes for the Emperor, and then say to it: 'Vote for the Republic,' and it votes for the Republic.

Those who direct it are also stupid; only, instead of obeying men, they obey principles which can only be stupid, sterile, and false, for the very reason that they are principles, that is to say, ideas which are considered as certain and unchangeable in this world where one is certain of nothing, since light is an illusion and noise is an illusion.

July 16. I saw some things yesterday that troubled me very much.

I was dining at the house of my cousin, Madame Sablé, whose husband is colonel of the 76th Chasseurs at Limoges. There were two young women there, one of whom had married a medical man, Dr. Parent, who devotes much attention to nervous diseases and to the remarkable manifestations taking place at this moment under the influence of hypnotism and suggestion.

He related to us at some length the wonderful results obtained by English scientists and by the doctors of the Nancy school; and the facts which he adduced appeared to me so strange that I declared that I was altogether incredulous.

'We are,' he declared, 'on the point of discovering one of the most important secrets of nature; I mean to say, one of its most important secrets on this earth, for there are certainly others of a different kind of importance up in the stars, yonder. Ever since man has thought, ever since he has been able to express and write down his thoughts, he has felt himself close to a mystery which is impenetrable to his gross and imperfect senses, and he endeavours to supplement through his intellect the inefficiency of his senses. As long as that intellect remained in its elementary stage, these apparitions of invisible spirits assumed forms that were commonplace, though terrifying. Thence sprang the popular belief in the supernatural, the legends of wandering spirits, of fairies, of gnomes, ghosts, I might even say the legend of God; for our conceptions of the workman-creator, from whatever religion they may have come down to us, are certainly the most mediocre, the most stupid and the most incredible inventions that ever sprang from the terrified brain of any human beings. Nothing is truer than what Voltaire says: "God made man in His own image, but man has certainly paid Him back in his own coin."

'However, for rather more than a century men seem to have had a presentiment of something new. Mesmer and some others have put us on an unexpected track, and, especially within the last two or three years, we have arrived at really surprising results.'

My cousin, who is also very incredulous, smiled, and Dr. Parent said to her: 'Would you like me to try and send you to sleep, madame?' 'Yes, certainly.'

She sat down in an easy chair, and he began to look at her fixedly, so as to fascinate her. I suddenly felt myself growing uncomfortable, my heart beating rapidly and a choking sensation in my throat. I saw Madame Sablé's eyes becoming heavy, her mouth twitching and her bosom heaving, and at the end of ten minutes she was asleep.

'Go behind her,' the doctor said to me, and I took a seat behind her. He put a visiting card into her hands, and said to her: 'This is a looking-glass; what do you see in it?' And she replied: 'I see my cousin.' 'What is he doing?' 'He is twisting his moustache.' 'And now?' 'He is taking a photograph out of his pocket.' 'Whose photograph is it?' 'His own.'

That was true, and the photograph had been given me that same evening at the hotel.

'What is his attitude in this portrait?' 'He is standing up with his hat in his hand.'

She saw, therefore, on that card, on that piece of white pasteboard, as if she had seen it in a mirror.

The young women were frightened and exclaimed: 'That is enough! Quite, quite enough!'

But the doctor said to Madame Sablé authoritatively: 'You will rise at eight o'clock to-morrow morning; then you will go and call on your cousin at his hotel and ask him to lend you five thousand francs which your husband demands of you, and which he will ask for when he sets out on his coming journey.'

Then he woke her up.

On returning to my hotel, I thought over this curious séance, and I was assailed by doubts, not as to my cousin's absolute and undoubted good faith, for I had known her as well as if she were my own sister ever since she was a child, but as to a possible trick on the doctor's part. Had he not, perhaps, kept a glass hidden in his hand, which he showed to the young woman in her sleep, at the same time as he did the card? Professional conjurors do things that are just as singular.

So I went home and to bed, and this morning, at about half-past eight, I was awakened by my valet, who said to me: 'Madame Sablé has asked to see you immediately, monsieur.' I dressed hastily and went to her.

She sat down in some agitation, with her eyes on the floor, and without raising her veil she said to me: 'My dear cousin, I am going to ask a great favour of you.' 'What is it, cousin?' 'I do not like to tell you, and yet I must. I am in absolute need of five thousand francs.' 'What, you?' 'Yes, I, or rather my husband, who has asked me to procure them for him.'

I was so thunderstruck that I stammered out my answers. I asked myself whether she had not really been making fun of me with Dr. Parent, if it was not merely a very well-acted farce which had been rehearsed beforehand. On looking at her attentively, however, all my doubts disappeared. She was trembling with grief, so painful was this step to her, and I was convinced that her throat was full of sobs.

I knew that she was very rich and I continued: 'What! Has not your husband five thousand francs at his disposal? Come, think. Are you sure that he commissioned you to ask me for them?'

She hesitated for a few seconds, as if she were making a great effort to search her memory, and then she replied: 'Yes . . . yes, I am quite sure of it.' 'He has written to you?'

She hesitated again and reflected, and I guessed the torture of her thoughts. She did not know. She only knew that she was to borrow five thousand francs of me for her husband. So she told a lie. 'Yes, he has written to me.' 'When, pray? You did not mention it to me yesterday.'

'I received his letter this morning.' 'Can you show it me?' 'No . . . no . . . no . . . it contains private matters . . . things too personal to ourselves. . . . I burned it.' 'So your husband runs into debt?'

She hestitated again, and then murmured: 'I do not know.' Thereupon I said bluntly: 'I have not five thousand francs at my disposal at this moment, my dear cousin.'

She uttered a kind of cry as if she were in pain and said: 'Oh! oh! I beseech you, I beseech you to get them for me. . . .'

She got excited and clasped her hands as if she were praying to me! I heard her voice change its tone; she wept and stammered, harassed and dominated by the irresistible order that she had received.

'Oh! oh! I beg you to . . . if you knew what I am suffering . . . I want them to-day.'

I had pity on her: 'You shall have them by and by, I swear to you.' 'Oh! thank you! thank you! How kind you are.'

I continued: 'Do you remember what took place at your house last night?' 'Yes.' 'Do you remember that Dr. Parent sent you to sleep?' 'Yes.' 'Oh! Very well, then he ordered you to come to me this morning to borrow five thousand francs, and at this moment you are obeying that suggestion.'

She considered for a few moments, and then replied: 'But as it is my husband who wants them—'

For a whole hour I tried to convince her, but could not succeed, and when she had gone I went to the doctor. He was just going out, and he listened to me with a smile, and said: 'Do you believe now?' 'Yes, I cannot help it.' 'Let us go to your cousin's.'

She was already half asleep on a reclining chair, overcome with fatigue. The doctor felt her pulse, looked at her for some time with one hand raised towards her eyes, which she closed by degrees under the irresistible power of this magnetic influence, and when she was asleep, he said:

'Your husband does not require the five thousand francs any longer! You must, therefore, forget that you asked your cousin to lend them to you, and, if he speaks to you about it, you will not understand him.'

Then he woke her up, and I took out a pocketbook and said: 'Here is what you asked me for this morning, my dear cousin.' But she was so surprised that I did not venture to persist; nevertheless, I tried to recall the circumstance to her, but she denied it vigorously, thought I was making fun of her, and, in the end, very nearly lost her temper.

There! I have just come back, and I have not been able to eat any lunch, for this experiment has altogether upset me.

July 19. Many people to whom I told the adventure laughed at me. I no longer know what to think. The wise man says: 'It may be!'

July 21. I dined at Bougival, and then I spent the evening at a boatman's ball. Decidedly everything depends on place and surroundings.

It would be the height of folly to believe in the supernatural on the Ile de la Grenouilliere ... but on the top of Mont Saint-Michel? ... and in India? We are terribly influenced by our surroundings. I shall return home next week.

July 30. I came back to my own house yesterday. Everything is going on well.

August 2. Nothing new; it is splendid weather, and I spent my days in watching the Seine flowing past.

August 4. Quarrels among my servants. They declare that the glasses are broken in the cupboards at night. The footman accuses the cook, who accuses the seamstress, who accuses the other two. Who is the culprit? It is a clever person who can tell.

August 6. This time I am not mad. I have seen ... I have seen ... I have seen! ... I can doubt no longer ... I have seen it! ...

I was walking at two o'clock among my rose trees, in the full sunlight ... in the walk bordered by autumn roses which are beginning to fall. As I stopped to look at a Géant de Bataille, which had three splendid blossoms, I distinctly saw the stalk of one of the roses near me bend, as if an invisible hand had bent it, and then break, as if that hand had picked it! Then the flower raised itself, following the curve which a hand would have described in carrying it towards a mouth, and it remained suspended in the transparent air, all alone and motionless, a terrible red spot, three yards from my eyes. In desperation I rushed at it to take it! I found nothing; it had disappeared. Then I was seized with furious rage against myself, for a reasonable and serious man should not have such hallucinations.

But was it an hallucination? I turned round to look for the stalk, and I found it at once, on the bush, freshly broken, between two other roses which remained on the branch. I returned home then, my mind greatly disturbed; for I am certain now, as certain as I am of the alternation of day and night, that there exists close to me an invisible being that lives on milk and water, that can touch objects, take them and change their places; that is, consequently, endowed with a material nature, although it is imperceptible to our senses, and that lives as I do, under my roof.

August 7. I slept tranquilly. He drank the water out of my decanter, but did not disturb my sleep.

I wonder if I am mad. As I was walking just now in the sun by the riverside, doubts as to my sanity arose in me; not vague doubts such as I have had hitherto, but definite, absolute doubts. I have seen mad people, and I have known some who have been quite intelligent, lucid, even clear-sighted at every concern of life, except on one point. They spoke clearly, readily, profoundly on everything, when suddenly their mind struck upon the shoals of their madness and broke to pieces there, and scattered and foundered in that furious and terrible sea, full of rolling waves, fogs and squalls, which I called *madness*.

I certainly should think that I was mad, absolutely mad, if I were not conscious, did not perfectly know my condition, did not fathom it by analysing it with the most complete lucidity. I should, in fact, be only a rational man who was labouring under an hallucination. Some unknown disturbance must have arisen in my brain, one of those disturbances which physiologists of the present day try to note and to verify; and that disturbance must have caused a deep gap in my mind and in the sequence and logic of my ideas. Similar phenomena occur in dreams which lead us among the most unlikely phantasmagoria, without causing us any surprise, because our verifying apparatus and our organ of control are asleep, while our imaginative faculty is awake and active. Is it not possible that one of the imperceptible notes of the cerebral keyboard has been paralysed in me? Some men lose the recollection of proper names, of verbs, or of numbers, or merely of dates, in consequence of an accident. The localization of all the variations of thought has been established nowadays; why, then, should it be surprising if my faculty of controlling the unreality of certain hallucinations were dormant in me for the time being?

I thought of all this as I walked by the side of the water. The sun shone brightly on the river and made earth delightful, while it filled me with a love for life, for the swallows, whose agility always delights my eye, for the plants by the riverside, the rustle of whose leaves is a pleasure to my ears.

By degrees, however, an inexplicable feeling of discomfort seized me. It seemed as if some unknown force were numbing and stopping me, were preventing me from going farther, and were calling me back. I felt that painful wish to return which oppresses you when you have left a beloved invalid at home, and when you are seized with a presentiment that he is worse.

I, therefore, returned in spite of myself, feeling certain that I should find some bad news awaiting me, a letter or a telegram. There was nothing, however, and I was more surprised and uneasy than if I had had another fantastic vision.

August 8. I spent a terrible evening yesterday. He does not show himself any more, but I feel that he is near me, watching me, looking at me, penetrating me, dominating me, and more redoubtable when he hides himself thus than if he were to manifest his constant and invisible presence by supernatural phenomena. However, I slept.

August 9. Nothing, but I am afraid.

August 10. Nothing; what will happen to-morrow?

August 11. Still nothing; I cannot stop at home with this fear hanging over me and these thoughts in my mind; I shall go away.

August 12. Ten o'clock at night. All day long I have been trying to get away, and have not been able. I wished to accomplish this simple and easy act of freedom – to go out – to get into my carriage in order to go to Rouen – and I have not been able to do it. What is the reason?

August 13. When we are attacked by certain maladies, all the springs of our physical being appear to be broken, all our energies destroyed, all our muscles relaxed; our bones, too, have become as soft as flesh, and our bodies as liquid as water. I am experiencing these sensations in my moral being in a strange and distressing manner. I have no longer any strength, any courage, any self-control, not even any power to set my own will in motion. I have no power left to will anything; but someone does it for me and I obey.

August 14. I am lost! Somebody possesses my soul and dominates it. Somebody orders all my acts, all my movements, all my thoughts. I am no longer anything in myself, nothing except an enslaved and terrified spectator of all the things I do. I wish to go out; I cannot. He does not wish to, and so I remain, trembling and distracted, in the armchair in which he keeps me sitting. I merely wish to get up and to rouse myself; I cannot! I am riveted to my chair, and my chair adheres to the ground in such a manner that no power could move us.

Then, suddenly, I must, I must go to the bottom of my garden to pick some strawberries and eat them, and I go there. I pick the strawberries and eat them! Oh, my God! My God! Is there a God? If there be one, deliver me! Save me! Succour me! Pardon! Pity! Mercy! Save me! Oh, what sufferings! What torture! What horror!

August 15. This is certainly the way in which my poor cousin was possessed and controlled when she came to borrow five thousand francs of me. She was under the power of a strange will which had entered into her, like another soul, like another parasitic and dominating soul. Is the world coming to an end?

But who is he, this invisible being that rules me? This unknowable being, this rover of a supernatural race?

Invisible beings exist, then! How is it, then, that since the beginning of the world they have never manifested themselves precisely as they do to me? I have never read of anything that resembles what goes on in my house. Oh, if I could only leave it, if I could only go away, escape, and never return! I should be saved, but I cannot.

August 16. I managed to escape to-day for two hours, like a prisoner who finds the door of his dungeon accidentally open. I suddenly felt that I was free and that he was far away, and so I gave orders to harness the horses as quickly as possible, and I drove to Rouen. Oh, how delightful to be able to say to a man who obeys you: 'Go to Rouen!'

I made him pull up before the library, and I begged them to lend me Dr. Herrmann Herestauss' treatise on the unknown inhabitants of the ancient and modern world.

Then, as I was getting into my carriage, I intended to say: 'To the railway station!' but instead of this I shouted – I did not say, but I shouted

– in such a loud voice that all the passers-by turned round; 'Home!' and I fell back on the cushion of my carriage, overcome by mental agony. He had found me again and regained possession of me.

August 17. Oh, what a night! What a night! And yet it seems to me that I ought to rejoice. I read until one o'clock in the morning! Herestauss, doctor of philosophy and theogony, wrote the history of the manifestation of all those invisible beings which hover around man, or of whom he dreams. He describes their origin, their domain, their power; but none of them resembles the one which haunts me. One might say that man, ever since he began to think, has had a foreboding fear of a new being, stronger than himself, his successor in this world, and that, feeling his presence, and not being able to foresee the nature of that master, he has, in his terror, created the whole race of occult beings, of vague phantoms born of fear.

Having, therefore, read until one o'clock in the morning, I went and sat down at the open window, in order to cool my forehead and my thoughts, in the calm night air. It was very pleasant and warm! How I should have enjoyed such a night formerly!

There was no moon, but the stars darted out their rays in the dark heavens. Who inhabits those worlds? What forms, what living beings, what animals are there yonder? What do the thinkers in those distant worlds know more than we do? What can they do more than we can? What do they see which we do not know? Will not one of them, some day or other, traversing space, appear on our earth to conquer it, just as the Norsemen formerly crossed the sea in order to subjugate nations more feeble than themselves?

We are so weak, so defenceless, so ignorant, so small, we who live on this particle of mud which revolves in a drop of water.

I fell asleep, dreaming thus in the cool night air, and when I had slept for about three-quarters of an hour, I opened my eyes without moving, awakened by I know not what confused and strange sensation. At first I saw nothing, and then suddenly it appeared to me as if a page of a book which had remained open on my table turned over of its own accord. Not a breath of air had come in at my window, and I was surprised, and waited. In about four minutes, I saw, I saw, yes saw with my own eyes, another page lift itself up and fall down on the others, as if a finger had turned it over. My armchair was empty, appeared empty, but I knew that he was there, he, and sitting in my place, and that he was reading. With a furious bound, the bound of an enraged wild beast that springs at its tamer, I crossed my room to seize him, to strangle him, to kill him! But before I could reach it, the chair fell over as if sombody had run away from me – my table rocked, my lamp fell and went out, and my window closed as if some thief had been surprised and had fled out into the night, shutting it behind him.

So he had run away; he had been afraid; he, afraid of me!

But – but – to-morrow – or later – some day or other – I should be able to hold him in my clutches and crush him against the ground! Do not dogs occasionally bite and strangle their masters?

August 18. I have been thinking the whole day long. Oh, yes, I will obey him, follow his impulses, fulfil all his wishes, show myself humble, submissive, a coward. He is the stronger; but the hour will come—

August 19. I know – I know – I know all! I have just read the following in the *Revue de Monde Scientifique*: 'A curious piece of news comes to us from Rio de Janeiro. Madness, an epidemic of madness, which may be compared to that contagious madness which attacked the people of Europe in the Middle Ages, is at this moment raging in the Province of San-Paolo. The terrified inhabitants are leaving their houses, saying that they are pursued, possessed, dominated like human cattle by invisible, though tangible, beings, a species of vampires, which feed on their life while they are asleep, and which, besides, drink water and milk without appearing to touch any other nourishment.

'Professor Don Pedro Henriques, accompanied by several medical savants, has gone to the Province of San-Paolo, in order to study the origin and the manifestations of this surprising madness on the spot, and to propose such measures to the Emperor as may appear to him to be most fitted to restore the mad population to reason.'

Ah! Ah! I remember now that fine Brazilian three-master which passed in front of my windows as she was going up the Seine, on the 8th day of last May! I thought she looked so pretty, so white and bright! That Being was on board of her, coming from there, where its race originated. And it saw me! It saw my house which was also white, and it sprang from the ship on to the land. Oh, merciful heaven!

Now I know, I can divine. The reign of man is over, and he has come. He who was feared by primitive man; whom disquieted priests exorcised; whom sorcerers evoked on dark nights, without having seen him appear, to whom the imagination of the transient masters of the world lent all the monstrous or graceful forms of gnomes, spirits, genii, fairies, and familiar spirits. After the coarse conceptions of primitive fear, more clear-sighted men foresaw it more clearly. Mesmer divined it, and ten years ago physicians accurately discovered the nature of his power, even before he exercised it himself. They played with this new weapon of the Lord, the sway of a mysterious will over the human soul, which had become a slave. They called it magnetism, hypnotism, suggestion – what do I know? I have seen them amusing themselves like rash children with this horrible power! Woe to us! Woe to man! He has come, the – the – what does he call himself – the – I fancy that he is shouting out his name to me and I do not hear him – the – yes – he is shouting it out – I am listening – I cannot – he repeats it – the – Horla – I hear – the Horla – it is he – the Horla – he has come!

Ah! the vulture has eaten the pigeon; the wolf has eaten the lamb; the lion has devoured the sharp-horned buffalo; man has killed the lion with an arrow, with a sword, with gunpowder; but the Horla will make of man what we have made of the horse and of the ox; his chattel, his slave, and his food, by the mere power of his will. Woe to us!

But, nevertheless, the animal sometimes revolts and kills the man who has subjugated it. I should also like – I shall be able to – but I must know him, touch him, see him! Scientists say that animals' eyes, being different from ours, do not distinguish objects as ours do. And my eye cannot distinguish this newcomer who is oppressing me.

Why? Oh, now I remember the words of the monk at Mont Saint-Michel: 'Can we see the hundred-thousandth part of what exists? See here; there is the wind, which is the strongest force in nature, which knocks men down, and wrecks buildings, uproots trees, raises the sea into mountains of water, destroys cliffs and casts great ships on the breakers; the wind which kills, which whistles, which sighs, which roars – have you ever seen it, and can you see it? It exists, for all that, however!'

And I went on thinking: my eyes are so weak, so imperfect, that they do not even distinguish hard bodies, if they are as transparent as glass! If a glass without tinfoil behind it were to bar my way, I should run into it, just as a bird which has flown into a room breaks its head against the window-panes. A thousand things, moreover, deceive man and lead him astray. Why should it then be surprising that he cannot perceive an unknown body through which the light passes?

A new being! Why not! It was assuredly bound to come! Why should we be the last? We do not distinguish it any more than all the others created before us! The reason is, that its nature is more perfect, its body finer and more finished than ours, that ours is so weak, so awkwardly constructed, encumbered with organs that are always tired, always on the strain like machinery that is too complicated, which lives like a plant and like a beast, nourishing itself with difficulty on air, herbs, and flesh, an animal machine which is a prey to maladies, tomalformations, to decay; broken-winded, badly regulated, simple and eccentric, ingeniously badly made, at one a coarse and a delicate piece of workmanship, the rough sketch of a being that might become intelligent and grand.

We are only a few, so few in this world, from the oyster up to man. Why should there not be one more, once that period is passed which separates the successive apparitions from all the different species?

Why not one more? Why not, also, other trees with immense, splendid flowers, perfuming whole regions? Why not other elements besides fire, air, earth, and water? There are four, only four, those nursing fathers of various beings! What a pity! Why are there not forty, four hundred, four thousand? How poor everything is, how mean and wretched! grudgingly produced, roughly constructed, clumsily made! Ah, the elephant and the hippopotamus, what grace! And the camel, what elegance!

But the butterfly, as you will say, a flying flower! I dream of one that should be as large as a hundred worlds, with wings whose shape, beauty, colour, and motion I cannot even express. But I see it – it flutters from star to star, refreshing them and perfuming them with the light and harmonious breath of its flight! And the people up there look at it as it passes in an ecstasy of delight!

What is the matter with me? It is he, the Horla, who haunts me, and who makes me think of these foolish things! He is within me, he is becoming my soul; I shall kill him!

August 29. I shall kill him. I have seen him! Yesterday I sat down at my table and pretended to write very assiduously. I knew quite well that he would come prowling round me, quite close to me, so close that I might perhaps be able to touch him, to seize him. And then – then I should have the strength of desperation; I should have my hands, my knees, my chest, my forehead, my teeth to strangle him, to crush him, to bite him, to tear him to pieces. And I watched for him with all my over-excited senses.

I had lighted my two lamps and the eight wax candles on my mantelpiece, as if with this light I could discover him.

My bedstead, my old oak post bedstead, stood opposite to me; on my right was the fireplace; on my left, the door which was carefully closed, after I had left it open for some time in order to attract him; behind me was a very high wardrobe with a looking-glass in it, before which I stood to shave and dress every day, and in which I was in the habit of glancing at myself from head to foot every time I passed it.

I pretended to be writing in order to deceive him, for he also was watching me, and suddenly I felt – I was certain that he was reading over my shoulder, that he was there, touching my ear.

I got up, my hands extended, and turned round so quickly that I almost fell. Eh! well? It was as bright as at midday, but I did not see my reflection in the mirror! It was empty, clear, profound, full of light! But my figure was not reflected in it – and I, I was opposite to it! I saw the large, clear glass from top to bottom, and I looked at it with unsteady eyes; and I did not dare to advance; I did not venture to make a movement, feeling that he was there, but that he would escape me again, he whose imperceptible body had absorbed my reflection.

How frightened I was! And then, suddenly, I began to see myself in a mist in the depths of the looking-glass, in a mist as it were a sheet of water; and it seemed to me as if this water were flowing clearer every moment. It was like the end of an eclipse. Whatever it was that hid me did not appear to possess any clearly defined outlines, but a sort of opaque transparency which gradually grew clearer.

At last I was able to distinguish myself completely, as I do every day when I look at myself.

I had seen it! And the horror of it remained with me, and makes me shudder even now.

August 30. How could I kill it, as I could not get hold of it? Poison? But it would see me mix it with the water; and then, would our poisons have any effect on its impalpable body? No – no – no doubt about the matter – Then – then?—

August 31. I sent for a blacksmith from Rouen, and ordered iron shutters for my room, such as some private hotels in Paris have on the ground floor, for fear of burglars, and he is going to make me an iron door as well. I have made myself out a coward, but I do not care about that!

September 10. Rouen, Hotel Continental. It is done – it is done – but is he dead? My mind is thoroughly upset by what I have seen.

Well, then, yesterday, the locksmith having put on the iron shutters and door, I left everything open until midnight, although it was getting cold.

Suddenly I felt that he was there, and joy, mad joy, took possession of me. I got up softly, and walked up and down for some time, so that he might not suspect anything; then I took off my boots and put on my slipper carelessly; then I fastened the iron shutters, and, going back to the door, quickly double-locked it with a padlock, putting the key into my pocket.

Suddenly I noticed that he was moving restlessly round me, that in his turn he was frightened and was ordering me to let him out. I nearly yielded; I did not, however, but, putting my back to the door, I half opened it, just enough to allow me to go out backward, and as I am very tall my head touched the casing. I was sure that he had not been able to escape, and I shut him up quite alone, quite alone. What happiness! I had him fast. Then I ran downstairs; in the drawing-room, which was under my bedroom, I took the two lamps and I poured all the oil on the carpet, the furniture, everywhere; then I set fire to it and made by escape, after having carefully double-locked the door.

I went and hid myself at the bottom of the garden, in a clump of laurel bushes. How long it seemed! How long it seemed! Everything was dark, silent, motionless, not a breath of air and not a star, but heavy banks of clouds which one could not see, but which weighed, oh, so heavily on my soul.

I looked at my house and waited. How long it was! I already began to think that the fire had gone out of its own accord, or that he had extinguished it, when one of the lower windows gave way under the violence of the flames, and a long, soft, caressing sheet of red flame mounted up the white wall, and enveloped it as far as the roof. The light fell on the trees, the branches, and the leaves, and a shiver of fear pervaded them also! The birds awoke, a dog began to howl, and it seemed to me as if the day were breaking! Almost immediately two other windows flew into fragments, and I saw that the whole of the lower part of my house was nothing but a terrible furnace. But a cry, a horrible, shrill, heart-rending cry, a woman's cry, sounded through the night, and two garret windows were opened! I had forgotten the servants! I saw their terror-stricken faces, and their arms waving frantically.

Then, overwhelmed with horror, I set off to run to the village, shouting: 'Help! help! fire! fire!' I met some people who were already coming to the scene, and I returned with them.

By this time the house was nothing but a horrible and magnificent funeral pile, a monstrous funeral pile which lit up the whole country, a funeral pile where men were burning, and where he was burning also, He, He, my prisoner, that new Being, the new master, the Horla!

Suddenly the whole roof fell in between the walls, and a volcano of flames darted up to the sky. Through all the windows which opened on that furnace, I saw the flames darting, and I thought that he was there, in that kiln, dead.

Dead? Perhaps.—His Body? Was not his body, which was transparent, indestructible by such means as would kill ours?

If he were not dead?—Perhaps time alone has power over that Invisible and Redoubtable Being. Why this transparent, unrecognizable body, this body belonging to a spirit, if it also has to fear ills, infirmities and premature destruction?

Premature destruction? All human terror spring from that! After man, the Horla. After him who can die every day, at any hour, at any moment, by any accident, comes the one who will die only at his own proper hour, day, and minute, because he has touched the limits of his existence!

No – no – without any doubt – he is not dead – Then – then – I suppose I must kill *myself!* . . .

Io

OLIVER ONIONS

AS THE YOUNG MAN put his hand to the uppermost of the four brass bell-knobs to the right of the fanlighted door he paused, withdrew the hand again, and then pulled at the lowest knob. The sawing of bell-wire answered him, and he waited for a moment, uncertain whether the bell had rung, before pulling again. Then there came from the basement a single cracked stroke; the head of a maid appeared in the whitewashed area below; and the head was withdrawn as apparently the maid recognised him. Steps were heard along the hall; the door was opened; and the maid stood aside to let him enter, the apron with which she had slipped the latch still crumpled in her greasy hand.

'Sorry, Daisy,' the young man apologised, 'but I didn't want to bring her down all those stairs. How is she? Has she been out to-day?'

The maid replied that the person spoken of had been out; and the young man walked along the wide carpeted passage.

It was cumbered like an antique-shop with alabaster busts on pedestals, dusty palms in faience vases, and trophies of spears and shields and assegais. At the foot of the stairs was a rustling portière of strung beads, and beyond it the carpet was continued up the broad, easy flight, secured at each step by a brass rod. Where the stairs made a turn, the fading light of the December afternoon, made still dimmer by a window of decalcomanied glass, shone on a cloudy green aquarium with sallow goldfish, a number of cacti on a shabby console table, and a large and dirty white sheepskin rug. Passing along a short landing, the young man began the ascent of the second flight. This also was carpeted, but with a carpet that had done duty in some dining- or bed-room before being cut up into strips of the width of the narrow space between the wall and the handrail. Then, as he still mounted, the young man's feet sounded loud on oilcloth; and when he finally paused and knocked at a door it was on a small landing of naked boards beneath the cold gleam of the skylight above the well of the stairs.

'Come in,' a girl's voice called.

The room he entered had a low sagging ceiling on which shone a low glow of firelight, making colder still the patch of eastern sky beyond the roofs and the cowls and hoods of chimneys framed by the square of the single window. The glow on the ceiling was reflected dully in the old dark mirror over the mantelpiece. An open door in the farther corner, hampered with skirts and blouses, allowed a glimpse of the girl's bedroom.

The young man set the paper bag he carried down on the littered round table and advanced to the girl who sat in an old wicker chair before the fire. The girl did not turn her head as he kissed her cheek, and he looked down at something that had muffled the sound of his steps as he had approached her.

'Hallo, that's new, isn't it, Bessie? Where did that come from?' he asked cheerfully.

The middle of the floor was covered with a common jute matting, but on the hearth was a magnificent leopard-skin rug.

'Mrs. Hepburn sent it up. There was a draught from under the door. It's much warmer for my feet.'

'Very kind of Mrs. Hepburn. Well, how are you feeling to-day, old girl?'

'Better, thanks, Ed.'

'That's the style. You'll be yourself again soon. Daisy says you've been out to-day?'

'Yes, I went for a walk. But not far; I went to the Museum and then sat down. You're early, aren't you?'

He turned away to get a chair, from which he had to move a mass of tissue-paper patterns and buckram linings. He brought it to the rug.

'Yes. I stopped last night late to cash up for Vedder, so he's staying to-night. Turn and turn about. Well, tell us all about it, Bess.'

Their faces were red in the firelight. Hers had the prettiness that the first glance almost exhausts, the prettiness, amazing in its quantity, that one sees for a moment under the light of the street lamps when shops and offices close for the day. She was short-nosed, pulpy-mouthed and faunish-eyed, and only the rather remarkable smallness of the head on the splendid thick throat saved her from ordinariness. He, too, might have been seen in his thousands at the close of any day, hurrying home to Catford or Walham Green or Tufnell Park to tea and an evening with a girl or in a billiard-room, or else dining cheaply 'up West' preparatory to smoking cigarettes from yellow packets in the upper circle of a music-hall. Four inches of white up-and-down collar encased his neck; and as he lifted his trousers at the knee to clear his purple socks, the pair of paper covers showed, that had protected his cuffs during the day at the office. He removed them, crumpled them up and threw them on the fire; and the momentary addition to the light of the upper chamber showed how curd-white was that superb neck of hers and how moody and tired her eyes.

From his face only one would have guessed, and guessed wrongly, that his preferences were for billiard-rooms and music-halls. His conversation showed them to be otherwise. It was of Polytechnic classes that he spoke, and of the course of lectures in English literature that had just begun. And, as if somebody had asserted that the pursuit of such studies was not compatible with a certain measure of physical development also, he announced that he was not sure that he should not devote, say, half an evening a week, on Wednesdays, to training in the gymnasium.

'*Mens sana in corpore sano*, Bessie,' he said; 'a sound mind in a sound body, you know. That's tremendously important, especially when a fellow spends the day in a stuffy office. Yes, I think I shall give it half Wednesdays, from eight-thirty to nine-thirty; sends you home in a glow. But I was going to tell you about the Literature Class. The second lecture's to-night. The first was splendid, all about the languages of Europe and Asia – what they call the Indo-Germanic languages, you know. Aryans. I can't tell you exactly without my notes, but the Hindoos and Persians, I think it was, they crossed the Himalaya Mountains and spread westward somehow, as far as Europe. That was the way it all began. It was splendid, the way the lecturer put it. English is a Germanic language, you know. Then came the Celts. I wish I'd brought my notes. I see you've been reading; let's look—'

A book lay on her knees, its back warped by the heat of the fire. He took it and opened it.

'Ah, Keats! Glad you like Keats, Bessie. We needn't be great readers, but it's important that what we do read should be all right. I don't know him, not *really* know him, that is. But he's quite all right – A1 in fact. And he's an example of what I've always maintained, that knowledge should be brought within the reach of all. It just shows. He was the son of a livery-stable keeper, you know, so what he'd have been if he'd really had chances, been to universities and so on, there's no knowing. But, of course, it's more from the historical standpoint that I'm studying these things. Let's have a look—'

He opened the book where a hairpin between the leaves marked a place. The firelight glowed on the page, and he read, monotonously and inelastically:

> '*And as I sat, over the light blue hills*
> *There came a noise of revellers; the rills*
> *Into the wide stream came of purple hue—*
> *'Twas Bacchus and his crew!*

The earnest trumpet spake, and silver thrills
From kissing cymbals made a merry din—
   'Twas Bacchus and his kin!
Like to a moving vintage down they came,
Crowned with green leaves, and faces all on flame
All madly dancing through the pleasant valley
   To scare thee, Melancholy!'

It was the wondrous passage from *Endymion*, of the descent of the
wild inspired rabble into India. Ed plucked for a moment at his lower
lip, and then, with a 'Hm! What's it all about, Bessie?' continued:

'Within his car, aloft, young Bacchus stood,
Trifling his ivy-dart, in dancing mood,
   With sidelong laughing;
And little rills of crimson wine imbrued
His plump white arms and shoulders, enough white
   For Venus' pearly bite;
And near him rode Silenus on his ass,
Pelted with flowers as he on did pass,
   Tipsily quaffing.'

'Hm! I see. Mythology. That's made up of tales, and myths, you know.
Like Odin and Thor and those, only those were Scandinavian Mythology.
So it would be absurd to take it too seriously. But I think, in a way,
things like that do harm. You see,' he explained, 'the more beautiful they
are the more harm they might do. We ought always to show virtue and
vice in their true colours, and if you look at it from that point of view this
is just drunkenness. That's rotten; destroys your body and intellect; as
I heard a chap say once, it's an insult to the beasts to call it beastly. I
joined the Blue Ribbon when I was fourteen and I haven't been sorry for
it yet. No. Now there's Vedder; he "went off on a bend," as he calls it,
last night, and even he says this morning it wasn't worth it. But let's read
on.'
Again he read, with unresilient movement:

'I saw Osirian Egypt kneel adown
Before the vine wreath crown!
   I saw parched Abyssinia rouse and sing
   To the silver cymbals' ring!
I saw the whelming vintage hotly pierce
   Old Tartary the fierce!
Great Brahma from his mystic heaven groans. . .'

'Hm! He was a Buddhist god, Brahma was; mythology again. As I say, if you take it seriously, it's just glorifying intoxication. – But I say; I can hardly see. Better light the lamp. We'll have tea first, then read. No, you sit still; I'll get it ready; I know where things are—'

He rose, crossed to a little cupboard with a sink in it, filled the kettle at the tap, and brought it to the fire. Then he struck a match and lighted the lamp.

The cheap glass shade was of a foolish corolla shape, clear glass below, shading to pink, and deepening to red at the crimped edge. It gave a false warmth to the spaces of the room above the level of the mantelpiece, and Ed's figure, as he turned the regulator, looked from the waist upwards as if he stood within that portion of a spectrum screen that deepens to the band of red. The bright concentric circles that spread in rings of red on the ceiling were more dimly reduplicated in the old mirror over the mantelpiece; and the wintry eastern light beyond the chimney-hoods seemed suddenly almost to die out.

Bessie, her white neck below the level of the lamp-shade, had taken up the book again; but she was not reading. She was looking over it at the upper part of the grate. Presently she spoke.

'I was looking at some of those things this afternoon, at the Museum.'

He was clearing from the table more buckram linings and patterns of paper, numbers of *Myra's Journal* and *The Delineator*. Already on his way to the cupboard he had put aside a red-bodiced dressmaker's 'shape' of wood and wire.

'What things?' he asked.

'Those you were reading about. Greek, aren't they?'

'Oh, the Greek room!. . . But those people, Bacchus and those, weren't people in the ordinary sense. Gods and goddesses, most of 'em; Bacchus was a god. That's what mythology means. I wish sometimes our course took in Greek literature, but it's a dead language after all. German's more good in modern life. It would be nice to know everything, but one has to select, you know. Hallo, I clean forgot; I brought you some grapes, Bessie; here they are, in this bag; we'll have 'em after tea, what?'

'But,' she said again after a pause, still looking at the grate, 'they had their priests and priestesses, and followers and people, hadn't they? It was their things I was looking at – combs and brooches and hairpins, and things to cut their nails with. They're all in a glass case there. And they had safety-pins, exactly like ours.'

'Oh, they were a civilised people,' said Ed cheerfully. 'It all gives you an idea. I only hope you didn't tire yourself out. You'll soon be all right, of course, but you have to be careful yet. We'll have a clean tablecloth, shall we?'

She had been seriously ill; her life had been despaired of; and somehow the young Polytechnic student seemed anxious to assure her that she was now all right again, or soon would be. They were to be married 'as soon as things brightened up a bit,' and he was very much in love with her.

He watched her head and neck as he continued to lay the table, and then, as he crossed once more to the cupboard, he put his hand lightly in passing on her hair.

She gave so quick a start that he too started. She must have been very deep in her reverie to have been so taken by surprise.

'I say, Bessie, don't jump like that!' he cried with involuntary quickness. Indeed, had his hand been red-hot, or ice-cold, or taloned, she could not have turned a more startled, even frightened, face to him.

'It was your touching me,' she muttered, resuming her gazing into the grate.

He stood looking anxiously down on her. It would have been better not to discuss her state, and he knew it; but in his anxiety he forgot it.

'That jumpiness is the effect of your illness, you know. I shall be glad when it's all over. It's made you so odd.'

She was not pleased that he should speak of her 'oddness.' For that matter, she, too, found him 'odd' – at any rate, found it difficult to realise that he was as he always had been. He had begun to irritate her a little. His club-footed reading of the verses had irritated her, and she had tried hard to hide from him that his cocksure opinions and the tone in which they were pronounced jarred on her. It was not that she was 'better' than he, 'knew' any more than he did, didn't (she supposed) love him still the same; these moods, that dated from her illness, had nothing to do with those things; she reproached herself sometimes that she was subject to such doldrums.

'It's all right, Ed, but please don't touch me just now,' she said.

He was in the act of leaning over her chair, but he saw her shrink, and refrained.

'Poor old girl!' he said sympathetically. 'What's the matter?'

'I don't know. It's awfully stupid of me to be like this, but I can't help it. I shall be better soon if you leave me alone.'

'Nothing's happened, has it?'

'Only those silly dreams I told you about.'

'Bother the dreams!' muttered the Polytechnic student.

During her illness she had had dreams, and had come to herself at intervals to find Ed or the doctor, Mrs. Hepburn or her aunt, bending over her. These kind, solicitous faces had been no more than a glimpse, and then she had gone off into the dreams again. The curious thing had been that the dreams had seemed to be her vivid waking life, and the other things – the anxious faces, the details of her dingy bedroom, the thermometer under her tongue – had been the dream. And, though she had come back to actuality, the dreams had never quite vanished. She could remember no more of them than that they had seemed to hold a high singing and jocundity, issuing from some region of haze and golden light; and they seemed to hover, ever on the point of being recaptured, yet ever eluding all her mental efforts. She was living now between reality and a vision.

She had fewer words than sensations, and it was a little pitiful to hear her vainly striving to make clear what she meant.

'It's so queer,' she said. 'It's like being on the edge of something – a sort of tiptoe – I can't describe it. Sometimes I could almost touch it with my hand, and then it goes away, but never *quite* away. It's like something just past the corner of my eye, over my shoulder, and I sit very still sometimes, trying to take it off its guard. But the moment I move my head it moves too – like this—'

Again he gave a quick start at the suddenness of her action. Very stealthily her faunish eyes had stolen sideways, and then she had swiftly turned her head.

'Here, I say, don't, Bessie!' he cried nervously. 'You look awfully uncanny when you do that! You're brooding,' he continued, 'that's what you're doing, brooding. You're getting into a low state. You want bucking up. I don't think I shall go to the Polytec. to-night; I shall stay and cheer you up. You know, I really don't think you're making an effort, darling.'

His last words seemed to strike her. They seemed to fit in with something of which she too was conscious. 'Not making an effort. . .' she wondered how he knew that. She felt in some vague way that it was important that she *should* make an effort.

For, while her dream ever evaded her, and yet never ceased to call her with such a voice as he who reads on a magic page of the calling of elves hears stilly in his brain, yet somehow behind the seduction was another and a sterner voice. There was warning as well as fascination. Beyond that edge at which she strained on tiptoe, mingled with the jocund calls to Hasten, Hasten, were deeper calls that bade her Beware. They puzzled her. Beware of what? Of what danger? And to whom?. . .

'How do you mean, I'm not making an effort, Ed?' she asked slowly, again looking into the fire, where the kettle now made a gnat-like singing.

'Why, an effort to get all right again. To be as you used to be – as, of course, you will be soon.'

'As I *used* to be?' The words came with a little check in her breathing.

'Yes, before all this. To be yourself, you know.'

'Myself?'

'All jolly, and without these jerks and jumps. I wish you could get away. A fortnight by the sea would do you all the good in the world.'

She knew not what it was in the words 'the sea' that caused her suddenly to breathe more deeply. The sea!. . . It was as if, by the mere uttering of them, he had touched some secret spring, brought to fulfilment some spell. What had he meant by speaking of the sea?. . . A fortnight before, had somebody spoken to her of the sea it would have been the sea of Margate, of Brighton, of Southend, that, supplying the image that a word calls up as if by conjuration, she would have seen before her; and

what other image could she supply, could she *possibly* supply, now?. . . .
Yet she did, or almost did, supply one. What new experience had she
had, or what old, old one had been released in her? With that confused,
joyous dinning just beyond the range of physical hearing there had
suddenly mingled a new illusion of sound – a vague, vast pash and rustle,
silky and harsh both at once, its tireless voice holding meanings of stillness
and solitude compared with which the silence that is mere absence of
sound was vacancy. It was part of her dream, invisible, intangible,
inaudible, yet there. As if he had been an enchanter, it had come into
being at the word upon his lips. Had he other such words? Had he the
Master Word that – (ah, she knew what the Master Word would do!)
– would make the Vision the Reality and the Reality the Vision? Deep
within her she felt something – her soul, herself, she knew not what –
thrill and turn over and settle again. . . .

'The sea,' she repeated in a low voice.

'Yes, that's what you want to set you up – rather! Do you remember
that fortnight at Littlehampton, you and me and your Aunt? Jolly that
was! I like Littlehampton. It isn't flash like Brighton, and Margate's
always so beastly crowded. And do you remember that afternoon by the
windmill? I did love you that afternoon, Bessie!'. . .

He continued to talk, but she was not listening. She was wondering
why the words 'the sea' were somehow part of it all – the pins and
brooches of the Museum, the book on her knees, the dream. She
remembered a game of hide-and-seek she had played as a child, in which
cries of 'Warm, warm, warmer!' had announced the approach to the
hidden object. Oh, she was getting warm – positively hot. . . .

He had ceased to talk, and was watching her. Perhaps it was the
thought of how he had loved her that afternoon by the windmill that had
brought him close to her chair again. She was aware of his nearness, and
closed her eyes for a moment as if she dreaded something. Then she said
quickly, 'Is tea nearly ready, Ed?' and, as he turned to the table, took up
the book again.

She felt that even to touch that book brought her 'warmer.' It fell open
at a page. She did not hear the clatter Ed made at the table, nor yet the
babble his words had evoked, of the pierrots and banjos and minstrels of
Margate and Littlehampton. It was to hear a gladder, wilder tumult that
she sat once more so still, so achingly listening. . . .

> 'The earnest trumpet spake, and silver thrills
> From kissing cymbals made a merry din—'

The words seemed to move on the page. In her eyes another light than
the firelight seemed to play. Her breast rose, and in her thick white throat
a little inarticulate sound twanged.

'Eh? Did you speak, Bessie?' Ed asked, stopping in his buttering of bread.

'Eh?. . . No.'

In answering, her head had turned for a moment, and she had seen him. Suddenly it struck her with force: what a shaving of a man he was! Desk-chested, weak-necked, conscious of his little 'important' lip and chin – yes, he needed a Polytechnic gymnastic course! Then she remarked how once, at Margate, she had seen him in the distance, as in a hired baggy bathing-dress he had bathed from a machine, in muddy water, one of a hundred others, all rather cold, flinging a polo-ball about and shouting stridently. 'A sound mind in a sound body!'. . . He was rather vain of his neat shoes, too, and doubtless stunted his feet; and she had seen the little spot on his neck caused by the chafing of his collar-stud. . . . No, she did not want him to touch her, just now at any rate. His touch would be too like a betrayal of another touch . . . somewhere, sometime, somehow . . . in that tantalising dream that refused to allow itself either to be fully remembered or quite forgotten. What *was* that dream? *What* was it? . . .

She continued to gaze into the fire.

Of a sudden she sprang to her feet with a choked cry of almost animal fury. The fool *had* touched her. Carried away doubtless by the memory of that afternoon by the windmill, he had, in passing once more to the kettle, crept softly behind her and put a swift burning kiss on the side of her neck.

Then he had retreated before her, stumbling against the table and causing the cups and saucers to jingle.

The basket-chair tilted up, but righted itself again.

'I told you – I told you —' she choked, her stockish figure shaking with rage, 'I told you – you—'

He put up his elbow as if to ward off a blow.

'*You* touch me – *you!* – *you!*' the words broke from her.

He had put himself farther round the table. He stammered.

'Here – dash it all, Bessie – what *is* the matter?'

'*You* touch me!'

'All right,' he said sullenly. 'I won't touch you again – no fear. I didn't know you were such a firebrand. All right, drop it now. I won't again. Good Lord!'

Slowly the white fist she had drawn back sank to her side again.

'All right now,' he continued to grumble resentfully. 'You needn't take on so. It's said – I won't touch you again.' Then, as if he remembered that after all she was ill and must be humoured, he began, while her bosom still rose and fell rapidly, to talk with an assumption that nothing much had happened. 'Come, sit down again, Bessie. The tea's in the pot and I'll have it ready in a couple of jiffs. What a ridiculous little girl you are, to take on like that! . . . And I say, listen! That's a muffin-bell, and there's a grand fire for toast! You sit down while I run out and get 'em. Give me your key, so I can let myself in again—'

He took her key from her bag, caught up his hat, and hastened out.

But she did not sit down again. She was no calmer for his quick disappearance. In that moment when he had recoiled from her she had had the expression of some handsome and angered snake, its hood puffed, ready to strike. She stood dazed; one would have supposed that that ill-advised kiss of his had indeed been the Master Word she sought, the Word she felt approaching, the Word to which the objects of the Museum, the book, that rustle of a sea she had never seen, had been but the ever 'warming' stages. Some merest trifle stood between her and those elfin cries, between her and that thin golden mist in which faintly seen shapes seemed to move – shapes almost of tossed arms, waving, brandishing objects strangely all but familiar. That roaring of the sea was *not* the rushing of her own blood in her ears, that rosy flush *not* the artificial glow of the cheap red lampshade. The shapes were almost as plain as if she saw them in some clear but black mirror, the sounds almost as audible as if she heard them through some not very thick muffling. . . .

'Quick – the book,' she muttered.

But even as she stretched out her hand for it, again came that solemn sound of warning. As if something sought to stay it, she had deliberately to thrust her hand forward. Again the high dinning calls of 'Hasten! Hasten!' were mingled with that deeper 'Beware!' She knew in her soul that, once over that terrible edge, the Dream would become the Reality and the Reality the Dream. She knew nothing of the fluidity of the thing called Personality – not a thing at all, but a state, a balance, a relation, a resultant of forces so delicately in equilibrium that a touch, and – *pff!* – the horror of Formlessness rushed over all.

As she hesitated a new light appeared in the chamber. Within the frame of the small square window, beyond the ragged line of the chimney-cowls, an edge of orange brightness showed. She leaned forward. It was the full moon, rusty and bloated and flattened by the earth-mist.

The next moment her hand had clutched at the book.

> 'Whence came ye, merry Damsels! Whence came ye
> So many, and so many, and such glee?
> Why have ye left your bowers desolate,
>   Your lutes, and gentler fate?
> "We follow Bacchus, Bacchus on the wing
>   A-conquering!
> Bacchus, young Bacchus! Good or ill betide
> We dance before him thorough kingdoms wide!
> Come hither, Lady fair, and joinèd be
>   To our wild minstrelsy!"'

There was an instant in which darkness seemed to blot out all else; then it rolled aside, and in a blaze of brightness was gone. It was gone, and she stood face to face with her Dream, that for two thousand years had slumbered in the blood of her and her line. She stood, with mouth agape and eyes that hailed, her thick throat full of suppressed clamour. The other was the Dream now, and *these!*. . . . they came down, mad and noisy and bright – Mænades, Thyades, satyrs, fauns – naked, in hides of beasts, ungirded, dishevelled, wreathed and garlanded, dancing, singing, shouting. The thudding of their hooves shook the ground, and the clash of their timbrels and the rustling of their thyrsi filled the air. They brandished frontal bones, the dismembered quarters of kids and goats; they struck the bronze cantharus, they tossed the silver obba up aloft. Down a cleft of rocks and woods they came, trooping to a wide seashore with the red of the sunset behind them. She saw the evening light on the sleek and dappled hides, the gilded ivory and rich brown of their legs and shoulders, the white of inner arms held up on high, their wide red mouths, the quivering of the twin flesh-gouts on the necks of the leaping fauns. And, shutting out the glimpse of sky at the head of the deep ravine, the god himself descended, with his car full of drunken girls who slept with the serpents coiled about them.

Shouting and moaning and frenzied, leaping upon one another with libidinous laughter and beating one another with the half-stripped thyrsi, they poured down to the yellow sands and the anemonied pools of the shore. They raced to the water, that gleamed pale as nacre in the deepening twilight in the eye of the evening star. They ran along its edge over their images in the wet sands, calling their lost companion.

'Hasten, hasten!' they cried; and one of them, a young man with a torso noble as the dawn and shoulder-lines strong as those of the eternal hills, ran here and there calling her name.

'Louder, louder!' she called back in an ecstasy.

Something dropped and tinkled against the fender. It was one of her hairpins. One side of her hair was in a loose tumble; she threw up the small head on the superb thick neck.

'Louder! – I cannot hear! Once more—'

The throwing up of her head that had brought down the rest of her hair had given her a glimpse of herself in the glass over the mantelpiece. For the last time that formidable 'Beware!' sounded like thunder in her ears; the next moment she had snapped with her fingers the ribbon that was cutting into her throbbing throat. He with the torso and those shoulders was seeking her. . . how should he know her in that dreary garret, in those joyless habiliments? He would as soon known his Own in that crimson-bodiced, wire-framed dummy by the window yonder!. . .

Her fingers clutched at the tawdry mercerised silk of her blouse. There was a rip, and her arms and throat were free. She panted as she tugged at something that gave with a short 'click-click,' as of steel fastenings;

something fell against the finder. . . . These also. . . She tore at them, and kicked them as they lay about her feet as leaves lie about the trunk of a tree in autumn. . . .

'*Ah!*'

And as she stood there, as if within the screen of a spectrum that deepened to the band of red, her eyes fell on the leopard-skin at her feet. She caught it up, and in doing so saw purple grapes – purple grapes that issued from the mouth of a paper bag on the table. With the dappled pelt about her she sprang forward. The juice spurted through them into the mass of her loosened hair. Down her body there was a spilth of seeds and pulp. She cried hoarsely aloud.

'Once more – oh, answer me! Tell me my name!'

Ed's steps were heard on the oilclothed portion of the staircase.

'My name – oh, my name!' she cried in an agony of suspense. . . . 'Oh, they will not wait for me! They have lighted the torches – they run up and down the shore with torches – oh, cannot you see me? . . .'

Suddenly she dashed to the chair on which the litter of linings and tissue-paper lay. She caught up a double handful and crammed them on the fire. They caught and flared. There was a call upon the stairs, and the sound of somebody mounting in haste.

'Once – once only – my name!'

The soul of the Bacchante rioted, struggled to escape from her eyes. Then as the door was flung open, she heard, and gave a terrifying shout of recognition.

'I hear – I almost hear – but once more. . . . IO! *Io, Io, Io!*'

Ed, in the doorway, stood for one moment agape; the next, ignorant of the full purport of his own words – ignorant that though man may come westwards he may yet bring his worship with him – ignorant that to make the Dream the Reality and the Reality the Dream is Heaven's dreadfullest favour – and ignorant that, that Edge once crossed, there is no return to the sanity and sweetness and light that are only seen clearly in the moment when they are lost for ever – he had dashed down the stairs crying in a voice hoarse and high with terror:

'She's mad! She's mad!'

The House and the Brain
EDWARD BULWER-LYTTON

A FRIEND OF MINE, who is a man of letters and a philosopher, said to me one day, as if between jest and earnest, 'Fancy! since we last met I have discovered a haunted house in the midst of London.'

'Really haunted? and by what – ghosts?'

'Well, I can't answer these questions; all I know is this: six weeks ago I and my wife were in search of a furnished apartment. Passing a quiet street, we saw on the window of one of the houses a bill, "Apartments Furnished." The situation suited us; we entered the house, liked the rooms, engaged them by the week, and left them the third day. No power on earth could have reconciled my wife to stay longer; and I don't wonder at it.'

'What did you see?'

'Excuse me; I have no desire to be ridiculed as a superstitious dreamer, nor, on the other hand, could I ask you to accept on my affirmation what you would hold to be incredible, without the evidence of your own senses. Let me only say this: it was not so much what we saw or heard (in which you might fairly suppose that we were the dupes of our own excited fancy, or the victims of imposture in others) that drove us away, as it was an undefinable terror which seized both of us whenever we passed by the door of a certain unfurnished room, in which we neither saw nor heard anything; and the strangest marvel of all was that for once in my life I agreed with my wife, silly woman though she be, and allowed after the third night that it was impossible to stay a fourth in that house.

'Accordingly, on the fourth morning I summoned the woman who kept the house and attended on us, and told her that the rooms did not quite suit us, and we would not stay out our week. She said dryly:

' "I know why; you have stayed longer than any other lodger. Few ever stayed a second night; none before you a third. But I take it that they have been very kind to you."

' "They – who?" I asked, affecting a smile.

' "Why, they who haunt the house, whoever they are; I don't mind them; I remember them many years ago, when I lived in this house not as a servant; but I know they will be the death of me some day. I don't care – I'm old and must die soon anyhow; and then I shall be with them, and in this house still."

'The woman spoke with so dreary a calmness that really it was a sort of awe that prevented my conversing with her further. I paid for my week, and too happy were I and my wife to get off so cheaply.'

'You excite my curiosity,' said I; 'nothing I should like better than to sleep in a haunted house. Pray give me the address of the one which you left so ignominiously.'

My friend gave me the address; and when we parted I walked straight towards the house thus indicated.

It is situated on the north side of Oxford Street, in a dull but respectable thoroughfare. I found the house shut up; no bill on the window, and no response to my knock. As I was turning away, a beer-boy, collecting pewter pots at the neighbouring areas, said to me, 'Do you want anyone at that house, sir?'

'Yes; I heard it was to be let.'

'Let! Why, the woman who kept it is dead; has been dead these three weeks; and no one can be found to stay there, though Mr. J— offered ever so much. He offered mother, who chars for him, one pound a week just to open and shut the windows, and she would not.'

'Would not! and why?'

'The house is haunted; and the old woman who kept it was found dead in her bed with her eyes wide open. They say the devil strangled her.'

'Pooh! You speak of Mr. J—. Is he the owner of the house?'

'Yes.'

'Where does he live?'

'In G— Street, No—.'

'What is he – in any business?'

'No, sir, nothing particular; a single gentleman.'

I gave the pot-boy the gratuity earned by his liberal information, and proceeded to Mr. J— in G— Street, which was close by the street that boasted the haunted house. I was lucky enough to find Mr. J— at home; an elderly man with intelligent countenance and prepossing manners.

I communicated my name and my business frankly. I said I heard the house was considered to be haunted; that I had a strong desire to examine a house with so equivocal a reputation; that I should be greatly obliged if he would allow me to hire it, though only for a night. I was willing to pay for that privilege whatever he might be inclined to ask.

'Sir,' said Mr. J—, with great courtesy, 'the house is at your service for as short or as long a time as you please. Rent is out of the question; the obligation will be on my side, should you be able to discover the cause of the strange phenomena which at present deprive it of all value. I cannot let it, for I cannot even get a servant to keep it in order or answer the door.

'Unluckily, the house is haunted, if I may use that expression, not only by night but by day; though at night the disturbances are of a more unpleasant and sometimes of a more alarming character. The poor old woman who died in it three weeks ago was a pauper whom I took out of a workhouse; for in her childhood she had been known to some of my family, and had once been in such good circumstances that she had rented that house of my uncle. She was a woman of superior education and strong mind, and was the only person I could ever induce to remain in the house. Indeed, since her death, which was sudden, and the coroner's inquest, which gave it a notoriety in the neighbourhood, I have so despaired of finding any person to take charge of it, much more a tenant, that I would most willingly let it rent free for a year to anyone who would pay its rates and taxes.'

'How long ago did the house acquire this character?'

'That I can scarcely tell you, but many years since; the old woman I spoke of said it was haunted when she rented it, between thirty and forty years ago. The fact is that my life has been spent in the East Indies, and in the civil service of the East India Company.

'I returned to England last year, on inheriting the fortune of an uncle, among whose possessions was the house in question. I found it shut up and uninhabited. I was told that it was haunted, and no one would inhabit it. I smiled at what seemed to me so idle a story.

'I spent some money in repainting and roofing it, added to its old-fashioned furniture a few modern articles, advertised it, and obtained a lodger for a year. He was a colonel retired on half pay. He came in with his family, a son and a daughter, and four or five servants; they all left the house the next day; and although they deponed that they had all seen something different, that something was equally terrible to all. I really could not in conscience sue, or even blame, the colonel for breach of agreement.

'Then I put in the old woman I have spoken of, and she was empowered to let the house in apartments. I never had one lodger who stayed more than three days. I do not tell you their stories; to no two lodgers have exactly the same phenomena been repeated. It is better that you should judge for yourself than enter the house with an imagination influenced by previous narratives; only be prepared to see and to hear something or other, and take whatever precautions you yourself please.'

'Have you never had a curiosity yourself to pass a night in that house?'

'Yes; I passed, not a night, but three hours in broad daylight alone in that house. My curiosity is not satisfied, but it is quenched. I have no desire to renew the experiment. You cannot complain you see, sir, that I am not sufficiently candid; and unless your interest be exceedingly eager and your nerves unusually strong, I honestly add that I advise you *not* to pass a night in that house.'

'My interest *is* exceedingly keen,' said I, 'and though only a coward will boast of his nerves in situations wholly unfamiliar to him, yet my nerves have been seasoned in such variety of danger that I have the right to rely on them, even in a haunted house.'

Mr. J— said very little more; he took the keys of the house out of his bureau, and gave them to me; and, thanking him cordially for his frankness and his urbane concession to my wish, I carried off my prize.

Impatient for the experiment, as soon as I reached home I summoned my confidential servant – a young man of gay spirits, fearless temper, and as free from superstitious prejudice as anyone I could think of.

'F—,' said I, 'you remember in Germany how disappointed we were at not finding a ghost in that old castle which was said to be haunted by a headless apparition? Well, I have heard of a house in London which, I have reason to hope, is decidedly haunted. I mean to sleep there to-night. From what I hear, there is no doubt that something will allow itself to be seen or to be heard – something perhaps excessively horrible. Do you think, if I take you with me, I may rely on your presence of mind, whatever may happen?'

'Oh, sir; pray trust me!' said he, grinning with delight.

'Very well, then, here are the keys of the house; this is the address. Go now, select for me any bedroom you please; and since the house has not been inhabited for weeks, make up a good fire, air the bed well; see, of course, that there are candles as well as fuel. Take with you my revolver and my dagger – so much for my weapons – arm youself equally well; and if we are not a match for a dozen ghosts, we shall be but a sorry couple of Englishmen.'

I was engaged for the rest of the day on business so urgent that I had not leisure to think much on the nocturnal adventure to which I had plighted my honour. I dined alone and very late, and while dining read, as is my habit. The volume I selected was one of Macaulay's essays. I thought to myself that I would take the book with me; there was so much of healthfulness in the style, and practical life in the subjects, that it would serve as an antidote against the influences of superstitious fancy.

Accordingly, about half-past nine I put the book into my pocket and strolled leisurely towards the haunted house. I took with me a favourite dog – an exceedingly sharp, bold, and vigilant bull-terrier, a dog fond of prowling about strange ghostly corners and passages at night in search of rats, a dog of dogs for a ghost.

It was a summer night, but chilly, the sky somewhat gloomy and overcast; still there was a moon – faint and sickly, but still a moon – and if the clouds permitted, after midnight it would be brighter.

99

I reached the house, knocked, and my servant opened with a cheerful smile.

'All right sir, and very comfortable.'

'Oh!' said I, rather disappointed; 'have you not seen nor heard anything remarkable?'

'Well, sir, I must own that I have heard something queer.'

'What? – what?'

'The sound of feet pattering behind me; and once or twice small noises like whispers close at my ear; nothing more.'

'You are not at all frightened?'

'I! Not a bit of it, sir!'

And the man's bold look reassured me on one point, namely, that, happen what might, he would not desert me.

We were in the hall, the street door closed, and my attention was now drawn to my dog. He had at first run in eagerly enough, but had sneaked back to the door, and was scratching and whining to get out. After I had patted him on the head and encouraged him gently, the dog seemed to reconcile himself to the situation, and followed me and F— through the house, but keeping close at my heels, instead of hurrying inquisitively in advance, which was his usual and normal habit in all strange places.

We first visited the subterranean apartments, the kitchen and other offices, and especially the cellars, in which last were two or three bottles of wine still left in a bin, covered with cobwebs, and evidently, by their appearance, undisturbed for many years. It was clear that the ghosts were not wine-bibbers.

For the rest, we discovered nothing of interest. There was a gloomy little back yard, with very high walls. The stones of this yard were very damp; and what with the damp and what with the dust and smoke-grime on the pavement, our feet left a slight impression where we passed.

And now appeared the first strange phenomenon witnessed by myself in this strange abode.

I saw, just before me, the print of a foot suddenly form itself, as it were. I stopped, caught hold of my servant, and pointed to it. In advance of that footprint as suddenly dropped another. We both saw it. I advanced quickly to the place; the footprints kept advancing before me; a small footprint – the foot of a child; the impression was too faint thoroughly to distinguish the shape, but it seemed to us both that it was the print of a naked foot.

This phenomenon ceased when we arrived at the opposite wall, nor did it repeat itself when we returned. We remounted the stairs and entered the rooms on the ground floor – a dining-parlour, a small back-parlour, and a still smaller third room that had probably been appropriated to a footman – all still as death.

We then visited the drawing-rooms, which seemed fresh and new. In the front room I seated myself in an arm-chair. F— placed on the table

the candlestick with which he had lighted us. I told him to shut the door.
As he turned to do so, a chair opposite to me moved from the wall quickly
and noiselessly, and dropped itself about a yard from my own chair,
immediately fronting it.

'Why, this is better than the turning-tables,' said I, laughing; and as
I laughed, my dog put back his head and howled.

F—, coming back, had not observed the movement of the chair. He
employed himself now in stilling the dog. I continued to gaze on the
chair, and fancied I saw on it a pale, blue, misty outline of a human
figure; but an outline so indistinct that I could only distrust my own
vision. The dog was now quiet.

'Put back the chair opposite to me,' said I to F—; 'put it back to the
wall.'

F— obeyed.

'Was that you, sir?' said he, turning abruptly.

'I – what?'

'Why, something struck me. I felt it sharply on the shoulder, just here.'

'No,' said I; 'but we have jugglers present, and though we may not
discover their tricks, we shall catch *them* before they frighten *us*.'

We did not stay long in the drawing-rooms; in fact, they felt so damp
and so chilly that I was glad to get to the fire upstairs. We locked the
doors of the drawing-rooms – a precaution which, I should observe, we
had taken with all the rooms we had searched below.

The bedroom my servant had selected for me was the best on the floor;
a large one, with two windows fronting the street. The four-posted
bedstead, which took up no inconsiderable space, was opposite to the fire,
which burned clear and bright: a door in the wall to the left, between the
bed and the window, communicated with the room which my servant
appropriated to himself. This last was a small room with a sofa-bed, and
had no communication with the landing-place; no other door but that
which conducted to the bedroom I was to occupy.

On either side of my fireplace was a cupboard, without locks, flush
with the wall, and covered with the same dull-brown paper. We examined
these cupboards; only hooks to suspend female dresses – nothing else. We
sounded the walls; evidently solid – the outer walls of the building.

Having finished the survey of these apartments, warmed myself a few
moments, and lighted my cigar, I then, still accompanied by F—, went
forth to complete my reconnoitre. In the landing-place there was another
door; it was closed firmly.

'Sir,' said my servant in surprise, 'I unlocked this door with all the
others when I first came in; it cannot have got locked from the inside, for
it is a—'

Before he had finished his sentence, the door, which neither of us was
then touching, opened quietly of itself. We looked at each other a single
instant. The same thought seized both: some human agency might be

detected here. I rushed in first, my servant followed. A small, blank, dreary room without furniture, a few empty boxes and hampers in a corner, a small window, the shutters closed – not even a fireplace – no other door but that by which we had entered, no carpet on the floor, and the floor seemed very old, uneven, worm-eaten, mended here and there, as was shown by the whiter patches on the wood; but no living being, and no visible place in which a living being could have hidden.

As we stood gazing round, the door by which we had entered closed as quietly as it had before opened; were were imprisoned.

For the first time I felt a creep of undefinable horror. Not so my servant.

'Why, they don't think to trap us, sir; I could break that trumpery door with a kick of my foot.'

'Try first if it will open to your hand,' said I, shaking off the vague apprehension that had seized me, 'while I open the shutters and see what is without.'

I unbarred the shutters; the window looked on the little back yard I have before described; there was no ledge without, nothing but sheer descent. No man getting out of that window would have found any footing till he had fallen on the stones below.

F— meanwhile was vainly attempting to open the door. He now turned round to me and asked my permission to use force. And I should here state, in justice to the servant, that, far from evincing any superstitious terror, his nerve, composure, and even gaiety amid circumstances so extraordinary, compelled my admiration and made me congratulate myself on having secured a companion in every way fitted to the occasion. I willingly gave him the permission he required. But, though he was a remarkably strong man, his force was as idle as his milder efforts; the door did not even shake to his stoutest kick.

Breathless and panting, he desisted. I then tried the door myself, equally in vain. As I ceased from the effort, again that creep of horror came over me; but this time it was more cold and stubborn, I felt as if somg strange and ghastly exhalation were rising from the chinks of that rugged floor and filling the atmosphere with a venomous influence hostile to human life.

The door now very slowly and quietly opened as of its own accord. We precipitated ourselves on to the landing-place. We both saw a large, pale light – as large as the human figure, but shapeless and unsubstantial – move before us and ascend the stairs that led from the landing into the attics.

I followed the light, and my servant followed me. It entered, to the right of the landing, a small garret, of which the door stood open. I entered in the same instant. The light then collapsed into a small globule, exceedingly brilliant and vivid; rested a moment on a bed in the corner, quivered, and vanished.

We approached the bed and examined it – a half-tester, such as is commonly found in attics devoted to servants. On the drawers that stood near it we perceived an old faded silk kerchief, with the needle still left in the rent half repaired. The kerchief was covered with dust; probably it had belonged to the old woman who had last died there, and this might have been her sleeping-room.

I had sufficient curiosity to open the drawers; there were a few odds and ends of female dress, and two letters tied round with a narrow ribbon of faded yellow. I took the liberty to possess myself of the letters. We found nothing else in the room worth noticing, nor did the light reappear; but we distinctly heard, as we turned to go, a pattering footfall on the floor just before us.

We went through the other attics (in all four), the footfall still preceding us. Nothing to be seen, nothing but the footfall heard. I had the letters in my hand; just as I was descending the stairs I distinctly felt my wrist seized, and a faint, soft effort made to draw the letters from my clasp. I only held them the more tightly, and the effort ceased.

We regained the bedchamber appropriated to myself, and I then remarked that my dog had not followed us when we had left it. He was thrusting himself close to the fire and trembling. I was impatient to examine the letters; and while I read them my servant opened a little box in which he had deposited the weapons I had ordered him to bring, took them out, placed them on a table close at my bed-head, and then occupied himself in soothing the dog, who, however, seemed to heed him very little.

The letters were short; they were dated – the dates exactly thirty-five years ago. They were evidently from a lover to his mistress, or a husband to some young wife. Not only the terms of expression, but a distinct reference to a former voyage indicated the writer to have been a seafarer. The spelling and handwriting were those of a man imperfectly educated; but still the language itself was forcible. In the expressions of endearment there was a kind of rough, wild love; but here and there were dark, unintelligible hints at some secret not of love – some secret that seemed of crime.

'We ought to love each other,' was one of the sentences I remember, 'for how everyone else would execrate us if all was known.'

Again: 'Don't let anyone be in the same room with you at night – you talk in your sleep.'

And again: 'What's done can't be undone; and I tell you there's nothing against us, unless the dead should come to life.'

Here was interlined, in a better handwriting (a female's), 'They do!'

At the end of the letter latest in date the same female hand had written these words:

'Lost at sea the 4th of June, the same day as—'

I put down the letters, and began to muse over their contents.

Fearing, however, that the train of thought into which I fell might unsteady my nerves, I fully determined to keep my mind in a fit state to cope with whatever of the marvellous the advancing night might bring forth. I roused myself, laid the letter on the table, stirred up the fire, which was still bright and cheering, and opened my volume of Macaulay.

I read quietly enough till about half-past eleven. I then threw myself dressed upon the bed, and told my servant he might retire to his own room, but must keep himself awake. I bade him leave open the doors between the two rooms. Thus alone I kept two candles burning on the table by my bed-head. I placed my watch beside the weapons and calmly resumed my Macaulay. Opposite to me the fire burned clear, and on the hearth-rug, seemingly asleep, lay the dog. In about twenty minutes I felt an exceedingly cold air pass by my cheek, like a sudden draught. I fancied the door to my right, communicating with the landing-place, must have got open; but no, it was closed.

I then turned my glance to the left, and saw the flames of the candles violently swayed as by a wind. At the same moment the watch beside the revolver softly slid from the table – softly, softly – no visible hand – it was gone. I sprang up, seizing the revolver with the one hand, the dagger with the other: I was not willing that my weapons should share the fate of the watch.

Thus armed, I looked round the floor: no sign of the watch. Three slow, loud, distinct knocks were now heard at the bed-head; my servant called out:

'Is that you, sir?'

'No; be on your guard.'

The dog now roused himself and sat on his haunches, his ears moving quickly backward and forward. He kept his eyes fixed on me with a look so strange that he concentrated all my attention on himself. Slowly he rose, all his hair bristling, and stood perfectly rigid, and with the same wild stare.

I had no time, however, to examine the dog. Presently my servant emerged from his room; and if I ever saw horror in the human face, it was then. I should not have recognized him had we met in the streets, so altered was every lineament. He passed by me quickly, saying, in a whisper that seemed scarcely to come from his lips:

'Run! run! It is after me!'

He gained the door to the landing, pulled it open, and rushed forth. I followed him on to the landing involuntarily, calling him to stop; but, without heeding me, he bounded down the stairs, clinging to the balusters and taking several steps at a time. I heard, where I stood, the street door open, heard it again clap to.

I was left alone in the haunted house.

It was but for a moment that I remained undecided whether or not to follow my servant; pride and curiosity alike forbade so dastardly a flight.

I re-entered my room, closing the door after me, and proceeded cautiously into the interior chamber. I encountered nothing to justify my servant's terror.

I again carefully examined the walls to see if there were any concealed door. I could find no trace of one – not even a seam in the full-brown paper with which the room was hung. How then had the THING, whatever it was, which had so scared him, obtained ingress, except through my own chamber?

I returned to my room, shut and locked the door that opened upon the interior one, and stood on the hearth, expectant and prepared.

I now perceived that the dog had slunk into an angle of the wall, and was pressing close against it, as if literally striving to force his way into it. I approached the animal and spoke to it; the poor brute was evidently beside itself with terror. It showed all its teeth, the slaver dropping from its jaws, and would certainly have bitten me if I had touched it. It did not seem to recognize me. Whoever has seen at the Zoological Gardens a rabbit fascinated by a serpent, cowering in a corner, may form some idea of the anguish which the dog exhibited.

Finding all efforts to soothe the animal in vain, and fearing that his bite might be as venomous in that state as if in the madness of hydrophobia, I left him alone, placed my weapons on the table beside the fire, seated myself, and recommenced my Macaulay.

Perhaps, in order not to appear seeking credit for a courage or rather a coolness, which the reader may conceive I exaggerate, I may be pardoned if I pause to indulge in one of two egotistical remarks.

As I hold presence of mind, or what is called courage, to be precisely proportioned to familiarity with the circumstances that lead to it, so I should say that I had been long sufficiently familiar with all experiments that appertain to the marvellous. I had witnessed many very extraordinary phenomena in various parts of the world – phenomena that would be either totally disbelieved if I stated them, or ascribed to supernatural agencies.

Now, my theory is that the supernatural is the impossible, and that what is called supernatural is only a something in the laws of nature of which we have been hitherto ignorant. Therefore, if a ghost rise before me, I have not the right to say, 'So, then, the supernatural is possible,' but rather, 'So, then, the apparition of a ghost is, contrary to received opinion, within the laws of nature, namely, not supernatural.'

Now, in all that I had hitherto witnessed, and indeed in all the wonders which the amateurs of mystery in our age record as facts, a material living agency is always required. On the Continent you will still find magicians who assert that they can raise spirits. Assume for a moment that they assert truly, still the living material form of the magician is present; he is the material agency by which, from some constitutional peculiarities, certain strange phenomena are represented to your natural senses.

Accept, again, as truthful the tales of spirit manifestation in America – musical or other sounds, writings on paper, produced by no discernible hand, articles of furniture moved without apparent human agency, or the actual sight and touch of hands, to which no bodies seem to belong – still there must be found the medium, or living being, with constitutional peculiarities capable of obtaining these signs.

In fine, in all such marvels, supposing even that there is no imposture, there must be a human being like ourselves, by whom or through whom the effects presented to human beings are produced. It is so with the now familiar phenomena of mesmerism or electrobiology; the mind of the person operated on is affected through a material living agent.

Nor, supposing it true that a mesmerized patient can respond to the will or passes of a mesmerizer a hundred miles distant, is the response less occasioned by a material being. It may be through a material fluid, call it Electric, call it Odic, call it what you will, which has the power of traversing space and passing obstacles, that the material effect is communicated from one to the other.

Hence, all that I had hitherto witnessed, or expected to witness, in this strange house, I believed to be occasioned through some agency or medium as mortal as myself; and this idea necessarily prevented the awe with which those who regard as supernatural things that are not within the ordinary operations of nature might have been impressed by the adventures of that memorable night.

As, then, it was my conjecture that all that was presented, or would be presented, to my senses, must originate in some human being gifted by constitution with the power so to present them, and having some motive so to do, I felt an interest in my theory which, in its way, was rather philosophical than superstitious. And I can sincerely say that I was in as tranquil a temper for observation as any practical experimentalist could be in awaiting the effects of some rare though perhaps perilous chemical combination. Of course, the more I kept my mind detached from fancy the more the temper fitted for observation would be obtained; and I therefore riveted eye and thought on the strong daylight sense in the page of my Macaulay.

I now became aware that something interposed between the page and the light: the page was overshadowed. I looked up and saw what I shall find very difficult, perhaps impossible, to describe.

It was a darkness shaping itself out of the air in very undefined outline. I cannot say it was of a human form, and yet it had more of a resemblance to a human force, or rather shadow, than anything else. As it stood, wholly apart and distinct from the air and the light around it, its dimensions seemed gigantic; the summit nearly touched the ceiling.

While I gazed, a feeling of intense cold seized me. An iceburg before me could not more have chilled me; nor could the cold of an iceberg have been more purely physical. I feel convinced that it was not the cold caused by fear. As I continued to gaze, I thought – but this I cannot say with precision – that I distinguished two eyes looking down on me from the height. One moment I seemed to distinguish them clearly, the next they seemed gone; but two rays of a pale, blue light frequently shot through the darkness, as from the height on which I half believed, half doubted, that I had encountered the eyes.

I strove to speak; my voice utterly failed me. I could only think to myself, 'Is this fear? it is *not* fear!' I strove to rise, in vain; I felt as weighed down by an irresistible force. Indeed my impression was that of an immense and overwhelming power opposed to my volition; that sense of utter inadequacy to cope with a force beyond man's, which one may feel *physically* in a storm at sea, in a conflagration, or when confronting some terrible wild beast, or rather, perhaps the shark of the ocean, I felt *morally*. Opposed to my will was another will, as far superior to its strength as storm, fire, and shark are superior in material force to the force of man.

And now, as this impression grew on me, now came, at last, horror – horror to a degree that no words can convey. Still I retained pride, if not courage; and in my own mind I said, 'This is horror, but it is not fear; unless I fear, I cannot be harmed; my reason rejects this thing; it is an illusion, I do not fear.'

With a violent effort I succeeded at last in stretching out my hand towards the weapon on the table; as I did so, on the arm and shoulder I received a strange shock, and my arm fell to my side powerless. And now, to add to my horror, the light began slowly to wane from the candles; they were not, as it were, extinguished, but their flame seemed very gradually withdrawn; it was the same with the fire, the light was extracted from the fuel; in a few minutes the room was in utter darkness.

The dread that came over me to be thus in the dark with that dark thing, whose power was so intensely felt, brought a reaction of nerve. In fact, terror had reached that climax that either my senses must have deserted me, or I must have burst through the spell.

I did burst through it.

I found voice, though the voice was a shriek. I remember that I broke forth with words like these, 'I do not fear, my soul does not fear'; and at the same time I found strength to rise.

Still in that profound gloom, I rushed to one of the windows, tore aside the curtain, flung open the shutters; my first thought was, LIGHT.

And when I saw the moon, high, clear, and calm, I felt a joy that almost compensated for the previous terror. There was the moon, there was also the light from the gas-lamps in the deserted, slumberous street. I turned to look back into the room; the moon penetrated its shadow very palely and partially, but still there was light. The dark thing, whatever it might be, was gone; except that I could yet see a dim shadow, which seemed the shadow of that shade, against the opposite wall.

My eye now rested on the table, and from under the table (which was without cloth or cover, an old mahogany round table) rose a hand, visible as far as the wrist. It was a hand, seemingly as much of flesh and blood as my own, but the hand of an aged person, lean, wrinkled, small too, a woman's hand. The hand very softly closed on the two letters that lay on the table; hand and letters both vanished. Then came the same three loud measured knocks I had heard at the bed-head before this extraordinary drama had commenced.

As these sounds slowly ceased, I felt the whole room vibrate sensibly; and at the far end rose, as from the floor, sparks or globules like bubbles of light, many-coloured – green, yellow, fire-red, azure – up and down, to and fro, hither, thither, as tiny will-o'-the wisps and sparks moved, slow or swift, each at its own caprice. A chair (as in the drawing-room below) was now advanced from the wall without apparent agency, and placed at the opposite side of the table.

Suddenly, as forth from the chair, grew a shape, a woman's shape. It was distinct as a shape of life, ghastly as a shape of death. The face was that of youth, with a strange, mournful beauty; the throat and shoulders were bare, the rest of the form in a loose robe of cloudy white.

It began sleeking its long yellow hair, which fell over its shoulders; its eyes were not turned towards me, but to the door; it seemed listening, watching, waiting. The shadow of the shade in the background grew darker, and again I thought I beheld the eyes gleaming out from the summit of the shadow, eyes fixed upon that shape.

As if from the door, though it did not open, grew out another shape, equally distinct, equally ghastly – a man's shape, a young man's. It was in the dress of the last century, or rather in a likeness of such dress; for both the male shape and the female, though defined, were evidently unsubstantial, impalpable – simulacre, phantasms; and there was something incongrous, grotesque, yet fearful, in the contrast between the elaborate finery, the courtly precision of that old-fashioned garb, with its ruffles and lace and buckles, and the corpse-like aspect and ghost-like stillness of the flitting wearer. Just as the male shape approached the female, the dark shadow darted from the wall, all three for a moment wrapped in darkness.

When the pale light returned, the two phantoms were as if in the grasp of the shadow that towered between them, and there was a bloodstain on the breast of the female; and the phantom male was leaning on its phantom sword, and blood seemed trickling fast from the ruffles, from the lace; and the darkness of the intermediate shadow swallowed them up – they were gone. And again the bubbles of light shot, and sailed, and undulated, growing thicker and thicker and more wildly confused in their movements.

The closet door to the right of the fireplace now opened, and from the aperture came the form of a woman, aged. In her hand she held letters – the very letters over which I had seen *the* hand close; and behind her I heard a footstep. She turned round as if to listen, and then she opened the letters and seemed to read: and over her shoulder I saw a livid face, the face as of a man long drowned – bloated, bleached, seaweed tangled in its dripping hair; and at her feet lay a form as of a corpse, and beside the corpse cowered a child, a miserable squalid child, with famine in its cheeks and fear in its eyes. As I looked in the old woman's face, the wrinkles and lines vanished, and it became a face of youth – hard-eyed, stony, but still youth; and the shadow darted forth and darkened over these phantoms, as it had darkened over the last.

Nothing now was left but the shadow, and on that my eyes were intently fixed, till again eyes grew out of the shadow – malignant, serpent eyes. And the bubbles of light again rose and fell, and in their disordered, irregular, turbulent maze mingled with the wan moonlight. And now from these globules themselves, as from the shell of an egg, monstrous things burst out; the air grew filled with them; larvae so bloodless and so hideous that I can in no way describe them except to remind the reader of the swarming life which the solar microscope brings before his eyes in a drop of water – things transparent, supple, agile, chasing each other, devouring each other – forms like naught ever beheld by the naked eye.

As the shapes were without symmetry, so their movements were without order. In their very vagrancies there was no sport; they came round me and round, thicker and faster and swifter, swarming over my head, crawling over my right arm, which was outstretched in involuntary command against all evil beings.

Sometimes I felt myself touched, but not by them; invisible hands touched me. Once I felt the clutch as of cold, soft fingers at my throat. I was still equally conscious that if I gave way to fear I should be in bodily peril, and I concentrated all my faculties in the single focus of resisting, stubborn will. And I turned my sight from the shadow, above all from those strange serpent eyes – eyes that had now become distinctly visible. For there, though in naught else around me, I was aware that there was a will, and a will of intense, creative, working evil, which might crush down my own.

The pale atmosphere in the room began now to redden as if in the air of some near conflagration. The larvae grew lurid as things that live in fire. Again the room vibrated; again were heard the three measured knocks; and again all things were swallowed up in the darkness of the dark shadow, as if out of that darkness all had come, into that darkness all returned.

As the gloom receded, the shadow was wholly gone. Slowly as it had been withdrawn, the flame grew again into the candles on the table, again into the fuel in the grate. The whole room came once more calmly, healthfully into sight.

The two doors were still closed, the door communicating with the servant's room still locked. In the corner of the wall, into which he had convulsively niched himself, lay the dog. I called to him – no movement; I approached – the animal was dead; his eyes protruded, his tongue out of his mouth, the froth gathered round his jaws. I took him in my arms; I brought him to the fire; I felt acute grief for the loss of my poor favourite, acute self-reproach; I accused myself of his death; I imagined he had died of fright. But what was my surprise on finding that his neck was actually broken – actually twisted out of the vertebrae. Had this been done in the dark? Must it not have been done by a hand human as mine? Must there not have been a human agency all the while in that room? Good cause to suspect it. I cannot tell. I cannot do more than state the fact fairly; the reader may draw his own inference.

Another surprising circumstance – my watch was restored to the table from which it had been so mysteriously withdrawn; but it had stopped at the very moment it was so withdrawn; nor, despite all the skill of the watchmaker, has it ever gone since – that is, it will go in a strange, erratic way for a few hours, and then come to a dead stop; it is worthless.

Nothing more chanced for the rest of the night; nor, indeed, had I long to wait before the dawn broke. Not till it was broad daylight did I quit the haunted house. Before I did so I revisited the little blind room in which my servant and I had been for a time imprisoned.

I had a strong impression, for which I could not account, that from that room had originated the mechanism of the phenomena, if I may use the term, which had been experienced in my chamber; and though I entered it now in the clear day, with the sun peering through the filmy window, I still felt, as I stood on its floor, the creep of the horror which I had first experienced there the night before, and which had been so aggravated by what had passed in my own chamber.

I could not, indeed, bear to stay more than half a minute within those walls. I descended the stairs, and again I heard the footfall before me; and when I opened the street door I thought I could distinguish a very low laugh. I gained my own home, expecting to find my runaway servant there. But he had not presented himself; nor did I hear more of him for three days, when I received a letter from him, dated from Liverpool, to this effect:

HONOURED SIR,—I humbly entreat your pardon, though I can scarcely hope that you will think I deserve it, unless – which heaven forbid! – you saw what I did. I feel that it will be years before I can recover myself; and as to being fit for service, it is out of the question. I am therefore going to my brother-in-law at Melbourne. The ship sails to-morrow. Perhaps the long voyage may set me up. I do nothg now but start and tremble, and fancy it is behind me. I humbly beg you, honoured sir, to order my clothes, and whatever wages are due to me, to be sent to my mother's at Walworth: John knows her address.

The letter ended with additional apologies, somewhat incoherent, and explanatory details as to effects that had been under the writer's charge.

This flight may perhaps warrant a suspicion that the man wished to go to Australia, and had been somehow or other fraudulently mixed up with the events of the night. I say nothing in refutation of that conjecture; rather, I suggest it as one that would seem to many persons the most probable solution of improbable occurrences.

My own theory remained unshaken. I returned in the evening to the house, to bring away in a hack cab the things I had left there, with my poor dog's body. In this task I was not disturbed, nor did any incident worth note befall me, except that still, on ascending and descending the stairs, I heard the same footfall in advance. On leaving the house, I went to Mr. J—'s. He was at home. I returned him the keys, told him that my curiosity was sufficiently gratified, and was about to relate quickly what had passed, when he stopped me and said, though with much politeness, that he had no longer any interest in a mystery which none had ever solved.

I determined at least to tell him of the two letters I had read, as well as of the extraordinary manner in which they had disappeared; and I then inquired if he thought they had been addressed to the woman who had died in the house, and if there were anything in her early history which could possibly confirm the dark suspicions to which the letters gave rise.

Mr. J— seemed startled, and after musing a few moments, answered:

'I know but little of the woman's earlier history, except, as I before told you, that her family were known to mine. But you revive some vague reminiscences to her prejudice. I will make inquiries, and inform you of their result. Still, even if we could admit the popular superstition that a person who had been either the perpetrator or the victim of dark crimes in life could revisit, as a restless spirit, the scene in which those crimes had been committed, I should observe that the house was infested by strange sights and sounds before the old woman died. You smile; what would you say?'

'I would say this: that I am convinced, if we could get to the bottom of these mysteries, we should find a living, human agency.'

'What! you believe it is all an imposture? For what object?'

'Not an imposture, in the ordinary sense of the word. If suddenly I were to sink into a deep sleep, from which you could not awake me, but in that deep sleep could answer questions with an accuracy which I could not pretend to when awake – tell you what money you had in your pocket, nay, describe your very thoughts – it is not necessarily an imposture, any more than it is necessarily supernatural. I should be, unconsciously to myself, under a mesmeric influence, conveyed to me from a distance by a human being who had acquired power over me by previous *rapport*.'

'Granting mesmerism, so far carried, to be a fact, you are right. And you would infer from this that a mesmerizer might produce the extraordinary effects you and others have witnessed over inanimate objects – fill the air with sights and sounds?'

'Or impress our senses with the belief in them, we never having been *en rapport* with the person acting on us? No. What is commonly called mesmerism could not do this; but there may be a power akin to mesmerism and superior to it – the power that in the old days was called magic. That such a power may extend to all inanimate objects of matter, I do not say; but if so, it would not be against nature, only a rare power in nature, which might be given to constitutions with certain peculiarities, and cultivated by practice to an extraordinary degree.

'That such a power might extend over the dead – that is, over certain thoughts and memories that the dead may still retain – and compel, not that which ought properly to be called the SOUL, and which is far beyond human reach, but rather a phantom of what has been most earth-stained on earth, to make itself apparent to our senses – is a very ancient though obsolete theory, upon which I will hazard no opinion. But I do not conceive the power would be supernatural.

'Let me illustrate what I mean, from an experiment which Paracelsus describes as not difficult, and which the author of the *Curiosities of Literature* cites as credible: A flower perishes; you burn it. Whatever were the elements of that flower while it lived are gone, dispersed, you know not whither; you can never discover nor re-collect them. But you can, by chemistry, out of the burnt dust of that flower, raise a spectrum of the flower, just as it seemed in life.

'It may be the same with a human being. The soul has as much escaped you as the essence or elements of the flower. Still you may make a spectrum of it. And this phantom, though in the popular superstition it is held to be the soul of the departed, must not be confounded with the true soul; it is but the eidolon of the dead form.

'Hence, like the best-attested stories of ghosts or spirits, the thing that most strikes us is the absence of what we hold to be soul – that is, of superior, emancipated intelligence. They come for little or no object; they seldom speak, if they do come; they utter no ideas above those of an ordinary person on earth. These American spiritseers have published volumes of communications in prose and verse, which they assert to be given in the names of the most illustrious dead – Shakespeare, Bacon, heaven knows whom.

'Those communications, taking the best, are certainly not of a whit higher order than would be communications from living persons of fair talent and education; they are wondrously inferior to what Bacon, Shakespeare, and Plato said and wrote when on earth. Nor, what is more notable, do they ever contain an idea that was not on the earth before.

'Wonderful, therefore, as such phenomena may be (granting them to be truthful), I see much that philosophy may question, nothing that it is incumbent on philosophy to deny, namely, nothing supernatural. They are but ideas conveyed somehow or other (we have not yet discovered the means) from one mortal brain to another. Whether in so doing tables walk of their own accord, or fiend-like shapes appear in a magic circle, or bodiless hands rise and remove material objects, or a thing of darkness, such as presented itself to me, freeze our blood – still am I persuaded that these are but agencies conveyed, as by electric wires, to my own brain from the brain of another.

'In some constitutions there is a natural chemistry, and these may produce chemic wonders; in others a natural fluid, call it electricity, and these produce electric wonders. But they differ in this from normal science: they are alike objectless, purposeless, puerile, frivolous. They lead on to no grand results, and therefore the world does not heed, and true sages have not cultivated them. But sure I am, that of all I saw or heard, a man, human as myself, was the remote originator; and, I believe, unconsciously to himself as to the exact effects produced, for this reason: no two persons, you say, have ever told you that they experience exactly the same thing; well, observe, no two persons ever experience exactly the same dream.

'If this were an ordinary imposture, the machinery would be arranged for results that would but little vary; if it were a supernatural agency permitted by the Almighty, it would surely be for some definite end. These phenomena belong to neither class. My persuasion is that they originate in some brain now far distant; that that brain has no distinct volition in anything that occurred; that what does occur reflects but its devious, motley, ever shifting, half-formed thoughts; in short, that it has been but the dreams of such a brain put into action and invested with a semi-substance.

'That this brain is of immense power, that it can set.matter into movement, that it is malignant and destructive, I believe. Some material force must have killed my dog; it might, for aught I know, have sufficed to kill myself, had I been as subjugated by terror as the dog – had my intellect or my spirit given me no countervailing resistance in my will.'

'It killed your dog! That is fearful! Indeed, it is strange that no animal can be induced to stay in that house; not even a cat. Rats and mice are never found in it.'

'The instincts of the brute creation detect influences deadly to their existence. Man's reason has a sense less subtle, because it has a resisting power more supreme. But enough; do you comprehend my theory?'

'Yes, though imperfectly; and I accept any crotchet (pardon the word), however odd, rather than embrace at once the notion of ghosts and hobgoblins we imbibed in our nurseries. Still, to my unfortunate house the evil is the same. What on earth can I do with the house?'

'I will tell you what I would do. I am convinced from my own internal feelings that the small unfurnished room, at right angles to the door of the bedroom which I occupied, forms a starting-point or receptacle for the influences which haunt the house; and I strongly advise you to have the walls opened, the floor removed, nay, the whole room pulled down. I observe that it is detached from the body of the house, built over the small back yard, and could be removed without injury to the rest of the building.'

'And you think that if I did that—'

'You would cut off the telegraph wires. Try it. I am so persuaded that I am right that I will pay half the expense if you will allow me to direct the operations.'

'Nay, I am well able to afford the cost; for the rest, allow me to write to you.'

About ten days afterwards I received a letter from Mr. J—, telling me that he had visited the house since I had seen him; that he had found the two letters I had described replaced in the drawer from which I had taken them; that he had read them with misgivings like my own; that he had instituted a cautious inquiry about the woman to whom I rightly conjectured they had been written.

It seemed that thirty-six years ago (a year before the date of the letters) she had married, against the wish of her relatives, an American of very suspicious character; in fact, he was generally believed to have been a pirate. She herself was the daughter of very respectable tradespeople, and had served in the capacity of nursery governess before her marriage. She had a brother, a widower, who was considered wealthy, and who had one child about six years old. A month after the marriage the body of this brother was found in the Thames, near London Bridge; there seemed some marks of violence about his throat, but they were not deemed sufficient to warrant the inquest in any other verdict than that of 'found drowned.'

The American and his wife took charge of the little boy, the deceased brother having by his will left his sister the guardian of his only child, and in the event of the child's death the sister inherited. The child died about six months afterwards; it was supposed to have been neglected and ill-treated. The neighbours deposed to have heard it shriek at night.

The surgeon who had examined it after death said that it was emaciated as if from want of nourishment, and the body was covered with livid bruises. It seemed that one winter night the child had sought to escape; had crept out into the back yard, tried to scale the wall, fallen back exhausted, and had been found at morning on the stones in a dying state.

But though there was some evidence of cruelty, there was none of murder; and the aunt and her husband had sought to palliate cruelty by alleging the exceeding stubbornness and perversity of the child, who was declared to be half-witted. Be that as it may, at the orphan's death the aunt inherited her brother's fortune.

Before the first wedded year was out, the American quitted England abruptly, and never returned to it. He obtained a cruising vessel, which was lost in the Atlantic two years afterwards. The widow was left in affluence; but reverses of various kinds had befallen her; a bank broke, an investment failed, she went into a small business and became insolvent, then she entered into service, sinking lower and lower, from housekeeper down to maid-of-all-work, never long retaining a place, though nothing peculiar against her character was ever alleged.

She was considered sober, honest, and peculiarly quiet in her ways; still nothing prospered with her. And so she had dropped into the workhouse, from which Mr. J— had taken her, to be placed in charge of the very house which she had rented as mistress in the first year of her wedded life.

Mr. J— added that he has passed an hour alone in the unfurnished room which I had urged him to destroy, and that his impressions of dread while there were so great, though he had neither heard nor seen anything, that he was eager to have the walls bared and the floors removed, as I had suggested. He had engaged persons for the work, and would commence any day I would name.

The day was accordingly fixed. I repaired to the haunted house; we went into the blind, dreary room, took up the skirting and then the floors. Under the rafters, covered with rubbish, was found a trap-door, quite large enough to admit a man. It was closely nailed down with clamps and rivets of iron. On removing these we descended into a room below, the existence of which had never been suspected.

In this room there had been a window and a flue, but they had been bricked over, evidently for many years. By the help of candles we examined this place; it still retained some mouldering furniture – three chairs, an oak settee, a table – all of the fashion of about eighty years ago.

There was a chest of drawers against the wall, in which we found, half rotted away, old-fashioned articles of a man's dress, such as might have been worn eighty or a hundred years ago, by a gentleman of some rank; costly steel buckles and buttons, like those yet worn in court-dresses, a handsome court-sword; in a waistcoat which had once been rich with gold lace, but which was now blackened and foul with damp, we found five guineas, a few silver coins, and an ivory ticket, probably for some place of entertainment long since passed away.

But our main discovery was in a kind of iron safe fixed to the wall, the lock of which it cost us much trouble to get picked.

In this safe were three shelves and two small drawers. Ranged on the shelves were several small bottles of crystal, hermetically stopped. They contained colourless volatile essences, of what nature I shall say no more than that they were not poisons; phosphor and ammonia entered into some of them. There were also some very curious glass tubes, and a small pointed rod of iron, with a large lump of rock crystal, and another of amber, also a lodestone of great power.

In one of the drawers we found a miniature portrait set in gold, and retaining the freshness of its colours most remarkably, considering the length of time it had probably been there. The portrait was that of a man who might be somewhat advanced in middle life, perhaps forty-seven or forty-eight.

It was a most peculiar face, a most impressive face. If you could fancy some mighty serpent transformed into man, preserving in the human lineaments the old serpent type, you would have a better idea of that countenance than long descriptions can convey; the width and flatness of frontal, the tapering elegance of contour, disguising the strength of the deadly jaw; the long, large, terrible eye, glittering and green as the emerald, and withal a certain ruthless calm, as if from the consciousness of an immense power.

The strange thing was this; the instant I saw the miniature I recognized a startling likeness to one of the rarest portraits in the world; the portrait of a man of rank only below that of royalty, who in his own day had made a considerable noise. History says little or nothing of him; but search the correspondence of his contemporaries, and you find reference to his wild daring, his bold profligacy, his restless spirit, his taste for the occult sciences.

While still in the meridian of life he died and was buried, so say the chronicles, in a foreign land. He died in time to escape the grasp of the law; for he was accused of crimes which would have given him to the headsman. After his death the portraits of him, which had been numerous, for he had been a munificent encourager of art, were bought up and destroyed, it was supposed by his heirs, who might have been glad could they have razed his very name from their splendid line.

He had enjoyed vast wealth; a large portion of this was believed to have been embezzled by a favourite astrologer or soothsayer; at all events, it had unaccountably vanished at the time of death. One portrait alone of him was supposed to have escaped the general destruction; I had seen it in the house of a collector some months before. It had made on me a wonderful impression, as it does on all who behold it – a face never to be forgotten; and there was that face in the miniature that lay within my hand. True that in the miniature the man was a few years older than in the portrait I had seen, or than the original was even at the time of his death. But a few years! – why, between the date in which flourished that direful noble and the date in which the miniature was evidently painted there was an interval of more than two centuries. While I was thus gazing, silent and wondering, Mr. J— said:

'But is it possible? I have known this man.'

'How? where?' cried I.

'In India. He was high in the confidence of the Rajah of—, and well-nigh drew him into a revolt which would have lost the Rajah his dominations. The man was a Frenchman; his name De V—; clever, bold, lawless; we insisted on his dismissal and banishment. It must be the same man, no two faces like his, yet this miniature seems nearly a hundred years old.'

Mechanically I turned round the miniature to examine the back of it, and on the back was engraved a pentacle; in the middle of the pentacle a ladder, and the third step of the ladder was formed by the date 1765. Examining still more minutely, I detected a spring; this, on being pressed, opened the back of the miniature as a lid.

Within-side the lid were engraved: 'Mariana, to thee. Be faithful in life and in death to—.'

Here follows a name that I will not mention, but it was not unfamiliar to me. I had heard it spoken of by old men in my childhood as the name borne by a dazzling charlatan, who had made a great sensation in London for a year or so, and had fled the country on the charge of a double murder within his own house – that of his mistress and his rival. I said nothing of this to Mr. J—, to whom reluctantly I resigned the miniature.

We had found no difficulty in opening the first drawer within the iron safe; we found great difficulty in opening the second: it was not locked, but it resisted all efforts, till we inserted in the chinks the edge of a chisel. When we had thus drawn it forth we found a very singular apparatus, in the nicest order.

Upon a small, thin book, or rather tablet, was placed a saucer of crystal; this saucer was filled with a clear liquid; on that liquid floated a kind of compass, with a needle shifting rapidly round; but instead of the usual points of a compass, were seven strange characters, not very unlike those used by astrologers to denote the planets.

A very peculiar, but not strong nor displeasing, odour came from this drawer, which was lined with a wood that we afterwards discovered to be hazel. Whatever the cause of this odour, it produced a material effect on the nerves. We all felt it, even the two workmen who were in the room; a creeping, tingling sensation, from the tips of the fingers to the roots of the hair.

Impatient to examine the tablet, I removed the saucer. As I did so, the needle of the compass went round and round with exceeding swiftness, and I felt a shock that ran through my whole frame, so that I dropped the saucer on the floor. The liquid was spilt, the saucer was broken, the compass rolled to the end of the room, and at that instant the walls shook to and fro as if a giant had swayed and rocked them.

The two workmen were so frightened that they ran up the ladder by which we had descended from the trap-door; but, seeing that nothing more happened, they were easily induced to return.

Meanwhile I had opened the tablet; it was bound in plain red leather, with a silver clasp; it contained but one sheet of thick vellum, and on that sheet were inscribed, within a double pentacle, words in old monkish Latin, which are literally to be translated thus:

On all that it can reach within these walls, sentient or inanimate, living or dead, as moves the needle, so works my will! Accursed be the house, and restless the dwellers therein.

We found no more. Mr. J— burned the tablet and its anathema. He razed to the foundation the part of the building containing the secret room, with the chamber over it. He had then the courage to inhabit the house himself for a month, and a quieter, better conditioned house could not be found in all London. Subsequently he let it to advantage, and his tenant has made no complaints.

But my story is not yet done. A few days after Mr. J— had removed into the house, I paid him a visit. We were standing by the open window and conversing. A van containing some articles of furniture which he was moving from his former house was at the door.

I had just urged on him my theory that all those phenomena regarded as supermundane had emanated from a human brain; adducing the charm, or rather curse we had found and destroyed, in support of my theory.

Mr. J— was observing in reply, 'that even if mesmerism, or whatever analogous power it might be called, could really thus work in the absence of the operator, and produce effects so extraordinary, still could those effects continue when the operator himself was dead? and if the spell had been wrought, and, indeed, the room walled up, more than seventy years ago, the probability was that the operator had long since departed this life' – Mr. J—, I say, was thus answering, when I caught hold of his arm and pointed to the street below.

A well-dressed man had crossed from the opposite side, and was accosting the carrier in charge of the van. His face, as he stood, was exactly fronting our window. It was the face of the miniature we had discovered; it was the face of the portrait of the noble three centuries ago.

'Good heavens!' cried Mr. J—, 'that is the face of De V—, and scarcely a day older than when I saw it in the Rajah's court in my youth!'

Seized by the same thought, we both hastened downstairs; I was first in the street, but the man had already gone. I caught sight of him, however, not many yards in advance, and in another moment I was by his side.

I had resolved to speak to him, but when I looked into his face I felt as if it were impossible to do so. That eye – the eye of the serpent – fixed and held me spellbound. And withal, about the man's whole person there was a dignity, an air of pride and station and superiority that would have made anyone, habituated to the usages of the world, hesitate long before venturing upon a liberty or impertinence.

And what could I say? What was it I could ask?

Thus ashamed of my first impulse, I fell a few paces back, still, however, following the stranger, undecided what else to do. Meanwhile he turned the corner of the street; a plain carriage was in waiting with a servant out of livery, dressed like a *valet de place*, at the carriage door. In another moment he had stepped into the carriage, and it drove off. I returned to the house.

Mr. J— was still at the street door. He had asked the carrier what the stranger had said to him.

'Merely asked whom that house now belonged to.'

The same evening I happened to go with a friend to a place in town called the Cosmopolitan Club, a place open to men of all countries, all opinions, all degrees. One orders one's coffee, smokes one's cigar. One is always sure to meet agreeable, sometimes remarkable persons.

I had not been two minutes in the room before I beheld at table, conversing with an acquaintance of mine, whom I will designate by the initial G—, the man, the original of the miniature. He was now without his hat, and the likeness was yet more startling, only I observed that while he was conversing there was less severity in the countenance; there was even a smile, though a very quiet and very cold one. The dignity of mien I had acknowledge in the street was also more striking; a dignity akin to that which invests some prince of the East, conveying the idea of supreme indifference and habitual, indisputable, indolent but resistless power.

G— soon after left the stranger, who then took up a scientific journal, which seemed to absorb his attention.

I drew G— aside.

'Who and what is that gentleman?'

'That? Oh, a very remarkable man indeed! I met him last year amid the caves of Petra, the Scriptural Edom. He is the best Oriental scholar I know. We joined company, had an adventure with robbers, in which he showed a coolness that saved our lives; afterwards he invited me to spend a day with him in a house he had bought at Damascus, buried among almond blossoms and roses – the most beautiful thing! He had lived there for some time, quite as an Oriental, in grand style.

'I half suspect he is a renegade, immensely rich, very odd; by the by, a great mesmerizer. I have seen him with my own eyes produce an effect on inanimate things. If you take a letter from your pocket and throw it to the other end of the room, he will order it to come to his feet, and you will see the letter wriggle itself along the floor till it has obeyed his command. 'Pon my honour 'tis true; I have seen him affect even the weather, disperse or collect clouds by means of a glass tube or wand. But he does not like talking of these matters to strangers. He has only just arrived in England; says he has not been here for a great many years; let me introduce him to you.'

'Certainly! He is English, then? What is his name?'

'Oh! a very homely one – Richards.'

'And what is his birth – his family?'

'How do I know? What does it signify? No doubt some *parvenu*; but rich, so infernally rich!'

G— drew me up to the stranger, and the introduction was effected. The manners of Mr. Richards were not those of an adventurous traveller. Travellers are in general gifted with high animal spirits; they are talkative, eager, imperious. Mr. Richards was calm and subdued in tone, with manners which were made distant by the loftiness of punctilious courtesy, the manners of a former age.

I observed that the English he spoke was not exactly of our day. I should even have said that the accent was slightly foreign. But then Mr. Richards remarked that he had been little in the habit for years of speaking in his native tongue.

The conversation fell upon the changes in the aspects of London since he had last visited our metropolis. G— then glanced off to the moral changes – literary, social, political – the great men who were removed from the stage within the last twenty years; the new great men who were coming on.

In all this Mr. Richards evinced no interest. He had evidently read none of our living authors, and seemed scarcely acquainted by name with our younger statemen. Once, and only once, he laughed; it was when G— asked him whether he had any thoughts of getting into Parliament; and the laugh was inward, sarcastic, sinister – a sneer raised into a laugh.

After a few minutes, G— left us to talk to some other acquaintances who had just lounged into the room, and I then said, quietly:

'I have seen a miniature of you, Mr. Richards, in the house you once inhabited, and perhaps built – if not wholly, at least in part – in Oxford Street. You passed by that house this morning.'

Not till I had finished did I raise my eyes to his, and then he fixed my gaze so steadfastly that I could not withdraw it – those fascinating serpent-eyes. But involuntarily, and as if the words that translated my thoughts were dragged from me, I added, in a low whisper, 'I have been a student in the mysteries of life and nature; of those mysteries I have known the occult professors. I have the right to speak to you thus.' And I uttered a certain password.

'Well, I concede the right. What would you ask?'

'To what extent human will in certain temperaments can extend?'

'To what extent can thought extend? Think, and before you draw breath you are in China!'

'True; but my thought has no power in China.'

'Give it expression, and it may have. You may write down a thought which, sooner or later, may alter the whole condition of China. What is a law but a thought? Therefore thought is infinite. Therefore thought has power; not in proportion to its value – a bad thought may make a bad law as potent as a good thought can make a good one.'

'Yes; what you say confirms my own theory. Through invisible currents one human brain may transmit is ideas to other human brains, with the same rapidity as a thought promulgated by visible means. And as thought is imperishable, as it leaves its stamp behind it in the natural world, even when the thinker has passed out of this world, so the thought of the living may have power to rouse up and revive the thoughts of the dead, such as those thoughts *were in life*, though the thought of the living cannot reach the thoughts which the dead *now* may entertain. Is it not so?'

'I decline to answer, if in my judgment thought has the limit you would fix to it. But proceed; you have a special question you wish to put.'

'Intense malignity is an intense will, engendered in a peculiar temperament, and aided by natural means within the reach of science, may produce effects like those ascribed of old to evil magic. It might thus haunt the walls of a human habitation with spectral revivals of all guilty thoughts and guilty deeds once conceived and done within those walls; all, in short, with which the evil will claims *rapport* and affinity – imperfect, incoherent, fragmentary snatches at the old dramas acted therein years ago.

'Thoughts thus crossing each other haphazard, as in the nightmare of a vision, growing up into phantom sights and sounds, and all serving to create horror; not because those sights and sounds are really visitations from a world without, but that they are ghastly, monstrous renewals of what have been in this world itself, set into malignant play by a malignant mortal. And it is through the material agency of that human brain that these things would acquire even a human power; would strike as with the shock of electricity, and might kill, if the thought of the person assailed did not rise superior to the dignity of the original assailer; might kill the most powerful animal, if unnerved by fear, but not injure the feeblest man, if, while his flesh crept, his mind stood out fearless.

'Thus when in old stories we read of a magician rent to pieces by the fiends he had invoked, or still more, in Eastern legends, that one magician succeeds by arts in destroying another, there may be so far truth, that a material being has clothed, from his own evil propensities, certain elements and fluids, usually quiescent or harmless, with awful shapes and terrific force; just as the lightning, that has lain hidden and innocent in the cloud, becomes by natural law suddenly visible, takes a distinct shape to the eye, and can strike destruction on the object to which it is attracted.'

'You are not without glimpses of a mighty secret,' said Mr. Richards composedly. 'According to your view, could a mortal obtain the power you speak of, he would necessarily be a malignant and evil being.'

'If the power were exercised as I have said, most malignant and most evil; though I believe in the ancient traditions that he could not injure the good. His will could only injure those with whom it has established an affinity, or over whom it forces unresisted sway. I will now imagine an example that may be within the laws of nature, yet seem wild as the fables of a bewildered monk.

'You will remember that Albertus Magnus, after describing minutely the process by which the spirits may be invoked and commanded, adds emphatically that the process will instruct and avail only to the few; that *a man must be born a magician!* – that is, born with a peculiar physical temperament, as a man is born a poet.

'Rarely are men in whose constitutions lurks this occult power of the highest order of intellect; usually in the intellect there is some twist, perversity, or disease. But on the other hand, they must possess, to an astonishing degree, the faculty to concentrate thought on a single object – the energic faculty that we call WILL. Therefore, though their intellect be not sound, it is exceedingly forcible for the attainment of what it desires. I will imagine such a person, pre-eminently gifted with this constitution and its concomitant forces. I will place him in the loftier grades of society.

'I will suppose his desires emphatically those of the sensualist; he has, therefore, a strong love of life. He is an absolute egotist; his will is concentred in himself; he has fierce passions; he knows no enduring, no holy affections, but he can covet eagerly what for the moment he desires; he can hate implacably what opposes itself to his objects; he can commit fearful crimes, yet feel small remorse; he resorts rather to curses upon others than to penitence for his misdeeds. Circumstances to which his constitution guides him, lead him to a rare knowledge of the natural secrets which may serve his egotism. He is a close observer where his passions encourage observation; he is a minute calculator, not from love of truth, but where love of self sharpens his faculties; therefore he can be a man of science.

'I suppose such a being, having by experience learned the power of his arts over others, trying what may be the power of will over his own frame, and studying all that in natural philosphy may increase that power. He loves life, he dreads death; *he wills to live on.* He cannot restore himself to youth; he cannot entirely stay the progress of death; he cannot make himself immortal in the flesh and blood. But he may arrest, for a time so long as to appear incredible if I said it, that hardening of the parts which constitutes old age.

'A year may age him no more than an hour ages another. His intense will, scientifically trained into system, operates in short, over the wear and tear of his own frame. He lives on. That he may not seem a portent and a miracle, he *dies*, from time to time, seemingly, to certain persons. Having schemed the transfer of a wealth that suffices to his wants, he disappears from one corner of the world, and contrives that his obsequies shall be celebrated.

'He reappears at another corner of the world, where he resides undetected, and does not visit the scenes of his former career till all who could remember his features are no more. He would be profoundly miserable if he had affections; he has none but for himself. No good man would accept his longevity; and to no man, good or bad, would he or could he communicate its true secret.

'Such a man might exist; such a man as I have described I see now before me – Duke of —, in the court of —, dividing time between lust and brawl, alchemists and wizards; again, in the last century, charlatan and criminal, with name less noble, domiciled in the house at which you gazed to-day, and flying from the law you had outraged, none knew whither; traveller once more revisiting London with the same earthly passion which filled your heart when races now no more walked through yonder streets; outlaw from the school of all the nobler and diviner mysteries. Execrable image of life in death and death in life, I warn you back from the cities and homes of healthful men! back to the ruins of departed empires! back to the deserts of nature unredeemed!'

There answered me a whisper so musical, so potently musical, that it seemed to enter into my whole being and subdue me despite myself. Thus it said:

'I have sought one like you for the last hundred years. Now I have found you, we part not till I know what I desire. The vision that sees through the past and cleaves through the veil of the future is in you at this hour – never before, never to come again. The vision of no pulling, fantastic girl, of no sick-bed somnambule, but of a strong man with a vigorous brain. Soar, and look forth!'

As he spoke, I felt as if I rose out of myself upon eagle wings. All the weight seemed gone from air, roofless the room, roofless the dome of space. I was not in the body – where, I knew not; but aloft over time, over earth.

Again I heard the melodious whisper:

'You say right. I have mastered great secrets by the power of will. True, by will and by science I can retard the process of years, but death comes not by age alone. Can I frustrate the accidents which bring death upon the young?'

'No; every accident is a providence. Before a providence snaps every human will.'

'Shall I die at last, ages and ages hence, by the slow though inevitable growth of time, or by the cause that I call accident?'

'By a cause you call accident.'

'Is not the end still remote?' asked the whisper, with a slight tremor.

'Regarded as my life regards time, it is still remote.'

'And shall I, before then, mix with the world of men as I did ere I learned these secrets; resume eager interest in their strife and their trouble; battle with ambition, and use the power of the sage to win the power that belongs to kings?'

'You will yet play a part on the earth that will fill earth with commotion and amaze. For wondrous designs have you, a wonder yourself, been permitted to live on through the centuries. All the secrets you have stored will then have their uses; all that now makes you a stranger amid the generations will contribute then to make you their lord. As the trees and the straws are drawn into a whirlpool, as they spin round, are sucked to the deep, and again tossed aloft by the eddies, so shall races and thrones be drawn into your vortex. Awful destroyer! but in destroying, made, against your own will, a constructor.'

'And that date, too, is far off?'

'Far off; when it comes, think your end in this world is at hand!'

'How and what is the end? Look east, west, south, and north.'

'In the north, where you never yet trod, towards the point whence your instincts have warned you, there a spectre will seize you. 'Tis Death! I see a ship; it is haunted; 'tis chased! it sails on. Baffled navies sail after that ship. It enters the region of ice. It passes a sky red with meteors. Two moons stand on high, over ice-reefs. I see the ship locked between white defiles; they are ice-rocks. I see the dead strew the decks, stark and livid, green mould on their limbs. All are dead but one man – it is you! But years, though so slowly they come, have then scathed you. There is the coming of age on your brow, and the will is relaxed in the cells of the brain. Still that will, though enfeebled, exceeds all that man knew before you; through the will you live on, gnawed with famine. And Nature no longer obeys you in that death-spreading region; the sky is a sky of iron, and the air has iron clamps, and the ice-rocks wedge in the ship. Hark how it cracks and groans! Ice will imbed it as amber imbeds a straw. And a man has gone forth, living yet, from the ship and its dead; and he has clambered up the spikes of an iceberg, and the two moons gaze down on his form. That man is yourself, and terror is on you – terror; and terror has swallowed up your will.

'And I see, swarming up the steep ice-rock, grey, grizzly things. The bears of the North have scented their quarry; they come nearer and nearer, shambling, and rolling their bulk. In that day every moment shall seem to you longer than the centuries through which you have passed. Heed this: after life, moments continued make the bliss or the hell of eternity.'

'Hush!' said the whisper. 'But the day, you assure me, is far off, very far! I go back to the almond and rose of Damascus! Sleep!'

The room swam before my eyes I became insensible. When I recovered, I found G— holding my hand and smiling. He said, 'You, who have always declared yourself proof against mesmerism, have succumbed at last to my friend Richards.'

'Where is Mr. Richards?'

'Gone, when you passed into a trance, saying quietly to me, "Your friend will not wake for an hour." '

I asked, as collectedly as I could, where Mr. Richards lodged.

'At the Trafalgar Hotel'

'Give me your arm,' said I to G—. 'Let us call on him; I have something to say.'

When we arrived at the hotel we were told that Mr. Richards had returned twenty minutes before, paid his bill, left directions with his servant (a Greek) to pack his effects, and proceed to Malta by the steamer that should leave Southampton the next day. Mr. Richards had merely said of his own movements that he had visits to pay in the neighbourhood of London, and it was uncertain whether he should be able to reach Southampton in time for that steamer; if not, he should follow in the next one.

The waiter asked me my name. On my informing him, he gave me a note that Mr. Richards had left for me in case I called.

The note was as follows:

I wished you to utter what was in your mind. You obeyed. I have therefore established power over you. For three months from this day you can communicate to no living man what has passed between us. You cannot even show this note to the friend by your side. During three months silence complete as to me and mine. Do you doubt my power to lay on you this command? Try to disobey me. At the end of the third month the spell is raised. For the rest, I spare you. I shall visit your grave a year and a day after it has received you.

So ends this strange story, which I ask no one to believe. I write it down exactly three months after I received the above note. I could not write it before, nor could I show to G—, in spite of his urgent request, the note which I read under the gas lamp by his side.

Fever Dream
RAY BRADBURY

THEY PUT HIM BETWEEN fresh, clean, laundered sheets and there was always a newly squeezed glass of thick orange juice on the table under the dim pink lamp. All Charles had to do was call and Mom or Dad would stick their heads into his room to see how sick he was. The acoustics of the room were fine; you could hear the toilet gargling its porcelain throat in the mornings, you could hear rain tap the roof or sly mice run in the secret walls, the canary singing in its cage downstairs. If you were very alert, sickness wasn't too bad.

He was fifteen, Charles was. It was mid September, with the land beginning to burn with autumn. He lay in the bed for three days before the terror overcame him.

His hand began to change. His right hand. He looked at it and it was hot and sweating there on the counterpane, alone. It fluttered, it moved a bit. Then it lay there, changing colour.

That afternoon the doctor came again and tapped his thin chest like a little drum. 'How are you?' asked the doctor, smiling. 'I know, don't tell me: "My *cold* is fine, Doctor, but I feel lousy!" Ha!' He laughed at his own oft-repeated joke.

Charles lay there and for him that terrible and ancient jest was becoming a reality. The joke fixed itself in his mind. His mind touched and drew away from it in a pale terror. The doctor did not know how cruel he was with his jokes! 'Doctor,' whispered Charles, lying flat and colourless. 'My *hand*, it doesn't *belong* to me any more. This morning it *changed* into something else. I want you to change it back, Doctor, Doctor!'

The doctor showed his teeth and patted his hand. 'It looks fine to me, son. You just had a little fever dream.'

'But it changed, Doctor, oh, Doctor,' cried Charles, pitifully holding up his pale wild hand. 'It *did*!'

The doctor winked. 'I'll give you a pink pill for that.' He popped a tablet on to Charles's tongue. 'Swallow!'

'Will it make my hand change back and become *me*, again?'

'Yes, yes.'

The house was silent when the doctor drove off down the road in his carriage under the quiet, blue September sky. A clock ticked far below in the kitchen world. Charles lay looking at his hand.

It did not change back. It was still – something else.

The wind blew outside. Leaves fell against the cool window.

At four o'clock his other hand changed. It seemed almost to become a fever, a chemical, a virus. It pulsed and shifted, cell by cell. It beat like a warm heart. The fingernails turned blue and then red. It took about an hour for it to change and when it was finished, it looked just like any ordinary hand. But it was not ordinary. It no longer was him any more. He lay in a fascinated horror and then fell into an exhausted sleep.

Mother brought the soup up at six. He wouldn't touch it. 'I haven't any hands,' he said, eyes shut.

'Your hands are perfectly good,' said Mother.

'No,' he wailed. 'My hands are gone. I feel like I have stumps. Oh, Mama, Mama, hold me, hold me, I'm scared!'

She had to feed him herself.

'Mama,' he said, 'get the doctor, please, again, I'm so sick.'

'The doctor'll be here tonight at eight,' she said, and went out.

At seven, with night dark and close around the house, Charles was sitting up in bed when he felt the thing happening to first one leg then the other. 'Mama! Come quick!' he screamed.

But when Mama came the thing was no longer happening.

When she went downstairs, he simply lay without fighting as his legs beat and beat, grew warm, red hot, and the room filled with the warmth of his feverish change. The glow crept up from his toes to his ankles and then to his knees.

'May I come in?' The doctor smiled in the doorway.

'Doctor!' cried Charles. 'Hurry, take off my blankets!'

The doctor lifted the blankets tolerantly. 'There you are. Whole and healthy. Sweating, though. A little fever. I told you not to move around, bad boy.' He pinched the moist pink cheek. 'Did the pills help? Did your hand change back?'

'No, no, now it's my other hand and my legs!'

'Well, well, I'll have to give you three more pills, one for each limb, eh, my little peach?' laughed the doctor.

'Will they help me? Please, please. What've I *got*?'

'A mild case of scarlet fever, complicated by a slight cold.'

'Is it a germ that lives and has more little germs in me?'

'Yes.'

'Are you *sure* it's scarlet fever? You haven't taken any tests!'

'I guess I know a certain fever when I see one,' said the doctor, checking the boy's pulse with cool authority.

Charles lay there, not speaking until the doctor was crisply packing his black kit. Then in the silent room, the boy's voice made a small, weak pattern, his eyes alight with remembrance. 'I read a book once. About petrified trees, wood turning to stone. About how trees fell and rotted and minerals got in and built up and they look just like trees, but they're not, they're stone.' He stopped. In the quiet warm room his breathing sounded.

'Well?' asked the doctor.

'I've been thinking,' said Charles, after a time. 'Do germs ever get big? I mean in biology class they told us about one-celled animals, amoebas and things, and how, millions of years ago, they got together until there was a bunch and they made the first body. And more and more cells got together and got bigger and then finally maybe there was a fish and finally here *we* are, and all we are is a bunch of cells that decided to get together, to help each other out. Isn't that right?' Charles wet his feverish lips.

'What's all this about?' The doctor bent over him.

'I've got to tell you this. Doctor, oh, I've got to!' he cried. 'What would happen, oh just pretend, please pretend, that just like in the old days, a lot of microbes got together and wanted to make a bunch, and reproduced and made more—'

His white hands were on his chest now, crawling towards his throat.

'And they decided to *take over* a person!' cried Charles.

'Take over a person?'

'Yes, *become* a person. *Me*, my hands, my feet! What if a disease somehow knew how to kill a person and yet live after him?'

He screamed.

The hands were on his neck.

The doctor moved forward, shouting.

At nine o'clock the doctor was escorted out to his carriage by the mother and father, who handed him up his bag. They conversed in the cool night wind for a few minutes. 'Just be sure his hands are kept strapped to his legs,' said the doctor. 'I don't want him hurting himself!'

'Will he be all right, Doctor?' The mother held to his arm a moment.

He patted her shoulder. 'Haven't I been your family physician for thirty years? It's the fever, he imagines things.'

'But those bruises on his throat, he almost choked himself.'

'Just you keep him strapped; he'll be all right in the morning.'

The horse and carriage moved off down the dark September road.

At three in the morning, Charles was still awake in his small back room. The bed was damp under his head and his back. He was very warm. Now he no longer had any arms or legs, and his body was beginning to change. He did not move on the bed, but looked at the vast blank ceiling space with insane concentration. For a while he had screamed and thrashed but now he was weak and hoarse from it, and his mother had gotten up a number of times to soothe his brow with a wet towel. Now he was silent, his hands strapped to his legs.

He felt the walls of his body change, the organs shift, the lungs catch fire like burning bellows of pink alcohol. The room was lighted up as with the flickerings of a hearthplace.

Now he had no body. It was all gone. It was under him, but it was filled with a vast pulse of some burning, lethargic drug. It was as if a guillotine had neatly lopped off his head and his head lay shining on a midnight pillow while the body, below, still alive, belonged to somebody else. The disease had eaten his body and from the eating had reproduced itself in feverish duplicate. There were the little hand-hairs and the fingernails and the scars and the toenails and the tiny mole on his right hip, all done again in perfect fashion.

I am dead, he thought. I've been killed, and yet I live. My body is dead, it is all disease and nobody will know. I will walk around and it will not be me, it will be something else. It will be something all bad, all evil, so big and so evil it's hard to understand or think about. Something that will buy shoes and drink water and get married some day maybe and do more evil in the world than has ever been done.

Now the warmth was stealing up his neck, into his cheeks, like a hot wine. His lips burned, his eyelids, like leaves, caught fire. His nostrils breathed out blue flame, faintly, faintly.

This will be all, he thought. I'll take my head and my brain and fix each eye and every tooth and all the marks in my brain, and every hair and every wrinkle in my ears, and there'll be nothing left of me.

He felt his brain fill with a boiling mercury. He felt his left eye clench in upon itself and, like a snail, withdraw, shift. He was blind in his left eye. It no longer belonged to him. It was enemy territory. His tongue was gone, cut out. His left cheek was numbed, lost. His left ear stopped hearing. It belonged to someone else now. This thing that was being born, this mineral thing replacing the wooden log, this disease replacing healthy animal cell.

He tried to scream and he was able to scream loud and high and sharply in the room, just as his brain flooded down, his right eye and right ear were cut out, he was blind and deaf, all fire and terror, all panic, all death.

His scream stopped before his mother ran through the door to his side.

It was a good, clear morning, with a brisk wind that helped carry doctor, horse and carriage along the road to halt before the house. In the window above, the boy stood, fully dressed. He did not wave when the doctor waved and called, 'What's this? Up? My God!'

The doctor almost ran upstairs. He came gasping into the bedroom.

'What are you doing out of bed?' he demanded of the boy. He tapped his thin chest, took his pulse and temperature. 'Absolutely amazing! Normal. Normal, by God!'

'I shall never be sick again in my life,' declared the boy, quietly, standing there, looking out of the wide window. 'Never.'

'I hope not. Why, you're looking fine, Charles.'

'Doctor?'

'Yes, Charles?'

'Can I go to school *now*?' asked Charles.

'Tomorrow will be time enough. You sound positively eager.'

'I am. I like school. All the kids. I want to play with them and wrestle with them, and spit on them and play with the girls' pigtails and shake the teacher's hand, and rub my hands on all the cloaks in the cloakroom, and I want to grow up and travel and shake hands with people all over the world, and be married and have lots of children, and go to libraries and handle books and – *all* of that I want tò!' said the boy looking off into the September morning. 'What's the name you called me?'

'What?' The doctor puzzled. 'I called you nothing but Charles.'

'It's better than no name at all, I guess,' Charles shrugged.

'I'm glad you want to go back to school,' said the doctor.

'I really anticipate it,' smiled the boy. 'Thank you for your help, Doctor. Shake hands.'

'Glad to.'

They shook hands gravely, and the clear wind blew through the open window. They shook hands for almost a minute, the boy smiling up at the old man and thanking him.

Then, laughing, the boy raced the doctor downstairs and out to his carriage. His mother and father followed for the happy farewell.

'Fit as a fiddle!' said the doctor. 'Incredible!'

'And strong,' said the father. 'He got out of his straps himself during the night. Didn't you, Charles?'

'Did I?' said the boy.

'You did! How?'

'Oh,' the boy said, 'that was a long time ago.'

'A long time ago!'

They all laughed, and while they were laughing, the quiet boy moved his bare foot on the pavement and brushed against a number of red ants that were scurrying about on the pavement. Secretly, his eyes shining, while his parents chatted with the old man, he saw the ants hesitate, quiver, and lie still on the cement. He knew they were cold now.

'Good-bye!'

The doctor drove away, waving.

The boy walked ahead of his parents. As he walked he looked away towards the town and began to hum 'School Days' under his breath.

'It's good to have him well again,' said the father.

'Listen to him. He's so looking forward to school!'

The boy turned quietly. He gave each of his parents a crushing hug. He kissed them both several times.

Then, without a word, he bounded up the steps into the house.

In the parlour, before the others entered, he quickly opened the birdcage, thrust his hand in, and petted the yellow canary, *once*.

Then he shut the cage door, stood back, and waited.

Green Tea

J. SHERIDAN LE FANU

THE REV. MR. JENNINGS is tall and thin. He is middleaged, and dresses with a natty, old-fashioned, high-church precision. He is naturally a little stately, but not at all stiff. His features, without being handsome, are well formed, and their expression extremely kind, but also shy.

I met him one evening at Lady Mary Heyduke's. The modesty and benevolence of his countenance are extremely prepossessing.

We were but a small party, and he joined agreeably enough in the conversation. He seems to enjoy listening very much more than contributing to the talk; but what he says is always to the purpose and well said. He is a great favourtie of Lady Mary's, who it seems, consults him upon many things, and thinks him the most happy and blessed person on earth. Little knows she about him.

The Rev. Mr. Jennings is a bachelor, and has, they say, sixty thousand pounds in the funds. He is a charitable man. He is most anxious to be actively employed in his sacred profession, and yet though always tolerably well elsewhere, when he goes down to his vicarage in Warwickshire, to engage in the actual duties of his sacred calling, his health soon fails him, and in a very strange way. So says Lady Mary.

There is no doubt that Mr. Jennings' health does break down in, generally a sudden and mysterious way, sometimes in the very act of officiating in his old and pretty church at Kenlis. It may be his heart, it may be his brain. But so it has happened three or four times, or oftener, that after proceeding a certain way in the service, he has on a sudden stopped short, and after a silence, apparently quite unable to resume, he has fallen into solitary, inaudible prayer, his hands and his eyes uplifted, and then pale as death, and in the agitation of a strange shame and horror, descended trembling, and got into the vestry-room, leaving his congregation, without explanation, to themselves. This occurred when his curate was absent. When he goes down to Kenlis now, he always takes care to provide a clergyman to share his duty, and to supply his place on the instant should he become thus suddenly incapacitated.

When Mr. Jennings breaks down quite, and beats a retreat from the vicarage, and returns to London, where, in a dark street off Piccadilly, he inhabits a very narrow house, Lady Mary says that he is always perfectly well. I have my own opinion about that. There are degrees of course. We shall see.

Mr. Jennings is a perfectly gentlemanlike man. People, however, remark something odd. There is an impression a little ambiguous. One thing which certainly contributes to it, people I think don't remember; or, perhaps, distinctly remark. But I did, almost immediately. Mr. Jennings has a way of looking sidelong upon the carpet, as if his eye followed the movements of something there. This, of course, is not always. It occurs only now and then. But often enough to give a certain oddity, as I have said to his manner, and in this glance travelling along the floor there is something both shy and anxious.

A medical philosopher, as you are good enough to call me, elaborating theories by the aid of cases sought out by himself, and by him watched and scrutinised with more time at command, and consequently infinitely more minuteness than the ordinary practitioner can afford, falls insensibly into habits of observation, which accompany him everywhere, and are exercised, as some people would say, impertinently, upon every subject that presents itself with the least likelihood of rewarding inquiry.

There was a promise of this kind in the slight, timid, kindly, but reserved gentleman, whom I met for the first time at this agreeable little evening gathering. I observed, of course, more than I here set down; but I reserve all that borders on the technical for a strictly scientific paper.

I may remark, that when I here speak of medical science, I do so, as I hope some day to see it more generally understood, in a much more comprehensive sense than its generally material treatment would warrant. I believe the entire natural world is but the ultimate expression of that spiritual world from which, and in which alone, it has its life. I believe that the essential man is a spirit, that the spirit is an organised substance, but as different in point of material from what we ordinarily understand by matter, as light or electricity is; that the material body is, in the most literal sense, a vesture, and death consequently no interruption of the living man's existence, but simply his extrication from the natural body – a process which commences at the moment of what we term death, and the completion of which, at furthest a few days later, is the resurrection 'in power.'

The person who weighs the consequences of these positions will probably see their practical bearing upon medical science. This is, however, by no means the proper place for displaying the proofs and discussing the consequences of this too generally unrecognized state of facts.

In pursuance of my habit, I was covertly observing Mr. Jennings, with all my caution – I think he perceived it – and I saw plainly that he was as cautiously observing me. Lady Mary happening to address me by my name, as Dr. Hesselius, I saw that he glanced at me more sharply, and then became thoughful for a few minutes.

After this, as I conversed with a gentleman at the other end of the room, I saw him look at me more steadily, and with an interest which I thought I understood. I then saw him take an opportunity of chatting with Lady Mary, and was, as one always is, perfectly aware of being the subject of a distant inquiry and answer.

This tall clergyman approached me by-and-by; and in a little time we had got into conversation. When two people, who like reading, and know books and places, having travelled, wish to discourse, it is very strange if they can't find topics. It was not accident that brought him near me, and led him into conversation. He knew German, and had read my Essays on Metaphysical Medicine which suggest more than they actually say.

This courteous man, gentle, shy, plainly a man of thought and reading, who moving and talking among us, was not altogether of us, and whom I already suspected of leading a life whose transactions and alarms were carefully concealed, with an impenetrable reserve from, not only the world, but his best beloved friends – was cautiously weighing in his own mind the idea of taking a certain step with regard to me.

I penetrated his thoughts without his being aware of it, and was careful to say nothing which could betray to his sensitive vigilance my suspicions respecting his position, or my surmises about his plans respecting myself.

We chatted upon indifferent subjects for a time; but at last he said:

'I was very much interested by some papers of yours, Dr. Hesselius, upon what you term Metaphysical Medicine – I read them in German, ten or twelve years ago – have they been translated?'

'No, I'm sure they have not – I should have heard. They would have asked my leave, I think.'

'I asked the publishers here, a few months ago, to get the book for me in the original German; but they tell me it is out of print.'

'So it is, and has been for some years; but it flatters me as an author to find that you have not forgotten my little book, although,' I added, laughing, 'ten or twelve years is a considerable time to have managed without it; but I suppose you have been turning the subject over again in your mind, or something has happened lately to revive your interest in it.'

At this remark, accompanied by a glance of inquiry, a sudden embarrassment disturbed Mr. Jennings, analogous to that which makes a young lady blush and look foolish. He dropped his eyes, and folded his hands together uneasily, and looked oddly, and you would have said, guiltily, for a moment.

I helped him out of his awkwardness in the best way, by appearing not to observe it, and going straight on, I said: 'Those revivals of interest in a subject happen to me often; one book suggests another, and often sends me back a wild-goose chase over an interval of twenty years. But if you still care to possess a copy, I shall be only too happy to provide you; I have still got two or three by me—and if you allow me to present one I shall be very much honoured.'

'You are very good indeed,' he said, quite at his ease again, in a moment: 'I almost despaired – I don't know how to thank you.'

'Pray don't say a word; the thing is really so little worth that I am only ashamed of having offered it, and if you thank me any more I shall throw it into the fire in a fit of modesty.'

Mr. Jennings laughed. He inquired where I was staying in London, and after a little more conversation on a variety of subjects, he took his departure.

'I like your vicar so much, Lady Mary,' said I, as soon as he was gone. 'He has read, travelled, and thought, and having also suffered, he ought to be an accomplished companion.'

'So he is, and, better still, he is a really good man,' said she. 'His advice is invaluable about my schools, and all my little undertakings at Dawlbridge, and he's so painstaking, he takes so much trouble – you have no idea – wherever he thinks he can be of use: he's so good-natured and so sensible.'

'It is pleasant to hear so good an account of his neighbourly virtues. I can only testify to his being an agreeable and gentle companion, and in addition to what you have told me, I think I can tell you two or three things about him,' said I.

'Really!'

'Yes, to begin with, he's unmarried.'

'Yes, that's right – go on.'

'He has been writing, that is he *was*, but for two or three years perhaps, he has not gone on with his work, and the book was upon some rather abstract subject – perhaps theology.'

'Well, he was writing a book, as you say; I'm not quite sure what it was about, but only that it was nothing that I cared for; very likely you are right, and he certainly did stop – yes.'

'And although he only drank a little coffee here to-night, he likes tea, at least, did like it, extravagantly.'

'Yes, that's *quite* true.'

'He drank green tea, a good deal, didn't he?' I pursued.

'Well, that's very odd! Green tea was a subject on which we used almost to quarrel.'

'But he has quite given that up,' said I.

'So he has.'

'And, now, one more fact. His mother or his father, did you know them?'

'Yes, both; his father is only ten years dead, and their place is near Dawlbridge. We knew them very well,' she answered.

'Well, either his mother or his father – I should rather think his father, saw a ghost,' said I.

'Well, you really are a conjurer, Dr. Hesselius.'

'Conjurer or no, haven't I said right?' I answered merrily.

'You certainly have, and it *was* his father: he was a silent, whimsical man, and he used to bore my father about his dreams, and at last he told him a story about a ghost he had seen and talked with, and a very odd story it was. I remember it particularly, because I was so afraid of him. This story was long before he died – when I was quite a child – and his ways were so silent and moping, and he used to drop in sometimes, in the dusk, when I was alone in the drawing-room, and I used to fancy there were ghosts about him.'

I smiled and nodded.

'And now, having established my character as a conjurer, I think I must say good-night,' said I.

'But how *did* you find it out?'

'By the planets, of course, as the gipsies do,' I answered, and so, gaily we said good-night.

Next morning I sent the little book he had been inquiring after, and a note to Mr. Jennings, and on returning late that evening, I found that he had called at my lodgings, and left his card. He asked whether I was at home, and asked at what hour he would be most likely to find me.

Does he intend opening his case, and consulting me 'professionally,' as they say. I hope so. I have already conceived a theory about him. It is supported by Lady Mary's answers to my parting questions. I should like much to ascertain from his own lips. But what can I do consistently with good breeding to invite a confession? Nothing. I rather think he meditates one.

Well, I have called at Blank Street.

On inquiring at the door, the servant told me that Mr. Jennings was engaged very particularly with a gentleman, a clergyman from Kenlis, his parish in the country. Intending to reserve my privilege, and to call again, I merely intimated that I should try another time, and had turned to go, when the servant begged my pardon, and asked me, looking at me a little more attentively than well-bred persons of his order usually do, whether I was Dr. Hesselius; and, on learning that I was, he said, 'Perhaps then, sir, you would allow me to mention it to Mr. Jennings, for I am sure he wishes to see you.'

The servant returned in a moment, with a message from Mr. Jennings, asking me to go into his study, which was in effect his back drawing-room, promising to be with me in a very few minutes.

This was really a study – almost a library. The room was lofty, with two tall slender windows, and rich dark curtains. It was much larger than I had expected, and stored with books on every side, from the floor to the ceiling. The upper carpet – for to my tread it felt that there were two or three – was a Turkey carpet. My steps fell noiselessly. The book-cases standing out, placed the windows, particularly narrow ones, in deep recesses. The effect of the room was, although extremely comfortable, and even luxurious decidedly gloomy, and aided by the silence, almost oppressive. Perhaps, however, I ought to have allowed something for association. My mind had connected peculiar ideas with Mr. Jennings. I stepped into this perfectly silent room, of a very silent house, with a peculiar foreboding; and its darkness, and solemn clothing of books, for except where two narrow looking-glasses were set in the wall, they were everywhere, helped this sombre feeling.

While awaiting Mr. Jennings' arrival, I amused myself by looking into some of the books with which his shelves were laden. Not among these, but immediately under them, with their backs upward, on the floor, I lighted upon a complete set of Swedenborg's 'Arcana Cælestia,' in the original Latin, a very find folio set, bound in the natty livery which theology affects, pure vellum, namely, gold letters, and carmine edges. There were paper markers in several of these volumes, I raised and placed them, one after the other, upon the table, and opening where these papers were placed, I read in the solemn Latin phraseology, a series of sentences indicated by a pencilled line at the margin. Of these I copy here a few, translating them into English.

'When man's interior sight is opened, which is that of his spirit, then there appear the things of another life, which cannot possibly be made visible to the bodily sight.' . . . .

'By the internal sight it has been granted me to see the things that are in the other life, more clearly than I see those that are in the world. From these considerations, it is evident that external vision exists from interior vision, and this from a vision still more interior, and·so on.' . . . .

'There are with every man at least two evil spirits.' . . . .

'With wicked genii there is also a fluent speech, but harsh and grating. There is also among them a speech which is not fluent, wherein the dissent of the thoughts is perceived as something secretly creeping along within it.'

'The evil spirits associated with man are, indeed from the hells, but when with man they are not then in hell, but are taken out thence. The place where they then are, is in the midst between heaven and hell, and is called the world of spirits – when the evil spirits who are with man, are in that world, they are not in any infernal torment, but in every thought and affection of the man, and so, in all that the man himself enjoys. But when they are remitted into their hell, they return to their former state.' . . . .

'If evil spirits could perceive that they were associated with man, and yet that they were spirits separate from him, and if they could flow in into the things of his body, they would attempt by a thousand means to destroy him; for they hate man with a deadly hatred.' . . . .

'Knowing, therefore, that I was a man in the body, they were continually striving to destroy me, not as to the body only, but especially as to the soul; for to destroy any man or spirit is the very delight of the life of all who are in hell; but I have been continually protected by the Lord. Hence it appears how dangerous it is for man to be in a living consort with spirits, unless he be in the good of faith.' . . . .

'Nothing is more carefully guarded from the knowledge of associate spirits than their being thus conjoint with a man, for if they knew it they would speak to him, with the intention to destroy him.' . . . .

'The delight of hell is to do evil to man, and to hasten his eternal ruin.'

A long note, written with a very sharp and fine pencil, in Mr. Jennings' neat hand, at the foot of the page, caught my eye. Expecting his criticism upon the text, I read a word or two, and stopped, for it was something quite different, and began with these words, *Deus misereatur mei*–'May God compassionate me.' Thus warned of its private nature, I averted my eyes, and shut the book, replacing all the volumes as I had found them, except one which interested me, and in which, as men studious and solitary in their habits will do, I grew so absorbed as to take no cognisance of the outer world, nor to remember where I was.

I was reading some pages which refer to 'representatives' and 'correspondents,' in the technical language of Swedenborg, and had arrived at a passage, the substance of which is that evil spirits, when seen by other eyes than those of their infernal associates, present themselves, by 'correspondence,' in the shape of the beast (*fera*) which represents their particular lust and life, in aspect direful and atrocious. This is a long passage, and particularises a number of those bestial forms.

I was running the head of my pencil-case along the line as I read it, and something caused me to raise my eyes.

Directly before me was one of the mirrors I have mentioned, in which I saw reflected the tall shape of my friend, Mr. Jennings, leaning over my shoulder, and reading the page at which I was busy, and with a face so dark and wild that I should hardly have known him.

I turned and rose. He stood erect also, and with an effort laughed a little, saying:

'I came in and asked you how you did, but without succeeding in awaking you from your book; so I could not restrain my curiosity, and very impertinently, I'm afraid, peeped over your shoulder. This is not your first time of looking into those pages. You have looked into Swedenborg, no doubt, long ago?'

'Oh dear, yes! I owe Swedenborg a great deal; you will discover traces of him in the little book on Metaphysical Medicine, which you were so good as to remember.'

Although my friend affected a gaiety of manner, there was a slight flush in his face, and I could perceive that he was inwardly much perturbed.

'I'm scarcely yet qualified, I know so little of Swedenborg. I've only had them a fortnight,' he answered, 'and I think they are rather likely to make a solitary man nervous – that is, judging from the very little I have read – I don't say that they have made me so,' he laughed; 'and I'm so very much obliged for the book. I hope you got my note?'

'I made all proper acknowledgments and modest disclaimers.

'I never read a book that I go with, so entirely, as that of yours,' he continued. 'I saw at once there is more in it than is quite unfolded. Do you know Dr. Harley?' he asked, rather abruptly.

In passing, the editor remarks that the physician here named was one of the most eminent who had ever practised in England.

I did, having had letters to him, and had experienced from him great courtesy and considerable assistance during my visit to England.

'I think that man one of the very greatest fools I ever met in my life,' said Mr. Jennings.

This was the first time I had ever heard him say a sharp thing of anybody, and such a term applied to so high a name a little startled me.

'Really! and in what way?' I asked.

'In his profession,' he answered.

I smiled.

'I mean this,' he said: 'he seems to me, one half, blind – I mean one half of all he looks at is dark – preternaturally bright and vivid all the rest; and the worst of it is, it seems *wilful*. I can't get him – I mean he won't – I've had some experience of him as a physician, but I look on him as, in that sense, no better than a paralytic mind, an intellect half dead. I'll tell you – I know I shall some time – all about it,' he said, with a little agitation. 'You stay some months longer in England. If I should be out of town during your stay for a little time, would you allow me to trouble you with a letter?'

'I should be only too happy,' I assured him.

'Very good of you. I am so utterly dissatisfied with Harley.'

'A little leaning to the materialistic school,' I said.

'A *mere* materialist,' he corrected me; 'you can't think how that wort of thing worries one who knows better. You won't tell any one – any of my friends you know – that I am hippish; now, for instance, no one knows – not even Lady Mary – that I have seen Dr. Harley, or any other doctor. So pray don't mention it; and, if I should have any threatening of an attack you'll kindly let me write, or, should I be in town, have a little talk with you.'

I was full of conjecture, and unconsciously I found I had fixed my eyes gravely on him, for he lowered his for a moment, and he said:

'I see you think I might as well tell you now, or else you are forming a conjecture; but you may as well give it up. If you were guessing all the rest of your life, you will never hit on it.'

He shook his head smiling, and over that wintry sunshine a black cloud suddenly came down, and he drew his breath in, through his teeth as men do in pain.

'Sorry, of course, to learn that you apprehend occasion to consult any of us; but, command me when and how you like, and I need not assure you that your confidence is sacred.'

He then talked of quite other things, and in a comparatively cheerful way and after a little time, I took my leave.

We parted cheerfully, but he was not cheerful, nor was I. There are certain expressions of that powerful organ of spirit – the human face – which, although I have seen them often, and possess a doctor's nerve, yet disturb me profoundly. One look of Mr. Jennings haunted me. It had seized my imagination with so dismal a power that I changed my plans for the evening, and went to the opera, feeling that I wanted a change of ideas.

I heard nothing of or from him for two or three days, when a note in his hand reached me. It was cheerful, and full of hope. He said that he had been for some little time so much better – quite well, in fact – that he was going to make a little experiment, and run down for a month or so to his parish, to try whether a little work might not quite set him up. There was in it a fervent religious expression of gratitude for his restoration, as he now almost hoped he might call it.

A day or two later I saw Lady Mary, who repeated what his note had announced, and told me that he was actually in Warwickshire, having resumed his clerical duties at Kenlis; and she added, 'I begin to think that he is really perfectly well, and that there never was anything the matter, more than nerves and fancy; we are all nervous, but I fancy there is nothing like a little hard work for that kind of weakness, and he has made up his mind to try it. I should not be surprised if he did not come back for a year.'

Notwithstanding all this confidence, only two days later I had this note, dated from his house off Piccadilly:

'DEAR SIR, – I have returned disappointed. If I should feel at all able to see you, I shall write to ask you kindly to call. At present, I am too low, and, in fact, simply unable to say all I wish to say. Pray don't mention my name to my friends. I can see no one. By-and-by, please

God, you shall hear from me. I mean to take a run into Shropshire, where some of my people are. God bless you! May we, on my return, meet more happily than I can now write.'

About a week after this I saw Lady Mary at her own house, the last person, she said, left in town, and just on the wing for Brighton, for the London season was quite over. She told me that she had heard from Mr. Jennings' niece, Martha, in Shropshire. There was nothing to be gathered from her letter, more than that he was low and nervous. In those words, of which healthy people think so lightly, what a world of suffering is sometimes hidden!

Nearly five weeks had passed without any further news of Mr. Jennings. At the end of that time I received a note from him. He wrote:

'I have been in the country, and have had change of air, change of scene, change of faces, change of everything and in everything – by *myself*. I have made up my mind, so far as the most irresolute creature on earth can do it, to tell my case fully to you. If your engagements will permit, pray come to me to-day, to-morrow, or the next day; but, pray defer as little as possible. You know not how much I need help. I have a quiet house at Richmond, where I now am. Perhaps you can manage to come to dinner, or to luncheon, or even to tea. You shall have no trouble in finding me out. The servant at Blank Street, who takes this note, will have a carriage at your door at any hour you please; and I am always to be found. You will say that I ought not to be alone. I have tried everything. Come and see.'

I called up the servant, and decided on going out the same evening, which accordingly I did.

He would have been much better in a lodging-house, or hotel, I thought, as I drove up through a short double row of sombre elms to a very old-fashioned brick house, darkened by the foliage of these trees, which overtopped, and nearly surrounded it. It was a perverse choice, for nothing could be imagined more triste and silent. The house, I found, belonged to him. He had stayed for a day or two in town, and, finding it for some cause insupportable, had come out here, probably because being furnished and his own, he was relieved of the thought and delay of selection, by coming here.

The sun had already set, and the red reflected light of the western sky illuminated the scene with the peculiar effect with which we are all familiar. The hall seemed very dark, but, getting to the back drawing-room, whose windows command the west, I was again in the same dusky light.

I sat down, looking out upon the richly-wooded landscape that glowed in the grand and melancholy light which was every moment fading. The corners of the room were already dark; all was growing dim, and the gloom was insensibly toning my mind, already prepared for what was

141

sinister. I was waiting alone for his arrival, which soon took place. The door communicating with the front room opened, and the tall figure of Mr. Jennings, faintly seen in the ruddy twilight, came, with quiet stealthy steps, into the room.

We shook hands, and, taking a chair to the window, where there was still light enough to enable us to see each other's faces, he sat down beside me, and, placing his hand upon my arm, with scarcely a word of preface began his narrative.

The faint glow of the west, the pomp of the then lonely woods of Richmond, were before us, behind and about us the darkening room, and on the stony face of the sufferer – for the character of his face, though still gentle and sweet, was changed – rested that dim, odd glow which seems to descend and produce, where it touches, lights, sudden though faint, which are lost, almost without gradation, in darkness. The silence, too, was utter; not a distant wheel, or bark, or whistle from without; and within the depressing stillness of an invalid bachelor's house.

I guessed well the nature, though not even vaguely the particulars of the revelations I was about to receive, from that fixed face of suffering that so oddly flushed stood out, like a portrait of Schalken's, before its background of darkness.

'It began,' he said, 'on the 15th of October, three years and eleven weeks ago, and two days – I keep very accurate count, for every day is torment. If I leave anywhere a chasm in my narrative tell me.

'About four years ago I began a work, which had cost me very much thought and reading. It was upon the religious metaphysics of the ancients.'

'I know,' said I, 'the actual religion of educated and thinking paganism, quite apart from symbolic worship? A wide and very interesting field.'

'Yes; but not good for the mind – the Christian mind, I mean. Paganism is all bound together in essential unity, and, with evil sympathy, their religion involves their art, and both their manners, and the subject is a degrading fascination and the Nemesis sure. God forgive me!

'I wrote a great deal; I wrote late at night. I was always thinking on the subject, walking about, wherever I was, everywhere. It thoroughly infected me. You are to remember that all the material ideas connected with it were more or less of the beautiful, the subject itself delightfully interesting, and I, then, without a care.'

He sighed heavily.

'I believe that every one who sets about writing in earnest does his work, as a friend of mine phrased it, *on* something – tea, or coffee, or tobacco. I suppose there is a material waste that must be hourly supplied in such occupations, or that we should grow too abstracted, and the mind, as it were, pass out of the body, unless it were reminded often of the connection by actual sensation. At all events, I felt the want, and I supplied it. Tea was my companion – at first the ordinary black tea, made in the usual way, not too strong: but I drank a good deal, and increased its strength as I went on. I never experienced an uncomfortable symptom from it. I began to take a little green tea. I found the effect pleasanter, it cleared and intensified the power of thought so. I had come to take it frequently, but not stronger than one might take it for pleasure. I wrote a great deal out here, it was so quiet, and in this room. I used to sit up very late, and it became a habit with me to sip my tea – green tea – every now and then as my work proceeded. I had a little kettle on my table, that swung over a lamp, and made tea two or three times between eleven o'clock and two or three in the morning, my hours of going to bed. I used to go into town every day. I was not a monk, and, although I spent an hour or two in a library, hunting up authorities and looking out lights upon my theme, I was in no morbid state as far as I can judge. I met my friends pretty much as usual and enjoyed their society, and, on the whole, existence had never been, I think, so pleasant before.

'I had met with a man who had some odd old books, German editions in mediæval Latin, and I was only too happy to be permitted access to them. This obliging person's books were in the City, a very out-of-the-way part of it. I had rather out-stayed my intended hour, and, on coming out, seeing no cab near, I was tempted to get into the omnibus which used to drive past this house. It was darker than this by the time the 'bus had reached an old house, you may have remarked, with four poplars at each side of the door, and there the last passenger but myself got out. We drove along rather faster. It was twilight now. I leaned back in my corner next the door ruminating pleasantly.

'The interior of the omnibus was nearly dark. I had observed in the corner opposite to me at the other side, and at the end next the horses, two small circular reflections, as it seemed to me of a reddish light. They were about two inches apart, and about the size of those small brass buttons that yachting men used to put upon their jackets. I began to speculate, as listless men will, upon this trifle, as it seemed. From what centre did that faint but deep red light come, and from what – glass beads, buttons, toy decorations – was it reflected? We were lumbering along gently, having nearly a mile still to go. I had not solved the puzzle, and it became in another minute more odd, for these two luminous points, with a sudden jerk, descended nearer the floor, keeping still their relative distance and horizontal position, and then, as suddenly, they rose to the level of the seat on which I was sitting and I saw them no more.

'My curiosity was now really excited, and, before I had time to think, I saw again these two dull lamps, again together near the floor; again they disappeared, and again in their old corner I saw them.

'So, keeping my eyes upon them, I edged quietly up my own side, towards the end at which I still saw these tiny discs of red.

'There was very little light in the 'bus. It was nearly dark. I leaned forward to aid my endeavour to discover what these little circles really were. They shifted their position a little as I did so. I began now to perceive an outline of something black, and I soon saw, with tolerable distinctness, the outline of a small black monkey, pushing its face forward in mimicry to meet mine; those were its eyes, and I now dimly saw its teeth grinning at me.

'I drew back, not knowing whether it might not meditate a spring. I fancied that one of the passengers had forgot this ugly pet, and wishing to ascertain something of its temper, though not caring to trust my fingers to it, I poked my umbrella softly towards it. It remained immovable – up to it – *through* it. For through it, and back and forward it passed, without the slightest resistance.

'I can't, in the least, convey to you the kind of horror that I felt. When I had ascertained that the thing was an illusion, as I then supposed, there came a misgiving about myself and a terror that fascinated me in impotence to remove my gaze from the eyes of the brute for some moments. As I looked, it made a little skip back, quite into the corner, and I, in a panic, found myself at the door, having put my head out, drawing deep breaths of the outer air, and staring at the lights and trees we were passing, too glad to reassure myself of reality.

'I stopped the 'bus and got out. I perceived the man look oddly at me as I paid him. I daresay there was something unusual in my looks and manner, for I had never felt so strangely before.'

'When the omnibus drove on, and I was alone upon the road, I looked carefully round to ascertain whether the monkey had followed me. To my indescribable relief I saw it nowhere. I can't describe easily what a shock I had received, and my sense of genuine gratitude on finding myself, as I supposed, quite rid of it.

'I had got out a little before we reached this house, two or three hundred steps. A brick wall runs along the footpath, and inside the wall is a hedge of yew, or some dark evergreen of that kind, and within that again the row of fine trees which you may have remarked as you came.

'This brick wall is about as high as my shoulder, and happening to raise my eyes I saw the monkey, with that stooping gait, on all fours, walking or creeping, close beside me on top of the wall. I stopped, looking at it with a feeling of loathing and horror. As I stopped so did it. It sat up on the wall with its long hands on its knees looking at me. There was not light enough to see it much more than in outline, nor was it dark enough to bring the peculiar light of its eyes into strong relief. I still saw, however, that red foggy light plainly enough. It did not show its teeth, nor exhibit any sign of irritation, but seemed jaded and sulky, and was observing me steadily.

'I drew back into the middle of the road. It was an unconscious recoil, and there I stood, still looking at it. It did not move.

'With an instinctive determination to try something – anything, I turned about and walked briskly towards town with askance look, all the time, watching the movements of the beast. I crept swiftly along the wall, at exactly my pace.

'Where the wall ends, near the turn of the road, it came down, and with a wiry spring or two brought itself close to my feet, and continued to keep up with me, as I quickened my pace. It was at my left side, so close to my leg that I felt every moment as if I should tread upon it.

'The road was quite deserted and silent, and it was darker every moment. I stopped dismayed and bewildered, turning as I did so, the other way – I mean, towards this house, away from which I had been walking. When I stood still, the monkey drew back to a distance of, I suppose, about five or six yards, and remained stationary, watching me.

'I had been more agitated than I have said. I had read, of course, as everyone has, something about "spectral illusions," as you physicians term the phenomena of such cases. I considered my situation, and looked my misfortune in the face.

'These affections, I had read, are sometimes transitory and sometimes obstinate. I had read of cases in which the appearance, at first harmless, had, step by step, degenerated into something direful and insupportable, and ended by wearing its victim out. Still as I stood there, but for my bestial companion, quite alone, I tried to comfort myself by repeating again and again the assurance, "the thing is purely disease, a well-known physical affection, as distinctly as small-pox or neuralgia. Doctors are all agreed on that, philosophy demonstrates it. I must not be a fool. I've been sitting up too late, and I daresay my digestion is quite wrong, and, with God's help, I shall be all right, and this is but a symptom of nervous dyspepsia." Did I believe all this? Not one word of it, no more than any other miserable being ever did who is once seized and riveted in this satanic captivity. Against my convictions, I might say my knowledge, I was simply bullying myself into a false courage.

'I now walked homeward. I had only a few hundred yards to go. I had forced myself into a sort of resignation, but I had not got over the sickening shock and the flurry of the first certainty of my misfortune.

'I made up my mind to pass the night at home. The brute moved close beside me, and I fancied there was the sort of anxious drawing toward the house, which one sees in tired horses or dogs, sometimes as they come toward home.

'I was afraid to go into town, I was afraid of any one's seeing and recognizing me. I was conscious of an irrepressible agitation in my manner. Also, I was afraid of any violent change in my habits, such as going to a place of amusement, or walking from home in order to fatigue myself. At the hall door it waited till I mounted the steps, and when the door was opened entered with me.

'I drank no tea that night. I got cigars and some brandy and water. My idea was that I should act upon my material system, and by living for a while in sensation apart from thought, send myself forcibly, as it were, into a new groove. I came up here to this drawing-room. I sat just here. The monkey then got upon a small table that then stood *there*. It looked dazed and languid. An irrepressible uneasiness as to its movements kept my eyes always upon it. Its eyes were half closed, but I could see them glow. It was looking steadily at me. In all situations, at all hours, it is awake and looking at me. That never changes.

'I shall not continue in detail my narrative of this particular night. I shall describe, rather, the phenomena of the first year, which never varied, essentially. I shall describe the monkey as it appeared in daylight. In the dark, as you shall presently hear, there are peculiarities. It is a small monkey, perfectly black. It had only one peculiarity – a character of malignity – unfathomable malignity. During the first year it looked sullen and sick. But this character of intense malice and vigilance was always underlying that surly languor. During all that time it acted as if on a plan of giving me as little trouble as was consistent with watching me. Its eyes were never off me. I have never lost sight of it, except in my sleep, light or dark, day or night, since it came here, excepting when it withdraws for some weeks at a time, unaccountably.

'In total dark it is visible as in daylight. I do not mean merely its eyes. It is *all* visible distinctly in a halo that resembles a glow of red embers, and which accompanies it in all its movements.

'When it leaves me for a time, it is always at night, in the dark, and in the same way. It grows at first uneasy, and then furious, and then advances towards me, grinning and shaking, its paws clenched, and, at the same time, there comes the appearance of fire in the grate. I never have any fire. I can't sleep in the room where there is any, and it draws nearer and nearer to the chimney, quivering, it seems, with rage, and when its fury rises to the highest pitch, it springs into the grate, and up the chimney, and I see it no more.

'When first this happened, I thought I was released. I was now a new man. A day passed – a night – and no return, and a blessed week – a week – another week. I was always on my knees, Dr. Hesselius, always, thanking God and praying. A whole month passed of liberty; but on a sudden, it was with me again.'

'It was with me, and the malice which before was torpid under a sullen exterior, was now active. It was perfectly unchanged in every other respect. This new energy was apparent in its activity and its looks, and soon in other ways.

'For a time, you will understand, the change was shown only in an increased vivacity, and an air of menace, as if it was always brooding over some atrocious plan. Its eyes, as before, were never off me.'

'Is it here now?' I asked.

'No,' he replied, 'it has been absent exactly a fortnight and a day – fifteen days. It has sometimes been away so long as nearly two months, once for three. Its absence always exceeds a fortnight, although it may be but by a single day. Fifteen days having past since I saw it last, it may return now at any moment.'

'Is its return,' I asked, 'accompanied by any peculiar manifestation?'

'Nothing – no,' he said. 'It is simply with me again. On lifting my eyes from a book, or turning my head, I see it, as usual, looking at me, and then it remains, as before, for its appointed time. I have never told so much and so minutely before to any one.'

I perceived that he was agitated, and looking like death, and he repeatedly applied his handkerchief to his forehead; I suggested that he might be tired, and told him that I would call, with pleasure, in the morning, but he said:

'No, if you don't mind hearing it all now. I have got so far, and I should prefer making one effort of it. When I spoke to Dr. Harley, I had nothing like so much to tell. You are a philosophic physician. You give spirit its proper rank. If this thing is real—'

He paused, looking at me with agitated inquiry.

'We can discuss it by-and-by, and very fully. I will give you all I think,' I answered, after an interval.

'Well – very well. If it is anything real, I say, it is prevailing, little by little, and drawing me more interiorly into hell. Optic nerves, he talked of. Ah! well – there are other nerves of communication. May God Almighty help me! You shall hear.

'Its power of action, I tell you, had increased. Its malice became, in a way aggressive. About two years ago, some questions that were pending between me and the bishop having been settled, I went down to my parish in Warwickshire, anxious to find occupation in my profession. I was not prepared for what happened, although I have since thought I might have apprehended something like it. The reason of my saying so is this—'

He was beginning to speak with a great deal more effort and reluctance, and sighed often, and seemed at times nearly overcome. But at this time his manner was not agitated. It was more like that of a sinking patient, who has given himself up.

'Yes, but I will first tell you about Kenlis, my parish.

'It was with me when I left this place for Dawlbridge. It was my silent travelling companion, and it remained with me at the vicarage. When I entered on the discharge of my duties, another change took place. The thing exhibited an atrocious determination to thwart me. It was with me in the church – in the reading-desk – in the pulpit – within the communion rails. At last, it reached this extremity, that while I was reading to the congregation, it would spring upon the open book and squat there, so that I was unable to see the page. This happened more than once.

'I left Dawlbridge for a time. I placed myself in Dr. Harley's hands. I did everything he told me. He gave my case a great deal of thought. It interested him, I think. He seemed successful. For nearly three months I was perfectly free from a return. I began to think I was safe. With his full assent I returned to Dawlbridge.

I travelled in a chaise. I was in good spirits. I was more – I was happy and grateful. I was returning, as I thought, delivered from a dreadful hallucination, to the scene of duties which I longed to enter upon. It was a beautiful sunny evening, everything looked serene and cheerful, and I was delighted. I remember looking out of the window to see the spire of my church at Kenlis among the trees, at the point where one has the earliest view of it. It is exactly where the little stream that bounds the parish passes under the road by a culvert, and where it emerges at the road-side, a stone with an old inscription is placed. As we passed this point, I drew my head in and sat down, and in the corner of the chaise was the monkey.

'For a moment I felt faint, and then quite wild with despair and horror. I called to the driver, and got out, and sat down at the road-side, and prayed to God silently for mercy. A despairing resignation supervened. My companion was with me as I re-entered the vicarage. The same persecution followed. After a short struggle I submitted, and soon I left the place.

'I told you,' he said, 'that the beast has before this become in certain ways aggressive. I will explain a little. It seemed to be actuated by intense and increasing fury, whenever I said my prayers, or even meditated prayer. It amounted at last to a dreadful interruption. You will ask, how could a silent immaterial phantom effect that? It was thus, whenever I meditated praying; it was always before me, and nearer and nearer.

'It used to spring on a table, on the back of a chair, on the chimney-piece, and slowly to swing itself from side to side, looking at me all the time. There is in its motion an indefinable power to dissipate thought, and to contract one's attention to that monotony, till the ideas shrink, as it were, to a point, and at last to nothing – and unless I had started up, and shook off the catalepsy I have felt as if my mind were on the point of losing itself. There are other ways,' he sighed heavily; 'thus, for instance, while I pray with my eyes closed, it comes closer and closer, and I see it. I know it is not to be accounted for physically, but I do actually see it, though my lids are closed, and so it rocks my mind, as it were, and overpowers me, and I am obliged to rise from my knees. If you had ever yourself known this, you would be acquainted with desperation.'

'I see, Dr. Hesselius, that you don't lose one word of my statement. I need not ask you to listen specially to what I am now going to tell you.

They talk of the optic nerves, and of spectral illusions, as if the organ of sight was the only point assailable by the influences that have fastened upon me – I know better. For two years in my direful case that limitation prevailed. But as food is taken in softly at the lips, and then brought under the teeth, as the tip of the little finger caught in a mill crank will draw in the hand, and the arm, and the whole body, so the miserable mortal who has been once caught firmly by the end of the finest fibre of his nerve, is drawn in and in, by the enormous machinery of hell, until he is as I am. Yes, Doctor, as *I* am, for while I talk to you, and implore relief, I feel that my prayer is for the impossible, and my pleading with the inexorable.'

I endeavoured to calm his visibly increasing agitation, and told him that he must not despair.

While we talked the night had overtaken us. The filmy moonlight was wide over the scene which the window commanded, and I said:

'Perhaps you would prefer having candles. This light, you know, is odd. I should wish you, as much as possible, under your usual conditions while I make my diagnosis, shall I call it – otherwise I don't care.'

'All lights are the same to me,' he said; 'except when I read or write, I care not if night were perpetual. I am going to tell you what happened about a year ago. The thing began to speak to me.'

'Speak! How do you mean – speak as a man does, do you mean?'

'Yes; speak in words and consecutive sentences, with perfect coherence and articulation; but there is a peculiarity. It is not like the tone of a human voice. It is not by my ears it reaches me – it comes like a singing through my head.

'This faculty, the power of speaking to me, will be my undoing. It won't let me pray, it interrupts me with dreadful blasphemies. I dare not go on, I could not. Oh! Doctor, can the skill, and thought, and prayers of man avail me nothing!'

'You must promise me, my dear sir, not to trouble yourself with unnecessarily exciting thoughts; confine yourself strictly to the narrative of *facts*; and recollect, above all, that even if the thing that infests you be, you seem to suppose, a reality with an actual independent life and will, yet it can have no power to hurt you, unless it be given from above: its access to your senses depends mainly upon your physical condition – this is, under God, your comfort and reliance: we are all alike environed. It is only that in your case, the "*paries*," the veil of the flesh, the screen, is a little out of repair, and sights and sounds are transmitted. We must enter on a new course, sir, – be encouraged. I'll give to-night to the careful consideration of the whole case.'

'You are very good, sir; you think it worth trying, you don't give me quite up; but, sir, you don't know, it is gaining such an influence over me: it orders me about, it is such a tyrant, and I'm growing so helpless. May God deliver me!'

'It orders you about – of course you mean by speech?'

'Yes, yes; it is always urging me to crimes, to injure others, or myself. You see, Doctor, the situation is urgent, it is indeed. When I was in Shropshire, a few weeks ago' (Mr. Jennings was speaking rapidly and trembling now, holding my arm with one hand, and looking in my face), 'I went out one day with a party of friends for a walk: my persecutor, I tell you, was with me at the time. I lagged behind the rest: the country near the Dee, you know, is beautiful. Our path happened to lie near a coal mine, and at the verge of the wood is a perpendicular shaft, they say, a hundred and fifty feet deep. My niece had remained behind with me – she knows, of course, nothing of the nature of my sufferings. She knew, however, that I had been ill, and was low, and she remained to prevent my being quite alone. As we loitered slowly on together, the brute that accompanied me was urging me to throw myself down the shaft. I tell you now – oh, sir, think of it! – the one consideration that saved me from that hideous death was the fear lest the shock of witnessing the occurrence should be too much for the poor girl. I asked her to go on and take her walk with her friends, saying that I could go no further. She made excuses, and the more I urged her the firmer she became. She looked doubtful and frightened. I suppose there was something in my looks or manner that alarmed her; but she would not go, and that literally saved me. You had no idea, sir, that a living man could be made so abject a slave of Satan,' he said, with a ghastly groan and a shudder.

There was a pause here, and I said, 'You *were* preserved nevertheless. It was the act of God. You are in His hands and in the power of no other being: be therefore confident for the future.'

I made him have candles lighted, and saw the room looking cheery and inhabited before I left him. I told him that he must regard his illness strictly as one dependent on physical, though *subtle* physical causes. I told him that he had evidence of God's care and love in the deliverance which he had just described, and that I had perceived with pain that he seemed to regard its peculiar features as indicating that he had been delivered over to spiritual reprobation. Than such a conclusion nothing could be, I insisted, less warranted; and not only so, but more contrary to facts, as disclosed in his mysterious deliverance from that murderous influence during his Shropshire excursion. First, his niece had been retained by his side without his intending to keep her near him; and, secondly, there had been infused into his mind an irresistible repugnance to execute the dreadful suggestion in her presence.

As I reasoned this point with him, Mr. Jennings wept. He seemed comforted. One promise I exacted, which was that should the monkey at any time return, I should be sent for immediately; and, repeating my assurance that I would give neither time nor thought to any other subject until I had thoroughly investigated his case, and that to-morrow he should hear the result, I took my leave.

Before getting into the carriage I told the servant that his master was far from well, and that he should make a point of frequently looking into his room.

My own arrangements I made with a view to being quite secure from interruption.

I merely called at my lodgings, and with a travelling-desk and carpet-bag, set off in a hackney carriage for an inn about two miles out of town, called 'The Horns,' a very quiet and comfortable house, with good thick walls. And there I resolved, without the possibility of intrusion or distraction, to devote some hours of the night, in my comfortable sitting-room, to Mr. Jennings' case, and so much of the morning as it might require.

I left town for the inn where I slept last night at half-past nine, and did not arrive at my room in town until one o'clock this afternoon. I found a letter in Mr. Jennings' hand upon my table. It had not come by post, and, on inquiry, I learned that Mr. Jennings' servant had brought it, and on learning that I was not to return until to-day, and that no one could tell him my address, he seemed very uncomfortable, and said that his orders from his master were that he was not to return without an answer.

I opened the letter and read:

'DEAR DR. HESSELIUS. – It is here. You had not been an hour gone when it returned. It is speaking. It knows all that has happened. It knows everything – it knows you, and is frantic and atrocious. It reviles. I send you this. It knows every word I have written – I write. This I promised, and I therefore write, but I fear very confused, very incoherently. I am so interrupted, disturbed.
      'Ever yours, sincerely yours,
        'ROBERT LYNDER JENNINGS'

'When did this come?' I asked.

'About eleven last night: the man was here again, and has been here three times to-day. The last time is about an hour since.'

Thus answered, and with the notes I had made upon his case in my pocket, I was in a few minutes driving towards Richmond, to see Mr. Jennings.

I by no means, as you perceive, despaired of Mr. Jennings' case. He had himself remembered and applied, though quite in a mistaken way, the principle which I lay down in my Metaphysical Medicine, and which governs all such cases. I was about to apply it in earnest. I was profoundly interested, and very anxious to see and examine him while the 'enemy' was actually present.

I drove up to the sombre house, and ran up the steps, and knocked. The door, in a little time, was opened by a tall woman in black silk. She looked ill, and as if she had been crying. She curtseyed, and heard my question, but she did not answer. She turned her face away, extending her hand towards two men who were coming down-stairs; and thus having, as it were, tacitly made me over to them, she passed through a side-door hastily and shut it.

The man who was nearest the hall, I at once accosted, but being now close to him, I was shocked to see that both his hands were covered with blood.

I drew back a little, and the man, passing down-stairs, merely said in a low tone, 'Here's the servant, sir.'

The servant had stopped on the stairs, confounded and dumb at seeing me. He was rubbing his hands in a handkerchief, and it was steeped in blood.

'Jones, what is it? what has happened?' I asked, while a sickening suspicion overpowered me.

The man asked me to come up to the lobby. I was beside him in a moment, and, frowning and pallid, with contracted eyes, he told me the horror which I already half guessed.

His master had made away with himself.

I went upstairs with him to the room – what I saw there I won't tell you. He had cut his throat with his razor. It was a frightful gash. The two men had laid him on the bed, and composed his limbs. It had happened, as the immense pool of blood on the floor declared, at some distance between the bed and the window. There was carpet round his bed, and a carpet under his dressing-table, but none on the rest of the floor, for the man said he did not like a carpet on his bedroom. In this sombre and now terrible room, one of the great elms that darkened the house was slowly moving the shadow of one of its great boughs upon this dreadful floor.

I beckoned to the servant, and we went downstairs together. I turned off the hall into an old-fashioned panelled room, and there standing, I heard all the servant had to tell. It was not a great deal.

'I concluded, sir, from your words, and looks, sir, as you left last night, that you thought my master seriously ill. I thought it might be that you were afraid of a fit, or something. So I attended very close to your directions. He sat up late, till past three o'clock. He was not writing or reading. He was talking a great deal to himself, but that was nothing unusual. At about that hour I assisted him to undress, and left him in his slippers and dressing-gown. I went back softly in about half-an-hour. He was in his bed, quite undressed, and a pair of candles lighted on the table beside his bed. He was leaning on his elbow, and looking out at the other side of the bed when I came in. I asked him if he wanted anything, and he said No.

'I don't know whether it was what you said to me, sir, or something a little unusual about him, but I was uneasy, uncommon uneasy about him last night.

'In another half hour, or it might be a little more, I went up again. I did not hear him talking as before. I opened the door a little. The candles were both out, which was not usual. I had a bedroom candle, and I let the light in, a little bit, looking softly round. I saw him sitting in that chair beside the dressing-table with his clothes on again. He turned round and looked at me. I thought it strange he should get up and dress, and put out the candles to sit in the dark, that way. But I only asked him again if I could do anything for him. He said, No, rather sharp, I thought. I asked if I might light the candles, and he said, "Do as you like, Jones." So I lighted them, and I lingered about the room, and he said, "Tell me truth, Jones; why did you come again – you did not hear anyone cursing?" "No, sir," I said, wondering what he could mean.

' "No," said he, after me, "of course, no;" and I said to him, "Wouldn't it be well, sir, you went to bed? It's just five o'clock;" and he said nothing but, "Very likely; good-night, Jones." So I went, sir, but in less than an hour I came again. The door was fast, and he heard me, and called as I thought from the bed to know what I wanted, and he desired me not to disturb him again. I lay down and slept for a little. It must have been between six and seven when I went up again. The door was still fast, and he made no answer, so I did not like to disturb him, and thinking he was asleep, I left him till nine. It was his custom to ring when he wished me to come, and I had no particular hour for calling him. I tapped very gently, and getting no answer, I stayed away a good while, supposing he was getting some rest then. It was not till eleven o'clock I grew really uncomfortable about him – for at the latest he was never, that I could remember, later than half-past ten. I got no answer. I knocked and called, and still no answer. So not being able to force the door, I called Thomas from the stables, and together we forced it, and found him in the shocking way you saw.'

Jones had no more to tell. Poor Mr. Jennings was very gentle, and very kind. All his people were fond of him. I could see that the servant was very much moved.

So, dejected and agitated, I passed from that terrible house, and its dark canopy of elms, and I hope I shall never see it more. While I write to you I feel like a man who has but half waked from a frightful and monotonous dream. My memory rejects the picture with incredulity and horror. Yet I know it is true. It is the story of the process of a poison, a poison which excites the reciprocal action of spirit and nerve, and paralyses the tissue that separates those cognate functions of the senses, the external and the interior. Thus we find strange bed-fellows, and the mortal and immortal prematurely make acquaintance.

The Inexperienced Ghost
H. G. WELLS

THE SCENE AMIDST WHICH Clayton told his last story comes back very
vividly to my mind. There he sat, for the greater part of the time, in the
corner of the authentic settle by the spacious open fire, and Sanderson
sat beside him smoking the Broseley clay that bore his name. There was
Evans, and that marvel among actors, Wish, who is also a modest man.
We had all come down to the Mermaid Club that Saturday morning,
except Clayton, who had slept there overnight – which indeed gave him
the opening of his story. We had golfed until golfing was invisible; we
had dined, and we were in that mood of tranquil kindliness when men
will suffer a story. When Clayton began to tell one, we naturally supposed
he was lying. It may be that indeed he was lying – of that the reader will
speedily be able to judge as well as I. He began, it is true, with an air
of matter-of-fact anecdote, but that we thought was only the incurable
artifice of the man.

'I say!' he remarked, after a long consideration of the upward rain of
sparks from the log that Sanderson had thumped, 'you know I was alone
here last night?'

'Except for the domestics,' said Wish.

'Who sleep in the other wing,' said Clayton. 'Yes. Well—' He pulled
at his cigar for some little time as though he still hesitated about his
confidence. Then he said, quite quietly, 'I caught a ghost!'

'Caught a ghost, did you?' said Sanderson. 'Where is it?'

And Evans, who admires Clayton immensely and has been four weeks
in America, shouted, '*Caught* a ghost, did you, Clayton? I'm glad of it!
Tell us all about it right now.'

Clayton said he would in a minute, and asked him to shut the door.

He looked apologetically at me. 'There's no eavesdropping of course,

but we don't want to upset our very excellent service with any rumours
of ghosts in the place. There's too much shadow and oak panelling to
trifle with that. And this, you know, wasn't a regular ghost. I don't think
it will come again – ever.'

'You mean to say you didn't keep it?' said Sanderson.

'I hadn't the heart to,' said Clayton.

And Sanderson said he was surprised.

We laughed, and Clayton looked aggrieved. 'I know,' he said, with the
flicker of a smile, 'but the fact is it really *was* a ghost, and I'm as sure
of it as I am that I am talking to you now. I'm not joking. I mean what
I say.'

Sanderson drew deeply at his pipe, with one reddish eye on Clayton,
and then emitted a thin jet of smoke more eloquent than many words.

Clayton ignored the comment. 'It is the strangest thing that has ever
happened in my life. You know I never believed in ghosts or anything
of the sort, before, ever; and then, you know, I bag one in a corner; and
the whole business is in my hands.'

He meditated still more profoundly and produced and began to pierce
a second cigar with a curious little stabber he affected.

'You talked to it?' asked Wish.

'For the space, probably, of an hour.'

'Chatty?' I said, joining the party of the sceptics.

'The poor devil was in trouble,' said Clayton, bowed over his cigar-
end and with the very faintest note of reproof.

'Sobbing?' someone asked.

Clayton heaved a realistic sigh at the memory. 'Good Lord!' he said;
'yes.' And then, 'Poor fellow! yes.'

'Where did you strike it?' asked Evans, in his best American accent.

'I never realised,' said Clayton, ignoring him, 'the poor sort of thing
a ghost might be,' and he hung us up again for a time, while he sought
for matches in his pocket and lit and warmed to his cigar.

'I took an advantage,' he reflected at last.

We were none of us in a hurry. 'A character,' he said, 'remains just
the same character for all that it's been disembodied. That's a thing we
too often forget. People with a certain strength or fixity of purpose may
have ghosts of a certain strength and fixity of purpose – most haunting
ghosts, you know, must be as one-idea'd as monomaniacs and as obstinate
as mules to come back again and again. This poor creature wasn't.' He
suddenly looked up rather queerly, and his eye went round the room.
'I say it,' he said, 'in all kindliness, but that is the plain truth of the case.
Even at the first glance he struck me as weak.'

He punctuated with the help of his cigar.

'I came upon him, you know, in the long passage. His back was
towards me and I saw him first. Right off I knew him for a ghost. He
was transparent and whitish; clean through his chest I could see the

155

glimmer of the little window at the end. And not only his physique but his attitude struck me as being weak. He looked, you know, as though he didn't know in the slightest whatever he meant to do. One hand was on the panelling and the other fluttered to his mouth. Like – *so!*'

'What sort of physique?' said Sanderson.

'Lean. You know that sort of young man's neck that has two great fluttings down the back, here and here – so! And a little, meanish head with scrubby hair and rather bad ears. Shoulders bad, narrower than the hips; turndown collar, ready-made short jacket, trousers baggy and a little frayed at the heels. That's how he took me. I came very quietly up the staircase. I did not carry a light, you know – the candles are on the landing table and there is that lamp – and I was in my list slippers, and I saw him as I came up. I stopped dead at that – taking him in. I wasn't a bit afraid. I think that in most of these affairs one is never nearly so afraid or excited as one imagines one would be. I was surprised and interested. I thought, "Good Lord! Here's a ghost at last! And I haven't believed for a moment in ghosts during the last five-and-twenty years."'

'Um,' said Wish.

'I suppose I wasn't on the landing a moment before he found out I was there. He turned on me sharply, and I saw the face of an immature young man, a weak nose, a scrubby little moustache, a feeble chin. So for an instant we stood – he looking over his shoulder at me – and regarded one another. Then he seemed to remember his high calling. He turned round, drew himself up, projected his face, raised his arms, spread his hands in approved ghost fashion – came towards me. As he did so his little jaw dropped, and he emitted a faint, drawn-out "Boo." No, it wasn't – not a bit dreadful. I'd dined. I'd had a bottle of champagne, and being all alone, perhaps two or three – perhaps even four or five – whiskies, so I was as solid as rocks and no more frightened than if I'd been assailed by a frog. "Boo!" I said. "Nonsense. You don't belong to *this* place. What are you doing here?"'

'I could see him wince. "Boo – oo," he said.

'"Boo – be hanged! Are you a member?" I said; and just to show I didn't care a pin for him I stepped through a corner of him and made to light my candle. "Are you a member?" I repeated, looking at him sideways.

'He moved a little so as to stand clear of me, and his bearing became crestfallen. "No," he said, in answer to the persistent interrogation of my eye; "I'm not a member – I'm a ghost."

'"Well, that doesn't give you the run of the Mermaid Club. Is there anyone you want to see, or anything of that sort?" And doing it as steadily as possible for fear that he should mistake the carelessness of whisky for the distraction of fear, I got my candle alight. I turned on him, holding it. "What are you doing here?" I said.

'He had dropped his hands and stopped his booing, and there he stood, abashed and awkward, the ghost of a weak, silly, aimless young man. "I'm haunting," he said.

"'You haven't any business to," I said in a quiet voice.

"'I'm a ghost," he said, as if in defence.

"'That may be, but you haven't any business to haunt here. This is a respectable private club; people often stop here with nursemaids and children, and, going about in the careless way you do, some poor little mite could easily come upon you and be scared out of her wits. I suppose you didn't think of that?"

"'No, sir," he said, "I didn't."

"'You should have done. You haven't any claim on the place, have you? Weren't murdered here, or anything of that sort?"

"'None, sir; but I thought as it was old and oak-panelled—"

"'That's *no* excuse," I regarded him firmly. "Your coming here is a mistake," I said, in a tone of friendly superiority. I feigned to see if I had my matches, and then looked up at him frankly. "If I were you I wouldn't wait for cock-crow – I'd vanish right away."

'He looked embarrassed. "The fact *is*, sir—" he began.

"'I'd vanish," I said, driving it home.

"'The fact is, sir, that – somehow – I can't."

"'You *can't*?"

"'No, sir. There's something I've forgotten. I've been hanging about here since midnight last night, hiding in the cupboards of the empty bedrooms and things like that. I'm flurried. I've never come haunting before, and it seems to put me out."

"'Put you out?"

"'Yes, sir. I've tried to do it several times, and it doesn't come off. There's some little thing has slipped me, and I can't get back."

'That, you know, rather bowled me over. He looked at me in such an abject way that for the life of me I couldn't keep up quite the high hectoring vein I had adopted. "That's queer," I said, and as I spoke I fancied I heard someone moving about down below. "Come into my room and tell me more about it," I said. I didn't of course, understand this, and I tried to take him by the arm. But, of course, you might as well have tried to take hold of a puff of smoke! I had forgotten my number, I think; anyhow, I remember going into several bedrooms – it was lucky I was the only soul in that wing – until I saw my traps. "Here we are," I said, and sat down in the armchair, "sit down and tell me all about it. It seems to me you have got yourself into a jolly awkward position, old chap."

'Well, he said he wouldn't sit down; he'd prefer to flit up and down the room if it was all the same to me. And so he did, and in a little while we were deep in a long and serious talk. And presently, you know, something of those whiskies and sodas evaporated out of me, and I began to realise just a little what a thundering rum and weird business it was that I was in. There he was, semi-transparent – the proper conventional phantom, and noiseless except for his ghost of a voice – flitting to and fro in that nice, clean, chintz-hung old bedroom. You could see the gleam of the copper candle-sticks through him, and the lights on the brass fender, and the corners of the framed engravings on the wall, and there he was telling me all about this wretched little life of his that had recently ended on earth. He hadn't a particularly honest face, you know, but being transparent, of course, he couldn't avoid telling the truth.'

'Eh?' said Wish, suddenly sitting up in his chair.

'What?' said Clayton.

'Being transparent – couldn't avoid telling the truth – I don't see it,' said Wish.

'*I* don't see it,' said Clayton, with inimitable assurance. 'But it *is* so, I can assure you nevertheless. I don't believe he got once a nail's breadth off the Bible truth. He told me how he had been killed – he went down into a London basement with a candle to look for a leakage of gas – and described himself as a senior English master in a London private school when that release occurred.'

'Poor wretch!' said I.

'That's what I thought, and the more he talked the more I thought it. There he was, purposeless in life and purposeless out of it. He talked of his father and mother and his schoolmaster, and all who had ever been anything to him in the world, meanly. He had been too sensitive, too nervous; none of them had ever valued him properly or understood him, he said. He had never had a real friend in the world, I think; he had never had a success. He had shirked games and failed examinations. "It's like that with some people," he said; "whenever I got into the examination-room or anywhere everything seemed to go." Engaged to be married of course to another over-sensitive person, I suppose – when the indiscretion with the gas escape ended his affairs. "And where are you now?" I asked. "Not in—?"

'He wasn't clear on that point at all. The impression he gave me was of a sort of vague, intermediate state, a special reserve for souls too non-existent for anything so positive as either sin or virtue. *I* don't know. He was much too egotistical and unobservant to give me any clear idea of the kind of place, kind of country, there is on the Other Side of Things. Wherever he was, he seems to have fallen in with a set of kindred spirits: ghosts of weak Cockney young men, who were on a footing of Christian names, and among these there was certainly a lot of talk about "going haunting" and things like that. Yes – going haunting! They seemed to think "haunting" a tremendous adventure, and most of them funked it all the time. And so primed, you know, he had come.'

'But really!' said Wish to the fire.

'These are the impressions he gave me, anyhow,' said Clayton, modestly. 'I may, of course, have been in a rather uncritical state, but that was the sort of background he gave to himself. He kept flitting up and down, with his thin voice going – talking, talking about his wretched self, and never a word of clear, firm statement from first to last. He was thinner and sillier and more pointless than if he had been real and alive. Only then, you know, he would not have been in my bedroom here – if he *had* been alive. I should have kicked him out.'

'Of course,' said Evans, 'there *are* poor mortals like that.'

'And there's just as much chance of their having ghosts as the rest of us,' I admitted.

'What gave a sort of point to him, you know, was the fact that he did .seem within limits to have found himself out. The mess he had made of haunting had depressed him terribly. He had been told it would be a "lark"; he had come expecting it to be a "lark," and here it was, nothing but another failure added to his record! He proclaimed himself an utter out-and-out failure. He said, and I can quite believe it, that he had never tried to do anything all his life that he hadn't made a perfect mess of – and through all the wastes of eternity he never would. If he had had sympathy, perhaps— He paused at that, and stood regarding me. He remarked that, strange as it might seem to me, nobody, not anyone, ever, had given him the amount of sympathy I was doing now. I could see what he wanted straight away, and I determined to head him off at once. I may be a brute, you know, but being the Only Real Friend, the recipient of the confidences of one of these egotistical weaklings, ghost or body, is beyond my physical endurance. I got up briskly. "Don't you brood on these things too much," I said. "The thing you've got to do is to get out of this – get out of this sharp. You pull yourself together and *try*." "I can't," he said. "You try," I said, and try he did.'

'Try!' said Sanderson. '*How?*'

'Passes,' said Clayton.

'Passes?'

'Complicated series of gestures and passes with the hands. That's how he had come in and that's how he had to get out again. Lord! what a business I had!'

'But how could *any* series of passes—' I began. 'My dear man,' said Clayton, turning on me and putting a great emphasis on certain words, 'you want *everything* clear. I don't know *how*. All I know is that you *do* – that *he* did, anyhow, at least. After a fearful time, you know, he got his passes right and suddenly disappeared.'

'Did you,' said Sanderson slowly, 'observe the passes?'

'Yes,' said Clayton, and seemed to think. 'It was tremendously queer,' he said. 'There we were, I and this thin vague ghost, in that silent room, in this silent, empty inn, in this silent little Friday-night town. Not a sound except our voices and a faint panting he made when he swung. There was the bedroom candle, and one candle on the dressing-table alight, that was all – sometimes one or other would flare up into a tall, lean, astonished flame for a space. And queer things happened. "I can't," he said; "I shall never—!" And suddenly he sat down on a little chair at the foot of the bed and began to sob and sob. Lord! what a harrowing, whimpering thing he seemed!

'"You pull yourself together," I said, and tried to pat him on the back, and . . . my confounded hand went through him! By that time, you know, I wasn't nearly so-massive as I had been on the landing. I got the queerness of it full. I remember snatching back my hand out of him, as it were, with a little thrill, and walking over to the dressing-table. "You pull yourself together," I said to him, "and try." And in order to encourage and help him I began to try as well.'

'What!' said Sanderson, 'the passes?'

'Yes, the passes.'

'But—' I said, moved by an idea that eluded me for a space. 'This is interesting,' said Sanderson, with his finger in his pipe-bowl. 'You mean to say this ghost of yours gave way—'

'Did his level best to give away the whole confounded barrier? *Yes.*'

'He didn't,' said Wish; 'he couldn't. Or you'd have gone there too.'

'That's precisely it,' I said, finding my elusive idea put into words for me.

'That *is* precisely it,' said Clayton, with thoughtful eyes upon the fire.

For just a little while there was silence.

'And at last he did it?' said Sanderson.

'At last he did it. I had to keep him up to it hard, but he did it at last – rather suddenly. He despaired, we had a scene, and then he got up abruptly and asked me to go through the whole performance, slowly, so that he might see. "I believe," he said, "if I could *see* I should spot what was wrong at once." And he did. "*I* know," he said. "What do you know?' said I. "*I* know," he repeated. Then he said, peevishly, "I *can't* do it, if you look at me – I really *can't*; it's been that, partly, all along. I'm such a nervous fellow that you put me out." Well, we had a bit of an argument. Naturally I wanted to see; but he was as obstinate as a mule, and suddenly I had come over as tired as a dog – he tired me out. "All right," I said, "*I* won't look at you," and turned towards the mirror, on the wardrobe, by the bed.

'He started off very fast. I tried to follow him by looking in the looking-glass, to see just what it was had hung. Round went his arms and his hands, so, and so, and so, and then with a rush came to the last gesture of all – you stand erect and open out your arms – and so, don't you know, he stood. And then he didn't! He didn't! He wasn't! I wheeled round from the looking-glass to him. There was nothing! I was alone, with the flaring candles and a staggering mind. What had happened? Had anything happened? Had I been dreaming? . . . And then, with an absurd note of finality about it, the clock upon the landing discovered the moment was ripe for striking *one*. So! – Ping! And I was as grave and sober as a judge, with all my champagne and whisky gone into the vast serene. Feeling queer, you know – confoundedly *queer!* Queer! Good Lord!'

He regarded his cigar-ash for a moment. 'That's all that happened,' he said.

'And then you went to bed?' asked Evans.

'What else was there to do?'

I looked Wish in the eye. We wanted to scoff, and there was something, something perhaps in Clayton's voice and manner, that hampered our desire.

'And about these passes?' said Sanderson.

'I believe I could do them now.'

'Oh!' said Sanderson, and produced a pen-knife and set himself to grub the dottel out of the bowl of his clay.

'Why don't you do them now?' said Sanderson, shutting his pen-knife with a click.

'That's what I'm going to do,' said Clayton.

'They won't work,' said Evans.

'If they do—' I suggested.

'You know, I'd rather you didn't,' said Wish, stretching out his legs.

'Why?' asked Evans.

'I'd rather he didn't,' said Wish.

'But he hasn't got 'em right,' said Sanderson, plugging too much tobacco into his pipe.

'All the same, I'd rather he didn't,' said Wish.

We argued with Wish. He said that for Clayton to go through those gestures was like mocking a serious matter. 'But you don't believe—?' I said. Wish glanced at Clayton, who was staring into the fire, weighing something in his mind. 'I do – more than half, anyhow, I do,' said Wish.

'Clayton,' said I, 'you're too good a liar for us. Most of it was all right. But that disappearance . . . happened to be convincing. Tell us, it's a tale of cock and bull.'

He stood up without heeding me, took the middle of the hearthrug, and faced me. For a moment he regarded his feet thoughtfully, and then for all the rest of the time his eyes were on the opposite wall, with an intent expression. He raised his two hands slowly to the level of his eyes and so began. . . .

Now Sanderson is a Freemason, a member of the lodge of the Four Kings, which devotes itself so ably to the study and elucidation of all the mysteries of Masonry past and present, and among the students of his lodge Sanderson is by no means the least. He followed Clayton's motions with a singular interest in his reddish eye. 'That's not bad,' he said, when it was done. 'You really do, you know, put things together, Clayton, in a most amazing fashion. But there's one little detail out.'

'I know,' said Clayton. 'I believe I could tell you which.'

'Well?'

'This,' said Clayton, and did a queer little twist and writhing and thrust of the hands.

'Yes.'

'That, you know, was what *he* couldn't get right.' said Clayton. 'But how do *you*—?'

'Most of this business, and particularly how you invented it, I don't understand at all,' said Sanderson, 'but just that phase – I do.' He reflected. 'These happen to be a series of gestures – connected with a certain branch of esoteric Masonry – Probably you know. Or else— *How*?' He reflected still further. 'I do not see I can do any harm in telling you just the proper twist. After all, if you know, you know; if you don't, you don't.'

'I know nothing,' said Clayton, 'except what the poor devil let out last night.'

'Well, anyhow,' said Sanderson, and placed his churchwarden very carefully upon the shelf over the fireplace. Then very rapidly he gesticulated with his hands.

'So?' said Clayton, repeating.

'So,' said Sanderson, and took his pipe in hand again.

'Ah, *now*,' said Clayton, 'I can do the whole thing – right.'

He stood up before the waning fire and smiled at us all. But I think there was just a little hesitation in his smile. 'If I begin—' he said.

'I wouldn't begin,' said Wish.

'It's all right!' said Evans. 'Matter is indestructible. You don't think any jiggery-pokery of this sort is going to snatch Clayton into the world of shades. Not it! You may try, Clayton, so far as I'm concerned, until your arms drop off at the wrists.'

'I don't believe that,' said Wish, and stood up and put his arm on Clayton's shoulder. 'You've made me half believe in that story somehow, and I don't want to see the thing done.'

'Goodness!' said I, 'here's Wish frightened!'

'I am,' said Wish, with real or admirably feigned intensity. 'I believe that if he goes through these motions right he'll *go*.'

'He'll not do anything of the sort,' I cried. 'There's only one way out of this world for men, and Clayton is thirty years from that. Besides . . . And such a ghost! Do you think—?'

Wish interrupted me by moving. He walked out from among our chairs and stopped beside the table and stood there. 'Clayton,' he said, 'you're a fool.'

Clayton, with a humorous light in his eyes, smiled back at him. 'Wish,' he said, 'is right and all you others are wrong. I shall go. I shall get to the end of these passes, and as the last swish whistles through the air, Presto! – this hearthrug will be vacant, the room will be blank amazement, and a respectably dressed gentleman of fifteen stone will plump into the world of shades. I'm certain. So will you be. I decline to argue further. Let the thing be tried.'

'*No,*' said Wish, and made a step and ceased, and Clayton raised his hands once more to repeat the spirit's passing.

By that time, you know, we were all in a state of tension – largely because of the behaviour of Wish. We sat all of us with our eyes on Clayton – I, at least, with a sort of tight, stiff feeling about me as though from the back of my skull to the middle of my thighs my body had been changed to steel. And there, with a gravity that was imperturbably serene, Clayton bowed and swayed and waved his hands and arms before us. As he drew towards the end one piled up, one tingled in one's teeth. The last gesture, I have said, was to swing the arms out wide open, with the face held up. And when at last he swung out to this closing gesture I ceased even to breathe. It was ridiculous, of course, but you know that ghost-story feeling. It was after dinner, in a queer, old shadowy house. Would he, after all—?

There he stood for one stupendous moment, with his arms open and his upturned face, assured and bright, in the glare of the hanging lamp. We hung through that moment as if it were an age, and then came from all of us something that was half a sigh of infinite relief and half a reassuring '*No!*' For visibly – he wasn't going. It was all nonsense. He had told an idle story, and carried it almost to conviction, that was all! . . . And then in that moment the face of Clayton changed.

It changed. It changed as a lit house changes when its lights are suddenly extinguished. His eyes were suddenly eyes that were fixed, his smile was frozen on his lips, and he stood there still. He stood there, very gently swaying.

That moment, too, was an age. And then, you know, chairs were scraping, things were falling, and we were all moving. His knees seemed to give, and he fell forward, and Evans rose and caught him in his arms. . .

It stunned us all. For a minute I suppose no one said a coherent thing. We believed it, yet could not believe it. . . . I came out of a muddled stupefaction to find myself kneeling beside him, and his vest and shirt were torn open, and Sanderson's hand lay on his heart. . . .

Well – the simple fact before us could very well wait our convenience; there was no hurry for us to comprehend. It lay there for an hour; it lies athwart my memory, black and amazing still, to this day. Clayton had, indeed, passed into the world that lies so near to and so far from our own, and he had gone thither by the only road that mortal man may take. But whether he did indeed pass there by that poor ghost's incantation, or whether he was stricken suddenly by apoplexy in the midst of an idle tale – as the coroner's jury would have us believe – is no matter for my judging; it is just one of those inexplicable riddles that must remain unsolved until the final solution of all things shall come. All

I certainly know is that, in the very moment, in the very instant, of concluding those passes, he changed, and staggered, and fell down before us – dead!

The Monk

MATTHEW LEWIS

First published in 1796, The Monk tells of the sinful fall of Ambrosio, proud and noble Abbot of the monastery of the Capuchins in medieval Madrid. Facing sentence of lingering death and torture for rape and murder, the Monk and his co-conspirator, Matilda, must make a hideous choice . . . .

THE DAY OF HIS SECOND examination was at hand. He had been compelled to swallow cordials, whose virtues were calculated to restore his bodily strength, and enable him to support the question longer. On the night preceding this dreaded day, his fears for the morrow permitted him not to sleep. His terrors were so violent, as nearly to annihilate his mental powers. He sat like one stupefied near the table on which his lamp was burning dimly. Despair chained up his faculties in idiotism, and he remained for some hours, unable to speak or move, or indeed to think.

'Look up, Ambrosio!' said a voice in accents well-known to him –

The Monk started, and raised his melancholy eyes. Matilda stood before him. She had quitted her religious habit. She now wore a female dress, at once elegant and splendid: a profusion of diamonds blazed upon her robes, and her hair was confined by a coronet of roses. In her right hand she held a small book: a lively expression of pleasure beamed upon her countenance; but still it was mingled with a wild imperious majesty, which inspired the Monk with awe, and represt in some measure his transports at seeing her.

'You here, Matilda?' He at length exclaimed: 'How have you gained entrance? Where are your chains? What means this magnificence, and the joy which sparkles in your eyes? Have our judges relented? Is there a chance of my escaping? Answer me for pity, and tell me, what I have to hope, or fear.'

'Ambrosio!' She replied with an air of commanding dignity; 'I have baffled the Inquisition's fury. I am free: A few moments will place kingdoms between these dungeons and me. Yet I purchase my liberty at a dear, at a dreadful price! Dare you pay the same, Ambrosio? Dare you spring without fear over the bounds, which separate men from angels? – You are silent. – You look upon me with eyes of suspicion and alarm – I read your thoughts and confess their justice. Yes, Ambrosio; I have sacrificed all for life and liberty. I am no longer a candidate for heaven! I have renounced God's service, and am enlisted beneath the banners of his foes. The deed is past recall: Yet were it in my power to go back, I would not. Oh! my friend, to expire in such torments! To die amidst curses and execrations! To bear the insults of an exasperated mob! To be exposed to all the mortifications of shame and infamy! Who can reflect without horror on such a doom? Let me then exult in my exchange. I have sold distant and uncertain happiness for present and secure: I have preserved a life, which otherwise I had lost in torture; and I have obtained the power of procuring every bliss, which can make that life delicious! The infernal spirits obey me as their sovereign: By their aid shall my days be past in every refinement of luxury and voluptuousness. I will enjoy unrestrained the gratification of my senses: Every passion shall be indulged, even to satiety; then will I bid my servants invent new pleasures, to revive and stimulate my glutted appetites! I go impatient to exercise my newly-gained dominion. I pant to be at liberty. Nothing should hold me one moment longer in this abhorred abode, but the hope of persuading you to follow my example. Ambrosio, I still love you: our mutual guilt and danger have rendered you dearer to me, then ever and I would fain save you from impending destruction. Summon then your resolution to your aid; and renounce for immediate and certain benefits the hopes of a salvation, difficult to obtain, and perhaps altogether erroneous. Shake off the prejudice of vulgar souls: abandon a god, who has abandoned you, and raise yourself to the level of superior beings!'

She paused for the Monk's reply: he shuddered, while he gave it.

'Matilda!' he said after a long silence in a low and unsteady voice; 'What price gave you for liberty?'

She answered him firm and dauntless.

'Ambrosio, it was my soul!'

'Wretched woman, what have you done? Pass but a few years, and how dreadful will be your sufferings!'

'Weak man, pass but this night, and how dreadful will be your own! Do you remember what you have already endured? To-morrow you must bear torments doubly exquisite. Do you remember the horrors of a fiery punishment? In two days you must be led a victim to the stake! What then will become of you? Still dare you hope for pardon? Still are you

beguiled with visions of salvation? Think upon your crimes! Think upon
your lust, your perjury, inhumanity, and hypocrisy! Think upon the
innocent blood, which cries to the throne of God for vengeance, and then
hope for mercy! Then dream of heaven, and sigh for worlds of light, and
realms of peace and pleasure! Absurd! Open your eyes, Ambrosio, and
be prudent. Hell is your lot; you are doomed to eternal perdition; nought
lies beyond your grave, but a gulf of devouring flames. And will you then
speed towards that hell? Will you clasp that perdition in your arms, ere
'tis needful? Will you plunge into those flames, while you still have the
power to shun them? 'Tis a madman's action. No, no, Ambrosio: let us
for awhile fly from divine vengeance. Be advised by me; purchase by one
moment's courage the bliss of years; enjoy the present, and forget that a
future lags behind.'

'Matilda, your counsels are dangerous: I dare not, I will not follow
them. I must not give up my claim to salvation. Monstrous are my crimes;
but God is merciful, and I will not despair of pardon.'

'Is such your resolution? I have no more to say. I speed to joy and
liberty, and abandon you to death and eternal torments.'

'Yet stay one moment, Matilda! You command the infernal dæmons:
You can force open these prison-doors; You can release me from these
chains, which weigh me down. Save me, I conjure you, and bear me from
these fearful abodes!'

'You ask the only boon beyond my power to bestow. I am forbidden
to assist a churchman and a partisan of God: renounce those titles, and
command me.'

'I will not sell my soul to perdition.'

'Persist in your obstinacy, till you find yourself at the stake: Then will
you repent your error, and sigh for escape when the moment is gone by.
I quit you. – Yet ere the hour of death arrives should wisdom enlighten
you, listen to the means of repairing your present fault. I leave with you
this book. Read the four first lines of the seventh page backwards: the
spirit whom you have already once beheld, will immediately appear to
you. If you are wise, we shall meet again: If not, farewell for ever!'

She let the book fall upon the ground. A cloud of blue fire wrapped
itself round her: she waved her hand to Ambrosio, and disappeared. The
momentary glare which the flames poured through the dungeon, on
dissipating suddenly, seemed to have increased its natural gloom. The
solitary lamp scarcely gave light sufficient to guide the Monk to a chair.
He threw himself into his seat, folded his arms, and leaning his head
upon the table, sank into reflections perplexing and unconnected.

He was still in this attitude, when the opening of the prison-door
roused him from his stupor. He was summoned to appear before the
Grand Inquisitor. He rose, and followed his gaoler with painful steps.
He was led into the same hall, placed before the same examiners, and
was again interrogated, whether he would confess. He replied as before,

that having no crimes, he could acknowledge none: but when the executioners prepared to put him to the question, when he saw the engines of torture, and remembered the pangs, which they had already inflicted, his resolution failed him entirely. Forgetting the consequences, and only anxious to escape the terrors of the present moment, he made an ample confession. He disclosed every circumstance of his guilt, and owned not merely the crimes with which he was charged, but those of which he had never been suspected. Being interrogated as to Matilda's flight which had created much confusion, he confessed that she had sold herself to Satan, and that she was indebted to sorcery for her escape. He still assured his judges, that for his own part he had never entered into any compact with the infernal spirits; but the threat of being tortured made him declare himself to be a sorcerer, and heretic, and whatever other title the inquisitors chose to fix upon him. In consequence of this avowal, his sentence was immediately pronounced. He was ordered to prepare himself to perish in the auto da fé, which was to be solemnised at twelve o'clock that night. This hour was chosen from the idea, that the horror of the flames being heightened by the gloom of midnight, the execution would have a greater effect upon the mind of the people.

Ambrosio rather dead than alive was left alone in his dungeon. The moment in which this terrible decree was pronounced, had nearly proved that of his dissolution. He looked forward to the morrow with despair, and his terrors increased with the approach of midnight. Sometimes he was buried in gloomy silence: at others he raved with delirious passion, wrung his hands, and cursed the hour, when he first beheld the light. In one of these moments his eye rested upon Matilda's mysterious gift. His transports of rage were instantly suspended. He looked earnestly at the book; he took it up, but immediately threw it from him with horror. He walked rapidly up and down his dungeon: then stopped, and again fixed his eyes on the spot where the book had fallen. He reflected, that here at least was a resource from the fate which he dreaded. He stooped, and took it up a second time. He remained for some time trembling and irresolute: he longed to try the charm, yet feared its consequences. The recollection of his sentence at length fixed his indecision. He opened the volume; but his agitation was so great, that he at first sought in vain for the page mentioned by Matilda. Ashamed of himself, he called all his courage to his aid. He turned to the seventh leaf. He began to read it aloud; but his eyes frequently wandered from the book, while he anxiously cast them round in search of the spirit, whom he wished, yet dreaded to behold. Still he persisted in his design; and with a voice unassured and frequent interruptions, he contrived to finish the four first lines of the page.

They were in a language, whose import was totally unknown to him. Scarce had he pronounced the last word, when the effects of the charm were evident. A loud burst of thunder was heard; the prison shook to its very foundations; a blaze of lightning flashed through the cell; and in the next moment, borne upon sulphurous whirl-winds, Lucifer stood before him a second time. But he came not, as when at Matilda's summons he borrowed the seraph's form to deceive Ambrosio. He appeared in all that ugliness, which since his fall from heaven had been his portion: his blasted limbs still bore marks of the Almighty's thunder: a swarthy darkness spread itself over his gigantic form: his hands and feet were armed with long talons: fury glared in his eyes, which might have struck the bravest heart with terror: over his huge shoulders waved two enormous sable wings; and his hair was supplied by living snakes, which twined themselves round his brows with frightful hissings. In one hand he held a roll of parchment, and in the other an iron pen. Still the lightning flashed around him, and the thunder with repeated bursts, seemed to announce the dissolution of nature.

Terrified at an apparition so different from what he had expected, Ambrosio remained gazing upon the fiend, deprived of the power of utterance. The thunder had ceased to roll: universal silence reigned through the dungeon.

'For what am I summoned hither?' said the dæmon, in a voice which sulphurous fogs had damped to hoarseness.

At the sound nature seemed to tremble: a violent earth-quake rocked the ground, accompanied by a fresh burst of thunder, louder and more appalling than the first.

Ambrosio was long unable to answer the dæmon's demand.

'I am condemned to die;' he said with a faint voice, his blood running cold, while he gazed upon his dreadful visitor. 'Save me! Bear me from hence!'

'Shall the reward of my services be paid me? Dare you embrace my cause? Will you be mine, body and soul? Are you prepared to renounce him who made you, and him who died for you? Answer but "Yes" and Lucifer is your slave.'

'Will no less price content you? Can nothing satisfy you but my eternal ruin? Spirit, you ask too much. Yet convey me from this dungeon: be my servant for one hour, and I will be yours for a thousand years. Will not this offer suffice?'

'It will not. I must have your soul; must have it mine, and mine for ever.'

'Insatiate dæmon, I will not doom myself to endless torments. I will not give up my hopes of being one day pardoned.'

'You will not? On what chimæra rest then your hopes? Short-sighted mortal! Miserable wretch! Are you not guilty? Are you not infamous in the eyes of men and angels. Can such enormous sins be forgiven? Hope you to escape my power? Your fate is already pronounced. The Eternal has abandoned you; mine you are marked in the book of destiny, and mine you must and shall be!'

'Fiend, 'tis false! Infinite is the Almighty's mercy, and the penitent shall meet his forgiveness. My crimes are monstrous, but I will not despair of pardon: Haply, when they have received due chastisement . . . .'

'Chastisement? Was Purgatory meant for guilt like yours? Hope you that your offences shall be bought off by prayers of superstitious dotards and droning monks? Ambrosio, be wise! Mine you must be: you are doomed to flames, but may shun them for the present. Sign this parchment: I will be you from hence, and you may pass your remaining years in bliss and liberty. Enjoy your existence: indulge in every pleasure to which appetite may lead you: but from the moment that it quits your body, remember that your soul belongs to me, and that I will not be defrauded of my right.'

The Monk was silent; but his looks declared, that the tempter's words were not thrown away. He reflected on the conditions proposed with horror: on the other hand, he believed himself doomed to perdition, and that, by refusing the dæmon's succour, he only hastened tortures which he never could escape. The fiend saw, that his resolution was shaken: he renewed his instances, and endeavoured to fix the Abbot's indecision. He described the agonies of death in the most terrific colours; and he worked so powerfully upon Ambrosio's despair and fears, that he prevailed upon him to receive the parchment. He then struck the iron pen which he held into a vein of the Monk's left-hand. It pierced deep, and was instantly filled with blood; yet Ambrosio felt no pain from the wound. The pen was put into his hand: it trembled. The wretch placed the parchment on the table before him, and prepared to sign it. Suddenly he held his hand: he started away hastily, and threw the pen upon the table.

'What am I doing?' he cried – then turning to the fiend with a desperate air, 'Leave me! Begone! I will not sign the parchment.'

'Fool! exclaimed the disappointed dæmon, darting looks so furious as penetrated the Friar's soul with horror; 'Thus am I trifled with? Go then! Rave in agony, expire in tortures, and then learn the extent of the Eternal's mercy! But beware how you make me again your mock! Call me no more, till resolved to accept my offers! Summon me a second time to dismiss me thus idly, and these talons shall rend you into a thousand pieces! Speak yet again; will you sign the parchment?'

'I will not! Leave me! Away!'

Instantly the thunder was heard to roll horribly: once more the earth trembled with violence: the dungeon resounded with loud shrieks, and the dæmon fled with blasphemy and curses.

At first, the Monk rejoiced at having resisted the seducer's arts, and obtained a triumph over mankind's enemy: but as the hour of punishment drew near, his former terrors revived in his heart. Their momentary repose seemed to have given fresh vigour. The nearer that the time approached, the more did he dread appearing before the throne of God. He shuddered to think how soon he must be plunged into eternity; how soon meet the eyes of his Creator, whom he had so grievously offended. The bell announced mid-night: It was the signal for being led to the stake! As he listened to the first stroke, the blood ceased to circulate in the Abbot's veins: he heard death and torture murmured in each succeeding sound. He expected to see the archers entering his prison; and as the bell forbore to toll, he seized the magic volume in a fit of despair. He opened it, turned hastily to the seventh page, and as if fearing to allow himself a moment's thought ran over the fatal lines with rapidity. Accompanied by his former terrors, Lucifer again stood before the trembler.

'You have summoned me,' said the fiend; 'Are you determined to be wise? Will you accept my conditions? You know them already. Renounce your claim to salvation, make over to me your soul, and I bear you from this dungeon instantly. Yet is it time. Resolve, or it will be too late. Will you sign the parchment?'

'I must! – Fate urges me! – I accept your conditions.'

'Sign the parchment!' replied the dæmon in an exulting tone.

The contract and the bloody pen still lay upon the table. Ambrosio drew near it. He prepared to sign his name. A moment's reflection made him hesitate.

'Hark!' cried the tempter; 'They come! Be quick! Sign the parchment, and I bear you from hence this moment.'

In effect, the archers were heard approaching, appointed to lead Ambrosio to the stake. The sound encouraged the Monk in his resolution.

'What is the import of this writing?' said he.

'It makes your soul over to me for ever, and without reserve.'

'What am I to receive in exchange?'

'My protection, and release from this dungeon. Sign it, and this instant I bear you away.'

Ambrosio took up the pen; he set it to the parchment. Again his courage failed him: he felt a pang of terror at his heart, and once more threw the pen upon the table.

'Weak and puerile!' cried the exasperated fiend: 'Away with this folly! Sign the writing this instant, or I sacrifice you to my rage!'

At this moment the bolt of the outward door was drawn back. The prisoner heard the rattling of chains; The heavy bar fell; the archers were on the point of entering. Worked up to frenzy by the urgent danger, shrinking from the approach of death, terrified by the dæmon's threats, and seeing no other means to escape destruction, the wretched Monk complied. He signed the fatal contract, and gave it hastily into the evil spirit's hands, whose eyes, as he received the gift, glared with malicious rapture.

'Take it!' said the God-abandoned; 'Now then save me! Snatch me from hence!'

'Hold! Do you freely and absolutely renounce your Creator and his Son?'

'I do! I do!'

'Do you make over your soul to me for ever?'

'For ever!'

'Without reserve or subterfuge? Without future appeal to the divine mercy?'

The last chain fell from the door of the prison: the key was heard turning in the lock: already the iron door grated heavily upon its rusty hinges.

'I am yours for ever and irrevocably!' cried the Monk wild with terror: 'I abandon all claim to salvation! I own no power but yours! Hark! Hark! They come! Oh! save me! Bear me away!'

'I have triumphed! You are mine past reprieve, and I fulfil my promise.'

While he spoke, the door unclosed. Instantly the dæmon grasped one of Ambrosio's arms, spread his broad pinions and sprang with him into the air. The roof opened as they soared upwards, and closed again when they had quitted the dungeon.

In the mean while, the gaoler was thrown into the utmost surprise by the disappearance of his prisoner. Though neither he nor the archers were in time to witness the Monk's escape, a sulphurous smell prevailing through the prison sufficiently informed them by whose aid he had been liberated. They hastened to make their report to the Grand Inquisitor. The story, how a sorcerer had been carried away by the Devil, was soon noised about Madrid; and for some days the whole city was employed in discussing the subject. Gradually it ceased to be the topic of conversation: other adventures arose whose novelty engaged universal attention; and Ambrosio was soon forgotten as totally, as if he never had existed. While this was passing, the Monk supported by his infernal guide, traversed the air with the rapidity of an arrow, and a few moments placed him upon a precipice's brink, the steepest in Sierra Morena.

Though rescued from the Inquisition, Ambrosio as yet was insensible of the blessings of liberty. The damning contract weighed heavy upon his mind; and the scenes in which he had been a principal actor, had left behind them such impressions, as rendered his heart the seat of anarchy and confusion. The objects now before his eyes, and which the full moon sailing through clouds permitted him to examine, were ill-calculated to inspire that calm, of which he stood so much in need. The disorder of his imagination was increased by the wildness of the surrounding scenery; by the gloomy caverns and steep rocks, rising above each other, and dividing the passing clouds; solitary clusters of trees scattered here and there, among whose thick-twined branches the wind of night sighed hoarsely and mournfully; the shrill cry of mountain eagles, who had built their nests among these lonely deserts; the stunning roar of torrents, as swelled by late rains they rushed violently down tremendous precipices;

and the dark waters of a silent sluggish stream which faintly reflected the moon-beams, and bathed the rock's base on which Ambrosio stood. The Abbot cast round him a look of terror. His infernal conductor was still by his side, and eyed him with a look of mingled malice, exultation, and contempt.

'Whither have you brought me?' said the Monk at length in an hollow trembling voice: 'Why am I placed in this melancholy scene? Bear me from it quickly! Carry me to Matilda!'

The fiend replied not, but continued to gaze upon him in silence. Ambrosio could not sustain his glance; He turned away his eyes, while thus spoke the dæmon:

'I have him then in my power! This model of piety! This being without reproach! This mortal who placed his puny virtues on a level with those of angels. He is mine! Irrevocably, eternally mine! Companions of my sufferings! Denizens of hell! How grateful will be my present!'

He paused; then addressed himself to the Monk—

'Carry you to Matilda?' he continued, repeating Ambrosio's words: 'Wretch! you shall soon be with her! You well deserve a place near her, for hell boasts no miscreant more guilty than yourself. Hark, Ambrosio, while I unveil your crimes! You have shed the blood of two innocents; Antonia and Elvira perished by your hand. That Antonia whom you violated, was your sister! That Elvira whom you murdered, gave you birth! Tremble, abandoned hypocrite! Inhuman parricide! Incestuous ravisher! Tremble at the extent of your offences! And you it was who thought yourself proof against temptation, absolved from human frailties, and free from error and vice! Is pride then a virtue? Is inhumanity no fault? Know, vain man! That I long have marked you for my prey: I watched the movements of your heart; I saw that you were virtuous from vanity, not principle, and I seized the fit moment of seduction. I observed your blind idolatry of the Madonna's picture. I bad a subordinate but crafty spirit assume a similar form, and you eagerly yielded to the blandishments of Matilda. Your pride was gratified by her flattery; your lust only needed an opportunity to break forth; you ran into the snare blindly, and scrupled not to commit a crime, which you blamed in another with unfeeling severity. It was I who threw Matilda in your way; it was I who gave you entrance to Antonia's chamber; it was I who caused the dagger to be given you which pierced your sister's bosom; and it was I who warned Elvira in dreams of your designs upon her daughter, and thus, by preventing your profiting by her sleep, compelled you to add rape as well as incest to the catalogue of your crimes. Hear, hear, Ambrosio! Had you resisted me one minute longer, you had saved your body and soul. The guards whom you heard at your prison-door, came to signify your pardon. But I had already triumphed: my plots had already succeeded. Scarcely could I propose crimes so quick as you performed them. You are mine, and Heaven itself cannot rescue you from my power. Hope not that your penitence will make void our contract. Here is your bond signed with your blood; you have given up your claim to mercy, and nothing can restore to you the rights which you have foolishly resigned. Believe you, that your secret thoughts escaped me? No, no, I read them all! You trusted that you should still have time for repentance. I saw your artifice, knew its falsity, and rejoiced in deceiving the deceiver! You are mine beyond reprieve: I burn to possess my right, and alive you quit not these mountains.'

During the dæmon's speech, Ambrosio had been stupefied by terror and surprise. This last declaration roused him.

'Not quit these mountains alive?' he exclaimed: 'Perfidious, what mean you? Have you forgotten our contract?'

The fiend answered by a malicious laugh:

'Our contract? Have I not performed my part? What more did I promise than to save you from your prison? Have I not done so? Are you not safe from the Inquisition – safe from all but from me? Fool that you were to confide yourself to a devil! Why did you not stipulate for life, and power, and pleasure? Then all would have been granted: now, your reflections come too late. Miscreant, prepare for death; you have not many hours to live!'

On hearing this sentence, dreadful were the feelings of the devoted wretch! He sank upon his knees, and raised his hands towards heaven. The fiend read his intention and prevented it—

'What?' He cried, darting at him a look of fury: 'Dare you still implore the Eternal's mercy? Would you feign penitence, and again act an hypocrite's part? Villain, resign your hopes of pardon. Thus I secure my prey!'

As he said this, darting his talons into the Monk's shaven crown, he sprang with him from the rock. The caves and mountains rang with Ambrosio's shrieks. The dæmon continued to soar aloft, till reaching a dreadful height, he released the sufferer. Headlong fell the Monk through the airy waste; the sharp point of a rock received him; and he rolled from precipice to precipice till bruised and mangled he rested on the river's banks. Life still existed in his miserable frame: He attempted in vain to raise himself; his broken and dislocated limbs refused to perform their office, nor was he able to quit the spot where he had first fallen. The sun now rose above the horizon; its scorching beams darted full upon the head of the expiring sinner. Myriads of insects were called forth by the warmth; they drank the blood which trickled from Ambrosio's wounds; he had no power to drive them from him, and they fastened upon his sores, darted their stings into his body, covered him with their multitudes, and inflicted on him tortures the most exquisite and insupportable. The eagles of the rock tore his flesh piecemeal, and dug out his eye-balls with their crooked beaks. A burning thirst tormented him; he heard the river's murmur as it rolled beside him, but strove in vain to drag himself towards the sound. Blind, maimed, helpless, and despairing, venting his rage in blasphemy and curses, execrating his existence, yet dreading the arrival of death destined to yield him up to greater torments, six miserable days did the villain languish. On the seventh a violent storm arose: the winds in fury rent up rocks and forests: the sky was now black with clouds, now sheeted with fire: the rain fell in torrents; it swelled the stream; the waves overflowed their banks; they reached the spot where Ambrosio lay, and when they abated carried with them into the river the corse of the despairing Monk.

The Mirror of Galadriel

J. R. R. TOLKIEN

The mission of Frodo and his companions is to cast the Great Ring he carries into the Crack of Doom, forever depriving the Dark Lord of Moria of its terrifying powers. In Lothlórien, the ancient kingdom of the Elves, Frodo is mysteriously forewarned of the greatest danger he will face . . . .

THE SUN WAS SINKING behind the mountains, and the shadows were deepening in the woods, when they went on again. Their paths now went into thickets where the dusk had already gathered. Night came beneath the trees as they walked, and the Elves uncovered their silver lamps.

Suddenly they came out into the open again and found themselves under a pale evening sky pricked by a few early stars. There was a wide treeless space before them, running in a great circle and bending away on either hand. Beyond it was a deep fosse lost in soft shadow, but the grass upon its brink was green, as if it glowed still in memory of the sun that had gone. Upon the further side there rose to a great height a green wall encircling a green hill thronged with mallorn-trees taller than any they had yet seen in all the land. Their height could not be guessed, but they stood up in the twilight like living towers. In their many-tiered branches and amid their ever-moving leaves countless lights were gleaming, green and gold and silver. Haldir turned towards the Company.

'Welcome to Caras Galadhon!' he said. 'Here is the city of the Galadhrim where dwell the Lord Celeborn and Galadriel the Lady of Lórien. But we cannot enter here, for the gates do not look northward. We must go round to the southern side, and the way is not short, for the city is great.'

There was a road paved with white stone running on the outer brink of the fosse. Along this they went westward, with the city ever climbing up like a green cloud upon their left; and as the night deepened more lights sprang forth, until all the hill seemed afire with stars. They came at last to a white bridge, and crossing found the great gates of the city: they faced south-west, set between the ends of the encircling wall that here overlapped, and they were tall and strong, and hung with many lamps.

Haldir knocked and spoke, and the gates opened soundlessly; but of guards Frodo could see no sign. The travellers passed within, and the gates shut behind them. They were in a deep lane between the ends of the wall, and passing quickly through it they entered the City of the Trees. No folk could they see, nor hear any feet upon the paths; but there were many voices, about them, and in the air above. Far away up on the hill they could hear the sound of singing falling from on high like soft rain upon leaves.

They went along many paths and climbed many stairs, until they came to the high places and saw before them amid a wide lawn a fountain shimmering. It was lit by silver lamps that swung from the boughs of trees, and it fell into a basin of silver, from which a white stream spilled. Upon the south side of the lawn there stood the mightiest of all the trees; its great smooth bole gleamed like grey silk, and up it towered, until its first branches, far above, opened their huge limbs under shadowy clouds of leaves. Beside it a broad white ladder stood, and at its foot three Elves were seated. They sprang up as the travellers approached, and Frodo saw that they were tall and clad in grey mail, and from their shoulders hung long white cloaks.

'Here dwell Celeborn and Galadriel,' said Haldir. 'It is their wish that you should ascend and speak with them.'

One of the Elf-wardens then blew a clear note on a small horn, and it was answered three times from far above. 'I will go first,' said Haldir. 'Let Frodo come next and with him Legolas. The others may follow as they wish. It is a long climb for those that are not accustomed to such stairs, but you may rest upon the way.'

As he climbed slowly up Frodo passed many flets: some on one side, some on another, and some set about the bole of the tree, so that the ladder passed through them. At a great height above the ground he came to a wide *talan*, like the deck of a great ship. On it was built a house, so large that almost it would have served for a hall of Men upon the earth. He entered behind Haldir, and found that he was in a chamber of oval shape, in the midst of which grew the trunk of the great mallorn, now tapering towards its crown, and yet making still a pillar of wide girth.

The chamber was filled with a soft light; its walls were green and silver and its roof of gold. Many Elves were seated there. On two chairs beneath the bole of the tree and canopied by a living bough there sat, side by side, Celeborn and Galadriel. They stood up to greet their guests, after the manner of Elves, even those who were accounted mighty kings. Very tall they were, and the Lady no less tall than the Lord; and they were grave and beautiful. They were clad wholly in white; and the hair of the Lady was of deep gold, and the hair of the Lord Celeborn was of silver long and bright; but no sign of age was upon them, unless it were in the depths of their eyes; for these were keen as lances in the starlight, and yet profound, the wells of deep memory.

Haldir led Frodo before them, and the Lord welcomed him in his own tongue. The Lady Galadriel said no word but looked long upon his face.

'Sit now beside my chair, Frodo of the Shire!' said Celeborn. 'When all have come we will speak together.'

Each of the companions he greeted courteously by name as they entered. 'Welcome Aragorn son of Arathorn!' he said. 'It is eight and thirty years of the world outside since you came to this land; and those years lie heavy on you. But the end is near, for good or ill. Here lay aside your burden for a while!'

'Welcome son of Thranduil! Too seldom do my kindred journey hither from the North.'

'Welcome Gimli son of Glóin! It is long indeed since we saw one of Durin's folk in Caras Galadhon. But today we have broken our long law. May it be a sign that though the world is now dark better days are at hand, and that friendship shall be renewed between our peoples.' Gimli bowed low.

When all the guests were seated before his chair the Lord looked at them again. 'Here there are eight,' he said. 'Nine were to set out: so said the messages. But maybe there has been some change of counsel that we have not heard. Elrond is far away, and darkness gathers between us, and all this year the shadows have grown longer.'

'Nay, there was no change of counsel,' said the Lady Galadriel, speaking for the first time. Her voice was clear and musical, but deeper than woman's wont. 'Gandalf the Grey set out with the Company, but he did not pass the borders of this land. Now tell us where he is; for I much desired to speak with him again. But I cannot see him from afar, unless he comes within the fences of Lothlórien: a grey mist is about him, and the ways of his feet and of his mind are hidden from me.'

'Alas!' said Aragorn. 'Gandalf the Grey fell into shadow. He remained in Moria and did not escape.'

At these words the Elves in the hall cried aloud in grief and amazement. 'These are evil tidings,' said Celeborn, 'the most evil that have been spoken here in long years full of grievous deeds.' He turned to Haldir. 'Why has nothing of this been told to me before?' he asked in the Elven-tongue.

'We have not spoken to Haldir of our deeds or our purpose,' said

Legolas. 'At first we were weary and danger was too close behind; and afterwards we almost forgot our grief for a time, as we walked in gladness on the fair paths of Lórien.'

'Yet our grief is great and our loss cannot be mended,' said Frodo. 'Gandalf was our guide, and he led us through Moria; and when our escape seemed beyond hope he saved us, and he fell.'

'Tell us now the full tale!' said Celeborn.

Then Aragorn recounted all that had happened upon the pass of Caradhras, and in the days that followed; and he spoke of Balin and his book, and the fight in the Chamber of Mazarbul, and the fire, and the narrow bridge, and the coming of the Terror. 'An evil of the Ancient World it seemed, such as I have never seen before,' said Aragorn. 'It was both a shadow and a flame, strong and terrible.'

'It was a Balrog of Morgoth,' said Legolas; 'of all elf-banes the most deadly, save the One who sits in the Dark Tower.'

'Indeed I saw upon the bridge that which haunts our darkest dreams, I saw Durin's Bane,' said Gimli in a low voice, and dread was in his eyes.

'Alas!' said Celeborn. 'We long have feared that under Caradhras a terror slept. But had I known that the Dwarves had stirred up this evil in Moria again, I would have forbidden you to pass the northern borders, you and all that went with you. And if it were possible, one would say that at the last Gandalf fell from wisdom into folly, going needlessly into the net of Moria.'

'He would be rash indeed that said that thing,' said Galadriel gravely. 'Needless were none of the deeds of Gandalf in life. Those that followed him knew not his mind and cannot report his full purpose. But however it may be with the guide, the followers are blameless. Do not repent of your welcome to the Dwarf. If our folk had been exiled long and far from Lothlórien, who of the Galadhrim, even Celeborn the Wise, would pass nigh and would not wish to look upon their ancient home, though it had become an abode of dragons?

'Dark is the water of Kheled-zâram, and cold are the springs of Kibil-nâla, and fair were the many pillared halls of Khazad-dûm in Elder Days before the fall of mighty kings beneath the stone.' She looked upon Gimli, who sat glowering and sad, and she smiled. And the Dwarf, hearing the names given in his own ancient tongue, looked up and met her eyes; and it seemed to him that he looked suddenly into the heart of an enemy and saw there love and understanding. Wonder came into his face, and then he smiled in answer.

He rose clumsily and bowed in dwarf-fashion, saying: 'Yet more fair is the living land of Lórien, and the Lady Galadriel is above all the jewels that lie beneath the earth!'

There was a silence. At length Celeborn spoke again. 'I did not know that your plight was so evil,' he said. 'Let Gimli forget my harsh words: I spoke the trouble of my heart. I will do what I can to aid you, each according to his wish and need, but especially that one of the little folk who bears the burden.'

'Your quest is known to us,' said Galadriel, looking at Frodo. 'But we will not here speak of it more openly. Yet not in vain will it prove, maybe, that you came to this land seeking aid, as Gandalf himself plainly purposed. For the Lord of the Galadhrim is accounted the wisest of the Elves of Middle-earth, and a giver of gifts beyond the power of kings. He has dwelt in the West since the days of dawn, and I have dwelt with him years uncounted; for ere the fall of Nargothrond or Gondolin I passed over the mountains, and together through ages of the world we have fought the long defeat.

'I it was who first summoned the White Council. And if my designs had not gone amiss, it would have been governed by Gandalf the Grey, and then mayhap things would have gone otherwise. But even now there is hope left. I will not give you counsel, saying do this, or do that. For not in doing or contriving, nor in choosing between thise course and another, can I avail; but only in knowing what was and is, and in part also what shall be. But this I will say to you: your Quest stands upon the edge of a knife. Stray but a little and it will fail, to the ruin of all. Yet hope remains while all the Company is true.'

And with that word she held them with her eyes, and in silence looked searchingly at each of them in turn. None save Legolas and Aragorn could long endure her glance. Sam quickly blushed and hung his head.

At length the Lady Galadriel released them from her eyes, and she smiled. 'Do not let your hearts be troubled,' she said. 'Tonight you shall sleep in peace.' Then they sighed and felt suddenly weary, as those who have been questioned long and deeply, though no words had been spoken openly.

'Go now!' said Celeborn. 'You are worn with sorrow and much toil. Even if your Quest did not concern us closely, you should have refuge in this City, until you were healed and refreshed. Now you shall rest, and we will not speak of your further road for a while.'

That night the Company slept upon the ground, much to the satisfaction of the hobbits. The Elves spread for them a pavilion among the trees near the fountain, and in it they laid soft couches; then speaking words of peace with fair elvish voices they left them. For a little while the travellers talked of their night before in the tree-tops, and of their day's journey, and of the Lord and Lady; for they had not yet the heart to look further back.

'What did you blush for, Sam?' said Pippin. 'You soon broke down. Anyone would have thought you had a guilty conscience. I hope it was nothing worse than a wicked plot to steal one of my blankets.'

'I never thought no such thing,' answered Sam, in no mood for jest. 'If you want to know, I felt as if I hadn't got nothing on, and I didn't like it. She seemed to be looking inside me and asking me what I would do if she gave me the chance of flying back home to the Shire to a nice little hole with – with a bit of garden of my own.'

'That's funny,' said Merry. 'Almost exactly what I felt myself; only, only well, I don't think I'll say any more,' he ended lamely.

All of them, it seemed, had fared alike; each had felt that he was offered a choice between a shadow full of fear that lay ahead, and something that he greatly desired: clear before his mind it lay, and to get it he had only to turn aside from the road and leave the Quest and the war against Sauron to others.

'And it seemed to me, too,' said Gimli, 'that my choice would remain secret and known only to myself.'

'To me it seemed exceedingly strange,' said Boromir. 'Maybe it was only a test, and she thought to read our thoughts for her own good purpose; but almost I should have said that she was tempting us, and offering what she pretended to have the power to give. It need not be said that I refused to listen. The Men of Minas Tirith are true to their word.' But what he thought that the Lady had offered him Boromir did not tell.

And as for Frodo, he would not speak, though Boromir pressed him with questions. 'She held you long in her gaze, Ring-bearer,' he said.

'Yes,' said Frodo; 'but whatever came into my mind then I will keep there.'

'Well, have a care!' said Boromir. 'I do not feel too sure of this Elvish Lady and her purposes.'

'Speak no evil of the Lady Galadriel!' said Aragorn sternly. 'You know not what you say. There is in her and in this land no evil, unless a man bring it hither himself. Then let him beware! But tonight I shall sleep without fear for the first time since I left Rivendell. And may I sleep deep, and forget for a while my grief ! I am weary in body and in heart.' He cast himself down upon his couch and fell at once into a long sleep.

The others soon did the same, and no sound or dream disturbed their slumber. When they woke they found that the light of day was broad upon the lawn before the pavilion, and the fountain rose and fell glittering in the sun.

They remained some days in Lothlórien, so far as they could tell or remember. All the while that they dwelt there the sun shone clear, save for a gentle rain that fell at times, and passed away leaving all things fresh and clean. The air was cool and soft, as if it were early spring, yet they felt about them the deep and thoughtful quiet of winter. It seemed to them that they did little but eat and drink and rest, and walk among the trees; and it was enough.

They had not seen the Lord and Lady again, and they had little speech

with the Elven-folk; for few of these knew or would use the Westron
tongue. Haldir had bidden them farewell and gone back again to the
fences of the North, where great watch was now kept since the tidings
of Moria that the Company had brought. Legolas was away much among
the Galadhrim, and after the first night he did not sleep with the other
companions, though he returned to eat and talk with them. Often he took
Gimli with him when he went abroad in the land, and the others
wondered at this change.

Now as the companions sat or walked together they spoke of Gandalf,
and all that each had known and seen of him came clear before their
minds. As they were healed of hurt and weariness of body the grief of
their loss grew more keen. Often they heard nearby Elvish voices singing,
and knew that they were making songs of lamentation for his fall, for
they caught his name among the sweet sad words that they could not
understand.

Mithrandir, Mithrandir sang the Elves, *O Pilgrim Grey!* For so they
loved to call him. But if Legolas was with the Company, he would not
interpret the songs for them, saying that he had not the skill, and that
for him the grief was still too near, a matter for tears and not yet for
song.

It was Frodo who first put something of his sorrow into halting words.
He was seldom moved to make song or rhyme; even in Rivendell he had
listened and had not sung himself, though his memory was stored with
many things that others had made before him. But now as he sat beside
the fountain in Lórien and heard about him the voices of the Elves, his
thought took shape in a song that seemed fair to him; yet when he tried
to repeat it to Sam only snatches remained, faded as a handful of withered
leaves.

> *When evening in the Shire was grey*
> *his footsteps on the Hill were heard;*
> *before the dawn he went away*
> *on journey long without a word.*
>
> *From Wilderland to Western shore,*
> *from northern waste to southern hill,*
> *through dragon-lair and hidden door*
> *and darkling woods he walked at will.*
>
> *With Dwarf and Hobbit, Elves and Men,*
> *with mortal and immortal folk,*
> *with bird on bough and beast in den,*
> *in their own secret tongues he spoke.*
>
> *A deadly sword, a healing hand,*
> *a back that bent beneath its load;*

> *a trumpet-voice, a burning brand,*
> *a weary pilgrim on the road.*
>
> *A lord of wisdom throned he sat,*
> *swift in anger, quick to laugh;*
> *an old man in a battered hat*
> *who leaned upon a thorny staff.*
>
> *He stood upon the bridge alone*
> *and Fire and Shadow both defied;*
> *his staff was broken on the stone,*
> *in Khazad-dûm his wisdom died.*

'Why, you'll be beating Mr. Bilbo next!' said Sam.

'No, I am afraid not,' said Frodo. 'But that is the best I can do yet.'

'Well, Mr. Frodo, if you do have another go, I hope you'll say a word about his fireworks,' said Sam. 'Something like this:

> *The finest rockets ever seen:*
> *they burst in stars of blue and green,*
> *or after thunder golden showers*
> *came falling like a rain of flowers.*

Though that doesn't do them justice by a long road.'

'No, I'll leave that to you, Sam. Or perhaps to Bilbo. But – well, I can't talk of it any more. I can't bear to think of bringing the news to him.'

One evening Frodo and Sam were walking together in the cool twilight. Both of them felt restless again. On Frodo suddenly the shadow of parting had fallen: he knew somehow that the time was very near when he must leave Lothlórien.

'What do you think of Elves now, Sam?' he said. 'I asked you the same question once before – it seems a very long while ago; but you have seen more of them since then.'

'I have indeed!' said Sam. 'And I reckon there's Elves and Elves. They're all elvish enough, but they're not all the same. Now these folk aren't wanderers or homeless, and seem a bit nearer to the likes of us: they seem to belong here, more even than Hobbits do in the Shire. Whether they've made the land, or the land's made them, it's hard to say, if you take my meaning. It's wonderfully quiet here. Nothing seems to be going on, and nobody seems to want it to. If there's any magic about, it's right down deep, where I can't lay my hands on it, in a manner of speaking.'

'You can see and feel it everywhere,' said Frodo.

'Well,' said Sam, 'you can't see nobody working it. No fireworks like poor Gandalf used to show. I wonder we don't see nothing of the Lord and Lady in all these days. I fancy now that *she* could do some wonderful things, if she had a mind. I'd dearly love to see some Elf-magic, Mr. Frodo!'

'I wouldn't,' said Frodo. 'I am content. And I don't miss Gandalf's fireworks, but his bushy eyebrows, and his quick temper, and his voice.'

'You're right,' said Sam. 'And don't think I'm finding fault. I've often wanted to see a bit of magic like what it tells of in old tales, but I've never heard of a better land than this. It's like being at home and on a holiday at the same time, if you understand me. I don't want to leave. All the same, I'm beginning to feel that if we've got to go, then we'd best get it over.

'It's the job that's never started as takes longest to finish, as my old gaffer used to say. And I don't reckon that these folk can do much more to help us, magic or no. It's when we leave this land that we shall miss Gandalf worse, I'm thinking.'

'I am afraid that's only too true, Sam,' said Frodo. 'Yet I hope very much that before we leave we shall see the Lady of the Elves again.'

Even as he spoke, they saw, as if she came in answer to their words, the Lady Galadriel approaching. Tall and white and fair she walked beneath the trees. She spoke no word, but beckoned to them.

Turning aside, she led them toward the southern slopes of the hill of Caras Galadhon, and passing through a high green hedge they came into an enclosed garden. No trees grew there, and it lay open to the sky. The evening star had risen and was shining with white fire above the western woods. Down a long flight of steps the Lady went into a deep green hollow, through which ran murmuring the silver stream that issued from the fountain on the hill. At the bottom, upon a low pedestal carved like a branching tree, stood a basin of silver, wide and shallow, and beside it stood a silver ewer.

With water from the stream Galadriel filled the basin to the brim, and breathed on it, and when the water was still again she spoke. 'Here is the Mirror of Galadriel,' she said. 'I have brought you here so that you may look in it, if you will.'

The air was very still, and the dell was dark, and the Elf-lady beside him was tall and pale. 'What shall we look for, and what shall we see?' asked Frodo, filled with awe.

'Many things I can command the Mirror to reveal,' she answered, 'and to some I can show what they desire to see. But the Mirror will also show things unbidden, and those are often stranger and more profitable than things which we wish to behold. What you will see, if you leave the Mirror free to work, I cannot tell. For it shows things that were, and things that are, and things that yet may be. But which it is that he sees, even the wisest cannot always tell. Do you wish to look?'

Frodo did not answer.

'And you?' she said, turning to Sam. 'For this is what your folk would call magic, I believe; though I do not understand clearly what they mean; and they seem also to use the same word of the deceits of the Enemy. But this, if you will, is the magic of Galadriel. Did you not say that you wished to see Elf-magic?'

'I did,' said Sam, trembling a little between fear and curiosity. 'I'll have a peep, Lady, if you're willing.'

'And I'd not mind a glimpse of what's going on at home,' he said in an aside to Frodo. 'It seems a terrible long time that I've been away. But there, like as not I'll only see the stars, or something that I won't understand.'

'Like as not,' said the Lady with a gentle laugh. 'But come, you shall look and see what you may. Do not touch the water!'

Sam climbed up on the foot of the pedestal and leaned over the basin. The water looked hard and dark. Stars were reflected in it.

'There's only stars, as I thought,' he said. Then he gave a low gasp, for the stars went out. As if a dark veil had been withdrawn, the Mirror grew grey, and then clear. There was sun shining, and the branches of trees were waving and tossing in the wind. But before Sam could make up his mind what it was that he saw, the light faded; and now he thought he saw Frodo with a pale face lying fast asleep under a great dark cliff. Then he seemed to see himself going along a dim passage, and climbing an endless winding stair. It came to him suddenly that he was looking urgently for something, but what it was he did not know. Like a dream the vision shifted and went back, and he saw the trees again. But this time they were not so close, and he could see what was going on: they were not waving in the wind, they were falling, crashing to the ground.

'Hi!' cried Sam in an outraged voice. 'There's that Ted Sandyman a-cutting down trees as he shouldn't. They didn't ought to be felled: it's that avenue beyond the Mill that shades the road to Bywater. I wish I could get at Ted, and I'd fell *him*!'

But now Sam noticed that the Old Mill had vanished, and a large red-brick building was being put up where it had stood. Lots of folk were busily at work. There was a tall red chimney nearby. Black smoke seemed to cloud the surface of the Mirror.

'There's some devilry at work in the Shire,' he said. 'Elrond knew what he was about when he wanted to send Mr. Merry back.' Then suddenly Sam gave a cry and sprang away. 'I can't stay here,' he said wildly. 'I must go home. They've dug up Bagshot Row, and there's the poor old gaffer going down the Hill with his bits of things on a barrow. I must go home!'

'You cannot go home alone,' said the Lady. 'You did not wish to go home without your master before you looked in the Mirror, and yet you knew that evil things might well be happening in the Shire. Remember that the Mirror shows many things, and not all have yet come to pass.

Some never come to be, unless those that behold the visions turn aside from their path to prevent them. The Mirror is dangerous as a guide of deeds.'

Sam sat on the ground and put his head in his hands. 'I wish I had never come here, and I don't want to see no more magic,' he said and fell silent. After a moment he spoke again thickly, as if struggling with tears. 'No, I'll go home by the long road with Mr. Frodo, or not at all,' he said. 'But I hope I do get back some day. If what I've seen turns out true, somebody's going to catch it hot!'

'Do you now wish to look, Frodo?' said the Lady Galadriel. 'You did not wish to see Elf-magic and were content.'

'Do you advise me to look?' asked Frodo.

'No,' she said. 'I do not counsel you one way or the other. I am not a counsellor. You may learn something, and whether what you see be fair or evil, that may be profitable, and yet it may not. Seeing is both good and perilous. Yet I think, Frodo, that you have courage and wisdom enough for the venture, or I would not have brought you here. Do as you will!'

'I will look,' said Frodo, and he climbed on the pedestal and bent over the dark water. At once the Mirror cleared and he saw a twilit land. Mountains loomed dark in the distance against a pale sky. A long grey road wound back out of sight. Far away a figure came slowly down the road, faint and small at first, but growing larger and clearer as it approached. Suddenly Frodo realized that it reminded him of Gandalf. He almost called aloud the wizard's name, and then he saw that the figure was clothed not in grey but in white, in a white that shone faintly in the dusk; and in its hand there was a white staff. The head was so bowed that he could see no face, and presently the figure turned aside round a bend in the road and went out of the Mirror's view. Doubt came into Frodo's mind: was this a vision of Gandalf on one of his many lonely journeys long ago, or was it Saruman?

The vision now changed. Brief and small but very vivid he caught a glimpse of Bilbo walking restlessly about his room. The table was littered with disordered papers; rain was beating on the windows.

Then there was a pause, and after it many swift scenes followed that Frodo in some way knew to be parts of a great history in which he had become involved. The mist cleared and he saw a sight which he had never seen before but knew at once: the Sea. Darkness fell. The sea rose and raged in the great storm. Then he saw against the Sun, sinking blood-red into a wrack of clouds, the black outline of a tall ship with torn sails riding up out of the West. Then a wide river flowing through a populous city. Then a white fortress with seven towers. And then again a ship with black sails, but now it was morning again, and the water rippled with light, and a banner bearing the emblem of a white tree shone in the sun. A smoke as of fire and battle arose, and again the sun went down in a burning red that faded into a grey mist; and into the mist a small ship passed away, twinkling with lights. It vanished, and Frodo sighed and prepared to draw away.

But suddenly the Mirror went altogether dark, as dark as if a hole had opened in the world of sight, and Frodo looked into emptiness. In the black abyss there appeared a single Eye that slowly grew, until it filled nearly all the Mirror. So terrible was it that Frodo stood rooted, unable to cry out or to withdraw his gaze. The Eye was rimmed with fire, but was itself glazed, yellow as a cat's, watchful and intent, and the black slit of its pupil opened on a pit, a window into nothing.

Then the Eye began to rove, searching this way and that; and Frodo knew with certainty and horror that among the many things that it sought he himself was one. But he also knew that it could not see him – not yet, not unless he willed it. The Ring that hung upon its chain about his neck grew heavy, heavier than a great stone, and his head was dragged downwards. The Mirror seemed to be growing hot and curls of steam were rising from the water. He was slipping forward.

'Do not touch the water!' said the Lady Galadriel softly. The vision faded, and Frodo found that he was looking at the cool stars twinkling in the silver basin. He stepped back shaking all over and looked at the Lady.

'I know what it was that you last saw,' she said; 'for that is also in my mind. Do not be afraid! But do not think that only by singing amid the trees, nor even by the slender arrows of elven-bows, is this land of Lothlórien maintained and defended against its Enemy. I say to you, Frodo, that even as I speak to you, I perceive the Dark Lord and know his mind, or all of his mind that concerns the Elves. And he gropes ever to see me and my thought. But still the door is closed!'

She lifted up her white arms, and spread out her hands towards the East in a gesture of rejection and denial. Eärendil, the Evening Star, most beloved of the Elves, shone clear above. So bright was it that the figure of the Elven-lady cast a dim shadow on the ground. Its rays glanced upon a ring about her finger; it glittered like polished gold overlaid with silver light, and a white stone in it twinkled as if the Even-star had come down to rest upon her hand. Frodo gazed at the ring with awe; for suddenly it seemed to him that he understood.

'Yes,' she said, divining his thought, 'it is not permitted to speak of it, and Elrond could not do so. But it cannot be hidden from the Ring-bearer, and one who has seen the Eye. Verily it is in the land of Lórien upon the finger of Galadriel that one of the Three remains. This is Nenya, the Ring of Adamant, and I am its keeper.

'He suspects, but he does not know – not yet. Do you not see now wherefore your coming is to us as the footstep of Doom? For if you fail, then we are laid bare to the Enemy. Yet if you succeed, then our power

187

is diminished, and Lothlórien will fade, and the tides of Time will sweep it away. We must depart into the West, or dwindle to a rustic folk of dell and cave, slowly to forget and to be forgotten.'

Frodo bent his head. 'And what do you wish?' he said at last.

'That what should be shall be,' she answered. 'The love of the Elves for their land and their works is deeper than the deeps of the Sea, and their regret is undying and cannot ever wholly be assuaged. Yet they will cast all away rather than submit to Sauron: for they know him now. For the fate of Lothlórien you are not answerable, but only for the doing of your own task. Yet I could wish, were it of any avail, that the One Ring had never been wrought, or had remained for ever lost.'

'You are wise and fearless and fair, Lady Galadriel,' said Frodo. 'I will give you the One Ring, if you ask for it. It is too great a matter for me.'

Galadriel laughed with a sudden clear laugh. 'Wise the Lady Galadriel may be,' she said, 'yet here she has met her match in courtesy. Gently are you revenged for my testing of your heart at our first meeting. You begin to see with a keen eye. I do not deny that my heart has greatly desired to ask what you offer. For many long years I had pondered what I might do, should the Great Ring come into my hands, and behold! it was brought within my grasp. The evil that was devised long ago works on in many ways, whether Sauron himself stands or falls. Would not that have been a noble deed to set to the credit of his Ring, if I had taken it by force or fear from my guest?

'And now at last it comes. You will give me the Ring freely! In place of the Dark Lord you will set up a Queen. And I shall not be dark, but beautiful and terrible as the Morning and the Night! Fair as the Sea and the Sun and the Snow upon the Mountain! Dreadful as the Storm and the Lightning! Stronger than the foundations of the earth. All shall love me and despair!'

She lifted up her hand and from the ring that she wore there issued a great light that illuminated her alone and left all else dark. She stood before Frodo seeming now tall beyond measurement, and beautiful beyond enduring, terrible and worshipful. Then she let her hand fall, and the light faded, and suddenly she laughed again, and lo! she was shrunken: a slender elf-woman, clad in simple white, whose gentle voice was soft and sad.

'I pass the test,' she said. 'I will diminish, and go into the West, and remain Galadriel.'

They stood for a long while in silence. At length the Lady spoke again. 'Let us return!' she said. 'In the morning you must depart, for now we have chosen, and the tides of fate are flowing.'

'I would ask one thing before we go,' said Frodo, 'a thing which I often meant to ask Gandalf in Rivendell. I am permitted to wear the One

Ring: why cannot I see all the others and know the thoughts of those that wear them?'

'You have not tried,' she said. 'Only thrice have you set the Ring upon your finger since you knew what you possessed. Do not try! It would destroy you. Did not Gandalf tell you that the rings give power according to the measure of each possessor? Before you could use that power you would need to become far stronger, and to train your will to the domination of others. Yet even so, as Ring-bearer and as one that has borne it on finger and seen that which is hidden, your sight is grown keener. You have perceived my thought more clearly than many accounted wise. You saw the Eye of him that holds the Seven and the Nine. And did you not see and recognize the ring upon my finger? Did you see my ring?' she asked turning to Sam.

'No, Lady,' he answered. 'To tell you the truth, I wondered what you were talking about. I saw a star through your finger. But if you'll pardon my speaking out, I think my master was right. I wish you'd take his Ring. You'd put things to rights. You'd stop them digging up the gaffer and turning him adrift. You'd make some folk pay for their dirty work.'

'I would,' she said. 'That is how it would begin. But it would not stop with that, alas! We will not speak more of it. Let us go!'

The Gray Wolf
GEORGE MACDONALD

ONE EVENING-TWILIGHT in spring, a young English student, who had wandered northwards as far as the outlying fragments of Scotland called the Orkney and Shetland Islands, found himself on a small island of the latter group, caught in a storm of wind and hail, which had come on suddenly. It was in vain to look about for any shelter; for not only did the storm entirely obscure the landscape, but there was nothing around him save a desert moss.

At length, however, as he walked on for mere walking's sake, he found himself on the verge of a cliff, and saw, over the brow of it, a few feet below him, a ledge of rock, where he might find some shelter from the blast, which blew from behind. Letting himself down by his hands, he alighted upon something that crunched beneath his tread, and found the bones of many small animals scattered about in front of a little cave in the rock, offering the refuge he sought. He went in, and sat upon a stone. The storm increased in violence, and as the darkness grew he became uneasy, for he did not relish the thought of spending the night in the cave. He had parted from his companions on the opposite side of the island, and it added to his uneasiness that they must be full of apprehension about him. At last there came a lull in the storm, and the same instant he heard a footfall, stealthy and light as that of a wild beast, upon the bones at the mouth of the cave. He started up in some fear, though the least thought might have satisfied him that there could be no very dangerous animals upon the island. Before he had time to think, however, the face of a woman appeared in the opening. Eagerly the wanderer spoke. She started at the sound of his voice. He could not see her well, because she was turned towards the darkness of the cave.

'Will you tell me how to find my way across the moor to Shielness?' he asked.

'You cannot find it tonight,' she answered, in a sweet tone, and with a smile that bewitched him, revealing the whitest of teeth.

'What am I to do, then?'

'My mother will give you shelter, but that is all she has to offer.'

'And that is far more than I expected a minute ago,' he replied. 'I shall be most grateful.'

She turned in silence and left the cave. The youth followed.

She was barefooted, and her pretty brown feet went cat-like over the sharp stones, as she led the way down a rocky path to the shore. Her garments were scanty and torn, and her hair blew tangled in the wind. She seemed about five and twenty, lithe and small. Her long fingers kept clutching and pulling nervously at her skirts as she went. Her face was very gray in complexion, and very worn, but delicately formed, and smooth-skinned. Her thin nostrils were tremulous as eyelids, and her lips, whose curves were faultless, had no colour to give sign of indwelling blood. What her eyes were like he could not see, for she had never lifted the delicate films of her eyelids.

At the foot of the cliff they came upon a little hut leaning against it, and having for its inner apartment a natural hollow within. Smoke was spreading over the face of the rock, and the grateful odour of food gave hope to the hungry student. His guide opened the door of the cottage; he followed her in, and saw a woman bending over a fire in the middle of the floor. On the fire lay a large fish broiling. The daughter spoke a few words, and the mother turned and welcomed the stranger. She had an old and very wrinkled, but honest face, and looked troubled. She dusted the only chair in the cottage, and placed it for him by the side of the fire opposite the one window, whence he saw a little patch of yellow sand over which the spent waves spread themselves out listlessly. Under this window there was a bench, upon which the daughter threw herself in an unusual posture, resting her chin upon her hand. A moment after, the youth caught the first glimpse of her blue eyes. They were fixed upon him with a strange look of greed, amounting to craving, but, as if aware that they belied or betrayed her, she dropped them instantly. The moment she veiled them, her face, notwithstanding its colourless complexion, was almost beautiful.

When the fish was ready, the old woman wiped the deal table, steadied it upon the uneven floor, and covered it with a piece of fine table-linen. She then laid the fish on a wooden platter, and invited the guest to help himself. Seeing no other provision, he pulled from his pocket a hunting knife, and divided a portion from the fish, offering it to the mother first.

'Come, my lamb,' said the old woman; and the daughter approached the table. But her nostrils and mouth quivered with disgust.

The next moment she turned and hurried from the hut.

'She doesn't like fish,' said the old woman, 'and I haven't anything else to give her.'

'She does not seem in good health,' he rejoined.

The woman answered only with a sigh, and they ate their fish with the help of a little rye bread. As they finished their supper, the youth heard the sound as of the pattering of a dog's feet upon the sand close to the door; but ere he had time to look out of the window, the door opened, and the young woman entered. She looked better, perhaps from having just washed her face. She drew a stool to the corner of the fire opposite him. But as she sat down, to his bewilderment, and even horror, the student spied a single drop of blood on her white skin within her torn dress. The woman brought out a jar of whisky, put a rusty old kettle on the fire, and took her place in front of it. As soon as the water boiled, she proceeded to make some toddy in a wooden bowl.

Meantime the youth could not take his eyes off the young woman, so that at length he found himself fascinated, or rather bewitched. She kept her eyes for the most part veiled with the loveliest eyelids fringed with darkest lashes, and he gazed entranced; for the red glow of the little oil-lamp covered all the strangeness of her complexion. But as soon as he met a stolen glance out of those eyes unveiled, his soul shuddered within him. Lovely face and craving eyes alternated fascination and repulsion.

The mother placed the bowl in his hands. He drank sparingly, and passed it to the girl. She lifted it to her lips, and as she tasted – only tasted it – looked at him. He thought the drink must have been drugged and have affected his brain. Her hair smoothed itself back, and drew her forehead backwards with it; while the lower part of her face projected towards the bowl, revealing, ere she sipped, her dazzling teeth in strange prominence. But the same moment the vision vanished; she returned the vessel to her mother, and rising, hurried out of the cottage.

Then the old woman pointed to a bed of heather in one corner with a murmured apology; and the student, wearied both with the fatigues of the day and the strangeness of the night, threw himself upon it, wrapped in his cloak. The moment he lay down, the storm began afresh, and the wind blew so keenly through the crannies of the hut, that it was only by drawing his cloak over his head that he could protect himself from its currents. Unable to sleep, he lay listening to the uproar which grew in violence, till the spray was dashing against the window. At length the door opened, and the young woman came in, made up the fire, drew the bench before it, and lay down in the same strange posture, with her chin propped on her hand and elbow, and her face turned towards the youth. He moved a little; she dropped her head, and lay on her face, with her arms crossed beneath her forehead. The mother had disappeared.

Drowsiness crept over him. A movement of the bench roused him, and he fancied he saw some four-footed creature as tall as a large dog trot quietly out of the door. He was sure he felt a rush of cold wind. Gazing fixedly through the darkness, he thought he saw the eyes of the damsel encountering his, but a glow from the falling together of the remnants of the fire revealed clearly enough that the bench was vacant. Wondering what could have made her go out in such a storm, he fell fast asleep.

In the middle of the night he felt a pain in his shoulder, came broad awake, and saw the gleaming eyes and grinning teeth of some animal close to his face. Its claws were in his shoulder, and its mouth in the act of seeking his throat. Before it had fixed its fangs, however, he had its throat in one hand, and sought his knife with the other. A terrible struggle followed; but regardless of the tearing claws, he found and opened his knife. He had made one futile stab, and was drawing it for a surer, when, with a spring of the whole body, and one wildly contorted effort, the creature twisted its neck from his hold, and with something betwixt a scream and a howl, darted from him. Again he heard the door open; again the wind blew in upon him, and it continued blowing; a sheet of spray dashed across the floor, and over his face. He sprung from his couch and bounded to the door.

It was a wild night – dark, but for the flash of whiteness from the waves as they broke within a few yards of the cottage; the wind was raving, and the rain pouring down the air. A gruesome sound as of mingled weeping and howling came from somewhere in the dark. He turned again into the hut and closed the door, but could find no way of securing it.

The lamp was nearly out, and he could not be certain whether the form of the young woman was upon the bench or not. Overcoming a strong repugnance, he approached it, and put out his hands – there was nothing there. He sat down and waited for the daylight: he dared not sleep any more.

When the day dawned at length, he went out yet again, and looked around. The morning was dim and gusty and gray. The wind had fallen, but the waves were tossing wildly. He wandered up and down the little strand, longing for more light.

At length he heard a movement in the cottage. By and by the voice of the old woman called to him from the door.

'You're up early, sir. I doubt you didn't sleep well.'

'Not very well,' he answered. 'But where is your daughter?'

'She's not awake yet,' said the mother. 'I'm afraid I have but a poor breakfast for you. But you'll take a dram and a bit of fish. It's all I've got.'

Unwilling to hurt her, though hardly in good appetite, he sat down at the table. While they were eating, the daughter came in, but turned her face away and went to the farther end of the hut. When she came forward after a minute or two, the youth saw that her hair was drenched, and her face whiter than before. She looked ill and faint, and when she raised her eyes, all their fierceness had vanished, and sadness had taken its place. Her neck was now covered with a cotton handkerchief. She was modestly attentive to him, and no longer shunned his gaze. He was gradually yielding to the temptation of braving another night in the hut, and seeing what would follow, when the old woman spoke.

'The weather will be broken all day, sir,' she said. 'You had better be going, or your friends will leave without you.'

Ere he could answer, he saw such a beseeching glance on the face of the girl, that he hesitated, confused. Glancing at the mother, he saw the flash of wrath in her face. She rose and approached her daughter, with her hand lifted to strike her. The young woman stooped her head with a cry. He darted round the table to interpose between them. But the mother had caught hold of her; the handkerchief had fallen from her neck; and the youth saw five blue bruises on her lovely throat – the marks of the four fingers and the thumb of a left hand. With a cry of horror he darted from the house, but as he reached the door he turned. His hostess was lying motionless on the floor, and a huge gray wolf came bounding after him.

There was no weapon at hand. Instinctively, he set himself firm, leaning a little forward, with half outstretched arms, and hands curved ready to clutch again at the throat upon which he had left those pitiful marks. But the creature as she sprung eluded his grasp, and just as he expected to feel her fangs, he found a woman weeping on his bosom, with her arms around his neck. The next instant, the gray wolf broke from him, and bounded howling up the cliff. Recovering himself as he best might, the youth followed, for it was the only way to the moor above, across which he must now make his way to find his companions.

All at once he heard the sound of a crunching of bones – not as if a creature was eating them, but as if they were ground by the teeth of rage and disappointment; looking up, he saw close above him the mouth of a little cavern in which he had taken refuge the day before. Summoning all his resolution, he passed it slowly and softly. From within came the sounds of a mingled moaning and growling.

Having reached the top, he ran at full speed for some distance across the moor before venturing to look behind him. When at length he did so, he saw, against the sky, the girl standing on the edge of the cliff, wringing her hands. One solitary wail crossed the space between. She made no attempt to follow him, and he reached the opposite shore in safety.

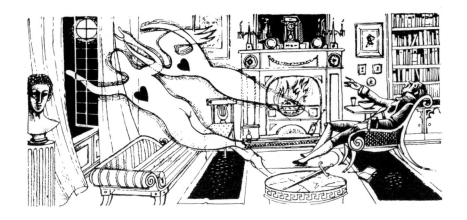

Lost Hearts

M. R. JAMES

IT WAS, AS FAR AS I can ascertain, in September of the year 1811 that a postchaise drew up before the door of Aswarby Hall, in the heart of Lincolnshire. The little boy who was the only passenger in the chaise, and who jumped out as soon as it had stopped, looked about him with the keenest curiosity during the short interval that elapsed between the ringing of the bell and the opening of the hall door. He saw a tall, square, red-brick house, built in the reign of Anne; a stone-pillared porch had been added in the purer classical style of 1790; the windows of the house were many, tall and narrow, with small panes and thick white woodwork. A pediment, pierced with a round window, crowned the front. There were wings to right and left, connected by curious glazed galleries, supported by colonnades, with the central block. These wings plainly contained the stables and offices of the house. Each was surmounted by an ornamental cupola with a gilded vane.

An evening light shone on the building, making the window-panes glow like so many fires. Away from the Hall in front stretched a flat park studded with oaks and fringed with firs, which stood out against the sky. The clock in the church-tower, buried in trees on the edge of the park, only its golden weather-cock catching the light, was striking six, and the sound came gently beating down the wind. It was altogether a pleasant impression, though tinged with the sort of melancholy appropriate to an evening in early autumn, that was conveyed to the mind of the boy who was standing in the porch waiting for the door to open to him.

He had just come from Warwickshire, and some six months ago had been left an orphan. Now, owing to the generous and unexpected offer of his elderly cousin, Mr. Abney, he had come to live at Aswarby. The offer was unexpected, because all who knew anything of Mr. Abney looked upon him as a somewhat austere recluse, into whose steady-going household the advent of a small boy would import a new and, it seemed, incongruous element. The truth is that very little was known of Mr. Abney's pursuits or temper. The Professor of Greek at Cambridge had been heard to say that no one knew more of the religious beliefs of the later pagans than did the owner of Aswarby. Certainly his library contained all the then available books bearing on the Mysteries, the Orphic poems, the worship of Mithras, and the Neo-Platonists. In the marble-paved hall stood a fine group of Mithras slaying a bull, which had been imported from the Levant at great expense by the owner. He had contributed a description of it to the *Gentleman's Magazine*, and he had written a remarkable series of articles in the *Critical Museum* on the superstitions of the Romans of the Lower Empire. He was looked upon, in fine, as a man wrapped up in his books, and it was a matter of great surprise among his neighbours that he should ever have heard of his orphan cousin, Stephen Elliott, much more that he should have volunteered to make him an inmate of Aswarby Hall.

Whatever may have been expected by his neighbours, it is certain that Mr. Abney – the tall, the thin, the austere – seemed inclined to give his young cousin a kindly reception. The moment the front-door was opened he darted out of his study, rubbing his hands with delight.

'How are you, my boy? – how are you? How old are you?' said he – 'that is, you are not too much tired, I hope, by your journey to eat your supper?'

'No, thank you, sir,' said Master Elliott; 'I am pretty well.'

'That's a good lad,' said Mr. Abney. 'And how old are you, my boy?'

It seemed a little odd that he should have asked the question twice in the first two minutes of their acquaintance.

'I'm twelve years old next birthday, sir,' said Stephen.

'And when is your birthday, my dear boy? Eleventh of September, eh? That's well – that's very well. Nearly a year hence, isn't it? I like – ha, ha! – I like to get these things down in my book. Sure it's twelve? Certain?'

'Yes, quite sure, sir.'

'Well, well! Take him to Mrs. Bunch's room, Parkes, and let him have his tea – supper – whatever it is.'

'Yes, sir,' answered the staid Mr. Parkes; and conducted Stephen to the lower regions.

Mrs. Bunch was the most comfortable and human person whom Stephen had as yet met in Aswarby. She made him completely at home; they were great friends in a quarter of an hour: and great friends they remained. Mrs. Bunch had been born in the neighbourhood some fifty-five years before the date of Stephen's arrival, and her residence at the Hall was of twenty years' standing. Consequently, if anyone knew the

ins and outs of the house and the district, Mrs. Bunch knew them; and
she was by no means disinclined to communicate her information.

Certainly there were plenty of things about the Hall and the Hall
gardens which Stephen, who was of an adventurous and inquiring turn,
was anxious to have explained to him. 'Who built the temple at the end
of the laurel walk? Who was the old man whose picture hung on the
staircase, sitting at a table, with a skull under his hand?' These and
many similar points were cleared up by the resources of Mrs. Bunch's
powerful intellect. There were others, however, of which the explanations
furnished were less satisfactory.

One November evening Stephen was sitting by the fire in the housekeeper's room reflecting on his surroundings.

'Is Mr. Abney a good man, and will he go to heaven?' he suddenly
asked, with the peculiar confidence which children possess in the ability
of their elders to settle these questions, the decision of which is believed
to be reserved for other tribunals.

'Good? – bless the child!' said Mrs. Bunch. 'Master's as kind a soul
as ever I see! Didn't I never tell you of the little boy as he took in out
of the street, as you may say, this seven years back? and the little girl,
two years after I first come here?'

'No. Do tell me all about them, Mrs. Bunch – now this minute!'

'Well,' said Mrs. Bunch, 'the little girl I don't seem to recollect so
much about. I know master brought her back with him from his walk
one day, and give orders to Mrs. Ellis, as was housekeeper then, as she
should be took every care with. And the pore child hadn't no one belonging
to her – she told me so her own self – and here she lived with us a
matter of three weeks it might be; and then, whether she were
somethink of a gipsy in her blood or what not, but one morning she out
of her bed afore any of us had opened a eye and neither track nor yet
trace of her have I set eyes on since. Master was wonderful put about,
and had all the ponds dragged; but it's my belief she was had away by
them gipsies, for there was singing round the house for as much as an
hour the night she went, and Parkes, he declare as he heard them a-
calling in the woods all that afternoon. Dear, dear! a hodd child she was,
so silent in her ways and all, but I was wonderful taken up with her, so
domesticated she was – surprising.'

'And what about the little boy?' said Stephen.

'Ah, that pore boy!' sighed Mrs. Bunch. 'He were a foreigner –
Jevanny he called his-self – and he come a-tweaking his'urdy-gurdy
round and about the drive one winter day, and master 'ad him in that
minute, and ast all about where he came from, and how old he was, and
how he made his way, and where was his relatives, and all as kind as
heart could wish. But it went the same way with him. They're a hunruly
lot, them foreign nations, I do suppose, and he was off one fine morning
just the same as the girl. Why he went and what he done was our

question for as much as a year after; for he never took his 'urdy-gurdy, and there it lays on the shelf.'

The remainder of the evening was spent by Stephen in miscellaneous cross-examination of Mrs. Bunch and in efforts to extract a tune from the hurdy-gurdy.

That night he had a curious dream. At the end of the passage at the top of the house, in which his bedroom was situated, there was an old disused bathroom. It was kept locked, but the upper half of the door was glazed, and, since the muslin curtains which used to hang there had long been gone, you could look in and see the lead-lined bath affixed to the wall on the right hand, with its head towards the window.

On the night of which I am speaking, Stephen Elliott found himself, as he thought, looking through the glazed door. The moon was shining through the window, and he was gazing at a figure which lay in the bath.

His description of what he saw reminds me of what I once beheld myself in the famous vaults of St. Michan's Church in Dublin, which possess the horrid property of preserving corpses from decay for centuries. A figure inexpressibly thin and pathetic, of a dusty leaden colour, enveloped in a shroud-like garment, the thin lips crooked into a faint and dreadful smile, the hands pressed tightly over the region of the heart.

As he looked upon it, a distant, almost inaudible moan seemed to issue from its lips, and the arms began to stir. The terror of the sight forced Stephen backwards, and he awoke to the fact that he was indeed standing on the cold boarded floor of the passage in the full light of the moon. With a courage which I do not think can be common among boys of his age, he went to the door of the bathroom to ascertain if the figure of his dream were really there. It was not, and he went back to bed.

Mrs. Bunch was much impressed next morning by his story, and went so far as to replace the muslin curtain over the glazed door of the bathroom. Mr. Abney, moreover, to whom he confided his experiences at breakfast, was greatly interested, and made notes of the matter in what he called 'his book.'

The spring equinox was approaching, as Mr. Abney frequently reminded his cousin, adding that this had been always considered by the ancients to be a critical time for the young: that Stephen would do well to take care of himself, and to shut his bedroom window at night; and that Censorinus had some valuable remarks on the subject. Two incidents that occurred about this time made an impression upon Stephen's mind.

The first was after an unusually uneasy and oppressed night that he had passed – though he could not recall any particular dream that he had had.

The following evening Mrs. Bunch was occupying herself in mending his nightgown.

'Gracious me, Master Stephen!' she broke forth rather irritably, 'how do you manage to tear your nightdress all to flinders this way? Look here, sir, what trouble you do give to poor servants that have to darn and mend after you!'

There was indeed a most destructive and apparently wanton series of slits or scorings in the garment, which would undoubtedly require a skilful needle to make good. They were confined to the left side of the chest – long, parallel slits, about six inches in length, some of them not quite piercing the texture of the linen. Stephen could only express his entire ignorance of their origin: he was sure they were not there the night before.

'But,' he said, 'Mrs. Bunch, they are just the same as the scratches on the outside of my bedroom door; and I'm sure I never had anything to do with making *them*'.

Mrs. Bunch gazed at him open-mouthed, then snatched up a candle, departed hastily from the room, and was heard making her way upstairs. In a few minutes she came down.

'Well,' she said, 'Master Stephen, it's a funny thing to me how them marks and scratches can 'a' come there – too high up for any cat or dog to 'ave made 'em, much less a rat: for all the world like a Chinaman's fingernails, as my uncle in the tea-trade used to tell us of when we was girls together. I wouldn't say nothing to master, not if I was you, Master Stephen, my dear; and just turn the key of the door when you go to your bed.'

'I always do, Mrs. Bunch, as soon as I've said my prayers.'

'Ah, that's a good child: always say your prayers, and then no one can't hurt you.'

Herewith Mrs. Bunch addressed herself to mending the injured night-gown, with intervals of meditation, until bed-time. This was on a Friday night in March, 1812.

On the following evening the usual duet of Stephen and Mrs. Bunch was augmented by the sudden arrival of Mr. Parkes, the butler, who as a rule kept himself rather *to* himself in his own pantry. He did not see that Stephen was there: he was, moreover, flustered and less slow of speech than was his wont.

'Master may get up his own wine, if he likes, of an evening,' was his first remark. 'Either I do it in the daytime or not at all, Mrs. Bunch. I don't know what it may be: very like it's the rats, or the wind got into the cellars; but I'm not so young as I was, and I can't go through with it as I have done.'

'Well, Mr. Parkes, you know it is a surprising place for the rats, is the Hall.'

'I'm not denying that, Mrs. Bunch; and, to be sure, many a time I've heard the tale from the men in the shipyards about the rat that could speak. I never laid no confidence in that before; but to-night, if I'd demeaned myself to lay my ear to the door of the further bin, I could pretty much have heard what they was saying.'

'Oh, there, Mr. Parkes, I've no patience with your fancies! Rats talking in the winecellar indeed!'

'Well, Mrs. Bunch, I've no wish to argue with you: all I say is, if you choose to go to the far bin, and lay your ear to the door, you may prove my words this minute.'

'What nonsense you do talk, Mr. Parkes – not fit for children to listen to! Why, you'll be frightening Master Stephen there out of his wits.'

'What! Master Stephen?' said Parkes, awaking to the consciousness of the boy's presence. 'Master Stephen knows well enough when I'm a-playing a joke with you, Mrs. Bunch.'

In fact, Master Stephen knew much too well to suppose that Mr. Parkes had in the first instance intended a joke. He was interested, not altogether pleasantly, in the situation; but all his questions were unsuccessful in inducing the butler to give any more detailed account of his experiences in the wine-cellar.

We have now arrived at March 24, 1812. It was a day of curious experiences for Stephen: a windy, noisy day, which filled the house and the gardens with a restless impression. As Stephen stood by the fence of the grounds, and looked out into the park, he felt as if an endless procession of unseen people were sweeping past him on the wind, borne on resistlessly and aimlessly, vainly striving to stop themselves, to catch at something that might arrest their flight and bring them once again into contact with the living world of which they had formed a part. After luncheon that day Mr. Abney said:

'Stephen, my boy, do you think you could manage to come to me to-night as late as eleven o'clock in my study? I shall be busy until that time, and I wish to show you something connected with your future life which it is most important that you should know. You are not to mention this matter to Mrs. Bunch nor to anyone else in the house; and you had better go to your room at the usual time.'

Here was a new excitement added to life: Stephen eagerly grasped at the opportunity of sitting up till eleven o'clock. He looked in at the library door on his way upstairs that evening, and saw a brazier, which he had often noticed in the corner of the room, moved out before the fire; an old silver-gilt cup stood on the table, filled with red wine, and some written sheets of paper lay near it. Mr. Abney was sprinkling some incense on the brazier from a round silver box as Stephen passed, but did not seem to notice his step.

The wind had fallen, and there was a still night and a full moon. At about ten o'clock Stephen was standing at the open window of his bedroom, looking out over the country. Still as the night was, the mysterious population of the distant moonlit woods was not yet lulled to rest. From time to time strange cries as of lost and despairing wanderers sounded from across the mere. They might be the notes of owls or water-birds, yet they did not quite resemble either sound. Were not they coming nearer? Now they sounded from the nearer side of the water, and in a few moments they seemed to be floating about among the shrubberies. Then they ceased; but just as Stephen was thinking of shutting the window and resuming his reading of 'Robinson Crusoe,' he caught sight of two figures standing on the gravelled terrace that ran along the garden side of the Hall – the figures of a boy and girl, as it seemed; they stood side by side, looking up at the windows. Something in the form of the girl recalled irresistibly his dream of the figure in the bath. The boy inspired him with more acute fear.

Whilst the girl stood still, half smiling, with her hands clasped over her heart, the boy, a thin shape, with black hair and ragged clothing, raised his arms in the air with an appearance of menace and of unappeasable hunger and longing. The moon shone upon his almost transparent hands, and Stephen saw that the nails were fearfully long and that the light shone through them. As he stood with his arms thus raised, he disclosed a terrifying spectacle. On the left side of his chest there opened a black and gaping rent; and there fell upon Stephen's brain, rather than upon his ear, the impression of one of those hungry and desolate cries that he had heard resounding over the woods of Aswarby all that evening. In another moment this dreadful pair had moved swiftly and noiselessly over the dry gravel, and he saw them no more.

Inexpressibly frightened as he was, he determined to take his candle and go down to Mr. Abney's study, for the hour appointed for their meeting was near at hand. The study or library opened out of the front-hall on one side, and Stephen, urged on by his terrors, did not take long in getting there. To effect an entrance was not so easy. It was not locked, he felt sure, for the key was on the outside of the door as usual. His repeated knocks produced no answer. Mr. Abney was engaged: he was speaking. What! why did he try to cry out? and why was the cry choked in his throat? Had he, too, seen the mysterious children? But now everything was quiet, and the door yielded to Stephen's terrified and frantic pushing.

On the table in Mr. Abney's study certain papers were found which explained the situation to Stephen Elliott when he was of an age to understand them. The most important sentences were as follows:

'It was a belief very strongly and generally held by the ancients – of whose wisdom in these matters I have had such experience as induces me to place confidence in their assertions – that by enacting certain processes, which to us moderns have something of a barbaric complexion, a very remarkable enlightenment of the spiritual faculties in man may be attained: that, for example, by absorbing the personalities of a certain number of his fellow-creatures, an individual may gain a complete ascendancy over those orders of spiritual beings which control the elemental forces of our universe.

'It is recorded of Simon Magus that he was able to fly in the air, to become invisible, or to assume any form he pleased, by the agency of the soul of a boy whom, to use the libellous phrase employed by the author of the "Clementine Recognitions," he had "murdered." I find it set down, moreover, with considerable detail in the writings of Hermes Trismegistus, that similar happy results may be produced by the absorption of the hearts of not less than three human beings below the age of twenty-one years. To the testing of the truth of this receipt I have devoted the greater part of the last twenty years, selecting as the *corpora vilia* of my experiment such persons as could conveniently be removed without occasioning a sensible gap in society. The first step I effected by the removal of one Phœbe Stanley, a girl of gipsy extraction, on March 24, 1792. The second, by the removal of a wandering Italian lad, named Giovanni Paoli, on the night of March 23, 1805. The final "victim" – to employ a word repugnant in the highest degree to my feelings – must be my cousin, Stephen Elliott. His day must be this March 24, 1812.

'The best means of effecting the required absorption is to remove the heart from the *living* subject, to reduce it to ashes, and to mingle them with about a pint of some red wine, preferably port. The remains of the first two subjects, at least, it will be well to conceal: a disused bath-room or wine-cellar will be found convenient for such a purpose. Some annoyance may be experienced from the psychic portion of the subjects, which popular language dignifies with the name of ghosts. But the man of philosophic temperament – to whom alone the experiment is appropriate – will be little prone to attach importance to the feeble efforts of these beings to wreak their vengeance on him. I contemplate with the liveliest satisfaction the enlarged and emancipated existence which the experiment, if successful, will confer on me; not only placing me beyond the reach of human justice (so-called), but eliminating to a great extent the prospect of death itself.'

Mr. Abney was found in his chair, his head thrown back, his face stamped with an expression of rage, fright, and mortal pain. In his left side was a terrible lacerated wound, exposing the heart. There was no blood on his hands, and a long knife that lay on the table was perfectly clean. A savage wild-cat might have inflicted the injuries. The window of the study was open, and it was the opinion of the coroner that Mr. Abney had met his death by the agency of some wild creature. But Stephen Elliott's study of the papers I have quoted led him to a very different conclusion.

The Overcoat
NIKOLAI GOGOL

IN ONE OF OUR GOVERNMENT departments . . . but perhaps I had better
not say exactly *which* one. For no one's more touchy than people in
government departments, regiments, chancelleries or indeed *any* kind of
official body. Nowadays every private citizen thinks the whole of society
is insulted when he himself is. They say that not so long ago a complaint
was lodged by a District Police Inspector (I cannot remember which town
he came from) and in this he made it quite plain that the State and all
its laws were going to rack and ruin, and that his own holy name had
been taken in vain without any shadow of doubt. To substantiate his
claim he appended as supplementary evidence an absolutely enormous
tome, containing a highly romantic composition, in which nearly every
ten pages a police commissioner made an appearance, sometimes in a
very drunken state. And so, to avoid any *further* unpleasantness, we had
better call the department in question *a certain department*.

In a certain department, then, there worked *a certain civil servant*. On
no account could he be said to have a memorable appearance; he was
shortish, rather pock-marked, with reddish hair, and also had weak
eyesight, or so it seemed. He had a small bald patch in front and both
cheeks were wrinkled. His complexion was the sort you find in those
who suffer from piles . . . but there's nothing anyone can do about that:
the Petersburg climate is to blame.

As for his rank in the civil service* (this must be determined before
we go any further) he belonged to the species known as perpetual titular
councillor, for far too long now, as we all know, mocked and jeered by
certain writers with the very commendable habit of attacking those who

*The civil service was graded into a hierarchy of fourteen ranks, introduced
by Peter the Great. A titular councillor belonged to the ninth grade. (Trans.)

are in no position to retaliate. His surname was Bashmachkin, which all too plainly was at some time derived from *bashmak*.*

But exactly when and what time of day and how the name originated is a complete mystery. Both his father and his grandfather, and even his brother-in-law and all the other Bashmachkins went around in boots and had them soled only three times a year. His name was Akaky Akakievich. This may appear an odd name to our reader and somewhat far-fetched, but we can assure him that no one went out of his way to find it, and that the way things turned out he just could not have been called *anything* else. This is how it all happened: Akaky Akakievich was born on the night of 22 March, if my memory serves me right. His late mother, the wife of a civil servant and a very fine woman, made all the necessary arrangements for the christening. At the time she was still lying in her bed, facing the door, and on her right stood the godfather, Ivan Ivanovich Yeroshkin, a most excellent gentleman who was a chief clerk in the Senate, and the godmother, Arina Semyonovna Belobrushkova, the wife of a district police inspector and a woman of the rarest virtue. The mother was offered a choice of three names: Mokkia, Sossia, or Khozdazat, after the martyr. 'Oh no,' his mother thought, 'such awful names they're going in for these days!' To try and please her they turned over a few pages in the calendar† and again three peculiar names popped up: Triphily, Dula and Varakhasy. 'It's sheer punishment sent from above!' the woman muttered. 'What names! For the life of me, I've never seen anything like them. Varadat or Varukh wouldn't be so bad but as for Triphily and Varakhasy!' They turned over yet another page and found Pavsikakhy and Vakhtisy. 'Well, it's plain enough that this is fate. So we'd better call him after his father. He was an Akaky, so let's call his son Akaky as well.' And that was how he became Akaky Akakievich. The child was christened and during the ceremony he burst into tears and made such a face it was plain that he knew there and then that he was fated to be a titular councillor. The reason for all this narrative is to enable our reader to judge for himself that the whole train of events was absolutely predetermined and that for Akaky to have any other name was quite impossible.

Exactly *when* he entered the department, and who was responsible for the appointment, no one can say for sure. No matter how many directors and principals came and went, he was always to be seen in precisely the same place, sitting in exactly the same position, doing exactly the same work – just routine copying, pure and simple. Subsequently everyone came to believe that he had come into this world already equipped for his job, complete with uniform and bald patch. No one showed him the least respect in the office. The porters not only remained seated when he

bashmak – shoe.

†The Orthodox Church calendar, containing a large number of saints' days, and their names. (Trans.)

went by, but they did not so much as give him a look – as though a common house-fly had just flown across the waiting-room. Some assistant to the head clerk would shove some papers right under his nose, without even so much as saying: 'Please copy this out', or 'Here's an interesting little job', or some pleasant remark you might expect to hear in refined establishments. He would take whatever was put in front of him without looking up to see who had put it there or questioning whether he had any right to do so, his eyes fixed only on his work. He would simply take the documents and immediately start copying them out. The junior clerks laughed and told jokes at his expense – as far as office wit would stretch – telling stories they had made up themselves, even while they were standing right next to him, about his seventy-year-old landlady, for example, who used to beat him, or so they said. They would ask when the wedding was going to be and shower his head with little bits of paper, calling them snow.

But Akaky Akakievich did not make the slightest protest, just as though there were nobody there at all. His work was not even affected and he never copied out one wrong letter in the face of all this annoyance. Only if the jokes became too unbearable – when somebody jogged his elbow, for example, and stopped him from working – would he say: 'Leave me alone, why do you have to torment me?' There was something strange in these words and the way he said them. His voice had a peculiar sound which made you feel sorry for him, so much so that one clerk who was new to the department, and who was about to follow the example of the others and have a good laugh at him, suddenly stopped dead in his tracks, as though transfixed, and from that time onwards saw everything in a different light. Some kind of supernatural power alienated him from his colleagues whom, on first acquaintance, he had taken to be respectable, civilized men. And for a long time afterwards, even during his gayest moments, he would see that stooping figure with a bald patch in front, muttering pathetically: 'Leave me alone, why do you have to torment me?' And in these piercing words he could hear the sound of others: 'I am your brother.' The poor young man would bury his face in his hands and many times later in life shuddered at the thought of how brutal men could be and how the most refined manners and breeding often concealed the most savage coarseness, even, dear God, in someone universally recognized for his honesty and uprightness . . .

One would be hard put to find a man anywhere who so lived for his work. To say he worked with zeal would be an understatement: no, he worked *with love*. In that copying of his he glimpsed a whole varied and pleasant world of his own. One could see the enjoyment on his face. Some letters were his favourites, and whenever he came to write them out he would be beside himself with excitement, softly laughing to himself and winking, willing his pen on with his lips, so you could tell what letter his pen was carefully tracing just by looking at him. Had his rewards been at all commensurate with his enthusiasm, he might perhaps have been promoted to state councillor, much to his own surprise. But as the wags in the office put it, all he got for his labour was a badge in his button-hole and piles on his backside. However, you could not say he was *completely* ignored. One of the directors, a kindly gentleman, who wished to reward him for his long service, once ordered him to be given something rather more important than ordinary copying – the preparation of a report for another department from a completed file. All this entailed was altering the title page and changing a few verbs from the first to the third person. This caused him so much trouble that he broke out in a sweat, kept mopping his brow, and finally said: 'No, you'd better let me stick to plain copying.' After that they left him to go on copying for ever and ever. Apart from this copying nothing else existed as far as he was concerned. He gave no thought at all to his clothes: his uniform was not what you might call green, but a mealy white tinged with red.

His collar was very short and narrow, so that his neck, which could not exactly be called long, appeared to stick out for miles, like those plaster kittens with wagging heads foreign street-pedlars carry around by the dozen. Something was always sure to be sticking to his uniform – a wisp of straw or piece of thread. What is more, he had the strange knack of passing underneath windows just as some rubbish was being emptied and this explained why he was perpetually carrying around scraps of melon rind and similar refuse on his hat. Not once in his life did he notice what was going on in the street he passed down every day, unlike his young colleagues in the Service, who are famous for their hawk-like eyes – eyes so sharp that they can even see whose trouser-strap has come undone on the other side of the pavement, something which never fails to bring a sly grin to their faces. But even if Akaky Akakievich did happen to notice something, all he ever saw were rows of letters in his own neat, regular handwriting.

Only if a horse's muzzle appeared from out of nowhere, propped itself on his shoulder and fanned his cheek with a gust from its nostrils – only then did he realize he was not in the middle of a sentence but in the middle of the street. As soon as he got home he would sit down at the table, quickly swallow his cabbage soup, and eat some beef and onions, tasting absolutely nothing and gulping everything down, together with whatever the Good Lord happened to provide at the time, flies included. When he saw that his stomach was beginning to swell he would get up from the table, fetch his inkwell and start copying out documents he had brought home with him. If he had no work from the office, he would copy out something else, just for his own personal pleasure – especially if the document in question happened to be remarkable not for its stylistic beauty, but because it was addressed to some newly appointed or important person.

Even at that time of day when the light has completely faded from the grey St Petersburg sky and the whole clerical brotherhood has eaten its fill, according to salary and palate; when everyone has rested from departmental pen-pushing and running around; when his own and everyone else's absolutely indispensable labours have been forgotten – as well as all those other things that restless man sets himself to do of his own free will – sometimes even more than is really necessary; when the civil servant dashes off to enjoy his remaining hours of freedom as much as he can (one showing a more daring spirit by careering off to the theatre; another sauntering down the street to spend his time looking at cheap little hats in the shop windows; another going off to a party to waste his time flattering a pretty girl, the shining light of some small circle of civil servants; while another – and this happens more often than not – goes off to visit a friend from the office living on the third or second floor, in two small rooms with hall and kitchen, and with some pretensions to fashion in the form of a lamp or some little trifle which has cost a great many sacrifices, refusals to invitations to dinner or country outings); in short, at that time of day when all the civil servants have dispersed to their friends' little flats for a game of whist, sipping tea from glasses and nibbling little biscuits, drawing on their long pipes, and giving an account while dealing out the cards of the latest scandal which has wafted down from high society – a Russian can *never* resist stories; or when there is nothing new to talk about, bringing out once again the old anecdote about the Commandant who was told that the tail of the horse in Falconet's statue* of Peter the Great had been cut off; briefly, when everyone was doing his best to amuse himself, Akaky Akakievich did not abandon himself to any such pleasures.

No one could remember ever having seen him at a party. After he had copied to his heart's content he would go to bed, smiling in anticipation of the next day and what God would send him to copy. So passed the uneventful life of a man quite content with his four hundred roubles a year; and this life might have continued to pass peacefully until ripe old age had it not been for the various calamities that lie in wait not only for titular councillors, but even privy, state, court and all types of councillor, even those who give advice to no one, nor take it from anyone.

St Petersburg harbours one terrible enemy of all those earning four hundred roubles a year – or thereabouts. This enemy is nothing else than our northern frost, although some people say it is very good for the health. Between eight and nine in the morning, just when the streets are crowded with civil servants on their way to the office, it starts dealing out indiscriminately such sharp nips to noses of every description that the poor clerks just do not know where to put them.

At this time of day, when the foreheads of even important officials

*This famous statue in St Petersburg (now Leningrad) shows the horse on its hind legs, with its tail as a third support. (Trans.)

ache from the frost and tears well up in their eyes, the humbler titular councillors are sometimes quite defenceless. Their only salvation lies in running the length of five or six streets in their thin, wretched little overcoats and then having a really good stamp in the lobby until their faculties and capacity for office work have thawed out. For some time now Akaky Akakievich had been feeling that his back and shoulders had become subject to really vicious onslaughts no matter how fast he tried to sprint the official distance between home and office. At length he began to wonder if his overcoat might not be at fault here.

After giving it a thorough examination at home he found that in two or three places – to be exact, on the back and round the shoulders – it now resembled coarse cheese-cloth: the material had worn so thin that it was almost transparent and the lining had fallen to pieces.

At this point it should be mentioned that Akaky Akakievich's coat was a standing joke in the office. It had been deprived of the status of overcoat and was called a dressing-gown instead. And there was really something very strange in the way it was made. With the passing of the years the collar had shrunk more and more, as the cloth from it had been used to patch up other parts. This repair work showed no sign of a tailor's hand, and made the coat look baggy and most unsightly. When he realized what was wrong, Akaky Akakievich decided he would have to take the overcoat to Petrovich, a tailor living somewhere on the third floor up some backstairs and who, in spite of being blind in one eye and having pockmarks all over his face, carried on quite a nice little business repairing civil servants' and other gentlemen's trousers and frock-coats, whenever – it goes without saying – he was sober and was not hatching some plot in that head of his.

Of course, there is not much point in wasting our time describing this tailor, but since it has become the accepted thing to give full details about every single character in a story, there is nothing for it but to take a look at this man Petrovich.

At first he was simply called Grigory and had been a serf belonging to some gentleman or other. People started calling him Petrovich after he had gained his freedom, from which time he began to drink rather heavily on every church holiday – at first only on the most important feast-days, but later on every single holiday marked by a cross in the calendar.* In this respect he was faithful to ancestral tradition, and when he had rows about this with his wife he called her a worldly woman and a German.

As we have now brought his wife up we might as well say something about her. Unfortunately, little is known of her except that she was Petrovich's wife and she wore a bonnet instead of a shawl. Apparently she had nothing to boast about as far as looks were concerned. At least

*In the calendar of the Orthodox Church the great festivals were printed in red and the less important saints' days marked with a cross. (Trans.)

only *guardsmen* were ever known to peep under her bonnet as they tweaked their moustaches and made a curious noise in their throats.

As he made his way up the stairs to Petrovich's (these stairs, to describe them accurately, were running with water and slops, and were saturated with that strong smell of spirit which makes the eyes smart and is a perpetual feature of all backstairs in Petersburg), Akaky Akakievich was already beginning to wonder how much Petrovich would charge and making up his mind not to pay more than two roubles. The door had been left open as his wife had been frying some kind of fish and had made so much smoke in the kitchen that not even the cockroaches were visible.

Mrs. Petrovich herself failed to notice Akaky Akakievich as he walked through the kitchen and finally entered a room where Petrovich was squatting on a broad, bare wooden table, his feet crossed under him like a Turkish Pasha. As is customary with tailors, he was working in bare feet. The first thing that struck Akaky was his familiar big toe with its deformed nail, thick and hard as tortoiseshell. A skein of silk and some thread hung round his neck and some old rags lay across his lap. For the past two or three minutes he had been trying to thread a needle without any success, which made him curse the poor light and even the thread itself. He grumbled under his breath: 'Why don't you go through, you swine! You'll be the death of me, you devil!'

Akaky Akakievich was not very pleased at finding Petrovich in such a temper: his real intention had been to place an order with Petrovich after he had been on the bottle, or, as his wife put it, 'after he'd bin swigging that corn brandy again, the old one-eyed devil!'

In this state Petrovich would normally be very amenable, invariably agreeing to any price quite willingly and even concluding the deal by bowing and saying thank you. It is true that afterwards his tearful wife would come in with the same sad story that that husband of hers was drunk again and had not charged enough. But even so, for another kopeck or two the deal was usually settled. But at this moment Petrovich was (or so it seemed) quite sober, and as a result was gruff, intractable and in the right mood for charging the devil's own price. Realizing this, Akaky Akakievich was all for making himself scarce, as the saying goes, but by then it was too late. Petrovich had already screwed up his one eye and was squinting steadily at him. Akaky Akakievich found himself saying:

'Good morning, Petrovich!'

'Good morning to you, sir,' said Petrovich, staring at Akaky's hand to see how much money he had on him.

'I . . . er . . . came about that . . . Petrovich.'

The reader should know that Akaky Akakievich spoke mainly in prepositions, adverbs, and resorted to parts of speech which had no meaning whatsoever. If the subject was particularly complicated he would even leave whole sentences unfinished, so that very often he would begin with: 'That is really exactly what . . .' and then forget to say anything more, convinced that he had said what he wanted to.

'What on earth's that?' Petrovich said, inspecting with his solitary eye every part of Akaky's uniform, beginning with the collar and sleeves, then the back, tails and buttonholes. All of this was very familiar territory, as it was his own work, but every tailor usually carries out this sort of inspection when he has a customer.

'I've er . . . come . . . Petrovich, that overcoat you know, the cloth . . . you see, it's quite strong in other places, only a little dusty. This makes it look old, but in fact it's quite new. Just a bit . . . you know . . . on the back and a little worn on one shoulder, and a bit . . . you know, on the other, that's all. Only a small job . . .'

Petrovich took the 'dressing-gown', laid it out on the table, took a long look at it, shook his head, reached out to the window-sill for his round snuff-box bearing the portrait of some general – exactly which one is hard to say, as someone had poked his finger through the place where his face should have been and it was pasted over with a square piece of paper.

Petrovich took a pinch of snuff, held the coat up to the light gave it another thorough scrutiny and shook his head again. Then he placed it with the lining upwards, shook his head once more, removed the snuff-box lid with the pasted-over general, filled his nose with snuff, replaced the lid, put the box away somewhere, and finally said: 'No, I can't mend that. It's in a *terrible* state!'

With these words Akaky Akakievich's heart sank.

'And why not, Petrovich?' he asked in the imploring voice of a child. 'It's only a bit worn on the shoulders. Really, you could *easily* patch it up.'

'I've got plenty of patches, plenty,' said Petrovich. 'But I can't sew them all up together. The coat's absolutely rotten. It'll fall to pieces if you so much as touch it with a needle.'

'Well, if it falls to bits you can patch it up again.'

'But it's too far gone. There's nothing for the patches to hold on to. You can hardly call it cloth at all. One gust of wind and the whole lot will blow away.'

'But patch it up just a *little*. It can't, hm, be, well . . .'

'I'm afraid it can't be done, sir,' replied Petrovich firmly. It's too far gone. You'd be better off if you cut it up for the winter and made some leggings with it, because socks aren't any good in the really cold weather. The Germans invented them as they thought they could make money out of them.' (Petrovich liked to have a dig at Germans.) 'As for the coat, you'll have to have a *new* one, sir.'

The word 'new' made Akaky's eyes cloud over and everything in the room began to swim round. All he could see clearly was the pasted-over face of the general on Petrovich's snuff-box.

'What do you mean, a *new* one?' he said as though in a dream. 'I've got no money.'

'Yes, you'll have to have a new one,' Petrovich said in a cruelly detached voice.

'Well, um, if I had a *new* one, how would, I mean to say, er . . .?'

'You mean, how much?'

'Yes.'

'You can reckon on three fifty-rouble notes or more,' said Petrovich pressing his lips together dramatically. He had a great liking for strong dramatic effects, and loved producing some remark intended to shock and then watching the expression on the other person's face out of the corner of his eye.

'A hundred and fifty roubles for an overcoat!' poor Akaky shrieked for what was perhaps the first time in his life – he was well known for his low voice.

'Yes, sir,' said Petrovich. 'And even then it wouldn't be much to write home about. If you want a collar made from marten fur and a silk-lined hood then it could set you back as much as two hundred.'

'Petrovich, please,' said Akaky imploringly, not hearing, or at least, trying not to hear Petrovich's 'dramatic' pronouncement, 'just do what you can with it, so I can wear it a little longer.'

'I'm afraid it's no good. It would be sheer waste of time and money,' Petrovich added, and with these words Akaky left, feeling absolutely crushed.

After he had gone Petrovich stayed squatting where he was for some time without continuing his work, his lips pressed together significantly. He felt pleased he had not cheapened himself or the rest of the sartorial profession.

Out in the street Akaky felt as if he were in a dream. 'What a to-do now,' he said to himself. 'I never thought it would turn out like this, for the life of me . . .' And then, after a brief silence, he added: 'Well now then! So this is how it's turned out and I would never have guessed it would end . . .' Whereupon followed a long silence, after which he murmured: 'So that's it! Really, to tell the truth, it's so unexpected that I never would have . . . such a to-do!' When he had said this, instead of going home, he walked straight off in the opposite direction, quite oblivious of what he was doing. On the way a chimney-sweeper brushed up against him and made his shoulder black all over. And then a whole hatful of lime fell on him from the top of a house that was being built. To this he was blind as well; and only when he happened to bump into a policeman who had propped his halberd up and was sprinkling some snuff he had taken from a small horn on to his wart-covered fist did he come to his senses at all, and only then because the policeman said:

'Isn't the pavement wide enough without you having to crawl right up my nose?'

This brought Akaky to his senses and he went off in the direction of home.

Not until he was there did he begin to collect his thoughts and properly assess the situation. He started talking to himself, not in incoherent phrases, but quite rationally and openly, as though he were discussing what had happened with a sensible friend in whom one could confide when it came to matters of the greatest intimacy.

'No, I can see it's impossible to talk to Petrovich now. He's a bit . . . and it looks as if his wife's been knocking him around. I'd better wait until Sunday morning: after he's slept off Saturday night he'll start his squinting again and will be dying for a drink to see him through his hangover. But his wife won't give him any money, so I'll turn up with a kopeck or two. That will soften him up, you know, and my overcoat . . .'

Akaky Akakievich felt greatly comforted by this fine piece of reasoning, and waiting until Sunday came went straight off to Petrovich's. He spotted his wife leaving the house some distance away. Just as he had expected, after Saturday night, Petrovich's eye really was squinting for all it was worth, and there he was, his head drooping towards the floor, and looking very sleepy. All the same, as soon as he realized why Akaky had come, he became wide awake, just as though the devil had given him a sharp kick.

'It's impossible, you'll have to have a new one.' At this point Akaky Akakievich shoved a ten-kopeck piece into his hand.

'Much obliged, sir. I'll have a quick pick-me-up on you,' said Petrovich. 'And I shouldn't worry about that overcoat of yours if I were you. It's no good at all. I'll make you a *marvellous* new one, so let's leave it at that.'

Akaky Akakievich tried to say something about having it repaired, but Petrovich pretended not to hear and said:

'Don't worry, I'll make you a brand-new one, you can depend on me to make a good job of it. And I might even get some silver clasps for the collar, like they're all wearing now.'

Now Akaky Akakievich realized he would *have* to buy a new overcoat and his heart sank. Where was the money coming from? Of course he could just about count on that holiday bonus. But this had been put aside for something else a long time ago. He needed new trousers, and then there was that long-standing debt to be settled with the shoemaker for putting some new tops on his old boots. And there were three shirts he had to order from the seamstress, as well as two items of underwear which cannot decently be mentioned in print. To cut a long story short, all his money was bespoke and he would not have enough even if the Director were so generous as to raise his bonus to forty-five or even fifty roubles. What was left was pure chicken-feed; in terms of *overcoat* finance, the merest drop in the ocean. Also, he knew very well that at times Petrovich would suddenly take it into his head to charge the most fantastic price, so that even his wife could not help saying about him:

'Has he gone out of his mind, the old fool! One day he'll work for next to nothing, and now the devil's making him charge more than he's worth himself!'

He knew very well, however, that Petrovich would take eighty roubles; but the question still remained, where was he to get them from? He could just about scrape half of it together, perhaps a little more. But what about the balance? Before we go into this, the reader should know where the *first* half was coming from.

For every rouble he spent, Akaky Akakievich would put half a kopeck away in a small box, which had a little slot in the lid for dropping money through, and which was kept locked. Every six months he would tot up his savings and change them into silver. He had been doing this for a long time, and over several years had amassed more than forty roubles. So, he had half the money, but what about the rest?

Akaky Akakievich thought and thought, and at last decided he would have to cut down on his day-to-day spending, for a year at least: he would have to stop drinking tea in the evenings; go without a candle; and, if he had copying to do, go to his landlady's room and work there. He would have to step as carefully and lightly as possible over the cobbles in the street – almost on tiptoe – to save the soles of his shoes; avoid taking his personal linen to the laundress as much as possible; and, to make his underclothes last longer, take them off when he got home and only wear his thick cotton dressing-gown – itself an ancient garment and one which time had treated kindly. Frankly, Akaky Akakievich found these privations quite a burden to begin with, but after a while he got used to them. He even trained himself to go without any food at all in the evenings, for his nourishment was *spiritual*, his thoughts always full of that overcoat which one day was to be his. From that time onwards his whole life seemed to have become richer, as though he had married and another human being was by his side. It was as if he was not alone at all but had some pleasant companion who had agreed to tread life's path together with him; and this companion was none other than the overcoat with its thick cotton-wool padding and strong lining, made to last a lifetime. He livened up and, like a man who has set himself a goal, became more determined.

His indecision and uncertainty – in short, the vague and hesitant side of his personality – just disappeared of its own accord. At times a fire shone in his eyes, and even such daring and audacious thoughts as: 'Now, what about having a *marten* collar?' flashed through his mind.

All these reflections very nearly turned his mind. Once he was not far from actually making a *copying mistake*, so that he almost cried out

'Ugh!' and crossed himself. At least once a month he went to Petrovich's to see how the overcoat was getting on and to inquire where was the best place to buy cloth, what colour they should choose, and what price they should pay. Although slightly worried, he always returned home contented, thinking of the day when all the material would be bought and the overcoat finished. Things progressed quicker than he had ever hoped. The Director allowed Akaky Akakievich not forty or forty-five, but a whole *sixty* roubles bonus, which was beyond his wildest expectations. Whether that was because the Director had some premonition that he needed a new overcoat, or whether it was just pure chance, Akaky Akakievich found himself with an extra twenty roubles. And as a result every thing was speeded up. After another two or three months of mild starvation Akaky Akakievich had saved up the eighty roubles. His heart, which usually had a very steady beat, started pounding away. The very next day off he went shopping with Petrovich. They bought some *very* fine material, and no wonder, since they had done nothing but discuss it for the past six months and scarcely a month had gone by without their calling in at all the shops to compare prices. What was more, even Petrovich said you could not buy better cloth anywhere. For the lining they simply chose calico, but calico so strong and of such high quality that, according to Petrovich, it was finer than silk and even had a smarter and glossier look.

They did not buy marten for the collar, because it was really too expensive, but instead they settled on cat fur, the finest cat they could find in the shops and which could easily be mistaken for marten from a distance. In all, Petrovich took two weeks to finish the overcoat as there was so much quilting to be done. Otherwise it would have been ready much sooner. Petrovich charged twelve roubles – anything less was out of the question. He had used silk thread everywhere, with fine double seams, and had gone over them with his teeth afterwards to make different patterns.

It was . . . precisely *which* day it is difficult to say, but without any doubt it was the most triumphant day in Akaky Akakievich's whole life when Petrovich at last delivered the overcoat. He brought it early in the morning, even before Akaky Akakievich had left for the office. The overcoat could not have arrived at a better time, since fairly severe frosts had already set in and were likely to get even worse. Petrovich delivered the overcoat in person – just as a good tailor should. Akaky Akakievich had never seen him looking so solemn before. He seemed to know full well that his was no mean achievement, and that he had suddenly shown by his own work the gulf separating tailors who only relined or patched up overcoats from those who make new ones, right from the beginning. He took the overcoat out of the large kerchief he had wrapped it in and which he had only just got back from the laundry. Then he folded the kerchief and put it in his pocket ready for use. Then he took the overcoat very proudly in both hands and threw it very deftly round Akaky Akakievich's shoulders. He gave it a sharp tug, smoothed it downwards on the back, and draped it round Akaky Akakievich, leaving some buttons in the front undone. Akaky Akakievich, who was no longer a young man, wanted to try it with his arms in the sleeves. Petrovich helped him, and even this way it was the right size. In short, the overcoat was a perfect fit, without any shadow of doubt. Petrovich did not forget to mention it was only *because* he happened to live in a small backstreet and *because* his workshop had no sign outside, and *because* he had known Akaky Akakievich such a long time, that he had charged him such a low price. If he had gone anywhere along Nevsky Avenue they would have rushed him seventy-five roubles for the labour alone. Akaky Akakievich did not feel like taking Petrovich up on this and in fact was rather intimidated by the large sums Petrovich was so fond of mentioning just to try and impress his clients. He settled up with him, thanked him and went straight off to the office in his new overcoat. Petrovich followed him out into the street, stood there for a long time having a look at the overcoat from some way off, and then deliberately made a small detour up a side street so that he could have a good view of the overcoat from the other side, i.e. coming straight towards him.

Meanwhile Akaky Akakievich continued on his way to the office in the most festive mood. Not one second passed without his being conscious of the new overcoat on his shoulders, and several times he even smiled from inward pleasure. And really the overcoat's advantages were two-fold: firstly, it was warm; secondly, it made him feel good. He did not notice where he was going at all and suddenly found himself at the office. In the lobby he took the overcoat off, carefully examined it all over, and then handed it to the porter for special safe-keeping.

No one knew how the news suddenly got round that Akaky Akakievich had a new overcoat and that his 'dressing-gown' was now no more. The moment he arrived everyone rushed out into the lobby to look at his new acquisition. They so overwhelmed him with congratulations and good wishes that he smiled at first and then he even began to feel quite embarrassed. When they all crowded round him saying they should have a drink on the new overcoat, and insisting that the *very least* he could do was to hold a party for all of them, Akaky Akakievich lost his head completely, not knowing what to do or what to answer or how to escape. Blushing all over, he tried for some considerable time, rather naively, to convince them it was not a new overcoat at all but really his old one. In the end one of the civil servants, who was nothing less than an assistant head clerk, and who was clearly anxious to show he was not at all snooty and could hobnob even with his inferiors, said: 'All right then, *I'll* throw a party instead. You're all invited over to my place this evening. It so happens it's my name-day.'

Naturally the others immediately offered the assistant head clerk their congratulations and eagerly accepted the invitation. When Akaky Akakievich tried to talk himself out of it, everyone said it was impolite, in fact quite shameful, and a refusal was out of the question. Later, however, he felt pleased when he remembered that the party would give him the opportunity of going out in his new overcoat that very same evening.

The whole day was like a triumphant holiday for Akaky Akakievich. He went home in the most jubilant mood, took off his coat, hung it up very carefully and stood there for some time admiring the cloth and lining. Then, to compare the two, he brought out his old 'dressing-gown', which by now had completely disintegrated. As he examined it he could not help laughing: what a *fantastic* difference! All through dinner the thought of his old overcoat and its shocking state made him smile. He ate his meal with great relish and afterwards did not do any copying but indulged in the luxury of lying on his bed until it grew dark. Then, without any further delay, he put his clothes on, threw his overcoat over his shoulders and went out into the street. Unfortunately the author cannot say exactly where the civil servant who was giving the party lived: his memory is beginning to let him down badly and everything in Petersburg, every house, every street, has become so blurred and mixed up in his mind that he finds it extremely difficult to say where *anything* is at all. All the same, we do at least know for certain that the civil servant lived in the *best part* of the city, which amounts to saying that he lived miles and miles away from Akaky Akakievich. At first Akaky Akakievich had to pass through some badly lit, deserted streets, but the nearer he got to the civil servant's flat the more lively and crowded they became, and the brighter the lamps shone. More and more people dashed by and he began to meet beautifully dressed ladies, and men with beaver collars. Here there were not so many cheap cabmen* with their wooden basketwork sleighs studded with gilt nails. Instead, there were dashing coachmen with elegant cabs, wearing crimson velvet caps, their sleighs lacquered and covered with bearskins. Carriages with draped boxes simply flew down the streets with their wheels screeching over the snow.

Akaky Akakievich surveyed this scene as though he had never witnessed anything like it in his life. For some years now he had not ventured out at all in the evenings.

Filled with curiosity, he stopped by a brightly lit shop window to look at a painting of a pretty girl who was taking off her shoe and showing her entire leg, which was not at all bad-looking, while behind her a gentleman with side-whiskers and a fine goatee was poking his head round the door of an adjoining room. Akaky Akakievich shook his head and smiled, then went on his way. Why did he smile? Perhaps because this was something he had never set eyes on before, but for which, nonetheless, each one of us has some instinctive feeling. Or perhaps, like

*Gogol here uses the word 'Vanka', diminutive of Ivan, the popular term for a cabman with an old, slow horse and ramshackle cab. (Trans.)

many other civil servants he thought: 'Oh, those Frenchmen! Of course, if they happen to fancy something, then really, I mean to say, to be exact, something . . .' Perhaps he was not thinking this at all, for it is impossible to probe deep into a man's soul and discover all his thoughts. Finally he arrived at the assistant head clerk's flat. This assistant head clerk lived in the grand style: a lamp shone on the staircase, and the flat was on the first floor.

As he entered the hall Akaky Akakievich saw row upon row of galoshes. Among them, in the middle of the room, stood a samovar, hissing as it sent out clouds of steam. The walls were covered with overcoats and cloaks; some of them even had beaver collars or velvet lapels. From the other side of the wall he could hear the buzzing of voices, which suddenly became loud and clear when the door opened and there emerged a footman carrying a tray laden with empty glasses, a jug of cream and a basketful of biscuits. There was no doubt at all that the clerks had been there a long time and had already drunk their first cup of tea.

When Akaky Akakievich had hung up his overcoat himself he went in and was struck all at once by the sight of candles, civil servants, pipes and card tables. His ears were filled with the blurred sound of little snatches of conversation coming from all over the room and the noise of chairs being shifted backwards and forwards. He stood very awkwardly in the middle of the room, looking around and trying to think what to do. But they had already spotted him and greeted him with loud shouts, everyone immediately crowding into the hall to have another look at the overcoat. Although he was somewhat overwhelmed by this reception, since he was a rather simple-minded and ingenuous person, he could not help feeling glad at the praises showered on his overcoat. And then, it goes without saying, they abandoned him, overcoat included, and turned their attention to the customary whist tables. All the noise and conversation and crowds of people – this was a completely new world for Akaky Akakievich. He simply did not know what to do, where to put his hands or feet or any other part of himself. Finally he took a seat near the card-players, looking at the cards, and examining first one player's face, then another's. In no time at all he started yawning and began to feel bored, especially as it was long after his usual bedtime.

He tried to take leave of his host, but everyone insisted on his staying to toast the new overcoat with a glassful of champagne. About an hour later supper was served. This consisted of mixed salad, cold veal, meat pasties, pastries and champagne. They made Akaky Akakievich drink two glasses, after which everything seemed a lot merrier, although he still could not forget that it was already midnight and that he should have left ages ago.

So that his host should not stop him on the way out, he crept silently from the room, found his overcoat in the hall (much to his regret it was lying on the floor), shook it to remove every trace of fluff, put it over his shoulders and went down the stairs into the street.

Outside it was still lit-up. A few small shops, which house-serfs and different kinds of people use as clubs at all hours of the day were open. Those which were closed had broad beams of light coming from chinks right the way down their doors, showing that there were still people talking inside, most probably maids and menservants who had not finished exchanging the latest gossip, leaving their masters completely in the dark as to where they had got to. Akaky Akakievich walked along in high spirits, and once, heavens know why, very nearly gave chase to some lady who flashed by like lightning, every part of her body showing an extraordinary mobility. However, he stopped in his tracks and continued at his previous leisurely pace, amazed at himself for breaking into that inexplicable trot. Soon there stretched before him those same empty streets which looked forbidding enough even in the daytime, let alone at night. Now they looked even more lonely and deserted. The street lamps thinned out more and more – the local council was stingy with its oil in this part of the town. Next he began to pass by wooden houses and fences. Not a soul anywhere, nothing but the snow gleaming in the streets and the cheerless dark shapes of low-built huts which, with their shutters closed, seemed to be asleep. He was now quite near the spot where the street was interrupted by an endless square with the houses barely visible on the other side: a terrifying desert. In the distance, God knows where, a light glimmered in a watchman's hut which seemed to be standing on the very edge of the world. At this point Akaky Akakievich's high spirits drooped considerably. As he walked out on to the square, he could not suppress the feeling of dread that welled up inside him, as though he sensed that something evil was going to happen. He looked back, then to both sides: it was as though he was surrounded by a whole ocean. 'No, it's best not to look,' he thought, and continued on his way with his eyes shut. When at last he opened them to see how much further he had to go he suddenly saw two men with moustaches right in front of him, although it was too dark to make them out exactly. His eyes misted over and his heart started pounding.

'Aha, that's *my* overcoat all right,' one of them said in a thunderous voice, grabbing him by the collar. Akaky Akakievich was about to shout for help, but the other man stuck a fist the size of a clerk's head right in his face and said: 'Just one squeak out of you!' All Akaky Akakievich knew was that they pulled his coat off and shoved a knee into him, making him fall backwards in the snow, after which he knew nothing more. A few minutes later he came to and managed to stand up, but by then there was no one to be seen. All he knew was that he was freezing and that his overcoat had gone, and he started shouting. But his voice would not carry across the vast square. Not once did he stop shouting as he ran desperately across the square towards a sentry box where a policeman stood propped up on his halberd looking rather intrigued as to who the devil was shouting and running towards him. When he had reached the policeman Akaky Akakievich (in between breathless gasps) shouted accusingly that he had been asleep, that he was neglecting his duty and could not even see when a man was being robbed under his very nose. The policeman replied that he had seen nothing, except for two men who had stopped him in the middle of the square and whom he had taken for his friends; and that instead of letting off steam he would be better advised to go the very next day to see the Police Inspector, who would get his overcoat back for him. Akaky Akakievich ran off home in the most shocking state: his hair – there was still some growing around the temples and the back of his head – was terribly dishevelled. His chest, his trousers, and his sides were covered with snow. When his old landlady heard a terrifying knocking at the door she leaped out of bed and rushed downstairs with only one shoe on, clutching her nightdress to her bosom out of modesty. But when she opened the door and saw the state Akaky Akakievich was in, she shrank backwards. After he had told her what had happened she clasped her hands in despair and told him to go straight to the District Police Superintendent, as the local officer was sure to try and put one over on him, make all kinds of promises and lead him right up the garden path. The best thing was to go direct to the Superintendent himself, whom she actually happened to know, as Anna, the Finnish girl who used to cook for her, was now a nanny at the Superintendent's house. She often saw him go past the houses and every Sunday he went to church, smiled at everyone as he prayed and to all intents and purposes was a thoroughly nice man. Akaky Akakievich listened to this advice and crept sadly up to his room. What sort of night he spent can best be judged by those who are able to put themselves in someone else's place. Early next morning he went to the Superintendent's house but was told that he was asleep. He returned at ten o'clock, but was informed that he was still asleep. He came back at eleven, and was told that he had gone out. When he turned up once again round about lunchtime, the clerks in the entrance hall would not let him through on any account, unless he told them first what his business was, why he had come, and what had happened. So in the end Akaky Akakievich, for the first time in his life, stood up for himself and told them in no uncertain terms that he wanted to see the Superintendent *in person*, that they dare not turn him away since he had come from a government department, and that they would know all about it if he made a complaint. The clerks did not have the nerve to argue and one of them went to fetch the Superintendent who reacted extremely strangely to the robbery. Instead of sticking to the main point of the story, he started cross-examining Akaky Akakievich with such questions as: 'What was he doing out so late?' or 'Had he been visiting a brothel?', which left Akaky feeling very embarrassed, and he went away completely in the dark as to whether they were going to take any action or not. The whole of that day he stayed away from the office – for the first time in his life.

The next morning he arrived looking very pale and wearing his old dressing-gown, which was in an even more pathetic state.

The story of the stolen overcoat touched many of the clerks, although a few of them could not refrain from laughing at Akaky Akakievich even then. There and then they decided to make a collection, but all they raised was a miserable little sum since, apart from any *extra* expense, they had nearly exhausted all their funds subscribing to a new portrait of the Director as well as to some book or other recommended by one of the heads of department – who happened to be a friend of the author. So they collected next to nothing.

One of them, who was deeply moved, decided he could at least help Akaky Akakievich with some good advice. He told him not to go to the local police officer, since although that gentleman might well recover his overcoat somehow or other in the hope of receiving a commendation from his superiors, Akaky did not have a chance of getting it out of the police station without the necessary legal proof that the overcoat was really his. The best plan was to apply to a certain *Important Person*, and this same Important Person, by writing to and contacting the proper people, would get things moving much faster. There was nothing else for it, so Akaky Akakievich decided to go and see this Important Person.

What exactly this Important Person did and what position he held remains a mystery to this day. All we need say is that this Important Person had become important only a short while before, and that until then he had been an *unimportant* person. However, even now his position was not considered very important if compared with others which were still more important. But you will always come across a certain class of people who consider something unimportant which for other people is in fact important. However, he tried all manners and means of buttressing his importance. For example, he was responsible for introducing the rule that all low-ranking civil servants should be waiting to meet him on the stairs when he arrived at the office; that no one, on any account, could walk straight into his office; and that everything must be dealt with in the *strictest* order of priority: the collegiate registrar was to report to the provincial secretary who in turn was to report to the titular councillor (or whoever it was he *had* to report to) so that in this way the matter reached him according to the prescribed procedure. In this Holy Russia of ours everything is infected by a mania for imitation, and everyone apes his superior. I have even heard say that when a certain titular councillor was appointed head of some minor government department he immediately partitioned off a section of his office into a special room for himself, an 'audience chamber' as he called it, and made two ushers in uniforms with red collars and gold braid stand outside to open the doors for visitors

– even though you would have a job getting an ordinary writing desk into this so-called chamber.

This Important Person's routine was very imposing and impressive, but nonetheless simple. The whole basis of his system was strict discipline. 'Discipline, discipline, and . . . discipline' he used to say, usually looking very solemnly into the face of the person he was addressing when he had repeated this word for the third time. However, there was really no good reason for this strict discipline, since the ten civil servants or so who made up the whole administrative machinery of his department were all duly terrified of him anyway. If they saw him coming from some way off they would stop what they were doing and stand to attention while the Director went through the office. His normal everyday conversation with his subordinates simply *reeked* of discipline and consisted almost entirely of three phrases: 'How dare you? Do you know who you're talking to? Do you realize who's standing before you?'

However, he was quite a good man at heart, pleasant to his colleagues and helpful. But his promotion to general's rank had completely turned his head; he became all mixed up, somehow went off the rails, and just could not cope any more. If he happened to be with someone of equal rank, then he was quite a normal person, very decent in fact and indeed far from stupid in many respects.

But put him with people only one rank lower, and he was really at sea. He would not say a single word, and one felt sorry to see him in such a predicament, all the more so as even *he* felt that he could have been spending the time far more enjoyably.

One could read this craving for interesting company and conversation in his eyes, but he was always inhibited by the thought: would this be going too far for someone in his position, would this be showing too much familiarity and therefore rather damaging to his status? For these reasons he would remain perpetually silent, producing a few monosyllables from time to time, and as a result acquired the reputation of being a terrible bore. This was the Important Person our Akaky Akakievich went to consult, and he appeared at the worst possible moment – most inopportune as far as *he* was concerned – but most opportune for the Important Person. The Important Person was in his office having a very animated talk with an old childhood friend who had just arrived in Petersburg and whom he had not seen for a few years.

At this moment the arrival of a certain Bashmachkin was announced. 'Who's he?' he asked abruptly and was told, 'Some clerk or other.' 'Ah, let him wait, I can't see him just now,' the Important Person replied. Here we should say that the Important Person told a complete lie: he had plenty of time, he had long since said all he wanted to his friend, and for some considerable time their conversation had been punctuated by very long silences broken only by their slapping each other on the thigh and saying:

'Quite so, Ivan Abramovich!' and 'Well yes; Stepan Varlamovich!'

Even so, he still ordered the clerk to wait, just to show his old friend (who had left the Service a fair time before and was now nicely settled in his country house) how long he could keep clerks standing about in his waiting-room. When they really had said all that was to be said, or rather, had sat there in the very comfortable easy chairs to their heart's content without saying a single word to each other, puffing away at their cigars, the Important Person suddenly remembered and told his secretary, who was standing by the door with a pile of papers in his hands: 'Ah yes now, I think there's some clerk or other waiting out there. Tell him to come in.' One look at the timid Akaky Akakievich in his ancient uniform and he suddenly turned towards him and said: 'What do *you* want?' in that brusque and commanding voice he had been practising especially, when he was alone in his room, in front of a mirror, a whole week before his present appointment and promotion to general's rank.

Long before this Akaky Akakievich had been experiencing that feeling of awe which it was proper and necessary for him to experience, and now, somewhat taken aback, he tried to explain, as far as his tongue would allow him and with an even greater admixture than ever before of 'wells' and 'that is to says', that his overcoat was a new one, that he had been robbed in the most barbarous manner, that he had come to ask the Important Person's help, so that through his influence, or by doing this or that, by writing to the Chief of Police or someone else (whoever it might be), the Important Person might get his overcoat back for him.

Heaven knows why, but the general found this approach rather too familiar.

'What do you mean by this, sir?' he snapped again. 'Are you unaware of the correct procedure? Where do you think you are? Don't you know how things are conducted here? It's high time you knew that first of all your application must be handed in at the main office, then taken to the chief clerk, then to the departmental director, then to my secretary, who *then* submits it to me for consideration...'

'But Your Excellency,' said Akaky Akakievich, trying to summon up the small handful of courage he possessed, and feeling at the same time that the sweat was pouring off him, 'I took the liberty of disturbing Your Excellency because, well, secretaries, you know, are a rather unreliable lot...'

'What, what, what?' cried the Important Person. 'Where did you learn such impudence? Where did you get those ideas from? What rebellious attitude has infected the young men these days?'

Evidently the Important Person did not notice that Akaky Akakievich was well past fifty. Of course, one might call him a young man, relatively speaking; that is, if you compared him with someone of seventy.

'Do you realize who you're talking to? Do you know who is standing before you? Do you understand, I ask you, do you understand? I'm asking you a question!'

At this point he stamped his foot and raised his voice to such a pitch that Akaky Akakievich was not the only one to be scared out of his wits. Akaky Akakievich almost fainted. He reeled forward, his body shook all over and he could hardly stand on his feet. If the porters had not rushed to his assistance he would have fallen flat on the floor. He was carried out almost lifeless. The Important Person, very satisfied that the effect he had produced exceeded even *his* wildest expectations, and absolutely delighted that a few words from him could deprive a man of his senses, peeped at his friend out of the corner of one eye to see what impression he had made. He was not exactly displeased to see that his friend was quite bewildered and was even beginning to show unmistakable signs of fear himself.

Akaky Akakievich remembered nothing about going down the stairs and out into the street. His hands and feet had gone dead. Never in his life had he received such a savage dressing-down from a general – and what is more, a general from another department.

He continually stumbled off the pavement as he struggled on with his mouth wide open in the face of a raging blizzard that whistled down the street. As it normally does in St Petersburg the wind was blowing from all four corners of the earth and from every single side-street. In a twinkling his throat was inflamed and when he finally dragged himself home he was unable to say one word. He put himself to bed and broke out all over in swellings. That is what a 'proper and necessary' dressing-down can sometimes do for you!

The next day he had a high fever. Thanks to the generous assistance of the Petersburg climate the illness made much speedier progress than one might have expected, and when the doctor arrived and felt his pulse, all he could prescribe was a poultice – and only then for the simple reason that he did not wish his patient to be deprived of the salutary benefits of medical aid. However, he *did* advance the diagnosis that Akaky Akakievich would not last another day and a half, no doubt about that, and then: *kaput*. After which he turned to the landlady and said:

'Now, don't waste any time and order a pine coffin right away, as he won't be able to afford oak.'

Whether Akaky Akakievich heard these fateful words – and if he did hear them, whether they shocked him into some feeling of regret for his wretched life – no one has the slightest idea, since he was feverish and delirious the whole time. Strange visions, each weirder than the last, paraded endlessly before him: in one he could see Petrovich the tailor and he was begging him to make an overcoat with special traps to catch the thieves that seemed to be swarming under his bed. Every other minute he called out to his landlady to drag one out which had actually crawled under the blankets.

In another he was asking why his old 'dressing-gown' was hanging up there when he had a *new* overcoat. Then he imagined himself standing next to the general and, after being duly and properly reprimanded, saying: 'I'm sorry, Your Excellency.' In the end he started cursing and swearing and let forth such a torrent of terrible obscenities that his good landlady crossed herself, as she had never heard the like from him in all her born days, especially as the curses always seemed to follow right after those 'Your Excellencies'. Later on he began to talk complete gibberish, until it was impossible to understand anything, except that this jumble of words and thoughts always centred on one and the same overcoat. Finally poor Akaky Akakievich gave up the ghost. Neither his room nor what he had in the way of belongings was sealed off,* in the first place, because he had no family, and in the second place, because his worldly possessions did not amount to very much at all: a bundle of goose quills, one quire of white government paper, three pairs of socks, two or three buttons that had come off his trousers, and the 'dressing-gown' with which the reader is already familiar. Whom all this went to, God only knows, and the author of this story confesses that he is not even interested. Akaky Akakievich was carted away and buried. And St Petersburg carried on without its Akaky Akakievich just as though he had never even existed.

So vanished and disappeared for ever a human being whom no one ever thought of protecting, who was dear to no one, in whom no one was the least interested, not even the naturalist who cannot resist sticking a pin in a common fly and examining it under the microscope; a being who endured the mockery of his colleagues without protesting, who went to his grave without any undue fuss, but to whom, nonetheless (although not until his last days) a shining visitor in the form of an overcoat suddenly appeared, brightening his wretched life for one fleeting moment; a being upon whose head disaster had cruelly fallen, just as it falls upon the kings and great ones of this earth . . .

A few days after his death a messenger was sent with instructions for him to report to the office *immediately*: it was the Director's own orders. But the messenger was obliged to return on his own and announced that Akaky would not be coming any more. When asked why not he replied: ''Cos 'e's dead, bin dead these four days.' This was how the office got to know about Akaky Akakievich's death, and on the very next day his place was taken by a new clerk, a much taller man whose handwriting was not nearly so upright and indeed had a pronounced slope.

But who would have imagined that this was not the last of Akaky Akakievich, and that he was destined to create quite a stir several days after his death, as though he were trying to make up for a life spent

*The police normally sealed off the house or flat of someone dying without any family or heirs. (Trans.)

being ignored by everybody? But this is what happened and it provides our miserable story with a totally unexpected, fantastic ending. Rumours suddenly started going round St Petersburg that a ghost in the form of a government clerk had been seen near the Kalinkin Bridge, and even further afield, and that this ghost appeared to be searching for a lost overcoat. To this end it was to be seen ripping all kinds of overcoats from everyone's shoulders, with no regard for rank or title: overcoats made from cat fur, beaver, quilted overcoats, raccoon, fox, bear – in short, overcoats made from every conceivable fur or skin that man has ever used to protect his own hide. One of the clerks from the department saw the ghost with his own eyes and immediately recognized it as Akaky Akakievich. He was so terrified that he ran off as fast as his legs would carry him, with the result he did not manage to have a very good look: all he could make out was someone pointing a menacing finger at him from the distance. Complaints continually poured in from all quarters, not only from titular councillors, but even from such high-ranking officials as privy councillors, who were being subjected to quite nasty colds in the back through this nocturnal ripping off of their overcoats. The police were instructed to run the ghost in, come what may, dead or alive, and to punish it most severely, as an example to others – and in this they very nearly succeeded. To be precise, a policeman, part of whose beat lay along Kirushkin Alley, was on the point of grabbing the ghost by the collar at the very scene of the crime, just as he was about to tear a woollen overcoat from the shoulders of a retired musician who, in his day, used to tootle on the flute. As he seized the ghost by the collar the policeman shouted to two of his friends to come and keep hold of it, just for a minute, while he felt in his boot for his birch-bark snuff-box to revive his nose (which had been slightly frost-bitten six times in his life). But the snuff must have been one of those blends even a ghost could not stand, for the policeman had barely managed to cover his right nostril with a finger and sniff half a handful up the other when the ghost sneezed so violently that they were completely blinded by the spray, all three of them. While they were wiping their eyes the ghost disappeared into thin air, so suddenly that the policemen could not even say for certain if they had ever laid hands on it in the first place. From then on the local police were so scared of ghosts that they were frightened of arresting even the living and would shout instead: 'Hey you, clear off!' – from a safe distance. The clerk's ghost began to appear even far beyond the Kalinkin Bridge, causing no little alarm and apprehension among fainter-hearted citizens. However, we seem to have completely neglected the Important Person, who, in fact, could almost be said to be the *real* reason for the fantastic turn this otherwise authentic story has taken. First of all, to give him his due, we should mention that soon after the departure of our poor shattered Akaky Akakievich the Important Person felt some twinges of regret. Compassion was not something new to him, and, although consciousness of his rank very often stifled them, his heart was not untouched by many generous impulses. As soon as his friend had left the office his thoughts turned to poor Akaky Akakievich.

Almost every day after that he had visions of the pale Akaky Akakievich, for whom an official wigging had been altogether too much. These thoughts began to worry him to such an extent that a week later he decided to send someone round from the office to the flat to ask how he was and if he could be of any help. When the messenger reported that Akaky Akakievich had died suddenly of a fever he was quite stunned. His conscience began troubling him, and all that day he felt off-colour.

Thinking that some light entertainment might help him forget that unpleasant experience he went off to a party given by one of his friends which was attended by quite a respectable crowd. He was particularly pleased to see that everyone there held roughly the same rank as himself, so there was no chance of any embarrassing situations. All this had an amazingly uplifting effect on his state of mind. He unwound completely, chatted very pleasantly, made himself agreeable to everyone, and in short, spent a very pleasant evening. Over dinner he drank one or two glasses of champagne, a wine which, as everyone knows, is not exactly calculated to dampen high spirits. The champagne put him in the mood for introducing several changes in his plans for that evening: he decided not to go straight home, but to call on a lady of his acquaintance, Karolina Ivanovna, who was of German origin and with whom he was on the friendliest terms. Here I should mention that the Important Person was no longer a young man but a good husband and the respected head of a family. His two sons, one of whom already had a job in the Civil Service, and a sweet sixteen-year-old daughter with a pretty little turned-up nose, came every day to kiss his hand and say 'Bonjour, Papa'. His wife, who still retained some of her freshness and had not even lost any of her good looks, allowed him to kiss her hand first, and then kissed his, turning it the other side up. But although the Important Person was thoroughly contented with the affection lavished on him by his family, he still did not think it wrong to have a lady friend in another part of the town. This lady friend was not in the least prettier or younger than his wife, but that is one of the mysteries of this world, and it is not for us to criticize. As I was saying, the Important Person went downstairs, climbed into his sledge and said to the driver: 'To Karolina Ivanovna's', while he wrapped himself snugly in his warm, very luxurious overcoat, revelling in that happy state of mind, so very dear to Russians, when one is thinking about absolutely nothing, but when, nonetheless, thoughts come crowding into one's head of their own accord, each more delightful than the last, and not even requiring one to make the mental effort of conjuring them up or chasing after them. He felt very contented as he recalled, without any undue exertion, all the gayest moments of the party, all the *bons mots* that had aroused loud guffaws in that little circle: some of them he even repeated quietly to himself and found just as funny as before, so that it was not at all surprising that he laughed very heartily. The boisterous wind, however, interfered with his enjoyment at times: blowing up God knows where or why, it cut right into his face, hurling lumps of snow at it, making his collar billow out like a sail, or blowing it back over his head with such supernatural force that he had the devil's own job extricating himself. Suddenly the Important Person felt a violent tug at his collar. Turning round, he saw a smallish man in an old, worn-out uniform, and not without a feeling of horror recognized him as Akaky Akakievich. The clerk's face was as pale as the snow and was just like a dead man's.

The Important Person's terror passed all bounds when the ghost's mouth became twisted, smelling horribly of the grave as it breathed on him and pronounced the following words: 'Ah, at last I've found you! Now I've, er, hm, collared you! It's *your* overcoat I'm after! You didn't care about mine, *and* you couldn't resist giving me a good ticking-off into the bargain! Now hand over *your* overcoat!' The poor Important Person nearly died. However much strength of character he displayed in the office (usually in the presence of his subordinates) – one only had to look at his virile face and bearing to say: '*There*'s a man for you!' – in this situation, like many of his kind who seem heroic at first sight, he was so frightened that he even began to fear (and not without reason) that he was in for a heart attack. He tore off his overcoat as fast as he could, without any help, and then shouted to his driver in a terrified voice: 'Home as fast as you can!'

The driver, recognizing the tone of voice his master used only in moments of crisis – a tone of voice usually accompanied by some much stronger encouragement – just to be on the safe side hunched himself up, flourished his whip and shot off like an arrow.

Not much more than six minutes later the Important Person was already at his front door. He was coatless, terribly pale and frightened out of his wits, and had driven straight home instead of going to Karolina Ivanovna's. Somehow he managed to struggle up to his room and spent a very troubled night, so much so that next morning his daughter said to him over breakfast: 'You look very pale today, Papa.' But Papa did not reply, did not say a single word to anyone about what had happened, where he had been and where he had originally intended going. The encounter had made a deep impression on him. From that time onwards he would seldom say: 'How dare you! Do you realize who is standing before you?' to his subordinates. And if he did have occasion to say this, it was never without first hearing what the accused had to say. But what was more surprising than anything else the ghostly clerk disappeared completely. Obviously the general's overcoat was a perfect fit. At least, there were no more stories about overcoats being torn off people's backs. However, many officious and over-cautious citizens would not be satisfied, insisting the ghost could still be seen in the remoter parts of the city, and in fact a certain police constable from the Kolomna district saw with his own eyes a ghost leaving a house. However, being rather weakly built – once a quite normal-sized, fully mature piglet which came tearing out of a private house knocked him off his feet, to the huge amusement of some cab-drivers who were standing near by, each of whom was made to cough up half a kopeck in snuff-money for his cheek – he simply did not have the nerve to make an arrest, but followed the ghost in the dark until it suddenly stopped, turned round, asked: 'What do *you* want?' and shook its fist at him – a fist the like of which you will never see in the land of the living. The constable replied: 'Nothing', and beat a hasty retreat. This ghost, however, was much taller than the first, had an absolutely enormous moustache and, apparently heading towards the Obukhov Bridge, was swallowed up in the darkness.

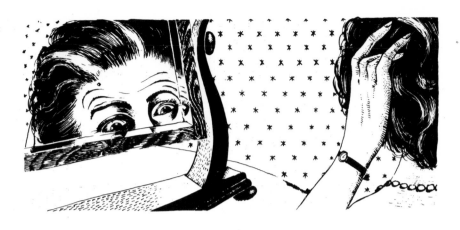

And Give Us Yesterday

SEABURY QUINN

FOR THE TENTH TIME Angela picked up the letter from the Quartermaster General with Form 345, Military, enclosed, the four options she might exercise; have him left near the beach where he fell, have him brought back for interment in a private cemetery, have him shipped to some foreign country, or sent back for burial in Arlington. She wanted none of them. She wanted her boy back, her Harold with his neat brown hair that waved a little just above the temples, steady hazel eyes and ready smile that lifted slightly more to the left than the right.

Three years ago when she received the formal notice from the War Department with its facsimile of the Adjutant General's signature she had felt betrayed, desolate, all her high hopes crumbled into fragments at her feet. She hadn't fainted, hadn't cried, but she had bitten her lips till the salty taste of blood was in her mouth as she sat with her hands demurely folded in her lap, all feeling gone from her eyes. She wanted desperately to cry, but there were no tears. She wanted desperately to pray, but couldn't; God seemed somehow terribly unreal. Then, with a feeling all her insides were becoming unfastened – and not the faintest notion what she could do about it – she walked slowly to his bedroom with the Japanese prints on the walls, the scarf of brown-blocked Java linen for a counterpane and her and Darcy's photographs on the dresser. She drew back the door of the closet where his suits draped in orderly array on hangers, tweeds, flannels, worsteds, dress and dinner kits, brown shoes and black on wooden trees set toe to toe, hats nearly brushed and put away in paste-board boxes. A little whiff of peat from Harris tweeds and Shetland weaves came to her, and the faint elusive scent of lavender and Russian leather and tobacco – odours redolent of him as carnation or violet may be of a beloved woman – and, scarce knowing what she did, she drew the sleeve of a camel's hair topcoat round her shoulders, sank her cheek in its soft silky fleece. 'Harold,' she murmured, her voice muffled by the yielding cloth. 'Oh, my boy; my boy!' Then she let her breath out slowly, with an odd jerk in it, as if she had not breathed for a long time and needed practice to pick up the way of it again.

Since that day nothing seemed to matter. 'Thank you, thank you, very much,' she had told the minister, 'Thank you,' to the kind old ladies of the congregation, 'Thank you,' to the laundry-man and grocer and the men who came to read the electric and gas meters, and the tone with which she voiced her thanks was flat, expressionless, almost mechanical. The War Department's citation and the Purple Heart had no more impact on her numbed senses than a fresh blow on a punch-drunk boxer. She ignored the stilted, sloppily typed communications from the Veterans' Administration. What need had she to ask insurance payments or pension? With health, sufficient money, more beauty than a woman in her middle forties had a right to dare hope for, she already had everything – and nothing.

Now, after three years came this latest message from the War Department and her heart that she had thought wrung dry of sorrow refilled itself from memories. She laid the papers down, her slim white fingers smoothing them almost caressingly, and tears slipped in big jewel-bright drops down her cheeks. She didn't sob, not so much as a sign escaped her; she just sat there in the big twilit room, her face like ivory, letting those big tears run down her cheeks. At last: 'O God,' she murmured, quoting something she had heard or read long, long ago, 'turn back Thy universe and give us yesterday!'

Her lips, as naturally pink as pigeons' feet and needing no rouge to define their perfection, joined in a smile as she finished. Her flexible mouth widened and her cheeks lifted a little; a dimple dented the smooth flesh beside her mouth, her sensitive nostrils expanded – all the components of a smile appeared in her face. But there was no smile. It was, rather, a bitter grimace of derision. 'But that would take a special kind of miracle, of course,' her voice seemed tired, so utterly weary it might have been that of an old woman, 'and miracles like that, are out of date, aren't they? You gave them up after Capernaum and Bethany.' Her acid laughter was a goading echo in the gathering dusk.

Something cool and black, faintly moist, insinuated itself into the hand she let trail idly beside her and a furred foot pawed her arm gently. 'Oh!' she exclaimed, a little startled then, 'Oh, it's you, Mr. Chips,' as she looked into the yellow eyes turned pleadingly to hers. 'You want to go for your walk? Very well, go get the lead.'

The honey-coloured cocker trotted off, nails clicking on the polished floor, and Angela rose half reluctantly, half eagerly to carry out the evening rite. Chips had come to them when he was a fist-sized bundle of soft fluffy fur about the shade of a Teddy bear. He had been Harold's dog, selected from a dozen sportive, friendly puppies at a pet shop on Fifth Avenue, and Harold had adored him, pampered him, looked after him from awkward, stumbling puppyhood to sedate middle age. When Harold went away to camp the duty of the daily run – which had slowed to a dignified amble with the years – developed on Angela.

They made a circuit of the square each evening just as dusk was deepening into dark. Chips strained at the lead, hanging back, investigating tree boxes, fire hydrants or the little bare spots of raw earth around the trees with an interrogative black nose, giving vent to subdued snorts of approval or muted whimpers of disfavour at what he discovered. Angela indulged him for as long as seemed reasonable, then her sharp, 'That's quite enough, Chips,' brought him from his olfactory researches, and he would trot sedately beside her till fresh locations roused the latent archaeologist in him again. In this way they effected complete encompassment of the Square, each occupied with his own thoughts, each tolerant of the other's privacy, as became gentle-folk, whether canine or human.

The air that flowed through the French windows of the drawing-room bore a faint mingled scent of flowers, new-mown grass and recently washed asphalt as she snapped the snaffle of the lead to the dog's harness and made for the street. Van Nostrand Square was like an etching in the July night. Inside the cast-iron grilles of the park cannas and geraniums bloomed, two fountains spurted jets of water which fell tinkling into iron basins, the freshly cut lawns smelt sweet and warm. Northwards, over the elms bordering the pavement, rose the tip of St. Jude's tower with its lighted clock dial round and bright and yellow as a harvest moon, across from it an ancient Quaker meeting house stood demurely in its small graveyard, and round the plaza ancient mansions, red-brick, white-marble trimmed, stood like old veterans in a hollow square. For the most part they had been made into 'maisonettes' for people in the upper-middle-income tax brackets, but outwardly they retained the air of hauteur they had worn when Oakey Hall was mayor and Boss Tweed a scandal in New York politics. The July moon hung low in the sky, a disc of scorched gold with the branches of the elms and sycamores on its face as if drawn with charcoal, and every park bench held its complement of lovers. Lovers strolled along the cement paths, each pair absorbed in themselves as if they had been the last people in the world; the tarnished moonlight was a mellow wonderland to them.

Angela caught her breath with a small sad sound that was not quite a sob, but something not far from it. She had been a young wife, almost a bride, when Darcy died, but she had found some measure of solace in the knowledge that beneath her heart she bore that which would give him immortality;

231

'To die would not be dying quite,
Leaving a little life behind. . . .'

And since she had been born with the proverbial silver spoon in her mouth she reared Darcy's son in a mellow atmosphere of ancestors, heirlooms and family tradition. All that came to him by nature had a chance to grow and develop and the final product was a slim brown man with curling hair and a quick friendly smile for whom the title 'gentleman' seemed to have been hand-tailored and to whom clung the faint fragrance of gentle living.

She loved him for his sweet and winsome self, but more than that she loved him as his father's surrogate. In him the high hopes she and Darcy had dreamed in their short ecstasy of marriage were to be fulfilled, he would perpetuate the Logan name; born in a world cleansed of the curse of war by countless bloody sacrifices of his father's generation he would achieve the thing that fate denied his father. Already he had shown a more than merely casual interest in the daughter of one of her classmates, and she had dreamed of being a grandmother before time had stolen strength and beauty from her.

Then December 7th, 1941, the blare of trumpets and the roll of drums and streets resounding to the pound of marching feet. Training camp ... letters from England ... the Normandy invasion ... 'the War Department regrets ...'.

There were tears in her heart that would not come to her eyes for relief as she heard a girl's low 'Always?' and her lover's promised 'Always and for ever, dear,' as a young couple passed her.

'There,' a shrill vindictive voice seemed whispering, 'there but for some drop stitch of Fate go Harold and Geraldine.' All at once she felt unutterably old. Old and tired. Her hands felt numb and in the hollows of her shoulders ached a fine pain. 'Oh, Harold, my poor, sweet boy,' she murmured hopelessly. Blinded with sudden tears, almost all life gone from her fine, pliant body, lost and forsaken as a derelict, she leaned against the park's iron fence, sobbing with short retching sobs like the breathing of a spent runner.

Mr. Chips strained at the leash, shrank fearfully into the shadow of a friendly tree, dropped upon his stomach with a terrified whimper. The pull upon the lead roused her, and she straightened, then stepped back with a short involuntary 'Oh!'

Within arm's length of her stood a small neat gentleman in black mohair with a Panama hat set jauntily on one side of his head and a gold-headed black malacca stick swung jauntily from his hand. His dark, lined face and short white beard and moustache were those of an old man but his bearing was decidedly sprightly and his eyes very bright. They were unusual eyes, dark but not black, with little flecks of garnet in them.

They seemed to have no division between the irises and pupils and their habitual expression was one of heavy-lidded weariness, as though they had looked too closely at life for a long time. Just then, however, they were bent on her with a look of dispassionate irony which seemed more curious than malicious.

'You are in trouble, Madame?' He spoke with the slightest of slight accents, in the almost colourless tone of the perfect linguist. There was a suave, foreign-bred something in his words and manner, and the gesture with which he doffed his wide hat was somehow reminiscent of a Versailles courtier in the days when Bourbons sat upon the throne of France.

Angela gave back a step. Without quite knowing why she was afraid of this small harmless-looking gentleman with courtly manners, but the fear was natural and intuitive as that felt when one gazes into a snake-pit at the zoo. 'There's nothing anyone can do to help,' she answered shortly, tightened her hold on the dog's leash and stepped towards the curb to pass the little man.

'One moment, if you please.' His voice, still soft, was mandatory in its even tone. 'You are in trouble, yet you say no one can help you. Are you sure?'

She braced herself as for a physical assault. Instinctively she knew something was coming, something which might change the whole rhythm of life. She took a short breath, let it out soundlessly, then, 'Of course, I'm sure.' Her tone was razor-sharp with finality.

'There you make a mistake, Madame,' the suave reply was compelling in its monotone. 'There is nothing – understand me, *nothing* – which we cannot have if we desire it enough and are willing to pay its price.'

'Pay?' her voice rose almost to a scream. 'Dear God, I'd pay anything—'

'Anything, Madame—' There was irony, perhaps a hint of malice in the echoed word.

'Anything!'

'Then listen carefully, Madame.' He fumbled in the pocket of his jacket and brought out a little doll-like image scarcely longer than her thumb. 'Take this for a talisman. Concentrate your thought – your wish – on it. If you are strong enough in your desire – and if you do not haggle at the price – you may attain your wish, though whether it will bring you happiness or not I should not care to say.'

Mechanically her fingers closed round the little puppet, and as she thanked him with an inclination of her head the little gentleman added, 'If you should need me again throw the charm away and call me.'

Despite herself Angela laughed. 'How can I call you? I don't even know your name.'

'You will know what name to call if the need comes, Madame.' The little man made her another bow which would have been a credit to a dancing master at the court of Louis XV. Then he replaced his hat at its slightly rakish angle and swinging his black cane strode off into the shadows.

Three times Angela made a gesture of casting the doll into the gutter as she walked back to her house, but each time, smiling mirthlessly at herself for her weakness, she refrained. Back in her drawing-room she snapped on the desk light and examined it.

It was carved or moulded of some hard substance, perhaps soap-stone or pottery, which had a velvety smoothness and retained an almost reptilian coolness despite the heat of the night and the warmth of her hand. The maker had shaped it to represent a man, or the grotesque of one, dressed in a medieval costume which consisted of long, pointed shoes, tight hose bound round with cross-garters, a loosely-hanging gabardine or cloak with foliated edges and sleeve-openings, and a close-fitting hood upon the head through which two openings had been cut to leave the ears exposed. The figure made her think of Punchinello, wide-shouldered, hunchbacked, with exaggeratedly sharp nose and chin, thick beetling brows above pop eyes, and a malicious, mocking grin. Somehow there was an air of hatefulness about it, an intimation of malevolence and animosity that repelled and yet fascinated her. The more she looked at it the more repulsive it seemed, and yet it had a certain charm like that which English bulldogs have by virtue of their very ugliness.

'He was an absurd little man,' she told herself, 'with all his foreign airs and graces, and his awful deadly earnestness. . . .' Her voice trailed off, became mute, for another thought had crowded into her brain. 'Use this as a talisman,' he had said, 'and concentrate your thought on it. If you are strong enough in your desire. . . .'

She rose, hands knotted into fists, and gazed at the small statuette. Her eyes were fixed, intense, half-closed, as if the violence of her gaze were too annihilating to be loosed direct; as if the substance of her soul and body would pour out of her set, staring orbs. 'My boy,' she whispered in a voice so low as to be hardly audible, but harsh as an abrasive scraped across metal. 'Give back my son – put back the universe and give us yesterday!'

Somewhere in the distance thunder rattled with a crackle like the sound of far-off musketry, into the heavy, humid air there crept a chill as tangible as smoke, and the sky shattered with a dazzling burst of yellow-green lightning.

She flinched from the flash as the telephone began ringing, at first querulously, then frantically, drilling at her, 'Hello?' she greeted somewhat shakily, still startled by the lightning.

'Mother?' Her stomach suddenly felt stiff and empty, she could not fight down the weakness that chilled her with pulse-stopping cold. Weak-kneed as a rag doll from which the stuffing has been ripped, she dropped into a chair. What line, if any, divides sanity from madness, were does sanity end and madness begin? she wondered. Was this a trick of overwrought senses and gnawing desire, or was she the victim of an unspeakably cruel hoax?

'Who – who is this?' she contrived at last, and in the little interval of silence she could hear the pounding of her heart like a jazz-drummer's rataplan.

'Whom do you think?'

Another silence, one that hummed electrically. Then: 'This joke's not in the best of taste,' her voice was hard and gritty.

'Oh, *maman*, you'll be what the Heinies couldn't – the death o' me!' It was the well-remembered laugh that stirred her pulses like a long note on a trumpet.

'But – but – you're – you were—'

'No, I'm not, I assure you. Officially or not, I'm still alive and likely to be kickin' if you don't snap out of it. The report of my death was greatly exaggerated, old dear. I did have a tough time, and spent a tour of duty in hospital *sans* memory, *sans* dog-tags, *sans* everything but life. But here I am like the proverbial bad penny, safe and moderately sound. Be with you in a little while – just landed at the airport.'

She was radiantly, arrogantly happy. Like one who wakens from a long dream-haunted night to find a morning with cool, limpid air and sunlight sparkling over everything. The twitterings of sparrow in the park seemed like a canticle: *For this my son was dead and is alive again; he was lost and is found.* Her face was transfigured by happiness as by a halo. The sunshine had a brighter gold, even when it rained the drops fell brightly, gleaming, jewel-like, on the trees and window panes.

At first she did not notice the small, subtle changes in him, the absence of the little niceties which had been as inherent as his breath. When he did not hold her chair at dinner or rise when she came into the room she overlooked it. War was dirty, dull, dangerous and degrading, small wonder it had rasped the patina of refinement from him. He had been meticulously neat, physically and mentally, now he was slovenly about his room, with clothes left carelessly on floor or chair or bed; in place of his alert, attentive manner he seemed oddly distraught. He would sit for minutes staring endlessly at nothing, his eyes strange, far-way, almost filmy with ennui, his shoulders slumping, as if nothing really mattered. Small blame to him, she thought. He had been to the very gates of hell; could she expect him to come back unmarked?

Even when he showed no interest in employment she made excuses. A man who had had death for a bedfellow and boon companion could hardly be expected to take interest in a desk job, or grow enthusiastic over selling things. No matter, she had plenty for them both.

But had she? When he asked her for five hundred dollars for 'a deal' she was delighted. He had determined to launch out for himself, not take an underling's position. When the deal fell through and he asked for a thousand she was more puzzled than worried. She had neither aptitude for nor experience in business, and knew only that men made or lost money in it. Harold, it appeared, was one of those who lost, for in a month he needed more, then more. Her income was derived from funds invested by the trust department of her bank, and earnings had not been as great this year as last. One morning came a notice from the bank that she was overdrawn. She made the necessary arrangements, sold off some bonds, and – had another notice of an overdraft within six weeks.

She knew she had not drawn five thousand dollars in one cheque, and went down to the bank to see about it. There it was, payable to Harold Logan, made out in her own handwriting, signed with her own signature. But the signature was not hers.

'Oh, yes, now I remember,' she told the cashier, and embarrassment brought a quick flush to her face. 'I had forgotten – this.'

The complete absence of expression in the banker's face voiced scepticism sharper than his words. 'That's your signature, Mrs. Logan?'

'Why, yes, of course,' she spoke with more than necessary emphasis. 'Of course, it's mine. Why do you ask?'

'Our teller was a little doubtful, but the cheque's entirely in your writing, and the payee is your son—'

'I don't think you need make yourself uneasy over any cheque my son presents.' She spaced her syllables precisely, so they sounded clipped and hard.

The visitor was not the sort of person she was used to entertaining. He was something less than middle height, dark-skinned, black-haired, curly-haired. His light grey, almost white suit had been pressed into knife-sharp creases, from the breast pocket of his jacket spilled a grey-silk handkerchief, he had been freshly shaved and manicured and exuded a faint odour of brandy, garlic and lilac perfume. His brown skin shone as if it had been rubbed with oil, his eyes danced with a light more sinister than merry, his full, too-red lips framed a smile more nearly contemptuous than good-humoured.

He did not, however, lack directions. 'You're Logan's old lady?' he asked.

'I am Mrs. Logan.'

'Uh-huh.' He looked at her, a little puzzled, just a little uneasy. His eyes swept up and down her as if they had been adding a column of figures and were not entirely satisfied with the answer. At last: 'You love 'im, don't you?'

'I'm sure you didn't call to ascertain the strength of my maternal affection, Mr.—' she paused interrogatively, and the cold, slightly amused contempt of her gaze seared him as an early frost withers a row of larkspur.

'Huh? Oh—' He fumbled for a word, then brought his reply out, and with it an oblong of green paper. 'I'll tell th' cockeyed world I didn't. I come here to get gelt for this.' He held the slip out, a cheque made payable to Joseph Lanzilotti in the sum of seven hundred dollars, signed with her name.

'I don't remember making any cheque to you, Mr. Lanzilotti.'

'Don't, huh? Then it's just too bad for your kid. That's all I gotta say.'

'I don't think I quite understand—'

'Lemme fill you in, lady. He rolled me Saturday night in a crap game, your kid, that is, an' when I took 'im for a half gran' he give me this IOU. Nex' day he come and gimme this' – he indicated the cheque – 'an' got two hun'nert fish in change for it. See? Then when I goes to th' bank this mornin' they reneges on th' signature. Says they gotta have your OK 'fore they'll lemme have th' money. Come clean, lady. Slap your OK on it, or little Harold goes to th' pokey. See?'

'You make it very clear, Mr. Lanzilotti.' She took the cheque, endorsed it, 'OK. Angela Logan,' and returned it. 'In future I'd advise you not to play games with my son,' she cautioned as she went with him to the door. 'I might not see your point so readily next time.'

Joe Lanzilotti knew when he was outclassed. Also, from long frequenting of race courses, he knew a thoroughbred when he saw one. 'Sure, lady,' he agreed as he tipped his pearl-grey Homburg with more than customary flourish, 'I won't never let th' bum come in my jernt ag'in, an' I'll top all th' other mugs to give 'im th' shoo-fly if he comes buzzin' round th' gallopin' dominoes.'

She had just the sort of dinner that delighted him that night, steak two inches thick, the tenderloin charred on the outside, pink as a poodle's tongue inside, lyonnaise potatoes, chicory salad and a chocolate pie. Since he no longer cared for sherry as an aperitif she chilled a shaker of Manhattans and had a bottle of Nuits St. Georges brought up from the cellar. But when he came in so late, the steak was ruined and the cocktails little more than ice water, he was slightly tipsy and more than a little truculent. 'Got here soon as I could,' he explained rather than apologized. 'That dam' subway—'.

She noted that he made no move to kiss her, and was stung by the omission. 'Oh, that's all right, son. If you can stand cold steak I'm sure the steak and I don't mind waiting—'

'Good Lord, steak again? I swear to God I'm getting so I daren't look a cow in the eye –' His nonchalance was poorly worn as he dropped into his chair.

She filled their glasses, tasted hers, then stared silently into its ruddy depths. 'A friend of yours was here today, Harold. A Mr. Lanzilotti – quite a character.'

'Eh?' She saw his eyes go suddenly wide, startled and questioning, a little frightened. 'What'd he want?'

'You ought to know—'

His chair crashed on the floor as he rose, glaring at her. 'Well, what're you going to do? Send me up for forgery—'

'Harold!'

'All right, you needn't be dramatic about it.' There was a morose recklessness about his pose as he stalked from the room, but at the doorway he came to a halt and in the courtly way he bowed his head before he left there was a echo of the old, aristocratic elegance that marked his every move in former days.

She lit a cigarette, stubbed out its fire before it had a chance to glow, than lit another. In her heart there was a dull ache and her knees felt weak and unsubstantial. She wasn't sure she could stand. Any moment, she knew, she might be sick.

The shrilling of the doorbell wakened her from her trancelike misery, and the tap-tap of high heels that followed was like a tonic. Geraldine Macfarland! Mightn't Gerry be the answer to her problem? Harold had been more than casually interested in her before he went away; she'd done everything she could to throw them together since his return. Angela was only nineteen years older than her son, but they were of different generations, just the same. She was not one of those fatuous fools who boasted she and her offspring were 'pals', but Gerry – perhaps romantic love could work a reformation where maternal affection failed.

'Gerry, dear,' she greeted, holding out slim bare arms to the girl, 'I'm so glad you – why, what's the matter, darling?'

Gerry's pretty pink-and-white face was ravaged as a garden following a savage storm, and the hands that seized hers were cold while the cheek that pressed against hers burned as if with fever. 'Aunt Angela,' the passionless, cold little voice went into her like a dentist's drill, 'I've got to talk to you – and Harold – right away.'

'Of course,' she led the way to the drawing-room and dropped down on a love seat, pulling the girl down beside her. 'Now, what is it, dear?'

Gerry's slender fingers wreathed and unwreathed, twisting blindly, futilely as worms. 'It's about Harold – me – us, Aunt Angela. I've been feeling miserable for some time, nauseated nearly every morning, nervous as a cat, pains in my chest. Today I called on Dr. Christy. He says I'm – we're – going to have—'

The world seemed suddenly to have stopped, and breathing with it. The silence was so overpowering Angela could hear the blood pound in her throat. Then, like a gallant boxer, beaten, but determined to fight to the final knockout, she rallied. '*Autres temps, autres moeurs*, dear,' somehow she contrived a smile which was a reasonable facsimile of the real thing. 'In my day this would have been a scandal, but you and Harold can be married quietly—'

'That's just it! He won't—'

'Oh, *no-o*!' Stark, utter misery made her voice quaver. 'He couldn't be such a cad. Not—'

His footsteps slightly unsteady, came down the stairs. He was humming:

> *'The minstrels sing of a jovial king;*
> *A wonderful king was he. . . .'*

He halted at the doorway. 'Goin' out, Mom. Goin' to give the gals a treat – Hi, Gerry,' he waved an indifferent greeting to the caller. 'Be seein' you around sometime—'

'Harold!' How she kept her voice from breaking, kept from screaming, Angela had no idea. 'Come here – sit down – I want to talk—'

'Eh?' He shot a sharp glance from her to the girl. 'Oh, I see, she's told you—'

'Yes, she's told me—'

'And just what are you goin' to do about it?'

'I think that you're the one to answer that.'

'Do, eh? Well, I can answer in one word; Nothing. How does she know that it was I – how do I know—'

'Oh, Harold!' Geraldine's voice was pitched shrill, but controlled. 'Oh, how could you – and I loved you so!'

He laughed, and Angela felt everything inside her shrivel as if touched with live flame.

This was no laugh of bravado, no brazen attempt to face indecency. He was amused – that was the devilish, unbelievable thing about it.

She had risen to face him, now she took a step back. Her lips opened, then shut again. With apocalyptic clarity she saw him as if for the first time. She could look through him distinctly as if using a spiritual X-ray. And he was bad. Rotten clear through as maggot-bitten fruit is rotten.

Raw misery was stark in her eyes as they swept round the room and came to momentary rest upon the figurine the little foreign gentleman had given her the night Harold came home. 'Saint Punchinello,' she had called the thing affectionately, the patron who had brought her dead back to her. Now her gaze hardened, froze like water into a sudden zero temperature. In three quick, almost stumbling steps she crossed the room and snatched the statuette from the desk. Something deep inside herself – or perhaps a thing outside – put the words she had never heard before in her mouth, '*Barran-Sathanas!*' she called in a voice that was like a dissonant chord. '*Barran-Sathanas!*' She hurled the image from her as if it had been a loathsome reptile.

Outside the November night was still as ice and bitter cold, the moonlight struck chill fire from frost-encrusted paving stones, the stars shone with a crystalline brightness, and not a cloud showed in the smalt-blue sky, but as the little figure struck the base-board and shattered as if it had been blown glass there came a distant cannonade of thunder and a zigzag lance of lightning slashed through the sky like a sword through flesh. The front door – she knew that it was latched and chained! – swung open and a step sounded in the hall.

'*Eh bien*, Madame,' said the small gentleman as he bowed in the doorway leading from the hall to the drawing-room, 'it seems you have repented of your bargain. You find the price too high?'

He wore a faultless dinner kit, black pearls glowed dully in his shirtfront, the thick white hair that sloped up from a widow's peak on his forehead was brushed back sleekly in a pompadour, his little white moustache and beard were neatness personified, but there was that in his lined face that bludgeoned her with horror. His features were not so much old as ancient, yet they seemed ageless too; he seemed to be a part of that which had been, was, and was to be.

Somehow she found her voice, forced throat and tongue and lips to function. 'The price?' she echoed, and her whisper was a queer small ghost of sound, 'Dear God, yes, it's too high! I would not call my boy – my fine, clean, gentle boy – back from his honoured grave to be a thing like this. I would not slake the thirst of my sorrow if quenching it means misery to Geraldine—'

'Your sentiments do you great credit, Madame, but should you not have thought of all that when you asked that the universe be turned back?'

'How could I know . . .?'

'True, Madame, how could you? But you were warned the price might be exorbitant—'

'Take me!' she broke in between chattering teeth. 'Kill my body, rend it, tear it – burn my wretched soul for all eternity in your hell, but put my dear, brave son back where he belongs with the honoured dead who died for decency and freedom. Let him lie in the earth hallowed by his blood, and by the blood of other mothers' sons—'

'Your soul, Madame?' He brushed his wisp of white moustache with the knuckle of a bent forefinger. 'You put extraordinary value on a bit of rather trumpery *bijouterie*, don't you? Besides, what need have I for more souls? From Rome, Berlin and Tokyo, from Moscow and Madrid—?' He waved a deprecating hand. 'Really, I suffer an embarrassment of riches. Sometimes I think I'll have to set a quota on the importations.'

She dropped to her knees, inched towards him, held up empty, supplicating hands. 'Barran – great Barran-Sathanas – Lord and Master—'

'Don't be a fool,' he said as casually as if refusing a second cup of coffee.

'Take me, take me, mighty Lord of the World, do with me as you will, only give my boy back to the earth made sacred by his blood—'

'You annoy me, Madame. Once every thousand years or so it pleases me to strike a bargain, then remit the *quid pro quo*. Think well; there is no turning back this time. You would not have your son restored to life; you are willing that he go down to the grave again—'

'I beg you, I beseech you; I entreat you—'

'So be it. Have it as you wish.' His sharp eyes bored into hers, and in them the small garnet speckings seemed to glow to incandescence. 'Have your wish, mother. And this' – he bent above her, laid two fingers on her bowed head – 'this is for remembering.'

Only once before had Angela felt anything like it. That was when as a child she had held the electrodes of a galvanic battery while a playmate ground the generator. Every nerve seemed suddenly knotted, all her muscles twisted into ropes of pain, a light as dazzling as aurora borealis flared before her eyes, her throat closed in quick, agonizing contraction, her breath stopped and she wilted to the floor with no more life in her than a dead thing.

Slowly consciousness returned. The big room echoed small sounds hollowly, like an empty auditorium. Outside she heard the splashing of the fountains and the distant gleeful shouts of children romping under street-showers. Somewhere not far away two cats indulging in illicit romance split the air with feline love calls and the big clock in the hall ticked with deliberate decorum. A little breeze stirred the curtains at the front windows, and over all was the soft, clinging sultriness of a July night.

She sat up, pressed the back of her hand to her forehead a bewildered moment, and got slowly to her feet. 'I dreamed it,' she told herself tremulously. 'How horrible!' Yet had it been only a dream? In olden days the Lord spoke to Jacob and Samuel, giving them a vision past their waking senses. Might she not have been vouchsafed such a boon? If Harold had come back and – 'Dear Lord, I thank Thee for this mercy,' she murmured. 'He's safe where he is, safe always and for ever, secure in honoured glory—'

She tottered to the desk, took up the Army form, wrote acceptance of the first option in a firm hand. Let the young oak lie where it had fallen; let him lie beside his comrades with his white cross above him, and over all, triumphantly, the flag he died to serve. . . . Some little spot of earth that is for ever home. . . .

She glanced up. In the glass above the desk she saw her reflection. Across the dark hair waved above her forehead was a double line of startling white, as if two fingers lightly dipped in flour had been laid on it.

The Old Nurse's Story

MRS. GASKELL

YOU KNOW, MY DEARS, that your mother was an orphan, and an only child; and I dare say you have heard that your grandfather was a clergyman up in Westmorland, where I come from. I was just a girl in the village school, when, one day, your grandmother came in to ask the mistress if there was any scholar there who would do for a nurse-maid; and mighty proud I was, I can tell ye, when the mistress called me up, and spoke to my being a good girl at my needle, and a steady honest girl, and one whose parents were very respectable, though they might be poor. I thought I should like nothing better than to serve the pretty young lady, who was blushing as deep as I was, as she spoke of the coming baby, and what I should have to do with it. However, I see you don't care so much for this part of my story, as for what you think is to come, so I'll tell you at once. I was engaged and settled at the parsonage before Miss Rosamond (that was the baby, who is now your mother) was born. To be sure, I had little enough to do with her when she came, for she was never out of her mother's arms, and slept by her all night long; and proud enough was I sometimes when missis trusted her to me. There never was such a baby before or since, though you've all of you been fine enough in your turns; but for sweet, winning ways, you've none of you come up to your mother. She took after her mother, who was a real lady born; a Miss Furnivall, a grand-daughter of Lord Furnivall's, in Northumberland. I believe she had neither brother nor sister, and had been brought up in my lord's family till she had married your grandfather, who was just a curate, son to a shopkeeper in Carlisle – but a clever, fine gentleman as ever was – and one who was a right-down hard worker in his parish, which was very wide, and scattered all abroad over the Westmorland Fells. When your mother, little Miss Rosamond, was about four or five years old, both her parents died in a fortnight – one after the other. Ah! that was a sad time. My pretty young mistress and me was looking for another baby, when my master came home from one of his long rides, wet, and tired, and took the fever he died of; and then she never held up her head again, but just lived to see her dead baby, and have it laid on her breast before she sighed away her life. My mistress had asked me, on her death-bed, never to leave Miss Rosamond; but if she had never spoken a word, I would have gone with the little child to the end of the world.

The next thing, and before we had well stilled our sobs, the executors and guardians came to settle the affairs. They were my poor young mistress's own cousin, Lord Furnivall, and Mr. Esthwaite, my master's brother, a shopkeeper in Manchester; not so well-to-do then as he was afterwards, and with a large family rising about him. Well! I don't know if it were their settling, or because of a letter my mistress wrote on her death-bed to her cousin, my lord; but somehow it was settled that Miss Rosamond and me were to go to Furnivall Manor House, in North-umberland, and my lord spoke as if it had been her mother's wish that she should live with his family, and as if he had no objections, for that one or two more or less could make no difference in so grand a household. So though that was not the way in which I should have wished the coming of my bright and pretty pet to have been looked at – who was like a sunbeam in any family, be it never so grand – I was well pleased that all the folks in the Dale should stare and admire, when they heard I was going to be the young lady's maid at my lord Furnivall's at Furnivall Manor.

But I made a mistake in thinking we were to go and live where my lord did. It turned out that the family had left Furnivall Manor house 50 years or more. I could not hear that my poor young mistress had ever been there, though she had been brought up in the family, and I was sorry for that, for I should have liked Miss Rosamond's youth to have passed where her mother's had been.

My lord's gentleman, from whom I asked so many questions as I durst, said that the Manor House was at the foot of the Cumberland Fells, and a very grand place; that an old Miss Furnivall, a great-aunt of my lord's lived there, with only a few servants; but that it was a very healthy place, and my lord had thought that it would suit Miss Rosamond very well for a few years, and that her being there might perhaps amuse his old aunt.

I was bidden by my lord to have Miss Rosamond's things ready by a certain day. He was a stern proud man, as they say all the Lords Furnivall were; and he never spoke a word more than was necessary. Folk did say he had loved my young mistress; but that, because she knew that his father would object, she would never listen to him, and married Mr. Esthwaite; but I don't know. He never married, at any rate. But he never took much notice of Miss Rosamond; which I thought he might have done if he had cared for her dead mother. He sent his gentleman with us to the Manor House, telling him to join him at Newcastle that same evening; so there was no great length of time for him to make us known to all the strangers before he, too, shook us off; and we were left, two lonely young things (I was not eighteen), in the great old Manor House. It seems like yesterday that we drove there. We had left our own dear parsonage very early, and we had both cried as if our hearts would break though we were travelling in my lord's carriage, which I thought so much of once. And now it was long past noon on a September day, and we stopped to change horses for the last time at a smoky town, all full of colliers and miners. Miss Rosamond had fallen asleep, but Mr. Henry told me to waken her, that she might see the park and the Manor House as we drove up. I thought it rather a pity; but I did what he bade me, for fear he should complain of me to my lord. We had left all signs of a town, or even a village, and were then inside the gates of a large wild park – not like the parks here in the north, but with rocks, and the noise of running water, and gnarled thorn-trees, and old oaks, all white and peeled with age.

The road went up about two miles, and then we saw a great and stately house, with many trees close around it, so close that in some places their branches dragged against the walls when the wind blew; and some hung broken down; for no one seemed to take much charge of the place; – to lop the wood, or to keep the moss-covered carriage-way in order. Only in front of the house all was clear. The great oval drive was without a weed; and neither tree nor creeper was allowed to grow over the long, many-windowed front; at both sides of which a wing projected, which were each the ends of other side fronts; for the house, although it was so desolate, was even grander than I expected. Behind it rose the Fells, which seemed unenclosed and bare enough; and on the left hand of the house, as you stood facing it, was a little, old-fashioned flower-garden, as I found out afterwards. A door opened out upon it from the west front; it had been scooped out of the thick dark wood for some old Lady Furnivall; but the branches of the great forest trees had grown and over-shadowed it again, and there were very few flowers that would live there at that time.

When we drove up to the great front entrance, and went into the hall I thought we should be lost – it was so large, and vast, and grand. There was a chandelier all of bronze, hung down from the middle of the ceiling; and I had never seen one before, and looked at it all in amaze. Then, at one end of the hall, was a great fireplace, as large as the sides of the houses in my country, with massy andirons and dogs to hold the wood; and by it were heavy old-fashioned sofas. At the opposite end of the hall, to the left as you went in – on the western side – was an organ built into the wall, and so large that it filled up the best part of that end. Beyond it, on the same side, was a door; and opposite, on each side of the fireplace were also doors leading to the east front; but those I never went through as long as I stayed in the house, so I can't tell you what lay beyond.

The afternoon was closing in, and the hall, which had no fire lighted in it, looked dark and gloomy, but we did not stay there a moment. The old servant, who had opened the door for us, bowed to Mr. Henry, and took us in through the door at the further side of the great organ, and led us through several small halls and passages into the west drawing-room, where he said that Miss Furnivall was sitting. Poor little Miss Rosamond held very tight to me, as if she were scared and lost in that great place, and as for myself, I was not much better. The west drawing-room was very cheerful-looking, with a warm fire it in, and plenty of good, comfortable furniture about. Miss Furnivall was an old lady not far from 80, I should think, but I do not know. She was thin and tall, and had a face as full of fine wrinkles as if they had been drawn all over it with a needle's point. Her eyes were very watchful, to make up, I suppose, for her being so deaf as to be obliged to use a trumpet. Sitting with her, working at the same great piece of tapestry, was Mrs. Stark, her maid and companion, and almost as old as she was. She had lived with Miss Furnivall ever since they were both young, and now she seemed more like a friend than a servant; she looked so cold and grey, and stony as if she had never loved or cared for anyone; and I don't suppose she did care for anyone, except her mistress; and, owing to the great deafness of the latter, Mrs. Stark treated her very much as if she were a child. Mr. Henry gave some message from my lord, and then he bowed good-bye to us all – taking no notice of my sweet little Rosamond's outstretched hand – and left us standing there, being looked at by the two old ladies through their spectacles.

I was right glad when they rung for the old footman who had shown us in at first, and told him to take us to our rooms. So we went out of that great drawing-room, and into another sitting-room, and out of that, and then up a great flight of stairs, and along a broad gallery – which was something like a library, having books all down one side, and windows and writing-tables all down the other – till we came to our rooms, which I was not sorry to hear were just over the kitchens; for I began to think I should be lost in that wilderness of a house. There was an old nursery that had been used for all the little lords and ladies long ago, with a pleasant fire burning in the grate, and the kettle boiling on the hob, and tea-things spread out on the table; and out of that room was the night-nursery, with a little crib for Miss Rosamond close to my bed. And old James called up Dorothy, his wife, to bid us welcome; and both he and she were so hospitable and kind, that by and by Miss Rosamond and me felt quite at home; and by the time tea was over, she was sitting on Dorothy's knee, and chattering away as fast as her little tongue could go. I soon found out that Dorothy was from Westmorland, and that bound her and me together, as it were; and I would never wish to meet with kinder people than were old James and his wife. James had lived pretty nearly all his life in my lord's family, and thought there was no one so grand as they. He even looked down a little on his wife, because, till he had married her, she had never lived in any but a farmer's household. But he was very fond of her, as well he might be. They had one servant under them, to do all the rough work. Bessy they called her; and she and me, and James and Dorothy, with Miss Furnivall and Mrs. Stark, made up the family; always remembering my sweet little Miss Rosamond! I used to wonder what they had done before she came, they thought so much of her now. Kitchen and drawing-room, it was all the same. The hard, sad Miss Furnivall, and the cold Mrs. Stark, looked pleased when she came fluttering in like a bird, playing and pranking hither and thither, with a continual murmur, and pretty prattle of gladness. I am sure, they were sorry many a time when she flitted away into the kitchen, though they were too proud to ask her to stay with them, and were a little surprised at her taste; though to be sure, as Mrs. Stark said, it was not to be wondered at, remembering what stock her father had come of. The great, old rambling house was a famous place for little Miss Rosamond. She made expeditions all over it, with me at her heels; all, except the east wing, which was never opened, and whither we never thought of going. But in the western and northern part was many a pleasant room; full of things that were curiosities to us, though they might not have been to people who had seen more. The windows were darkened by the sweeping boughs of the trees, and the ivy which had overgrown them: but, in the green gloom, we could manage to see old China jars and carved ivory boxes, and great heavy books, and, above all, the old pictures!

Once, I remember, my darling would have Dorothy go with us to tell us who they all were; for they were all portraits of some of my lord's family, though Dorothy could not tell us the names of every one. We had gone through most of the rooms, when we came to the old state drawing-room over the hall, and there was a picture of Miss Furnivall; or, as she was called in those days, Miss Grace, for she was the younger sister. Such a beauty she must have been! but with such a set, proud look, and such scorn looking out of her handsome eyes, with her eyebrows just a little raised, as if she were wondering how anyone could have the impertinence to look at her; and her lips curled at us, as we stood there gazing. She had a dress on, the like of which I had never seen before, but it was all the fashion when she was young: a hat of some soft white stuff like beaver, pulled a little over her brows, and a beautiful plume of feathers sweeping round it on one side; and her gown of blue satin was open in front to a quilted white stomacher.

'Well, to be sure!' said I, when I had gazed my fill. 'Flesh is grass,

THE OLD NURSE'S STORY

they do say; but who would have thought that Miss Furnivall had been such an out-and-out beauty, to see her now?'

'Yes,' said Dorothy. 'Folks change sadly. But if what my master's father used to say was true, Miss Furnivall, the elder sister, was handsomer than Miss Grace. Her picture is here somewhere; but, if I show it you, you must never let on, even to James, that you have seen it. Can the little lady hold her tongue, think you?' asked she.

I was not so sure, for she was such a little sweet, bold outspoken child, so I set her to hide herself; and then I helped Dorothy to turn a great picture, that leaned with its face towards the wall, and was not hung up as the others were. To be sure, it beat Miss Grace for beauty; and, I think, for scornful pride, too, though in that matter it might be hard to choose. I could have looked at it an hour, but Dorothy seemed half frightened at having shown it to me, and hurried it back again, and bade me run and find Miss Rosamond, for that there were some ugly places about the house, where she should like ill for the child to be. I was a brave, high-spirited girl, and thought little of what the old woman said, for I liked hide-and-seek as well as any child in the parish; so off I ran to find my little one.

As winter drew on, and the days grew shorter, I was sometimes almost certain that I heard a noise as if someone was playing on the great organ in the hall. I did not hear it every evening; but, certainly, I did very often; usually when I was sitting with Miss Rosamond, after I had put her to bed, and keeping quite still and silent in the bedroom. Then I used to hear it booming and swelling away in the distance. The first night, when I went down to my supper, I asked Dorothy who had been playing music, and James said very shortly that I was a gowk to take the wind soughing among the trees for music: but I saw Dorothy look at him very fearfully, and Bessy, the kitchen-maid, said something beneath her breath, and went quite white. I saw they did not like my question, so I held my peace till I was with Dorothy alone, when I knew I could get a good deal out of her. So, the next day, I watched my time, and I coaxed and asked her who it was that played the organ; for I knew that it was the organ and not the wind well enough, for all I had kept silence before James. But Dorothy had had her lesson, I'll warrant, and never a word could I get from her. So then I tried Bessy, though I had always held my head rather above her, as I was evened to James and Dorothy, and she was little better than their servant. So she said I must never, never tell; and, if I ever told, I was never to say *she* had told me; but it was a very strange noise, and she had heard it many a time, but most of all on winter nights, and before storms; and folks did say, it was the old lord playing on the great organ in the hall, just as he used to do when he was alive; but who the old lord was, or why he played, and why he played on stormy winter evenings in particular, she either could not or would not tell me. Well! I told you I had a brave heart; and I thought it was rather pleasant to have that grand music rolling about the house, let who would be the player; for now it rose above the great gusts of wind, and wailed and triumphed just like a living creature, and then it fell to a softness most complete; only it was always music and tunes, so it was nonsense to call it the wind. I thought at first that it might be Miss Furnivall who played, unknown to Bessy; but one day when I was in the hall by myself, I opened the organ and peeped all about it and around it, as I had done to the organ in Crosthwaite Church once before, and I saw it was all broken and destroyed inside, though it looked so brave and fine; and then, though it was noonday, my flesh began to creep a little, and I shut it up, and ran away pretty quickly to my own bright nursery; and I did not like hearing the music for some time after that, any more than James and Dorothy did. All this time Miss Rosamond was making herself more and more beloved. The old ladies liked her to dine with them at their early dinner; James still behind Miss Furnivall's chair, and I behind Miss Rosamond's all in state; and, after dinner, she would play about in a corner of the great drawing-room, as still as any mouse, while Miss Furnivall slept, and I had my dinner in the kitchen. But she was glad enough to come to me in the nursery afterwards; for, as she said, Miss Furnivall was so sad, and Mrs. Stark so dull; but she and I were merry enough; and, by-and-by, I got not to care for that weird rolling music, which did one no harm, if we did not know where it came from.

That winter was very cold. In the middle of October the frosts began, and lasted many, many weeks. I remember, one day at dinner, Miss Furnivall lifted up her sad, heavy eyes, and said to Mrs. Stark, 'I am afraid we shall have a terrible winter,' in a strange kind of meaning way. But Mrs. Stark pretended not to hear, and talked very loud of something else. My little lady and I did not care for the frost; not we! As long as it was dry we climbed up the steep brows, behind the house, and went up on the Fells, which were bleak, and bare enough, and there we ran races in the fresh, sharp air: and once we came down by a new path that took us past the two old gnarled holly-trees, which grew about halfway down by the east side of the house. But the days grew shorter and shorter; and the old lord, if it was he, played more and more stormily and sadly on the great organ. One Sunday afternoon – it must have been towards the end of November – I asked Dorothy to take charge of little Missey when she came out of the drawing-room, after Miss Furnivall had had her nap; for it was too cold to take her with me to church, and yet I wanted to go. And Dorothy was glad enough to promise, and was so fond of the child that all seemed well; and Bessy and I set off very briskly, though the sky hung heavy and black over the white earth, as if the night had never fully gone away; and the air, though still, was very biting and keen.

'We shall have a fall of snow,' said Bessy to me. And sure enough, even while we were in church, it came down thick, in great large flakes, so thick it almost darkened the windows. It had stopped snowing before we came out, but it lay soft, thick and deep beneath our feet, as we tramped home. Before we got to the hall the moon rose, and I think it was lighter then – what with the moon, and what with the white dazzling snow – than it had been when we went to church, between two and three o'clock. I have not told you that Miss Furnivall and Mrs. Stark never went to church: they used to read the prayers together, in their quiet gloomy way; they seemed to feel the Sunday very long without their tapestry-work to be busy at. So when I went to Dorothy in the kitchen, to fetch Miss Rosamond and take her upstairs with me, I did not much wonder when the old woman told me that the ladies had kept the child with them, and that she had never come to the kitchen, as I had bidden her, when she was tired of behaving pretty in the drawing-room. So I took off my things and went to find her, and bring her to her supper in the nursery. But when I went into the best drawing-room there sat the two old ladies, very still and quiet, dropping out a word now and then but looking as if nothing so bright and merry as Miss Rosamond had ever been near them. Still I thought she might be hiding from me; it was one of her pretty ways; and that she had persuaded them to look as if they knew nothing about her; so I went softly peeping under this sofa, and behind that chair, making believe I was sadly frightened at not finding her.

'What's the matter, Hester?' said Mrs. Stark, sharply. I don't know if Miss Furnivall had seen me, for, as I told you, she was very deaf, and she sat quite still, idly staring into the fire, with her hopeless face. 'I'm only looking for my little Rosy-Posy,' replied I, still thinking that the child was there, and near me, though I could not see her.

'Miss Rosamond is not here,' said Mrs. Stark. 'She went away more than an hour ago to find Dorothy.' And she too turned and went on looking into the fire.

My heart sank at this, and I began to wish I had never left my darling. I went back to Dorothy and told her. James was gone out for the day, but she and me and Bessy took lights and went up into the nursery first, and then roamed over the great large house, calling and entreating Miss Rosamond to come out of her hiding-place, and not frighten us to death in that way. But there was no answer; no sound.

'Oh!' said I at last, 'Can she have gone into the east wing and hidden there?'

But Dorothy said it was not possible, for that she herself had never been there; that the doors were always locked; and my lord's steward had the keys, she believed; at any rate, neither she nor James had ever seen them; so I said I would go back, and see if, after all, she was not hidden in the drawing-room, unknown to the old ladies; and if I found her there, I said, I would whip her well for the fright she had given me; but I never meant to do it. Well, I went back to the west drawing-room, and I told Mrs. Stark we could not find her anywhere, and asked for leave to look all about the furniture there, for I thought now, that she might have fallen asleep in some warm hidden corner; but no! we looked, Miss Furnivall got up and looked, trembling all over, and she was nowhere there; then we set off again, everyone in the house, and looked in all the places we had searched before, but we could not find her. Miss Furnivall shivered and shook so much that Mrs. Stark took her back into the warm drawing-room; but not before they had made me promise to bring her to them when she was found. Well-a-day! I began to think she never would be found, when I bethought me to look out into the great front court, all covered with snow. I was upstairs when I looked out; but it was such clear moonlight, I could see, quite plain, two little footprints, which might be traced from the hall door, and round the corner of the east wing. I don't know how I got down, but I tugged open the great, stiff hall door; and, throwing the skirt of my gown over my head for a cloak, I ran out. I turned the east corner, and there a black shadow fell on the snow; but when I came again into the moonlight, there were the little footmarks going up – up to the Fells. It was bitter cold; so cold that the air almost took the skin off my face as I ran, but I ran on, crying to think how my poor little darling must be perished, and frightened. I was within sight of the holly-trees when I saw a shepherd coming down the hill, bearing something in his arms wrapped in his maud. He shouted to me, and asked me if I had lost a bairn; and, when I could not speak for crying, he bore towards me, and I saw my wee bairnie lying still, and white, and stiff, in his arms, as if she had been dead. He told me he had been up the Fells to gather in his sheep, before the deep cold of night came on, and that under the holly-trees (black marks on the hillside, where no other bush was for miles around) he had found my little lady – my lamb – my queen – my darling – stiff and cold, in the terrible sleep which is frost-begotten. Oh! the joy, and the tears of having her in my arms once again! for I would not let him carry her; but took her, maud and all, into my own arms, and held her near my own warm neck and heart, and felt the life stealing slowly back again into her little gentle limbs. But she was still insensible when we reached the hall, and I had no breath for speech. We went in by the kitchen door.

'Bring the warming-pan,' said I; and I carried her upstairs and began undressing her by the hursery fire, which Bessy had kept up. I called my little lammie all the sweet and playful names I could think of – even while my eyes were blinded by my tears; and at last, oh! at length she opened her large blue eyes. Then I put her into her warm bed, and sent Dorothy down to tell Miss Furnivall that all was well; and I made up my mind to sit by my darling's bedside the live-long night. She fell away into a soft sleep as soon as her pretty head had touched the pillow, and

I watched by her until morning light; when she wakened up bright and clear – or so I thought at first – and, my dears, so I think now.

She said that she had fancied that she should like to go to Dorothy, for that both the old ladies were asleep, and it was very dull in the drawing-room; and that, as she was going through the west lobby, she saw the snow through the high window falling – soft and steady; but she wanted to see it lying pretty and white on the ground; so she made her way into the great hall; and then, going to the window, she saw it bright and soft upon the drive; but while she stood there, she saw a little girl, not so old as she was, 'but so pretty', said my darling, 'and this little girl beckoned to me to come out; and oh, she was so pretty and so sweet, I could not choose but go.' And then this other little girl had taken her by the hand, and side by side the two had gone round the east corner.

'Now you are a naughty little girl, and telling stories,' said I. 'What would your good mamma, that is in heaven, and never told a story in her life, say to her little Rosamond, if she heard her – and I dare say she does – telling stories!'

'Indeed, Hester,' sobbed out my child, 'I'm telling you true. Indeed I am.'

'Don't tell me!' said I, very stern. 'I tracked you by your footmarks through the snow; there were only yours to be seen: and if you had had a little girl to go hand-in-hand with you up the hill, don't you think the footprints would have gone along with yours?'

'I can't help it, dear, dear Hester,' said she, crying. 'If they did not; I never looked at her feet, but she held my hand fast and tight in her little one, and it was very, very cold. She took me up the Fell-path, up to the holly-trees; and there I saw a lady weeping and crying; but when she saw me, she hushed her weeping, and smiled very proud and grand, and took me on her knee, and began to lull me to sleep; and that's all, Hester – but that is true; and my dear mamma knows it is,' said she, crying. So I thought the child was in a fever, and pretended to believe her, as she went over her story – over and over again, and always the same. At last Dorothy knocked at the door with Miss Rosamond's breakfast; and she told me the old ladies were down in the eating parlour, and that they wanted to speak to me. They had both been into the night-nursery the evening before, but it was after Miss Rosamond was asleep; so they had only looked at her – not asked me any questions.

'I shall catch it,' thought I to myself, as I went along the north gallery. 'And yet,' I thought, taking courage, 'it was in their charge I left her; and it's they that's to blame for letting her steal away unknown and unwatched.' So I went in boldly, and told my story. I told it all to Miss Furnivall, shouting it close to her ear; but when I came to the mention of the other little girl out in the snow, coaxing and tempting her out, and willing her up to the grand and beautiful lady by the holly-tree, she

threw her arms up – her old and withered arms – and cried aloud. 'Oh!
Heaven, forgive! Have mercy!'

Mrs. Stark took hold of her; roughly enough, I thought; but she was
past Mrs. Stark's management, and spoke to me, in a kind of wild
warning and authority.

'Hester! keep her from that child! It will lure her to her death! That
evil child! Tell her it is a wicked, naughty child.' Then Mrs. Stark
hurried me out of the room; where, indeed, I was glad enough to go; but
Miss Furnivall kept shrieking out, 'Oh! have mercy! Wilt Thou never
forgive! It is many a long year ago'—

I was very uneasy in my mind after that. I durst never leave Miss
Rosamond, night or day, for fear lest she might slip off again, after some
fancy or other; and all the more because I thought I could make out that
Miss Furnivall was crazy, from their odd ways about her; and I was
afraid lest something of the same kind (which might be in the family, you
know) hung over my darling. And the great frost never ceased all this
time; and whenever it was a more stormy night than usual, between the
gusts, and through the wind, we heard the old lord playing on the great
organ. But, old lord, or not, wherever Miss Rosamond went, there I
followed; for my love for her, pretty helpless orphan, was stronger than
my fear for the grand and terrible sound. Besides, it rested with me to
keep her cheerful and merry, as beseemed her age. So we played together,
and wandered together, here and there, and everywhere; for I never dared
to lose sight of her again in that large and rambling house. And so it
happened, that one afternoon, not long before Christmas Day, we were
playing together on the billiard-table in the great hall (not that we knew
the way of playing, but she liked to roll the smooth ivory balls with her
pretty hands, and I liked to do whatever she did); and, by-and-by, without
our noticing it, it grew dusk indoors, though it was still light in the open
air, and I was thinking of taking her back into the nursery, when, all of
a sudden, she cried out:

'Look, Hester! Look! there is my poor little girl out in the snow!'

I turned towards the long narrow windows, and there, sure enough,
I saw a little girl, less than my Miss Rosamond – dressed all unfit to be
out-of-doors such a bitter night – crying, and beating against the
window-panes, as if she wanted to be let in. She seemed to sob and wail,
till Miss Rosamond could bear it no longer, and was flying to the door
to open it, when, all of a sudden, and close up upon us, the great organ
pealed out so loud and thundering, it fairly made me tremble; and all the
more, when I remembered me that, even in the stillness of that dead-cold
weather, I had heard no sound of little battering hands upon the
window-glass, although the Phantom Child had seemed to put forth all
its force; and, although I had seen it wail and cry, no faintest touch of
sound had fallen upon my ears. Whether I remembered all this at the
very moment, I do not know; the great organ sound had so stunned me

into terror; but this I know, I caught up Miss Rosamond before she got the hall-door opened, and clutched her, and carried her away, kicking and screaming, into the large bright kitchen, where Dorothy and Bessy were busy with their mince-pies.

'What is the matter with my sweet one?' cried Dorothy, as I bore in Miss Rosamond, who was sobbing as if her heart would break.

'She won't let me open the door for my little girl to come in; and she'll die if she is out on the Fells all night. Cruel, naughty Hester,' she said, slapping me; but she might have struck harder, for I had seen a look of ghastly terror on Dorothy's face, which made my very blood run cold.

'Shut the back-kitchen door fast, and bolt it well,' said she to Bessy. She said no more; she gave me raisins and almonds to quiet Miss Rosamond: but she sobbed about the little girl in the snow, and would not touch any of the good things. I was thankful when she cried herself to sleep in bed. Then I stole down to the kitchen, and told Dorothy I had made up my mind. I would carry my darling back to my father's house in Applethwaite; where, if we lived humbly, we lived at peace. I said I had been frightened enough with the old lord's organ-playing; but now that I had seen for myself this little moaning child, all decked out as no child in the neighbourhood could be, beating and battering to get in, yet always without any sound or noise – with the dark wound on its right shoulder; and that Miss Rosamond had known it again for the phantom that had nearly lured her to her death (which Dorothy knew was true); I would stand it no longer.

I saw Dorothy change colour once or twice. When I had done, she told me she did not think I could take Miss Rosamond with me, for that she was my lord's ward, and I had no right over her; and she asked me, would I leave the child that I was so fond of, just for sounds and sights that could do me no harm; and that they had all had to get used to in their turns? I was all in a hot, trembling passion; and I said it was very well for her to talk, that knew what these sights and noises betokened, and that had, perhaps, had something to do with the Spectre-Child while it was alive. And I taunted her so, that she told me all she knew, at last; and then I wished I had never been told, for it only made me afraid more than ever.

She said she had heard the tale from old neighbours, that were alive when she was first married; when folks used to come to the hall sometimes, before it had got such a bad name in the countryside; it might not be true, or it might, what she had been told.

The old lord was Miss Furnivall's father – Miss Grace as Dorothy called her, for Miss Maude was the elder, and Miss Furnivall by rights. The old lord was eaten up with pride. Such a proud man was never seen or heard of; and his daughters were like him. No one was good enough to wed them, although they had choice enough; for they were the great beauties of their day, as I had seen by their portraits, where they hung in the state drawing-room. But, as the old saying is, 'Pride will have a fall'; and these two haughty beauties fell in love with the same man, and he no better than a foreign musician, whom their father had down from London to play music with him at the Manor House. For, above all things, next to his pride, the old lord loved music. He could play on nearly every instrument that ever was heard of: and it was a strange thing it did not soften him; but he was a fierce dour old man, and had broken his poor wife's heart with his cruelty, they said. He was mad after music, and would any money for it. So he got this foreigner to come; who made such beautiful music, that they said the very birds on the trees stopped their singing to listen. And, by degrees, this foreign gentleman got such a hold over the old lord, that nothing would serve him but that he must come every year; and it was he that had the great organ brought from Holland, and built up in the hall, where it stood now. He taught the old lord to play on it; but many and many a time, when Lord Furnivall was thinking of nothing but his fine organ, and his finer music, the dark foreigner was walking abroad in the woods with one of the young ladies; now Miss Maude, and then Miss Grace.

Miss Maude won the day and carried off the prize, such as it was; and he and she were married, all unknown to anyone; and before he made his next yearly visit, she had been confined of a little girl at a farm-house on the Moors, while her father and Miss Grace thought she was away at Doncaster Races. But though she was a wife and a mother, she was not a bit softened, but as haughty and as passionate as ever; and perhaps more so, for she was jealous of Miss Grace, to whom her foreign husband paid a deal of court – by way of blinding her – as he told his wife. But Miss Grace triumphed over Miss Maude, and Miss Maude grew fiercer and fiercer, both with her husband and with her sister; and the former – who could easily shake off what was disagreeable, and hide himself in foreign countries – went away a month before his usual time that summer, and half-threatened that he would never come back again. Meanwhile, the little girl was left at the farm-house, and her mother used to have her horse saddled and gallop wildly over the hills to see her once every week, at the very least – for where she loved, she loved; and where she hated, she hated. And the old lord went on playing – playing on his organ; and the servants thought the sweet music he made had soothed down his awful temper, of which (Dorothy said) some terrible tales could be told. He grew infirm too, and had to walk with a crutch; and his son – that was the present Lord Furnivall's father – was with the army in America, and the other son at sea; so Miss Maude had it pretty much her own way, and she and Miss Grace grew colder and bitterer to each other every day; till at last they hardly ever spoke, except when the old lord was by. The foreign musician came again the next summer, but it was for the last time; for they led him such a life with their jealousy and their passions, that he grew weary, and went away, and never was heard of again. And Miss Maude, who had always meant to have her marriage acknowledged when her father should be dead, was left now a deserted wife – whom nobody knew to have been married – with a child that she dared not own, although she loved it to distraction; living with a father whom she feared, and a sister whom she hated. When the next summer passed over and the dark foreigner never came, both Miss Maude and Miss Grace grew gloomy and sad; they had a haggard look about them, though they looked handsome as ever. But by-and-by Miss Maude brightened; for her father grew more and more infirm, and more than ever carried away by his music; and she and Miss Grace lived almost entirely apart, having separate rooms, the one on the west side, Miss Maude on the east – those very rooms which were now shut up. So she thought she might have her little girl with her, and no one need ever know except those who dared not speak about it, and were bound to believe that it was, as she said, a cottager's child she had taken a fancy to. All this, Dorothy said, was pretty well known; but what came afterwards no one knew, except Miss Grace, and Mrs. Stark, who was even then her maid, and much more of a friend to her than ever her sister had been. But the servants supposed, from words that were dropped, that Miss Maude had triumphed over Miss Grace, and told her that all the time the dark foreigner had been mocking her with pretended love – he was her own husband; the colour left Miss Grace's cheek and lips that very day for ever, and she was heard to say many a time that sooner or later she would have her revenge; and Mrs. Stark was for ever spying about the east rooms.

One fearful night, just after the New Year had come in, when the snow was lying thick and deep, and the flakes were still falling – fast enough to blind anyone who might be out and abroad – there was a great and violent noise heard, and the old lord's voice above all, cursing and swearing awfully – and the cries of a little child – and the proud defiance of a fierce woman – and the sound of a blow – and a dead stillness – and moans and wailings dying away on the hillside! Then the old lord summoned all his servants, and told them, with terrible oaths, and words more terrible, that his daughter had disgraced herself, and that he had turned her out of doors – her, and her child – and that if ever they gave her help – or food – or shelter – he prayed that they might never enter Heaven. And, all the while, Miss Grace stood by him, white and still as any stone; and when he had ended she heaved a great sigh, as much as to say her work was done, and her end was accomplished. But the old lord never touched his organ again, and died within the year; and no wonder! for, on the morrow of that wild and fearful night, the shepherds, coming down the Fell side, found Miss Maude sitting, all crazy and smiling, under the holly-trees, nursing a dead child – with a terrible mark on its right shoulder. 'But that was not what killed it,' said Dorothy; 'it was the frost and the cold – every wild creature was in its hole, and every beast in its fold – while the child and its mother were turned out to wander on the Fells! And now you know all! and I wonder if you are less frightened now?'

I was more frightened than ever; but I said I was not. I wished Miss Rosamond and myself well out of that dreadful house for ever; but I would not leave her, and I dared not take her away. But oh! how I watched her, and guarded her! We bolted the doors and shut the window-shutters fast, an hour or more before dark, rather than leave them open five minutes too late. But my little lady still heard the weird child crying and mourning; and not all we could do or say could keep her from wanting to go to her, and let her in from the cruel wind and the snow. All this time, I kept away from Miss Furnivall and Mrs. Stark, as much as ever I could; for I feared them – I knew no good could be about them, with their grey hard faces, and their dreamy eyes, looking back into the ghastly years that were gone. But, even in my fear, I had a kind of pity – for Miss Furnivall, at least. Those gone down to the pit can hardly have a more hopeless look than that which was ever on her face. At last I even got so sorry for her – who never said a word but what was quite forced from her – that I prayed for her; and I taught Miss Rosamond to pray for one who had done a deadly sin; but often when she came to those words, she would listen, and start up from her knees, and say, 'I hear my little girl plaining and crying very sad – Oh! let her in, or she will die!'

One night – just after New Year's Day had come at last, and the long winter had taken a turn, as I hoped – I heard the west drawing-room bell ring three times, which was a signal for me. I would not leave Miss Rosamond alone, for all she was asleep – for the old lord had been playing wilder than ever – and I feared lest my darling should waken to hear the spectre child; see her I knew she could not. I had fastened the windows too well for that. So I took her out of her bed and wrapped her up in such outer clothes as were most handy, and carried her down to the drawing-room, where the old ladies sat at their tapestry work as usual. They looked up when I came in, and Mrs. Stark asked, quite astounded, 'Why did I bring Miss Rosamond there, out of her warm bed?' I had begun to whisper, 'Because I was afraid of her being tempted out while I was away, by the wild child in the snow,' when she stopped me short (with a glance at Miss Furnivall), and said Miss Furnivall wanted me to undo some work she had done wrong, and which neither of them could see to unpick. So I laid my pretty dear on the sofa, and sat down on a stool by them, and hardened my heart against them, as I heard the wind rising and howling.

Miss Rosamond slept on sound, for all the wind blew so; and Miss Furnivall said never a word, nor looked round when the gusts shook the windows. All at once she started up to her full height, and put up one hand, as if to bid us listen.

'I hear voices!' said she, 'I hear terrible screams – I hear my father's voice!'

Just at that moment my darling wakened with a sudden start: 'My little girl is crying, oh, how she is crying!' and she tried to get up and go to her, but she got her feet entangled in the blanket, and I caught her up; for my flesh had begun to creep at these noises, which they heard while we could catch no sound. In a minute or two the noises came, and gathered fast, and filled our ears; we, too, heard voices and screams, and no longer heard the winter's wind that raged abroad. Mrs. Stark looked at me, and I at her, but we dared not speak. Suddenly Miss Furnivall went towards the door, out into the ante-room, through the west lobby, and opened the door into the great hall. Mrs. Stark followed, and I durst not be left, though my heart almost stopped beating for fear. I wrapped my darling tight in my arms, and went out with them. In the hall the screams were louder than ever; they sounded to come from the east wing – nearer and nearer – close on the other side of the locked-up doors – close behind them. Then I noticed that the great bronze chandelier seemed all alight, though the hall was dim, and that a fire was blazing in the vast hearth-place, though it gave no heat; and I shuddered up with terror, and folded my darling closer to me. But as I did so, the east door shook, and she, suddenly struggling to get free from me, cried, 'Hester! I must go! My little girl is there; I hear her; she is coming! Hester, I must go!'

I held her tight with all my strength; with a set will I held her. If I had died, my hands would have grasped her still, I was so resolved in my mind. Miss Furnivall stood listening, and paid no regard to my darling, who had got down to the ground, and whom I, upon my knees now, was holding with both my arms clasped round her neck; she still striving and crying to get free.

All at once the east door gave way with a thundering crash, as if torn open in a violent passion, and there came into that broad and mysterious light, the figure of a tall old man, with grey hair and gleaming eyes. He drove before him, with many a relentless gesture of abhorrence, a stern and beautiful woman, with a little child clinging to her dress.

'Oh Hester! Hester!' cried Miss Rosamond. 'It's the lady! the lady below the holly-trees; and my little girl is with her. Hester! Hester! let me go to her; they are drawing me to them. I feel them – I feel them. I must go!'

Again she was almost convulsed by her efforts to get away; but I held her tighter and tighter, till I feared I should do her a hurt; but rather that than let her go towards those terrible phantoms. They passed along towards the great hall-door, where the winds howled and ravened for their prey; but before they reached that, the lady turned; and I could see that she defied the old man with a fierce and proud defiance; but then she quailed – and then she threw up her arms wildly and piteously to save her child – her little child – from a blow from his uplifted crutch.

And Miss Rosamond was torn as by a power stronger than mine, and writhed in my arms, and sobbed (for by this time the poor darling was growing faint).

'They want me to go with them on to the Fells – they are drawing me to them. On, my little girl! I would come, but cruel, wicked Hester holds me very tight.' But when she saw the uplifted crutch she swooned away, and I thanked God for it. Just at this moment – when the tall old man, his hair streaming as in the blast of a furnace, was going to strike the little shrinking child – Miss Furnivall, the old woman by my side, cried out, 'Oh, Father! Father! spare the little innocent child!' But just then I saw – we all saw – another phantom shape itself, and grow clear out of the blue and misty light that filled the hall; we had not seen her till now, for it was another lady who stood by the old man, with a look of relentless hate and triumphant scorn. That figure was very beautiful to look upon, with a soft white hat drawn down over the proud brows and a red and curling lip. It was dressed in an open robe of blue satin. I had seen that figure before. It was the likeness of Miss Furnivall in her youth; and the terrible phantoms moved on, regardless of old Miss Furnivall's wild entreaty – and the uplifted crutch fell on the right shoulder of the little child, and the younger sister looked on, stony and deadly serene. But at that moment the dim lights, and the fire that gave no heat, went out of themselves, and Miss Furnivall lay at our feet stricken down by the palsy – death-stricken.

Yes! she was carried to her bed that night never to rise again. She lay with her face to the wall muttering low but muttering away: 'Alas! alas! what is done in youth can never be undone in age! What is done in youth can never be undone in age!'

A Ghost Story

MARK TWAIN

I TOOK A LARGE ROOM, far up New York's Broadway, in a huge old building whose upper storeys had been wholly unoccupied for years until I came. The place had long been given up to dust and cobwebs, to solitude and silence. I seemed groping among the tombs and invading the privacy of the dead, that first night I climbed up to my quarters. For the first time in my life a superstitious dread came over me; and as I turned a dark angle of the stairway and an invisible cobweb swung its slazy woof in my face and clung there, I shuddered as one who had encountered a phantom.

I was glad enough when I reached my room and locked out the mould and the darkness. A cheery fire was burning in the grate, and I sat down before it with a comfortable sense of relief. For two hours I sat there, thinking of bygone times; recalling old scenes, and summoning half-forgotten faces out of the mists of the past; listening, in fancy, to voices that long ago grew silent for all time, and to once familiar songs that nobody sings now. And as my reverie softened down to a sadder and sadder pathos, the shrieking of the winds outside softened to a wail, the angry beating of the rain against the panes diminished to a tranquil patter, and one by one the noises in the street subsided, until the hurrying footsteps of the last belated straggler died away in the distance and left no sound behind.

The fire had burned low. A sense of loneliness crept over me. I arose and undressed, moving on tiptoe about the room, doing stealthily what I had to do, as if I were environed by sleeping enemies whose slumbers it would be fatal to break. I covered up in bed, and lay listening to the rain and wind and the faint creaking of distant shutters, till they lulled me to sleep.

I slept profoundly, but how long I do not know. All at once I found myself awake, and filled with a shuddering expectancy. All was still. All but my own heart – I could hear it beat. Presently the bedclothes began to slip slowly towards the foot of the bed, as if some one were pulling them! I could not stir; I could not speak. Still the blankets slipped deliberately away, till my chest was uncovered. Then with a great effort I seized them and drew them over my head. I waited, listened, waited. Once more that steady pull began, and once more I lay torpid a century of dragging seconds till my chest was once more uncovered. At last I roused my energies and snatched the covers back to their place and held them with a strong grip. I waited. By and by I felt a faint tug, and took a fresh grip. The tug strengthened to a steady strain – it grew stronger and stronger. My hold parted, and for the third time the blankets slid away. I groaned. An answering groan came from the foot of the bed! Beaded drops of sweat stood upon my forehead. I was more dead than alive. Presently I heard a heavy footstep in my room – the step of an elephant, it seemed to me – it was not like anything human. But it was moving *from* me – there was relief in that. I heard it approach the door – pass out without moving bolt or lock – and wander away among the dismal corridors, straining the floors and joists till they creaked again as it passed – and then silence reigned once more.

When my excitement had calmed, I said to myself, 'This is a dream – simply a hideous dream.' And so I lay thinking it over until I convinced myself that it *was* a dream, and then a comforting laugh relaxed my lips and I was happy again. I got up and struck a light; and when I found that the locks and bolts were just as I had left them, another soothing laugh welled in my heart and rippled from my lips. I took my pipe and lit it, and was just sitting down before the fire, when – down went the pipe out of my nerveless fingers, the blood forsook my cheeks, and my placid breathing was cut short with a gasp! In the ashes on the hearth, side by side with my own bare footprint, was another, so vast that in comparison mine was but an infant's! Then I *had* had a visitor, and the elephantine tread was explained.

I put out the light and returned to bed, palsied with fear. I lay a long time, peering into the darkness, and listening. Then I heard a grating noise overhead, like the dragging of a heavy body across the floor; then the throwing down of the body, and the shaking of my windows in response to the concussion. In distant parts of the building I heard the muffled slamming of doors. I heard, at intervals, stealthy footsteps creeping in and out among the corridors, and up and down the stairs. Sometimes these noises approached my door, hesitated, and went away again. I heard the clanking of chains faintly, in remote passages, and listened while the clanking grew nearer – while it wearily climbed the stairways, marking each move by the loose surplus of chain that fell with an accented rattle upon each succeeding step as the goblin that bore it advanced. I heard muttered sentences; half uttered screams that seemed smothered violently; and the swish of invisible garments, the rush of invisible wings. Then I became conscious that my chamber was invaded – that I was not alone. I heard sighs and breathings about my bed, and mysterious whisperings. Three little spheres of soft phosphorescent light appeared on the ceiling directly over my head, clung and glowed there a moment, and then dropped – two of them upon my face and one upon the pillow. They spattered liquidly and felt warm. Intuition told me they had turned to gouts of blood as they fell – I needed no light to satisfy myself of that. Then I saw pallid faces, dimly luminous, and white uplifted hands, floating bodiless in the air – floating a moment and then disappearing. The whispering ceased, and the voices and the sounds, and a solemn stillness followed. I waited and listened. I felt that I must have light or die. I was weak with fear. I slowly raised myself towards a sitting posture, and my face came in contact with a clammy hand! All strength went from me apparently, and I fell back like a stricken invalid. Then I heard the rustle of a garment – it seemed to pass to the door and go out.

When everything was still once more, I crept out of bed, sick and feeble, and lit the gas with a hand that trembled as if it were aged with a hundred years. The light brought some little cheer to my spirits. I sat down and fell into a dreamy contemplation of that great footprint in the ashes. By and by its outlines began to waver and grow dim. I glanced up and the broad gas-flame was slowly wilting away. In the same moment I heard that elephantine tread again. I noted its approach, nearer and nearer, along the musty halls, and dimmer and dimmer the light waned. The tread reached my very door and paused – the light had dwindled to a sickly blue, and all things about me lay in a spectral twilight. The door did not open, and yet I felt a faint gust of air fan my cheek, and presently was conscious of a huge, cloudy presence before me. I watched it with fascinated eyes. A pale glow stole over the Thing; gradually its cloudy folds took shape – an arm appeared, then legs, then a body, and last a great sad face looked out of the vapour. Stripped of its filmy housings, naked, muscular and comely, that petrified, prehistoric man, the so-called Cardiff Giant loomed above me!

All my misery vanished – for a child might know that no harm could come with that benignant countenance. My cheerful spirits returned at once, and in sympathy with them the gas flamed up brightly again. Never was a lonely outcast so glad to welcome company as I was to greet the friendly giant. I said:

'Why, is it nobody but you? Do you know, I have been scared to death for the last two or three hours? I am most honestly glad to see you. I wish I had a chair— Here, here, don't try to sit down in that thing!'

But it was too late. He was in it before I could stop him, and down he went – I never saw a chair so shivered in my life.

'Stop, stop, you'll ruin ev—'

Too late again. There was another crash, and another chair was resolved into its original elements.

'Confound it, haven't you got any judgement at all? Do you want to ruin all the furniture in the place? Here, here, you petrified fool—'

But it was no use. Before I could arrest him he had sat down on the bed, and it was a melancholy ruin.

'Now what sort of a way is that to do? First you come lumbering about the place bringing a legion of vagabond goblins along with you to worry me to death, and when I overlook an indelicacy of costume, which would not be tolerated anywhere by cultivated people except in a respectable theatre, and not even there if the nudity were of *your* sex, you repay me by wrecking all the furniture you can find to sit down on. And why will you? You damage yourself as much as you do me. You have broken off the end of your spinal column, and littered up the floor with chips of your hams till the place looks like a marble yard. You ought to be ashamed of yourself – you are big enough to know better.'

'Well, I will not break any more furniture. But what am I to do? I have not had a chance to sit down for a century.' And the tears came into his eyes.

'Poor devil,' I said, 'I should not have been so harsh with you. And you are an orphan too, no doubt. But sit down on the floor here – nothing else can stand your weight – and besides, we cannot be sociable with you away up there above me; I want you down where I can perch on this high counting-house stool and gossip with you face to face.'

So he sat down on the floor, and lit a pipe which I gave him, threw one of my red blankets over his shoulders, inverted my hip-bath on his head, helmet fashion, and made himself picturesque and comfortable. Then he crossed his ankles, while I renewed the fire, and exposed the flat, honeycombed bottoms of his prodigious feet to the grateful warmth.

'What is the matter with the bottom of your feet and the back of your legs, that they are gouged up so?'

'Infernal chilblains – I caught them clear up to the back of my head, roosting out there under Newell's farm where they dug me up. But I love the place; love it as one loves his old home. There is no peace like the peace I feel when I am there.'

We talked along for half an hour, and then I noticed that he looked tired, and spoke of it.

'Tired?' said he. 'Well, I should think so. And now I will tell you all about it, since you have treated me so well. I am the spirit of the petrified man that lies across the street there in the museum. I am the ghost of the Cardiff Giant. I can have no rest, no peace, till they have given that poor body burial again. Now what was the most natural thing for me to do, to make men satisfy this wish? Terrify them into it! haunt the place where the body lay! So I haunted the museum night after night. I even got other spirits to help me. But it did no good, for nobody ever came to the museum at midnight. Then it occurred to me to come over the way and haunt this place a little. I felt that if I ever got a hearing I must succeed, for I had the most efficient company that perdition could furnish. Night after night we have shivered around through these mildewed halls, dragging chains, groaning, whispering, tramping up and down stairs, till, to tell you the truth, I am almost worn out. But when I saw a light in your room tonight I roused my energies again and went at it with a deal of the old freshness. But I'm tired out – entirely fagged out. Give me, I beseech you, give me some hope!'

I lit off my perch in a burst of excitement, and exclaimed:

'This transcends everything! Everything that ever did occur. Why, you poor blundering old fossil, you have had all your trouble for nothing – you have been haunting a *plaster cast* of yourself – the real Cardiff Giant is in Albany! Confound it, don't you know your own remains?"

It was a fact. The original fraud was ingeniously and fraudulently duplicated, and exhibited in New York as the 'only genuine' Cardiff Giant (to the unspeakable disgust of the owners of the real colossus) at the very same time that the latter was drawing crowds at a museum in Albany.

Well, when I explained all this, I never saw such an eloquent look of shame, of pitiable humiliation, overspread a countenance before.

The petrified man rose slowly to his feet, and said:

'Honestly, *is* that true?'

'As true as I am sitting here.'

He took the pipe from his mouth and laid it on the mantel, then stood irresolute a moment, dropping his chin on his chest, and finally said:

'Well – I *never* felt so absurd before. The petrified man has sold everybody else, and now the mean fraud has ended by selling its own ghost! My son, if there is any charity left in your heart for a poor friendless phantom like me, don't let this get out. Think how *you* would feel if you had made such an ass of yourself.'

I heard his stately tramp die away, step by step down the stairs and out into the deserted street, and felt sorry that he was gone, poor fellow – and sorrier still that he had carried off my red blanket and my bath-tub.

The Picture of Dorian Gray
OSCAR WILDE

In nineteenth century London, Dorian Gray has retained his unblemished youthful appearance in spite of his abandonment to depravity. His portrait, however, locked away in an attic, mysteriously reveals the truth of his life. Its painter, Basil Hallward, becomes the victim of cold-blooded murder when he urges Dorian to reform before it is too late . . . .

A COLD RAIN BEGAN to fall, and the blurred street-lamps looked ghastly in the dipping mist. The public-houses were just closing and dim men and women were clustering in broken groups round their doors. From some of the bars came the sound of horrible laughter. In others, drunkards brawled and screamed.

Lying back in the hansom, with his hat pulled over his forehead, Dorian Gray watched with listless eyes the sordid shame of the great city, and now and then he repeated to himself the words that Lord Henry had said to him on the first day they had met, 'To cure the soul by means of the senses, and the senses by means of the soul.' Yes, that was the secret. He had often tried it, and would try it again now. There were opium-dens, where one could buy oblivion, dens of horror where the memory of old sins could be destroyed by the madness of sins that were new.

The moon hung low in the sky like a yellow skull. From time to time a huge misshapen cloud stretched a long arm across and hid it. The gas-lamps grew fewer, and the streets more narrow and gloomy. Once the man lost his way, and had to drive back half a mile. A steam rose from the horse as it splashed up the puddles. The side-windows of the hansom were clogged with a grey-flannel mist.

'To cure the soul by means of the senses, and the senses by means of the soul!' How the words rang in his ears! His soul, certainly was sick to death. Was it true that the senses could cure it? Innocent blood had been spilt. What could atone for that? Ah! for that there was no atonement; but though forgiveness was impossible, forgetfulness was possible still, and he was determined to forget, to stamp the thing out, to crush it as one would crush the adder that had stung one. Indeed, what right had Basil to have spoken to him as he had done? Who had made him a judge over others? He had said things that were dreadful, horrible, not to be endured.

On and on plodded the hansom, going slower, it seemed to him, at each step. He thrust up the trap, and called to the man to drive faster. The hideous hunger for opium began to gnaw at him. His throat burned, and his delicate hands twitched nervously together. He struck at the horse madly with his stick. The driver laughed, and whipped up. He laughed in answer, and the man was silent.

The way seemed interminable, and the streets like the black web of some sprawling spider. The monotony became unbearable, and, as the mist thickened, he felt afraid.

Then they passed by lonely brickfields. The fog was lighter here, and he could see the strange bottle shaped kilns with their orange fan-like tongues of fire. A dog barked as they went by, and far away in the darkness some wandering sea-gull screamed. The horse stumbled in a rut, then swerved aside, and broke into a gallop.

After some time they left the clay road, and rattled again over rough-paven streets. Most of the windows were dark, but now and then fantastic shadows were silhouetted against some lamp-lit blind. He watched them curiously. They moved like monstrous marionettes, and made gestures like live things. He hated them. A dull rage was in his heart. As they turned a corner a woman yelled something at them from an open door, and two men ran after the hansom for about a hundred yards. The driver beat at them with his whip.

It is said that passion makes one think in a circle. Certainly with hideous iteration the bitten lips of Dorian Gray shaped and reshaped those subtle words that dealt with soul and sense, till he had found in them the full expression, as it were, of his mood, and justified, by intellectual approval, passions that without such justification would still have dominated his temper. From cell to cell of his brain crept the one thought; and the wild desire to live, most terrible of all man's appetites, quickened into force each trembling nerve and fibre. Ugliness that had once been hateful to him because it made things real, became dear to him now for that very reason. Ugliness was the one reality. The coarse brawl, the loathsome den, the crude violence of disordered life, the very vileness of thief and outcast, were more vivid, in their intense actuality of impression, than all the gracious shapes of Art, the dreamy shadows of

Song. They were what he needed for forgetfulness. In three days he would be free.

Suddenly the man drew up with a jerk at the top of a dark lane. Over the low roofs and jagged chimney stacks of the houses rose the black masts of ships. Wreaths of white mist clung like ghostly sails to the yards.

'Somewhere about here, sir, ain't it?' he asked huskily through the trap.

Dorian started, and peered round. 'This will do,' he answered, and, having got out hastily, and given the driver the extra fare he had promised him, he walked quickly in the direction of the quay. Here and there a lantern gleamed at the stern of some huge merchantman. The light shook and splintered in the puddles. A red glare came from an outward-bound steamer that was coaling. The slimy pavement looked like a wet mackintosh.

He hurried on towards the left, glancing back now and then to see if he was being followed. In about seven or eight minutes he reached a small shabby house, that was wedged in between two gaunt factories. In one of the top-windows stood a lamp. He stopped, and gave a peculiar knock.

After a little time he heard steps in the passage, and the chain being unhooked. The door opened quietly, and he went in without saying a word to the squat misshapen figure that flattened itself into the shadow as he passed. At the end of the hall hung a tattered green curtain that swayed and shook in the gusty wind which had followed him in from the street. He dragged it aside, and entered a long, low room which looked as if it had once been a third-rate dancing-salon. Shrill flaring gas jets, dulled and distorted in the fly-blown mirrors that faced them, were ranged round the walls. Greasy reflectors of ribbed tin backed them, making quivering discs of light. The floor was covered with ochre-coloured sawdust, trampled here and there into mud, and stained with dark rings of spilt liquor. Some Malays were crouching by a little charcoal stove playing with bone counters and showing their white teeth as they chattered. In one corner, with his head buried in his arms, a sailor sprawled over a table, and by the tawdrily-painted bar that ran across one complete side stood two haggard women mocking an old man who was brushing the sleeves of his coat with an expression of disgust. 'He thinks he's got red ants on him,' laughed one of them, as Dorian passed by. The man looked at her in terror and began to whimper.

At the end of the room there was a little staircase, leading to a darkened chamber. As Dorian hurried up its three rickety steps, the heavy odour of opium met him. He heaved a deep breath, and his nostrils quivered with pleasure. When he entered, a young man with smooth yellow hair, who was bending over a lamp, lighting a long thin pipe, looked up at him, and nodded in a hesitating manner.

'You here, Adrian?' muttered Dorian.

266

'Where else should I be?' he answered, listlessly. 'None of the chaps will speak to me now.'

'I thought you had left England.'

'Darlington is not going to do anything. My brother paid the bill at last. George doesn't speak to me either. . . . I don't care,' he added, with a sigh. 'As long as one has this stuff, one doesn't want friends. I think I have had too many friends.'

Dorian winced, and looked round at the grotesque things that lay in such fantastic postures on the ragged mattresses. The twisted limbs, the gaping mouths, the staring lustreless eyes, fascinated him. He knew in what strange heavens they were suffering, and what dull hells were teaching them the secret of some new joy. They were better off than he was. He was prisoned in thought. Memory, like a horrible malady, was eating his soul away. From time to time he seemed to see the eyes of Basil Hallward looking at him. Yet he felt he could not stay. The presence of Adrian Singleton troubled him. He wanted to be where no man would know who he was. He wanted to escape from himself.

'I am going on to the other place,' he said, after a pause.

'On the wharf?'

'Yes.'

'That mad-cat is sure to be there. They won't have her in this place now.'

Dorian shrugged his shoulders. 'I am sick of women who love one. Women who hate one are much more interesting. Besides, the stuff is better.'

'Much the same.'

'I like it better. Come and have something to drink. I must have something.'

'I don't want anything,' murmured the young man.

'Never mind.'

Adrian Singleton rose up wearily, and followed Dorian to the bar. A half-caste, in a ragged turban and a shabby ulster, grinned a hideous greeting as he thrust a bottle of brandy and two tumblers in front of them. The women sidled up, and began to chatter. Dorian turned his back on them, and said something in a low voice to Adrian Singleton.

A crooked smile, like a Malay crease, writhed across the face of one of the women.

'We are very proud to-night,' she sneered.

'For God's sake don't talk to me,' cried Dorian, stamping his foot on the ground. 'What do you want? Money? Here it is. Don't ever talk to me again.'

Two red sparks flashed for a moment in the woman's sodden eyes, then flickered out, and left them dull and glazed. She tossed her head, and raked the coins off the counter with greedy fingers. Her companion watched her enviously.

'It's no use,' sighed Adrian Singleton. 'I don't care to go back. What does it matter? I am quite happy here.'

'You will write to me if you want anything, won't you?' said Dorian after a pause.

'Perhaps.'

'Good-night, then.'

'Good-night,' answered the young man, passing up the steps, and wiping his parched mouth with a handkerchief.

Dorian walked to the door with a look of pain in his face. As he drew the curtain aside a hideous laugh broke from the painted lips of the woman who had taken his money. 'There goes the devil's bargain!' she hiccoughed, in a hoarse voice.

'Curse you!' he answered, 'don't call me that.'

She snapped her fingers. 'Prince Charming is what you like to be called, ain't it?' she yelled after him.

The drowsy sailor leapt to his feet as she spoke, and looked wildly round. The sound of the shutting of the hall door fell on his ear. He rushed out as if in pursuit.

Dorian Gray hurried along the quay through the drizzling rain. His meeting with Adrian Singleton had strangely moved him, and he wondered if the ruin of that young life was really to be laid at his door, as Basil Hallward had said to him with such infamy of insult. He bit his lip, and for a few seconds his eyes grew sad. Yet, after all, what did it matter to him? One's days were too brief to take the burden of another's errors on one's shoulders. Each man lived his own life, and paid his own price for living it. The only pity was one had to pay so often for a single fault. One had to pay over and over again, indeed. In her dealings with man Destiny never closed her accounts.

There are moments, psychologists tell us, when the passion for sin, or for what the world calls sin, so dominates a nature, that every fibre of the body, as every cell of the brain, seems to be instinct with fearful impulses. Men and women at such moments lose the freedom of their will. They move to their terrible end as automatons move. Choice is taken from them, and conscience is either killed, or, if it lives at all, lives but to give rebellion its fascination, and disobedience its charm. For all sins, as theologians weary not of reminding us, are sins of disobedience. When that high spirit, that morning-star of evil, fell from heaven, it was as a rebel that he fell.

Callous, concentrated on evil, with stained mien, and soul hungry for rebellion, Dorian Gray hastened on, quickening his step as he went, but as he darted aside into a dim archway, that had served him often as a short cut to the ill-famed place where he was going, he felt himself suddenly seized from behind, and before he had time to defend himself he was thrust back against the wall, with a brutal hand round his throat.

He struggled madly for life, and by a terrible effort wrenched the tightening fingers away. In a second he heard the click of a revolver, and saw the gleam of a polished barrel pointing straight at his head, and the dusky form of a short thick-set man facing him.

'What do you want?' he gasped.

'Keep quiet,' said the man. 'If you stir, I shoot you.'

'You are mad. What have I done to you?'

'You wrecked the life of Sibyl Vane,' was the answer, 'and Sibyl Vane was my sister. She killed herself. I know it. Her death is at your door. I swore I would kill you in return. For years I have sought you. I had no clue, no trace. The two people who could have described you were dead. I knew nothing of you but the pet name she used to call you. I heard it to-night by chance. Make your peace with God, for to-night you are going to die.'

Dorian Gray grew sick with fear. 'I never knew her,' he stammered. 'I never heard of her. You are mad.'

'You had better confess your sin, for as sure as I am James Vane, you are going to die.' There was a horrible moment. Dorian did not know what to say or do. 'Down on your knees!' growled the man. 'I give you one minute to make your peace – no more. I go on board to-night for India, and I must do my job first. One minute. That's all.'

Dorian's arms fell to his side. Paralysed with terror, he did not know what to do. Suddenly a wild hope flashed across his brain. 'Stop,' he cried. 'How long ago is it since your sister died? Quick, tell me!'

'Eighteen years,' said the man. 'Why do you ask me? What do years matter?'

'Eighteen years,' laughed Dorian Gray, with a touch of triumph in his voice. 'Eighteen years! Set me under a lamp and look at my face!'

James Vane hesistated for a moment, not understanding what was meant. Then he seized Dorian Gray and dragged him from the archway.

Dim and wavering as was the wind-blown light, yet it served to show him the hideous error, as it seemed, into which he had fallen, for the face of the man he had sought to kill had all the bloom of boyhood, all the unstained purity of youth. He seemed little older than a lad of twenty summers, hardly older, if older indeed at all, than his sister had been when they had parted so many years ago. It was obvious that this was not the man who had destroyed her life.

He loosened his hold and reeled back. 'My God! my God!' he cried, 'and I would have murdered you!'

Dorian Gray drew a long breath. 'You have been on the brink of committing a terrible crime, my man,' he said, looking at him sternly. 'Let this be a warning to you not to take vengeance into your own hands.'

'Forgive me, sir,' muttered James Vane. 'I was deceived. A chance word I heard in that damned den set me on the wrong track.'

'You had better go home, and put that pistol away, or you may get into trouble,' said Dorian, turning on his heel, and going slowly down the street.

James Vane stood on the pavement in horror. He was trembling from head to foot. After a little while a black shadow that had been creeping along the dripping wall moved out into the light and came close to him with stealthy footsteps. He felt a hand laid on his arm and looked round with a start. It was one of the women who had been drinking at the bar.

'Why didn't you kill him?' she hissed out, putting her haggard face quite close to his. 'I knew you were following him when you rushed out from Daly's. You fool! You should have killed him. He has lots of money, and he's as bad as bad.'

'He is not the man I am looking for,' he answered, 'and I want no man's money. I want a man's life. The man whose life I want must be nearly forty now. This one is little more than a boy. Thank God, I have not got his blood upon my hands.'

The woman gave a bitter laugh. 'Little more than a boy!' she sneered. 'Why, man, it's nigh on eighteen years since Prince Charming made me what I am.'

'You lie!' cried James Vane.

She raised her hand up to heaven. 'Before God I am telling the truth,' she cried.

'Before God?'

'Strike me dumb if it ain't so. He is the worst one that comes here. They say he has sold himself to the devil for a pretty face. It's nigh on eighteen years since I met him. He hasn't changed much since then. I have though,' she added, with a sickly leer.

'You swear this?'

'I swear it,' came in hoarse echo from her flat mouth. 'But don't give me away to him,' she whined; 'I am afraid of him. Let me have some money for my night's lodging.'

He broke from her with an oath, and rushed to the corner of the street, but Dorian Gray had disappeared. When he looked back, the woman had vanished also.

A week later Dorian Gray was sitting in the conservatory at Selby Royal talking to the pretty Duchess of Monmouth, who with her husband, a jaded-looking man of sixty, was amongst his guests. It was tea-time, and the mellow light of the huge lace-covered lamp that stood on the table lit up the delicate china and hammered silver of the service at which the Duchess was presiding. Her white hands were moving daintily among the cups, and her full red lips were smiling at something that Dorian had whispered to her. Lord Henry was lying back in a silk-draped wicker chair looking at them. On a peach-coloured divan sat Lady Narborough pretending to listen to the Duke's description of the last Brazilian beetle that he had added to his collection. Three young men in elaborate

THE PICTURE OF DORIAN GRAY

smoking-suits were handing tea-cakes to some of the women. The house-party consisted of twelve people, and there were more expected to arrive on the next day.

'What are you two talking about?' said Lord Henry, strolling over to the table, and putting his cup down. 'I hope Dorian has told you about my plan for rechristening everything, Gladys. It is a delightful idea.'

'But I don't want to be rechristened, Harry,' rejoined the Duchess, looking up at him with her wonderful eyes. 'I am quite satisfied with my own name, and I am sure Mr. Gray should be satisfied with his.'

'My dear Gladys, I would not alter either name for the world. They are both perfect. I was thinking chiefly of flowers. Yesterday I cut an orchid, for my buttonhole. It was a marvellous spotted thing, as effective as the seven deadly sins. In a thoughtless moment I asked one of the gardeners what it was called. He told me it was a fine specimen of *Robinsoniana*, or something dreadful of that kind. It is a sad truth, but we have lost the faculty of giving lovely names to things. Names are everything. I never quarrel with actions. My one quarrel is with words. That is the reason I hate vulgar realism in literature. The man who could call a spade a spade should be compelled to use one. It is the only thing he is fit for.'

'Then what should we call you, Harry?' she asked.

'His name is Prince Paradox,' said Dorian.

'I recognise him in a flash,' exclaimed the Duchess.

'I won't hear of it,' laughed Lord Henry, sinking into a chair. 'From a label there is no escape! I refuse the title.'

'Royalties may not abdicate,' fell as a warning from pretty lips.

'You wish me to defend my throne, then?'

'Yes.'

'I give the truths of to-morrow.'

'I prefer the mistakes of to-day,' she answered.

'You disarm me, Gladys,' he cried, catching the wilfulness of her mood.

'Of your shield, Harry: not of your spear.'

'I never tilt against beauty,' he said, with a wave of his hand.

'That is your error, Harry, believe me. You value beauty far too much.'

'How can you say that? I admit that I think that it is better to be beautiful than to be good. But on the other hand no one is more ready than I am to acknowledge that it is better to be good than to be ugly.'

'Ugliness is one of the seven deadly sins, then?' cried the Duchess. 'What becomes of your simile about the orchid?'

'Ugliness is one of the seven deadly virtues, Gladys. You, as a good Tory, must not underrate them. Beer, the Bible, and the seven deadly virtues have made our England what she is.'

'You don't like your country, then?' she asked.

'I live in it.'

'That you may censure it the better.'

'Would you have me take the verdict of Europe on it?' he inquired.

'What do they say of us?'

'That Tartuffe has emigrated to England and opened a shop.'

'Is that yours, Harry?'

'I give it to you.'

'I could not use it. It is too true.'

'You need not be afraid. Our countrymen never recognise a description.'

'They are practical.'

'They are more cunning than practical. When they make up their ledger, they balance stupidity by wealth, and vice by hypocrisy.'

'Still, we have done great things.'

'Great things have been thrust on us, Gladys.'

'We have carried their burden.'

'Only as far as the Stock Exchange.'

She shook her head. 'I believe in the race,' she cried.

'It represents the survival of the pushing.'

'It has development.'

'Decay fascinates me more.'

'What of Art?' she asked.

'It is a malady.'

'Love?'

'An illusion.'

'Religion?'

'The fashionable substitute for Belief.'

'You are a sceptic.'

'Never! Scepticism is the beginning of Faith.'

'What are you?'

'To define is to limit.'

'Give me a clue.'

'Threads snap. You would lose your way in the labyrinth.'

'You bewilder me. Let us talk of some one else.'

'Our host is a deiightful topic. Years ago he was christened Prince Charming.'

'Ah! don't remind me of that,' cried Dorian Gray.

'Our host is rather horrid this evening,' answered the Duchess, colouring. 'I believe he thinks that Monmouth married me on purely scientific principles as the best specimen he could find of a modern butterfly.'

'Well, I hope he won't stick pins into you, Duchess,' laughed Dorian.

'Oh, my maid does that already, Mr. Gray, when she is annoyed with me.'

'And what does she get annoyed with you about, Duchess?'

'For the most trivial things, Mr. Gray, I assure you. Usually because

I come in at ten minutes to nine and tell her that I must be dressed by half-past eight.'

'How unreasonable of her! You should give her warning.'

'I daren't, Mr. Gray. Why, she invents hats for me. You remember the one I wore at Lady Hilstone's garden-party? You don't, but it is nice of you to pretend that you do. Well, she made it out of nothing. All good hats are made out of nothing.'

'Like all good reputations, Gladys,' interrupted Lord Henry. 'Every effect that one produces gives one an enemy. To be popular one must be a mediocrity.'

'Not with women,' said the Duchess, shaking her head; 'and women rule the world. I assure you we can't bear mediocrities. We women, as some one says, love with our ears, just as you men love with your eyes, if you ever love at all.'

'It seems to me that we never do anything else,' murmured Dorian.

'Ah! then, you never really love, Mr. Gray,' answered the Duchess, with mock sadness.

'My dear Gladys!' cried Lord Henry. 'How can you say that? Romance lives by repetition, and repetition converts an appetite into an art. Besides, each time that one loves is the only time one has ever loved. Difference of object does not alter singleness of passion. It merely intensifies it. We can have in life but one great experience at best, and the secret of life is to reproduce that experience as often as possible.'

'Even when one has been wounded by it, Harry?' asked the Duchess, after a pause.

'Especially when one has been wounded by it,' answered Lord Henry.

The Duchess turned and looked at Dorian Gray with a curious expression in her eyes. 'What do you say to that, Mr. Gray?' she inquired.

Dorian hesitated for a moment. Then he threw his head back and laughed. 'I always agree with Harry, Duchess.'

'Even when he is wrong?'

'Harry is never wrong, Duchess.'

'And does his philosophy make you happy?'

'I have never searched for happiness. Who wants happiness? I have searched for pleasure.'

'And found it, Mr. Gray?'

'Often. Too often.'

The Duchess sighed. 'I am searching for peace,' she said, 'and if I don't go and dress, I shall have none this evening.'

'Let me get you some orchids, Duchess,' cried Dorian, starting to his feet, and walking down the conservatory.

'You are flirting disgracefully with him,' said Lord Henry to his cousin. 'You had better take care. He is very fascinating.'

'If he were not, there would be no battle.'

'Greek meets Greek, then?'

'I am on the side of the Trojans. They fought for a woman.'

'They were defeated.'

'There are worse things than capture,' she answered.

'You gallop with a loose rein.'

'Pace gives life,' was the *riposte*.

'I shall write it in my diary to-night.'

'What?'

'That a burnt child loves the fire.'

'I am not even singed. My wings are untouched.'

'You can use them for everything except flight.'

'Courage has passed from men to women. It is a new experience for us.'

'You have a rival.'

'Who?'

He laughed. 'Lady Narborough,' he whispered. 'She perfectly adores him.'

'You fill me with apprehension. The appeal to Antiquity is fatal to us who are romanticists.'

'Romanticists! You have all the methods of science.'

'Men have educated us.'

'But not explained you.'

'Describe us as a sex,' was her challenge.

'Sphynxes without secrets.'

She looked at him, smiling. 'How long Mr. Gray is!' she said. 'Let us go and help him. I have not yet told him the colour of my frock.'

'Ah! you must suit your frock to his flowers, Gladys.'

'That would be a premature surrender.'

'Romantic Art begins with its climax.'

'I must keep an opportunity for retreat.'

'In the Parthian manner?'

'They found safety in the desert. I could not do that.'

'Women are not always allowed a choice,' he answered, but hardly had he finished the sentence before from the far end of the conservatory came a stifled groan, followed by the dull sound of a heavy fall. Everybody started up. The Duchess stood motionless in horror. And with fear in his eyes Lord Henry rushed through the flapping palms to find Dorian Gray lying face downwards on the tiled floor in a death-like swoon.

He was carried at once into the blue drawing-room, and laid upon one of the sofas. After a short time he came to himself, and looked round with a dazed expression.

'What has happened?' he asked. 'Oh! I remember. Am I safe here, Harry?' He began to tremble.

'My dear Dorian,' answered Lord Henry, 'you merely fainted. That was all. You must have overtired yourself. You had better not come down to dinner. I will take your place.'

'No, I will come down,' he said, struggling to his feet. 'I would rather come down. I must not be alone.'

He went to his room and dressed. There was a wild recklessness of gaiety in his manner as he sat at table, but now and then a thrill of terror ran through him when he remembered that, pressed against the window of the conservatory, like a white handkerchief, he had seen the face of James Vane watching him.

The next day he did not leave the house, and indeed, spent most of the time in his own room, sick with a wild terror of dying, and yet indifferent to life itself. The consciousness of being hunted, snared, tracked down, had begun to dominate him. If the tapestry did but tremble in the wind, he shook. The dead leaves that were blown against the leaded panes seemed to him like his own wasted resolutions and wild regrets. When he closed his eyes, he saw again the sailor's face peering through the mist-stained glass, and horror seemed once more to lay its hand upon his heart.

But perhaps it had been only his fancy that had called vengeance out of the night, and set the hideous shapes of punishment before him. Actual life was chaos, but there was something terribly logical in the imagination. It was the imagination that set remorse to dog the feet of sin. It was the imagination that made each crime bear its misshapen brood. In the common world of fact the wicked were not punished, nor the good rewarded. Success was given to the strong, failure thrust upon the weak. That was all. Besides, had any stranger been prowling round the house he would have been seen by the servants or the keepers. Had any footmarks been found on the flower-beds, the gardeners would have reported it. Yes: it had been merely fancy. Sibyl Vane's brother had not come back to kill him. He had sailed away in his ship to founder in some winter sea. From him, at any rate, he was safe. Why, the man did not know who he was, could not know who he was. The mask of youth had saved him.

And yet if it had been merely an illusion, how terrible it was to think that conscience could raise such fearful phantoms, and give them visible form, and make them move before one! What sort of life would his be, if day and night, shadows of his crime were to peer at him from silent corners, to mock him from secret places, to whisper in his ear as he sat at the feast, to wake him with icy fingers as he lay asleep! As the thought crept through his brain, he grew pale with terror, and the air seemed to him to have become suddenly colder. Oh! in what a wild hour of madness he had killed his friend! How ghastly the mere memory of the scene! He saw it all again. Each hideous detail came back to him with added horror. Out of the black cave of Time, terrible and swathed in scarlet, rose the image of his sin. When Lord Henry came in at six o'clock, he found him crying as one whose heart will break.

It was not till the third day that he ventured to go out. There was something in the clear, pine-scented air of that winter morning that seemed to bring him back his joyousness and his ardour for life. But it was not merely the physical conditions of environment that had caused the change. His own nature had revolted against the excess of anguish that had sought to maim and mar the perfection of its calm. With subtle and finely-wrought temperaments it is always so. Their strong passions must either bruise or bend. They either slay the man, or themselves die. Shallow sorrows and shallow loves live on. The loves and sorrows that are great are destroyed by their own plenitude. Besides, he had convinced himself that he had been the victim of a terror-stricken imagination, and looked back now on his fears with something of pity and not a little of contempt.

After breakfast he walked with the Duchess for an hour in the garden, and then drove across the park to join the shooting-party. The crisp frost lay like salt upon the grass. The sky was an inverted cup of blue metal. A thin film of ice bordered the flat reed-grown lake.

At the corner of the pine-wood he caught sight of Sir Geoffrey Clouston, the Duchess's brother, jerking two spent cartridges out of his gun. He jumped from the cart, and having told the groom to take the mare home, made his way towards his guest through the withered bracken and rough undergrowth.

'Have you had good sport, Geoffrey?' he asked.

'Not very good, Dorian. I think most of the birds have gone to the open. I dare say it will be better after lunch, when we get to new ground.'

Dorian strolled along by his side. The keen aromatic air, the brown and red lights that glimmered in the wood, the hoarse cries of the beaters ringing out from time to time, and the sharp snaps of the guns that followed, fascinated him, and filled him with a sense of delightful freedom. He was dominated by the carelessness of happiness, by the high indifference of joy.

Suddenly from a lumpy tussock of old grass, some twenty yards in front of them, with black-tipped ears erect, and long hinder limbs throwing it forward, started a hare. It bolted for a thicket of alders. Sir Geoffrey put his gun to his shoulder, but there was something in the animal's grace of movement that strangely charmed Dorian Gray, and he cried out at once, 'Don't shoot it, Geoffrey. Let it live.'

'What nonsense, Dorian!' laughed his companion, and as the hare bounded into the thicket he fired. There were two cries heard, the cry of a hare in pain, which is dreadful, the cry of a man in agony, which is worse.

'Good heavens! I have hit a beater!' exclaimed Sir Geoffrey. 'What an ass the man was to get in front of the guns! Stop shooting there!' he called out at the top of his voice. 'A man is hurt.'

The head-keeper came running up with a stick in his hand.

'Where, sir? Where is he?' he shouted. At the same time the firing ceased along the line.

'Here,' answered Sir Geoffrey, angrily, hurrying towards the thicket. 'Why on earth don't you keep your men back? Spoiled my shooting for the day.'

Dorian watched them as they plunged into the alder-clump, brushing the lithe, swinging branches aside. In a few moments they emerged, dragging a body after them into the sunlight. He turned away in horror. It seemed to him that misfortune followed wherever he went. He heard Sir Geoffrey ask if the man was really dead, and the affirmative answer of the keeper. The wood seemed to him to have become suddenly alive with faces. There was the trampling of myriad feet, and the low buzz of voices. A great copper-breasted pheasant came beating through the boughs overhead.

After a few moments, that were to him, in his perturbed state, like endless hours of pain, he felt a hand laid on his shoulder. He started, and looked round.

'Dorian,' said Lord Henry. 'I had better tell them that the shooting is stopped for to-day. It would not look well to go on.'

'I wish it were stopped for ever, Harry,' he answered bitterly. 'The whole thing is hideous and cruel. Is the man . . .?'

He could not finish the sentence.

'I am afraid so,' rejoined Lord Henry. 'He got the whole charge of shot in his chest. He must have died almost instantaneously. Come; let us go home.'

They walked side by side in the direction of the avenue for nearly fifty yards without speaking. Then Dorian looked at Lord Henry, and said, with a heavy sigh, 'It is a bad omen, Harry, a very bad omen.'

'What is?' asked Lord Henry. 'Oh, this accident, I suppose. My dear fellow, it can't be helped. It was the man's own fault. Why did he get in front of the guns? Besides, it's nothing to us. It is rather awkward for Geoffrey, of course. It does not do to pepper beaters. It makes people think that one is a wild shot. And Geoffrey is not; he shoots very straight. But there is no use talking about the matter.'

Dorian shook his head. 'It is a bad omen, Harry. I feel as if something horrible were going to happen to some of us. To myself, perhaps,' he added, passing his hand over his eyes, with a gesture of pain.

The elder man laughed. 'The only horrible thing in the world is *ennui*, Dorian. That is the one sin for which there is no forgiveness. But we are not likely to suffer from it, less these fellows keep chattering about this thing at dinner. I must tell them that the subject is to be tabooed. As for omens, there is no such thing as an omen. Destiny does not send us heralds. She is too wise or too cruel for that. Besides, what on earth could happen to you, Dorian? You have everything in the world that a man

TALES FROM BEYOND THE GRAVE

can want. There is no one who would not be delighted to change places with you.'

'There is no one with whom I would not change places, Harry. Don't laugh like that. I am telling you the truth. The wretched peasant who has just died is better off than I am. I have no terror of Death. It is the coming of Death that terrifies me. Its monstrous wings seem to wheel in the leaden air around me. Good heavens! don't you see a man moving behind the trees there, watching me, waiting for me?'

Lord Henry looked in the direction in which the trembling gloved hand was pointing. 'Yes,' he said, smiling, 'I see the gardener waiting for you. I suppose he wants to ask you what flowers you wish to have on the table to-night. How absurdly nervous you are, my dear fellow! You must come and see my doctor, when we get back to town.'

Dorian heaved a sigh of relief as he saw the gardener approaching. The man touched his hat, glanced for a moment at Lord Henry in a hesitating manner, and then produced a letter, which he handed to his master. 'Her Grace told me to wait for an answer,' he murmured.

Dorian put the letter into his pocket. 'Tell her Grace that I am coming in,' he said, coldly. The man turned round, and went rapidly in the direction of the house.

'How fond women are of doing dangerous things!' laughed Lord Henry. 'It is one of the qualities in them that I admire most. A woman will flirt with anybody in the world as long as other people are looking on.'

'How fond you are of saying dangerous things, Harry! In the present instance you are quite astray. I like the Duchess very much, but I don't love her.'

'And the Duchess loves you very much, but she likes you less, so you are excellently matched.'

'You are talking scandal, Harry, and there is never any basis for scandal.'

'The basis for every scandal is an immoral certainty,' said Lord Henry, lighting a cigarette.

'You would sacrifice anybody, Harry, for the sake of an epigram.'

'The world goes to the altar of its own accord,' was the answer.

'I wish I could love,' cried Dorian Gray, with a deep note of pathos in his voice. 'But I seem to have lost the passion, and forgotten the desire. I am too much concentrated on myself. My own personality has become a burden to me. I want to escape, to go away, to forget. It was silly of me to come down here at all. I think I shall send a wire to Harvey to have the yacht got ready. On a yacht one is safe.'

'Safe from what, Dorian? You are in some trouble. Why not tell me what it is? You know I would help you.'

'I can't tell you, Harry,' he answered, sadly. 'And I dare say it is only a fancy of mine. This unfortunate accident has upset me. I have a horrible presentiment that something of the kind may happen to me.'

'What nonsense!'

'I hope it is, but I can't help feeling it. Ah! here is the Duchess, looking like Artemis in a tailor-made gown. You see we have come back, Duchess.'

'I have heard all about it, Mr. Gray,' she answered. 'Poor Geoffrey is terribly upset. And it seems that you asked him not to shoot the hare. How curious!'

'Yes, it was very curious. I don't know what made me say it. Some whim, I suppose. It looked the loveliest of little live things. But I am sorry they told you about the man. It is a hideous subject.'

'It is an annoying subject,' broke in Lord Henry. 'It has no psychological value at all. Now if Geoffrey had done the thing on purpose, how interesting he would be! I should like to know some one who had committed a real murder.'

'How horrid of you, Harry!' cried the Duchess. 'Isn't it, Mr. Gray? Harry, Mr. Gray is ill again. He is going to faint.'

Dorian drew himself up with an effort, and smiled. 'It is nothing, Duchess,' he murmured; 'my nerves are dreadfully out of order. That is all. I am afraid I walked too far this morning. I didn't hear what Harry said. Was it very bad? You must tell me some other time. I think I must go and lie down. You will excuse me, won't you?'

They had reached the great flight of steps that led from the conservatory on to the terrace. As the glass door closed behind Dorian, Lord Henry turned and looked at the Duchess with his slumberous eyes. 'Are you very much in love with him?' he asked.

She did not answer for some time, but stood gazing at the landscape. 'I wish I knew,' she said at last.

He shook his head. 'Knowledge would be fatal. It is the uncertainty that charms one. A mist makes things wonderful.'

'One may lose one's way.'

'All ways end at the same point, my dear Gladys.'

'What is that?'

'Disillusion.'

'It was my *début* in life,' she sighed.

'It came to you crowned.'

'I am tired of strawberry leaves.'

'They become you.'

'Only in public.'

'You would miss them,' said Lord Henry.

'I will not part with a petal.'

'Monmouth has ears.'

'Old age is dull of hearing.'

'Has he never been jealous?'

'I wish he had been.'

He glanced about as if in search of something. 'What are you looking for?' she inquired.

'The button from your foil,' he answered. 'You have dropped it.'

She laughed. 'I have still the mask.'

'It makes your eyes lovelier,' was the reply.

She laughed again. Her teeth showed like white seeds in a scarlet fruit.

Upstairs, in his own room, Dorian Gray was lying on a sofa, with terror in every tingling fibre of his body. Life had suddenly become too hideous a burden for him to bear. The dreadful death of the unlucky beater, shot in the thicket like a wild animal, had seemed to him to prefigure death for himself also. He had nearly swooned at what Lord Henry had said in a chance mood of cynical jesting.

At five o'clock he rang his bell for his servant and gave him orders to pack his things for the night-express to town, and to have the brougham at the door by eight-thirty. He was determined not to sleep another night at Selby Royal. It was an ill-omened place, Death walked there in the sunlight. The grass of the forest had been spotted with blood.

Then he wrote a note to Lord Henry, telling him that he was going up to town to consult his doctor, and asking him to entertain his guests in his absence. As he was putting it into the envelope, a knock came to the door, and his valet informed him that the head-keeper wished to see him. He frowned, and bit his lip. 'Send him in,' he muttered after some moments' hesitation.

As soon as the man entered Dorian pulled his cheque-book out of a drawer, and spread it out before him.

'I suppose you have come about the unfortunate accident of this morning, Thornton?' he said, taking up a pen.

'Yes, sir,' answered the gamekeeper.

'Was the poor fellow married? Had he any people dependent on him?' asked Dorian, looking bored. 'If so, I should not like them to be left in want, and will send them any sum of money you may think necessary.'

'We don't know who he is, sir. That is what I took the liberty of coming to you about.'

'Don't know who he is?' said Dorian, listlessly. 'What do you mean? Wasn't he one of your men?'

'No, sir. Never saw him before. Seems like a sailor, sir.'

The pen dropped from Dorian Gray's hand, and he felt as if his heart had suddenly stopped beating. 'A sailor?' he cried out. 'Did you say a sailor?'

'Yes, sir. He looks as if he had been a sort of sailor; tattooed on both arms, and that kind of thing.'

'Was there anything found on him?' said Dorian, leaning forward and looking at the man with startled eyes. 'Anything that would tell his name?'

'Some money, sir – not much, and a six-shooter. There was no name

THE PICTURE OF DORIAN GRAY

of any kind. A decent-looking man, sir, but rough-like. A sort of sailor, we think.'

Dorian started to his feet. A terrible hope fluttered past him. He clutched at it madly. 'Where is the body?' he exclaimed. 'Quick! I must see it at once.'

'It is in an empty stable in the Home Farm, sir. The folk don't like to have that sort of thing in their houses. They say a corpse brings bad luck.'

'The Home Farm! Go there at once and meet me. Tell one of the grooms to bring my horse round. No. Never mind. I'll go to the stables myself. It will save time.'

In less than a quarter of an hour Dorian Gray was galloping down the long avenue as hard as he could go. The trees seemed to sweep past him in spectral procession, and wild shadows to fling themselves across his path. Once the mare swerved at a white gate-post and nearly threw him. He lashed her across the neck with his crop. She cleft the dusky air like an arrow. The stones flew from her hoofs.

At last he reached the Home Farm. Two men were loitering in the yard. He leapt from the saddle and threw the reins to one of them. In the farthest stable a light was glimmering. Something seemed to tell him that the body was there, and he hurried to the door, and put his hand upon the latch.

There he paused for a moment, feeling that he was on the brink of a discovery that would either make or mar his life. Then he thrust the door open, and entered.

On a heap of sacking in the far corner was lying the dead body of a man dressed in a coarse shirt and a pair of blue trousers. A spotted handkerchief had been placed over the face. A coarse candle, stuck in a bottle, spluttered beside it.

Dorian Gray shuddered. He felt that his could not be the hand to take the handkerchief away, and called out to one of the farm-servants to come to him.

'Take that thing off the face. I wish to see it,' he said, clutching at the doorpost for support.

When the farm-servant had done so, he stepped forward. A cry of joy broke from his lips. The man who had been shot in the thicket was James Vane.

He stood there for some minutes looking at the dead body. As he rode home, his eyes were full of tears, for he knew he was safe.

'There is no use in your telling me that you are going to be good,' cried Lord Henry, dipping his white fingers into a red copper bowl filled with rose-water. 'You're quite perfect. Pray, don't change.'

Dorian Gray shook his head. 'No, Harry, I have done too many dreadful things in my life. I am not going to do any more. I began my good actions yesterday.'

'Where were you yesterday?'

'In the country, Harry. I was staying at a little inn by myself.'

'My dear boy,' said Lord Henry, smiling, 'anybody can be good in the country. There are no temptations there. That is the reason why people who live out of town are so absolutely uncivilised. Civilisation is not by any means an easy thing to attain to. There are only two ways by which man can reach it. One is by being cultured, the other by being corrupt. Country people have no opportunity of being either, so they stagnate.'

'Culture and corruption,' echoed Dorian. 'I have known something of both. It seems terrible to me now that they should ever be found together. For I have a new ideal, Harry. I am going to alter. I think I have altered.'

'You have not yet told me what your good action was. Or did you say you had done more than one?' asked his companion, as he spilt into his plate a little crimson pyramid of seeded strawberries, and through a perforated shell-shaped spoon snowed white sugar upon them.

'I can tell you, Harry. It is not a story I could tell to any one else. I spared somebody. It sounds vain, but you understand what I mean. She was quite beautiful, and wonderfully like Sibyl Vane. I think it was that which first attracted me to her. You remember Sibyl, don't you? How long ago that seems! Well, Hetty was not one of our own class, of course. She was simply a girl in a village. But I really loved her. I am quite sure that I loved her. All during this wonderful May that we have been having, I used to run down and see her two or three times a week. Yesterday she met me in a little orchard. The apple-blossoms kept tumbling down on her hair, and she was laughing. We were to have gone away together this morning at dawn. Suddenly I determined to leave her as flower-like as I had found her.'

'I should think the novelty of the emotion must have given you a thrill of real pleasure, Dorian,' interrupted Lord Henry. 'But I can finish your idyll for you. You gave her good advice, and broke her heart. That was the beginning of your reformation.'

'Harry, you are horrible! You mustn't say these dreadful things. Hetty's heart is not broken. Of course she cried, and all that. But there is no disgrace upon her. She can live, like Perdita, in her garden of mint and marigold.'

'And weep over a faithless Florizel,' said Lord Henry, laughing, as he leant back in his chair. 'My dear Dorian, you have the most curiously boyish moods. Do you think this girl will ever be really contented now with any one of her own rank? I suppose she will be married some day to a rough carter or a grinning ploughman. Well, the fact of having met you, and loved you, will teach her to despise her husband, and she will be wretched. From a moral point of view, I cannot say that I think much of your great renunciation. Even as a beginning, it is poor. Besides, how do you know that Hetty isn't floating at the present moment in some star-lit millpond, with lovely water-lilies round her, like Ophelia?'

'I can't bear this, Harry! You mock at everything, and then suggest the most serious tragedies. I am sorry I told you now. I don't care what you say to me. I know I was right in acting as I did. Poor Hetty! As I rode past the farm this morning, I saw her white face at the window, like a spray of jasmine. Don't let us talk about it any more, and don't try to persuade me that the first good action I have done for years, the first little bit of self-sacrifice I have ever known, is really a sort of sin. I want to be better. I am going to be better. Tell me something about yourself. What is going on in town? I have not been to the club for days.'

'The people are still discussing poor Basil's disappearance.'

'I should have thought they had got tired of that by this time,' said Dorian, pouring himself out some wine, and frowning slightly.

'My dear boy, they have only been talking about it for six weeks, and the British public are really not equal to the mental strain of having more than one topic every three months. They have been very fortunate lately, however. They have had my own divorce case, and Alan Campbell's suicide. Now they have got the mysterious disappearance of an artist. Scotland Yard still insists that the man in the grey ulster who left for Paris by the midnight train on the ninth of November was poor Basil, and the French police declare that Basil never arrived in Paris at all. I suppose in about a fortnight we shall be told that he has been seen in San Francisco. It is an odd thing, but every one who disappears is said to be seen at San Francisco. It must be a delightful city, and possess all the attractions of the next world.'

'What do you think has happened to Basil?' asked Dorian, holding up his Burgundy against the light, and wondering how it was that he could discuss the matter so calmly.

'I have not the slightest idea. If Basil chooses to hide himself, it is no business of mine. If he is dead, I don't want to think about him. Death is the only thing that ever terrifies me. I hate it.'

'Why?' said the younger man, wearily.

'Because,' said Lord Henry, passing beneath his nostrils the gilt trellis of an open vinaigrette box, 'one can survive everything nowadays except that. Death and vulgarity are the only two facts in the nineteenth century that one cannot explain away. Let us have our coffee in the music-room, Dorian. You must play Chopin to me. The man with whom my wife ran away played Chopin exquisitely. Poor Victoria! I was very fond of her. The house is rather lonely without her. Of course married life is merely a habit, a bad habit. But then one regrets the loss even of one's worst habits. Perhaps one regrets them the most. They are such an essential part of one's personality.'

Dorian said nothing, but rose from the table and, passing into the next room, sat down to the piano and let his fingers stray across the white and black ivory of the keys. After the coffee had been brought in, he stopped, and, looking over at Lord Henry, said, 'Harry, did it ever occur to you that Basil was murdered?'

Lord Henry yawned. 'Basil was very popular, and always wore a Waterbury watch. Why should he have been murdered? He was not clever enough to have enemies. Of course he had a wonderful genius for painting. But a man can paint like Velasquez and yet be as dull as possible. Basil was really rather dull. He only interested me once, and that was when he told me, years ago, that he had a wild adoration for you, and that you were the dominant motive of his art.'

'I was very fond of Basil,' said Dorian, with a note of sadness in his voice. 'But don't people say that he was murdered?'

'Oh, some of the papers do. It does not seem to me to be at all probable. I know there are dreadful places in Paris, but Basil was not the sort of man to have gone to them. He had no curiosity. It was his chief defect.'

'What would you say, Harry, if I told you that I had murdered Basil?' said the younger man. He watched him intently after he had spoken.

'I would say, my dear fellow, that you were posing for a character that doesn't suit you. All crime is vulgar, just as all vulgarity is crime. It is not in you, Dorian, to commit a murder. I am sorry if I hurt your vanity by saying so, but I assure you it is true. Crime belongs exclusively to the lower orders. I don't blame them in the smallest degree. I should fancy that crime was to them what art is to us, simply a method of procuring extraordinary sensations.'

'A method of procuring sensations? Do you think, then, that a man who has once committed a murder could possibly do the same crime again? Don't tell me that.'

'Oh! anything becomes a pleasure if one does it too often,' cried Lord Henry, laughing. 'That is one of the most important secrets of life. I should fancy, however, that murder is always a mistake. One should never do anything that one cannot talk about after dinner. But let us pass from poor Basil. I wish I could believe that he had come to such a really romantic end as you suggest; but I can't. I dare say he fell into the Seine off an omnibus, and that the conductor hushed up the scandal. Yes: I should fancy that was his end. I see him lying now on his back under those dull-green waters with the heavy barges floating over him, and long weeds catching in his hair. Do you know, I don't think he would have done much more good work. During the last ten years his painting had gone off very much.'

Dorian heaved a sigh, and Lord Henry strolled across the room and began to stroke the head of a curious Java parrot, a large grey-plumaged bird, with pink crest and tail, that was balancing itself upon a bamboo perch. As his pointed fingers touched it, it dropped the white scurf of crinkled lids over black glass-like eyes, and began to sway backwards and forwards.

'Yes,' he continued, turning round, and taking his handkerchief out of his pocket; 'his painting had quite gone off. It seemed to me to have lost something. It had lost an ideal. When you and he ceased to be great friends, he ceased to be a great artist. What was it separated you? I suppose he bored you. If so, he never forgave you. It's a habit bores have. By the way, what has become of that wonderful portrait he did of you? I don't think I have ever seen it since he finished it. Oh! I remember your telling me years ago that you had sent it down to Selby, and that it had got mislaid or stolen on the way. You never got it back? What a pity! It was really a masterpiece. I remember I wanted to buy it. I wish I had now. It belonged to Basil's best period. Since then, his work was that curious mixture of bad painting and good intentions that always entitles a man to be called a representative British artist. Did you advertise for it? You should.'

'I forget,' said Dorian. 'I suppose I did. But I never really liked it. I am sorry I sat for it. The memory of the thing is hateful to me. Why do you talk of it? It used to remind me of those curious lines in some play – *Hamlet* I think – how do they run? –

> 'Like the painting of a sorrow,
> A face without a heart.'

Yes: that is what it was like.'

Lord Henry laughed. 'If a man treats life artistically, his brain is his heart,' he answered, sinking into an arm-chair.

Dorian Gray shook his head, and struck some soft chords on the piano. ' "Like the painting of a sorrow," ' he repeated, ' "a face without a heart." '

The elder man lay back and looked at him with half-closed eyes. 'By the way, Dorian,' he said, after a pause, 'what does it profit a man if he gain the whole world and lose' – how does the quotation run? – 'his own soul"?'

The music jarred and Dorian Gray started, and stared at his friend. 'Why do you ask me that, Harry?'

'My dear fellow,' said Lord Henry, elevating his eyebrows in surprise, 'I asked you because I thought you might be able to give me an answer. That is all. I was going through the Park last Sunday, and close by the Marble Arch there stood a little crowd of shabby looking people listening to some vulgar street-preacher. As I passed by, I heard the man yelling out that question to his audience. It struck me as being rather dramatic. London is very rich in curious effects of that kind. A wet Sunday, an uncouth Christian in a mackintosh, a ring of sickly white faces under a broken roof of dripping umbrellas, and a wonderful phrase flung into the air by shrill, hysterical lips – it was really very good in its way, quite a suggestion. I thought of telling the prophet that Art had a soul, but that man had not. I am afraid, however, he would not have understood me.'

'Don't' Harry. The soul is a terrible reality. It can be bought, and sold, and bartered away. It can be poisoned, or made perfect. There is a soul in each one of us. I know it.'

'Do you feel quite sure of that, Dorian?'

'Quite sure.'

'Ah! then it must be an illusion. The things one feels absolutely certain about are never true. That is the fatality of Faith, and the lesson of Romance. How grave you are! Don't be so serious. What have you or I to do with the superstitions of our age? No: we have given up our belief in the soul. Play me something. Play me a nocturne, Dorian, and, as you play, tell me, in a low voice, how you have kept your youth. You must have some secret. I am only ten years older than you are, and I am wrinkled, and worn, and yellow. You are really wonderful, Dorian. You have never looked more charming than you do to-night. You remind me of the day I saw you first. You were rather cheeky, very shy, and absolutely extraordinary. You have changed, of course, but not in appearance. I wish you would tell me your secret. To get back my youth I would do anything in the world, except take exercise, get up early, or be respectable. Youth! There is nothing like it. It's absurd to talk of the ignorance of youth. The only people to whose opinions I listen now with any respect are people much younger than myself. They seem in front of me. Life has revealed to them her latest wonder. As for the aged, I always contradict the aged. I do it on principle. If you ask them their opinion on something that happened yesterday, they solemnly give you the opinions current in 1820, when people wore high stocks, believed in everything, and knew absolutely nothing. How lovely that thing you are playing is! I wonder did Chopin write it at Majorca, with the sea weeping round the villa, and the salt spray dashing against the panes? It is marvellously romantic. What a blessing it is that there is one art left to us that is not imitative! Don't stop. I want music to-night. It seems to me that you are the young Apollo, and that I am Marsyas listening to you. I have sorrows, Dorian, of my own, that even you know nothing of. The tragedy of old age is not that one is old, but that one is young. I am amazed sometimes at my own sincerity. Ah, Dorian, how happy you are! What an exquisite life you have had! You have drunk deeply of everything. You have crushed the grapes against your palate. Nothing has been hidden from you. And it has all been to you no more than the sound of music. It has not marred you. You are still the same.'

'I am not the same, Harry.'

'Yes: you are the same. I wonder what the rest of your life will be. Don't spoil it by renunciations. At present you are a perfect type. Don't make yourself incomplete. You are quite flawless now. You need not shake your head: you know you are. Besides, Dorian, don't deceive yourself. Life is not governed by will or intention. Life is a question of nerves, and fibres, and slowly built-up cells in which thought hides itself and passion has its dreams. You may fancy yourself safe, and think yourself strong. But a chance tone of colour in a room or a morning sky, a particular perfume that you had once loved and that brings subtle memories with it, a line from a forgotten poem that you had come across again, a cadence from a piece of music that you had ceased to play – I tell you, Dorian, that it is on things like these that our lives depend. Browning writes about that somewhere; but our own senses will imagine them for us. There are moments when the odour of *lilas blanc* passes suddenly across me, and I have to live the strangest month of my life over again. I wish I could change places with you, Dorian. The world has cried out against us both, but it has always worshipped you. It always will worship you. You are the type of what the age is searching for, and what it is afraid it has found. I am so glad that you have never done anything, never carved a statue, or painted a picture, or produced anything outside of yourself! Life has been your art. You have set yourself to music. Your days are your sonnets.'

Dorian rose up from the piano, and passed his hand through his hair. 'Yes, life has been exquisite,' he murmured, 'but I am not going to have the same life, Harry. And you must not say these extravagant things to me. You don't know everything about me. I think that if you did, even you would turn from me. You laugh. Don't laugh.'

'Why have you stopped playing, Dorian? Go back and give me the nocturne over again. Look at that great honey-coloured moon that hangs in the dusky air. She is waiting for you to charm her, and if you play she will come closer to the earth. You won't? Let us go to the club, then. It has been a charming evening, and we must end it charmingly. There is some one at White's who wants immensely to know you – young Lord Poole, Bournemouth's eldest son. He has already copied your neckties, and has begged me to introduce him to you. He is quite delightful, and rather reminds me of you.'

'I hope not,' said Dorian, with a sad look in his eyes. 'But I am tired to-night, Harry. I shan't go to the club. It is nearly eleven, and I want to go to bed early.'

'Do stay. You have never played so well as to-night. There was something in your touch that was wonderful. It had more expression than I had ever heard from it before.'

'It is because I am going to be good,' he answered, smiling. 'I am a little changed already.'

'You cannot change to me, Dorian,' said Lord Henry. 'You and I will always be friends.'

'Yet you poisoned me with a book once. I should not forgive that. Harry, promise me that you will never lend that book to any one. It does harm.'

'My dear boy, you are really beginning to moralise. You will soon be going about the converted, and the revivalist, warning people against all the sins of which you have grown tired. You are much too delightful to do that. Besides, it is no use. You and I are what we are, and will be what we will be. As for being poisoned by a book, there is no such thing as that. Art has no influence upon action. It annihilates the desire to act. It is superbly sterile. The books that the world calls immoral are books that show the world its own shame. That is all. But we won't discuss literature. Come round to-morrow. I am going to ride at eleven. We might go together, and I will take you to lunch afterwards with Lady Branksome. She is a charming woman, and wants to consult you about some tapestries she is thinking of buying. Mind you come. Or shall we lunch with our little Duchess? She says she never sees you now. Perhaps you are tired of Gladys? I thought you would be. Her clever tongue gets on one's nerves. Well, in any case, be here at eleven.'

'Must I really come, Harry?'

'Certainly. The Park is quite lovely now. I don't think there have been such lilacs since the year I met you.'

'Very well. I shall be here at eleven,' said Dorian 'Good-night, Harry.' As he reached the door he hesitated for a moment, as if he had something more to say. Then he sighed and went out.

It was a lovely night, so warm that he threw his coat over his arm, and did not even put his silk scarf round his throat. As he strolled home, smoking his cigarette, two young men in evening dress passed him. He heard one of them whisper to the other, 'That is Dorian Gray.' He remembered how pleased he used to be when he was pointed out, or stared at, or talked about. He was tired of hearing his own name now. Half the charm of the little village where he had been so often lately was that no one knew who he was. He had often told the girl whom he had lured to love him that he was poor, and she had believed him. He had told her once that he was wicked, and she had laughed at him, and answered that wicked people were always very old and very ugly. What a laugh she had! – just like a thrush singing. And how pretty she had been in her cotton dress and her large hats! She knew nothing, but she had everything that he had lost.

When he reached home, he found his servant waiting up for him. He sent him to bed, and threw himself down on the sofa in the library, and began to think over some of the things that Lord Henry had said to him.

Was it really true that one could never change? He felt a wild longing for the unstained purity of his boyhood – his rose-white boyhood, as Lord Henry had once called it. He knew that he had tarnished himself, filled his mind with corruption, and given horror to his fancy; that he had been an evil influence to others, and had experienced a terrible joy in being so; and that, of the lives that had crossed his own, it had been the fairest and the most full of promise that he had brought to shame. But was it all irretrievable? Was there no hope for him?

Ah! in what a monstrous moment of pride and passion he had prayed that the portrait should bear the burden of his days, and he keep the unsullied splendour of eternal youth! All his failure had been due to that. Better for him that each sin of his life had brought its sure, swift penalty along with it. There was purification in punishment. Not 'Forgive us our sins,' but 'Smite us for our iniquities,' should be the prayer of a man to a most just God.

The curiously carved mirror that Lord Henry had given to him, so many years ago now, was standing on the table, and the white-limbed Cupids laughed round it as of old. He took it up, as he had done on that night of horror, when he had first noted the change in the fatal picture, and with wild, tear-dimmed eyes looked into its polished shield. Once, some one who had terribly loved him had written to him a mad letter, ending with these idolatrous words: 'The world is changed because you are made of ivory and gold. The curves of your lips rewrite history.' The phrases came back to his memory, and he repeated them over and over to himself. Then he loathed his own beauty, and, flinging the mirror on the floor, crushed it into silver splinters beneath his heal. It was his beauty that had ruined him, his beauty and the youth that he had prayed for. But for those two things, his life might have been free from stain. His beauty had been to him but a mask, his youth but a mockery. What was youth at best? A green, an unripe time, a time of shallow moods and sickly thoughts. Why had he worn its livery? Youth had spoiled him.

It was better not to think of the past. Nothing could alter that. It was of himself, and of his own future, that he had to think. James Vane was hidden in a nameless grave in Selby Churchyard. Alan Campbell had shot himself one night in his laboratory, but had not revealed the secret that he had been forced to know. The excitement, such as it was, over Basil Hallward's disappearance would soon pass away. It was already waning. He was perfectly safe there. Nor, indeed, was it the death of Basil Hallward that weighed most upon his mind. It was the living death of his own soul that troubled him. Basil had painted the portrait that had marred his life. He could not forgive him that. It was the portrait that had done everything. Basil had said things to him that were unbearable, and that he had yet borne with patience. The murder had been simply the madness of a moment. As for Alan Campbell, his suicide had been his own act. He had chosen to do it. It was nothing to him.

A new life! That was what he wanted. That was what he was waiting for. Surely he had begun it already. He had spared one innocent thing, at any rate. He would never again tempt innocence. He would be good.

As he thought of Hetty Merton, he began to wonder if the portrait in the locked room had changed. Surely it was not still so horrible as it had been? Perhaps if his life became pure, he would be able to expel every sign of evil passion from the face. Perhaps the signs of evil had already gone away. He would go and look.

He took the lamp from the table and crept upstairs. As he unbarred the door a smile of joy flitted across his strangely young-looking face and lingered for a moment about his lips. Yes, he would be good, and the hideous thing that he had hidden away would no longer be a terror to him. He felt as if the load had been lifted from him already.

He went in quietly, locking the door behind him, as was his custom, and dragged the purple hanging from the portrait. A cry of pain and indignation broke from him. He could see no change save that in the eyes there was a look of cunning, and in the mouth the curved wrinkle of the hypocrite. The thing was still loathsome – more loathsome, if possible, than before – and the scarlet dew that spotted the hand seemed brighter, and more like blood newly spilt. Then he trembled. Had it been merely vanity that had made him do his one good deed? Or the desire for a new sensation, as Lord Henry had hinted, with his mocking laugh? Or that passion to act a part that sometimes makes us do things finer than we are ourselves? Or, perhaps, all these? And why was the red stain larger than it had been? It seemed to have crept like a horrible disease over the wrinkled fingers. There was blood on the painted feet, as though the thing had dripped – blood even on the hand that had not held the knife. Confess? Did it mean that he was to confess? To give himself up, and be put to death? He laughed. He felt that the idea was monstrous. Besides, even if he did confess, who would believe him? There was no trace of the murdered man anywhere. Everything belonging to him had been destroyed. He himself had burned what had been below-stairs. The world would simply say that he was mad. They would shut him up if he persisted in his story.... Yet it was his duty to confess, to suffer public shame, and to make public atonement. There was a God who called upon men to tell their sins to earth as well as to heaven. Nothing that he could do would cleanse him till he had told his own sin. His sin? He shrugged his shoulders. The death of Basil Hallward seemed very little to him. He was thinking of Hetty Merton. For it was an unjust mirror, this mirror of his soul that he was looking at. Vanity? Curiosity? Hypocrisy? Had there been nothing more in his renunciation than that? There had been something more. At least he thought so. But who could tell? ... No. There had been nothing more. Through vanity he had spared her. In hypocrisy he had worn the mask of goodness. For curiosity's sake he had tried the denial of self. He recognised that now.

But this murder – was it to dog him all his life? Was he always to be burdened by his past? Was he really to confess? Never. There was only one bit of evidence left against him. The picture itself – that was evidence. He would destroy it. Why had he kept it so long? Once it had given him pleasure to watch it changing and growing old. Of late he had felt no such pleasure. It had kept him awake at night. When he had been away,

THE PICTURE OF DORIAN GRAY

he had been filled with terror lest other eyes should look upon it. It had
brought melancholy across his passions. Its mere memory had marred
many moments of joy. It had been like conscience to him. Yes, it had
been conscience. He would destroy it.

He looked round, and saw the knife that had stabbed Basil Hallward.
He had cleaned it many times, till there was no stain left upon it. It was
bright, and glistened. As it had killed the painter, so it would kill the
painter's work, and all that that meant. It would kill the past and when
that was dead he would be free. It would kill this monstrous soul-life,
and, without its hideous warnings, he would be at peace. He seized the
thing, and stabbed the picture with it.

There was a cry heard, and a crash. The cry was so horrible in its
agony that the frightened servants woke, and crept out of their rooms.
Two gentlemen, who were passing in the Square below, stopped, and
looked up at the great house. They walked on till they met a policeman,
and brought him back. The man rang the bell several times, but there
was no answer. Except for a light in one of the top windows, the house
was all dark. After a time, he went away and stood in an adjoining
portico and watched.

'Whose house is that, constable?' asked the elder of the two gentlemen.

'Mr. Dorian Gray's, sir,' answered the policeman.

They looked at each other, as they walked away, and sneered. One of
them was Sir Henry Ashton's uncle.

Inside, in the servants' part of the house, the half-clad domestics were
talking in low whispers to each other. Old Mrs. Leaf was crying and
wringing her hands. Francis was as pale as death.

After about quarter of an hour, he got the coachman and one of the
footmen and crept upstairs. They knocked, but there was no reply. They
called out. Everything was still. Finally, after vainly trying to force the
door, they got on the roof, and dropped down on to the balcony. The
windows yielded easily; their bolts were old.

When they entered they found, hanging upon the wall, a splendid
portrait of their master as they had last seen him, in all the wonder of
his exquisite youth and beauty. Lying on the floor was a dead man, in
evening dress, with a knife in his heart. He was withered, wrinkled, and
loathsome of visage. It was not till they had examined the rings that they
recognised who it was.

Yours Truly, Jack the Ripper
ROBERT BLOCH

I LOOKED AT THE STAGE Englishman. He looked at me.

'Sir Guy Hollis?' I asked.

'Indeed. Have I the pleasure of addressing John Carmody, the psychiatrist?'

I nodded. My eyes swept over the figure of my distinguished visitor. Tall, lean, sandy-haired—with the traditional tufted moustache. And the tweeds. I suspected a monocle concealed in a vest pocket, and wondered if he'd left his umbrella in the outer office.

But more than that, I wondered what the devil had impelled Sir Guy Hollis of the British Embassy to seek out a total stranger here in Chicago.

Sir Guy didn't help matters any as he sat down. He cleared his throat, glanced around nervously, tapped his pipe against the side of the desk. Then he opened his mouth.

'What do you think of London?' he said.

'Why—'

'I'd like to discuss London with you, Mr. Carmody.'

I meet all kinds. So I merely smiled, sat back, and gave him his head.

'Have you ever noticed anything strange about that city?' he asked.

'Well, the fog is famous.'

'Yes, the fog. That's important. It usually provides the perfect setting.'

'Setting for what?'

Sir Guy Hollis gave me an enigmatic grin.

'Murder,' he murmured.

'Murder?'

'Yes. Hasn't it struck you that London, of all cities, has a peculiar affinity for those who contemplate homicide?'

They don't talk that way, except in books. Still, it was an interesting thought. London as an ideal spot for a murder!

'As you mentioned,' said Sir Guy, 'there is a natural reason for this. The fog is an ideal background. And then too the British have a peculiar attitude in such matters. You might call it their sporting instinct. They regard murder as sort of a game.'

I sat up straight. Here was a theory.

'Yes, I needn't bore you with homicide statistics. The record is there. Aesthetically, temperamentally, the Englishman is interested in crimes of violence.

'A man commits murder. Then the excitement begins. The game starts. Will the criminal outwit the police? You can read between the lines in their newspaper stories. Everybody is waiting to see who will score.

'British law regards a prisoner as innocent until proved guilty. That's *their* advantage. But first they must catch their prisoner. And London bobbies are not allowed to carry fire-arms. That's a point for the fugitive. You see? All part of the rules of the game.'

I wondered what Sir Guy was driving at. Either a point or a strait-jacket. But I kept my mouth shut and let him continue.

'The logical result of this British attitude towards murder is— Sherlock Holmes,' he said.

'Have you ever noticed how popular the theme of murder is in British fiction and drama?'

I smiled. I was back on familiar ground.

'*Angel Street*,' I suggested.

'*Ladies in Retirement*,' he continued. '*Night Must Fall.*'

'*Payment Deferred*,' I added. '*Laburnum Grove. Kind Lady. Love from a Stranger. Portrait of a Man with Red Hair. Black Limelight.*'

He nodded. 'Think of the motion pictures of Alfred Hitchcock and Emlyn Williams. The actors – Wilfred Lawson and Leslie Banks.'

'Charles Laughton,' I continued for him. 'Edmund Gwenn. Basil Rathbone. Raymond Massey. Sir Cedric Hardwicke.'

'You're quite an expert on this sort of thing yourself,' he told me.

'Not at all.' I smiled. 'I'm a psychiatrist.'

Then I leaned forward. I didn't change my tone of voice. 'All I want to know,' I said sweetly, 'is why you come up to my office and discuss murder melodramas with me.'

It stung him. He sat back and blinked a little.

'That isn't my intention,' he murmured. 'No. Not at all. I was just advancing a theory—'

'Stalling,' I said. 'Stalling. Come on, Sir Guy – spit it out.'

Talking like a gangster is all part of the applied psychiatric technique. At least, it worked for me.

It worked this time.

Sir Guy stopped bleating. His eyes narrowed. When he leaned forward again he meant business.

'Mr. Carmody,' he said, 'have you ever heard of – Jack the Ripper?'

'The murderer?' I asked.

'Exactly. The greatest monster of them all. Worse then Spring-heel Jack or Crippen. Jack the Ripper. Red Jack.'

'I've heard of him,' I said.

'Do you know his history?'

I got tough again. 'Listen, Sir Guy,' I muttered. 'I don't think we'll get any place swapping old wives' tales about famous crimes of history.'

Another bull's-eye. He took a deep breath.

'This is no old wives' tale. It's a matter of life or death.'

He was so wrapped up in his obsession he even talked that way. Well – I was willing to listen. We psychiatrists get paid for listening.

'Go ahead,' I told him. 'Let's have the story.'

Sir Guy lit a cigarette and began to talk.

'London, 1888,' he began. 'Late summer and early autumn. That was the time. Out of nowhere came the shadowy figure of Jack the Ripper – a stalking shadow with a knife, prowling through London's East End. Haunting the squalid dives of Whitechapel, Spitalfields. Where he came from no one knew. But he brought death. Death in a knife.

'Six times that knife descended to slash the throats and bodies of London's women. Drabs and alley sluts. August 7 was the date of the first butchery. They found her body lying there with thirty-nine stab wounds. A ghastly murder. On August 31 another victim. The press became interested. The slum inhabitants were more deeply interested still.

'Who was this unknown killer who prowled in their midst and struck at will in the deserted alleyways of night-town? And what was more important – when would he strike again?

'September 8 was the date. Scotland Yard assigned special deputies. Rumours ran rampant. The atrocious nature of the slayings was the subject for shocking speculation.

'The killer used a knife – expertly. He cut throats. He chose victims and settings with a fiendish deliberation. No one saw him or heard him. But watchmen making their grey rounds in the dawn would stumble across the hacked and horrid thing that was the Ripper's handiwork.

'Who was he? What was he? A mad surgeon? A butcher? An insane scientist? A pathological degenerate escaped from an asylum? A deranged nobleman? A member of the London police?

'Then the poem appeared in the newspapers. The anonymous poem, designed to put a stop to speculations – but which only aroused public interest to a further frenzy. A mocking little stanza:

I'm not a butcher, I'm not a kid
Nor yet a foreign skipper,

> *But I'm your own true loving friend,*
> *Yours truly – Jack the Ripper.*

'And on September 30, two more throats were slashed open.'

I interrupted Sir Guy for a moment.

'Very interesting,' I commented. I'm afraid a faint hint of sarcasm crept into my voice.

He winced, but didn't falter in his narrative.

'There was silence, then, in London for a time. Silence, and a nameless fear. When would Red Jack strike again? They waited through October. Every figment of fog concealed his phantom presence. Concealed it well – for nothing was learned of the Ripper's identity, or his purpose. The drabs of London shivered in the raw wind of early November. Shivered, and were thankful for the coming of each morning's sun.

'November 9. They found her in her room. She lay there very quietly, limbs neatly arranged. And beside her, with equal neatness, were laid her head and heart. The Ripper had outdone himself in execution.

'Then, panic. But needless panic. For though press, police and populace alike awaited in sick dread, Jack the Ripper did not strike again.

'Months passed. A year. The immediate interest died, but not the memory. They said Jack had skipped to America. That he had committed suicide. They said – and they wrote. They've written ever since. Theories, hypotheses, arguments, treatises. But to this day no one knows who Jack the Ripper was. Or why he killed. Or why he stopped killing.'

Sir Guy was silent. Obviously he expected some comment from me.

'You tell the story well,' I remarked. 'Though with a slight emotional bias.'

'I've got all the documents,' said Sir Guy Hollis. 'I've made a collection of existing data and studied it.'

I stood up. 'Well,' I yawned, in mock fatigue, 'I've enjoyed your little bedtime story a great deal, Sir Guy. It was kind of you to abandon your duties at the British Embassy to drop in on a poor psychiatrist and regale him with your acecdotes.'

Goading him always did the trick.

'I suppose you want to know why I'm interested?' he snapped.

'Yes. That's exactly what I'd like to know. Why are you interested?'

'Because,' said Sir Guy Hollis, 'I am on the trail of Jack the Ripper now. I think he's here – in Chicago!'

I sat down again. This time I did the blinking act.

'Say that again,' I stuttered.

'Jack the Ripper is alive, in Chicago, and I'm out to find him.'

'Wait a minute,' I said. 'Wait – a – minute!'

He wasn't smiling. It wasn't a joke.

'See here,' I said. 'What was the date of these murders?'

'August to November 1888.'

'1888? But if Jack the Ripper was an able-bodied man in 1888, he'd surely be dead today! Why look, man – if he were merely *born* in that year, he'd be fifty-five years old today!'

'Would he?' smiled Sir Guy Hollis. 'Or should I say "Would she?" Because Jack the Ripper may have been a woman. Or any number of things.'

'Sir Guy,' I said. 'You came to the right person when you looked me up. You definitely need the services of a psychiatrist.'

'Perhaps. Tell me, Mr. Carmody, do you think I'm crazy?'

I looked at him and shrugged. But I had to give him a truthful answer.

'Frankly – no.'

'Then you might listen to the reasons I believe Jack the Ripper is alive today.'

'I might.'

'I've studied these cases for thirty years. Been over the actual ground. Talked to officials. Talked to friends and acquaintances of the poor drabs who were killed. Visited with men and women in the neighbourhood. Collected an entire library of material touching on Jack the Ripper. Studied all the wild theories or crazy notions.

'I learned a little. Not much, but a little. I won't bore you with my conclusions. But there was another branch of inquiry that yielded more fruitful returns. I have studied unsolved crimes. Murders.

'I could show you clippings from the papers of half the world's great cities. San Francisco. Shanghai. Calcutta. Omsk. Paris. Berlin. Pretoria. Cairo. Milan. Adelaide.

'The trail is there, the pattern. Unsolved crimes. Slashed throats of women. With the peculiar disfigurations and removals. Yes, I've followed a trail of blood. From New York westward across the continent. Then to the Pacific. From there to Africa. During the Great War it was Europe. After that, South America. And since 1930, the United States again. Eighty-seven such murders – and to the trained criminologist, all bear the stigma of the Ripper's handiwork.

'Recently there were the so-called Cleveland torso slayings. Remember? A shocking series. And finally, two recent deaths in Chicago. Within the past six months. One out on South Dearborn, the other somewhere up on Halsted. Same type of crime, same technique. I tell you, there are unmistakable indications in all these affairs – indications of the work of Jack the Ripper!'

I smiled.

'A very tight theory,' I said. 'I'll not question your evidence at all, or the deductions you draw. You're the criminologist, and I'll take your word for it. Just one thing remains to be explained. A minor point, perhaps, but worth mentioning.'

'And what is that?' asked Sir Guy.

'Just how could a man of, let us say, eighty-five years, commit these crimes? For if Jack the Ripper was around thirty in 1888 and lived, he'd be eighty-five today!'

Sir Guy Hollis was silent. I had him there. But—

'*Suppose he didn't get any older?*' whispered Sir Guy.

'What's that?'

'Suppose Jack the Ripper didn't grow old? Suppose he is still a young man today.'

'All right,' I said. 'I'll suppose for a moment. Then I'll stop supposing and call for my nurse to restrain you.'

'I'm serious,' said Sir Guy.

'They all are,' I told him. 'That's the pity of it all, isn't it? They *know* they hear voices and see demons. But we lock them up just the same.'

It was cruel, but it got results. He rose and faced me.

'It's a crazy theory, I grant you,' he said. 'All the theories about the Ripper are crazy. The idea that he was a doctor. Or a maniac. Or a woman. The reasons advanced for such beliefs are flimsy enough. There's nothing to go by. So why should my notion be any worse?'

'Because people grow older,' I reasoned with him. 'Doctors, maniacs and women alike.'

'What about – *sorcerers?*'

'Sorcerers?'

'Necromancers. Wizards. Practisers of black magic?'

'What's the point?'

'I studied,' said Sir Guy. 'I studied everything. After a while I began to study the dates of the murders. The pattern those dates formed. The rhythm. The solar, lunar, stellar rhythm. The sidereal aspect. The astrological significance.'

He *was* crazy. But I still listened.

'Suppose Jack the Ripper didn't murder for murder's sake alóne? Suppose he wanted to make – a sacrifice?'

'What kind of a sacrifice?'

Sir Guy shrugged. 'It is said that if you offer blood to the dark gods they grant boons. Yes, if a blood offering is made at the proper time when the moon and the stars are right – and with the proper ceremonies – they grant boons. Boons of youth. Eternal youth.'

'But that's nonsense!'

'No. That's – Jack the Ripper.'

I stood up. 'A most interesting theory,' I told him. 'But Sir Guy – there's just one thing I'm interested in. Why do you come here and tell it to me? I'm not an authority on witchcraft. I'm not a police official or criminologist. I'm a practising psychiatrist. What's the connection?'

Sir Guy smiled.

'You are interested, then?'

'Well, yes. There must be some point.'

'There is. But I wished to be assured of your interest first. Now I can tell you my plan.'

'And just what is that plan?'

Sir Guy gave me a long look. Then he spoke.

'John Carmody,' he said, 'you and I are going to capture Jack the Ripper.'

That's the way it happened. I've given the gist of that first interview in all its intricate and somewhat boring detail because I think it's important. It helps to throw some light on Sir Guy's character and attitude. And in view of what happened after that—

But I'm coming to those matters.

Sir Guy's thought was simple. It wasn't even a thought. Just a hunch.

'You know the people here,' he told me. 'I've inquired. That's why I came to you as the ideal man for my purpose. You number among your acquaintances many writers, painters, poets. The so-called intelligentsia. The Bohemians. The lunatic fringe from the near north side.

'For certain reasons – never mind what they are – my clues lead me to infer that Jack the Ripper is a member of that element. He chooses to pose as an eccentric. I've a feeling that with you to take me around and introduce me to your set, I might hit on the right person.'

'It's all right with me,' I said. 'But just how are you going to look for him? As you say, he might be anybody, anywhere. And you have no idea what he looks like. He might be young or old. Jack the Ripper – a jack of all trades? Rich man, poor man, beggar man, thief, doctor, lawyer – how will you know?'

'We shall see.' Sir Guy sighed heavily. 'But I must find him. At once.'

'Why the hurry?'

Sir Guy sighed again. 'Because in two days he will kill again.'

'Are you sure?'

'Sure as the stars. I've plotted his chart, you see. All eighty-seven of the murders correspond to certain astrological rhythm patterns. If, as I suspect, he makes a blood sacrifice to renew his youth, he must murder within two days. Notice the pattern of his first crimes in London. August 7. Then August 31. September 8. September 30. November 9. Intervals of twenty-four days, nine days, twenty-two days – he killed two this time – and then forty days. Of course there were crimes in between. There had to be. But they weren't discovered and pinned on him.

'At any rate, I've worked out a pattern for him, based on all my data. And I say that within the next two days he kills. So I must seek him out, somehow, before then.'

'And I'm still asking you what you want me to do.'

'Take me out,' said Sir Guy. 'Introduce me to your friends. Take me to parties.'

'But where do I begin? As far as I know, my artistic friends, despite their eccentricities, are all normal people.'

'So is the Ripper. Perfectly normal. Except on certain nights.' Again that faraway look in Sir Guy's eyes. 'Then he becomes an ageless pathological monster, crouching to kill, on evenings when the stars blaze down in the blazing patterns of death.'

'All right,' I said. 'All right. I'll take you to parties, Sir Guy. I want to go myself, anyway. I need the drinks they'll serve there after listening to your kind of talk.'

We made our plans. And that evening I took him over to Lester Baston's studio.

As we ascended to the penthouse roof in the elevator I took the opportunity to warn Sir Guy.

'Baston's a real screwball,' I cautioned him. 'So are his guests. Be prepared for anything and everything.'

'I am.' Sir Guy Hollis was perfectly serious. He put his hand in his trouser pocket and pulled out a gun.

'What the—' I began.

'If I see him I'll be ready,' Sir Guy said. He didn't smile, either.

'But you can't go running around at a party with a loaded revolver in your pocket, man!'

'Don't worry, I won't behave foolishly.'

I wondered. Sir Guy Hollis was not, to my way of thinking, a normal man.

We stepped out of the elevator and went towards Baston's apartment door.

'By the way,' I murmured, 'just how do you wish to be introduced? Shall I tell them who you are and what you are looking for?

'I don't care. Perhaps it would be best to be frank.'

'But don't you think that the Ripper – if by some miracle he or she is present – will immediately get the wind up and take cover?'

'I think the shock of the announcement that I am hunting the Ripper would provoke some kind of betraying gesture on his part,' said Sir Guy.

'You'd make a pretty good psychiatrist yourself,' I conceded. 'It's a fine theory. But I warn you, you're going to be in for a lot of ribbing. This is a wild bunch.'

Sir Guy smiled.

'I'm ready,' he announced. 'I have a little plan of my own. Don't be shocked by anything I do,' he warned me.

I nodded and knocked on the door.

Baston opened it and poured out into the hall. He teetered back and forth regarding us very gravely. He squinted at my square-cut Homburg hat and Sir Guy's moustache.

'Aha,' he intoned. 'The Walrus and the Carpenter.'

I introduced Sir Guy.

'Welcome,' said Baston, gesturing us inside with over-elaborate courtesy. He stumbled after us into the garish parlour.

I stared at the crowd that moved restlessly through the fog of cigarette smoke.

It was the shank of the evening for this mob. Every hand held a drink. Every face held a slightly hectic flush. Over in one corner the piano was going full blast.

Sir Guy got a monocle-full right away. He saw LaVerne Gonnister, the poetess, hit Hymie Kralik in the eye. He saw Hymie sit down on the floor and cry until Dick Pool accidentally stepped on his stomach as he walked through to the dining-room for a drink.

He heard Nadia Vilinoff, the commercial artist, tell Johnny Odcutt that she thought his tattooing was in dreadful taste.

His zoological observations might have continued indefinitely if Lester Baston hadn't stepped to the centre of the room and called for silence by dropping a vase on the floor.

'We have distinguished visitors in our midst,' bawled Lester, waving his empty glass in our direction. 'None other than the Walrus and the Carpenter. The Walrus is Sir Guy Hollis, a something-or-other from the British Embassy. The Carpenter, as you all know, is our own John Carmody, the prominent dispenser of libido-liniment.'

He turned and grabbed Sir Guy by the arm, dragging him to the middle of the carpet. For a moment I thought Hollis might object, but a quick wink reassured me. He was prepared for this.

'It is our custom, Sir Guy,' said Baston, loudly, 'to subject our new friends to a little cross-examination. Just a little formality at these very formal gatherings, you understand. Are you prepared to answer questions?'

Sir Guy nodded and grinned.

'Very well,' Baston muttered. 'Friends – I give you this bundle from Britain. Your witness.'

Then the ribbing started. I meant to listen, but at that moment Lydia Dare saw me and dragged me off into the vestibule for one of those Darling-I-waited-for-your-call-all-day routines.

By the time I got rid of her and went back, the impromptu quiz session was in full swing. From the attitude of the crowd, I gathered that Sir Guy was doing all right for himself.

Then Baston himself interjected a question that upset the apple-cart.

'And what, may I ask, brings you to our midst tonight? What is your mission, oh Walrus?'

'I'm looking for Jack the Ripper.'

Nobody laughed.

Perhaps it struck them all the way it did me. I glanced at my neighbours and began to *wonder*.

LaVerne Gonnister. Hymie Kralik. Harmless. Dick Pool. Nadia

Vilinoff. Johnny Odcutt and his wife. Barclay Melton. Lydia Dare. All harmless.

But what a forced smile on Dick Pool's face! And that sly, self-conscious smirk that Barclay Melton wore!

Oh, it was absurd, I grant you. But for the first time I saw these people in a new light. I wondered about their lives – their secret lives beyond the scenes of parties.

How many of them were playing a part, concealing something?

Who here would worship Hecate and grant that horrid goddess the dark boon of blood?

Even Lester Baston might be masquerading.

The mood was upon us all, for a moment. I saw questions flicker in the circle of eyes around the room.

Sir Guy stood there, and I could swear he was fully conscious of the situation he'd created, and enjoyed it.

I wondered idly just what was *really* wrong with him. Why he had this odd fixation concerning Jack the Ripper. Maybe he was hiding secrets, too . . .

Baston, as usual, broke the mood. He burlesqued it.

'The Walrus isn't kidding, friends,' he said. He slapped Sir Guy on the back and put his arm around him as he orated. 'Our English cousin is really on the trail of the fabulous Jack the Ripper. You all remember Jack the Ripper, I presume? Quite a cut-up in the old days, as I recall. Really had some ripping good times when he went out on a tear.

'The Walrus has some idea that the Ripper is still alive, probably prowling around Chicago with a boy scout knife. In fact' – Baston paused impressively and shot it out in a rasping stage-whisper – '*in fact, he has reason to believe that Jack the Ripper might even be right here in our midst tonight.*'

There was the expected reaction of giggles and grins. Baston eyed Lydia Dare reprovingly. 'You girls needn't laugh,' he smirked. 'Jack the Ripper might be a woman, too, you know. Sort of a Jill the Ripper.'

'You mean you actually suspect one of us?' shrieked LaVerne Gonnister, simpering up to Sir Guy. 'But that Jack the Ripper person disappeared ages ago, didn't he? In 1888?

'Aha!' interrupted Baston. 'How do you know so much about it, young lady? Sounds suspicious! Watch her, Sir Guy – she may not be as young as she appears. These lady poets have dark pasts.'

The tension was gone, the mood was shattered, and the whole thing was beginning to degenerate into a trivial party joke.

Then Baston caught it.

'Guess what?' he yelled. 'The Walrus has a gun.'

His embracing arm had slipped and encountered the hard outline of the gun in Sir Guy's pocket. He snatched it out before Hollis had the opportunity to protest.

I stared hard at Sir Guy, wondering if this thing had carried far enough. But he flicked a wink my way and I remembered he had told me not to be alarmed.

So I waited as Baston broached a drunken inspiration.

'Let's play fair with our friend the Walrus,' he cried. 'He came all the way from England to our party on this mission. If none of you is willing to confess, I suggest we give him a chance to find out – the hard way.'

'What's up?' asked Johnny Odcutt.

'I'll turn out the lights for one minute. Sir Guy can stand here with his gun. If anyone in this room is the Ripper he can either run for it or take the opportunity to – well, eradicate his pursuer. Fair enough?'

It was even sillier than it sounds, but it caught the popular fancy. Sir Guy's protests went unheard in the ensuing babble. And before I could stride over and put in my two cents' worth, Lester Baston had reached the light switch.

'Don't anybody move,' he announced, with fake solemnity. 'For one minute we will remain in darkness – perhaps at the mercy of a killer. At the end of that time, I'll turn up the lights again and look for bodies. Choose your partners, ladies and gentlemen.'

The lights went out.

Somebody giggled.

I heard footsteps in the darkness. Mutterings.

A hand brushed my face.

The watch on my wrist ticked violently. But even louder, rising above it, I heard another thumping. The beating of my heart.

Absurd. Standing in the dark with a group of tipsy fools. And yet there was real terror lurking here, rustling through the velvet blackness.

Jack the Ripper prowled in darkness like this. And Jack the Ripper had a knife. Jack the Ripper had a madman's brain and a madman's purpose.

But Jack the Ripper was dead, dead and dust these many years – by every human law.

Only there are no human laws when you feel yourself in the darkness, when the darkness hides and protects and the outer mask slips off your face and you feel something welling up within you, a brooding shapeless purpose that is brother to the blackness.

Sir Guy Hollis shrieked.

There was a grisly thud.

Baston had the lights on.

Everybody screamed.

Sir Guy Hollis lay sprawled on the floor in the centre of the room. The gun was still clutched in his hand.

I glanced at the faces, marvelling at the variety of expressions human beings can assume when confronting horror.

All the faces were present in the circle. Nobody had fled. And yet Sir Guy Hollis lay there. . .

LaVerne Gonnister was wailing and hiding her face.

'All right.'

Sir Guy rolled over and jumped to his feet. He was smiling.

'Just an experiment, eh? If Jack the Ripper *were* among those present, and thought I had been murdered, he would have betrayed himself in some way when the lights went on and he saw me lying there.

'I am convinced of your individual and collective innocence. Just a gentle spoof, my friends.'

Hollis stared at the goggling Baston and the rest of them crowding in behind him.

'Shall we leave, John?' he called to me. 'It's getting late, I think.'

Turning, he headed for the closet. I followed him. Nobody said a word.

It was a pretty dull party after that.

I met Sir Guy the following evening as we agreed, on the corner of 29th Street and South Halsted.

After what had happened the night before, I was prepared for almost anything. But Sir Guy seemed matter-of-fact enough as he stood huddled against a grimy doorway and waited for me to appear.

'Boo!' I said, jumping out suddenly. He smiled. Only the betraying gesture of his left hand indicated that he'd instinctively reached for his gun when I startled him.

'All ready for our wild goose chase?' I asked.

'Yes.' He nodded. 'I'm glad that you agreed to meet me without asking questions,' he told me. 'It shows you trust my judgment.' He took my arm and edged me along the street slowly.

'It's foggy tonight, John,' said Sir Guy. 'Like London.'

I nodded.

'Cold, too, for November.'

I nodded again and half-shivered my agreement.

'Curious,' he mused. 'London fog and November. The place and the time of the Ripper murders.'

I grinned through darkness. 'Let me remind you, Sir Guy, that this isn't London, but Chicago. And it isn't November 1888. It's over fifty years later.

Sir Guy returned my grin, but without mirth. 'I'm not so sure, at that,' he murmured. 'Look about you. These tangled alleys and twisted streets. They're like the East End. Mitre Square. And surely they are as ancient as fifty years, at least.'

'You're in the poor neighbourhood off South Clark Street,' I said, shortly. 'And why you dragged me down here I still don't know.'

'It's a hunch,' Sir Guy admitted. 'Just a hunch on my part, John. I want to wander around down here. There's the same geographical conformation in these streets as in those courts where the Ripper roamed and slew. That's where we'll find him, John. Not in the bright lights of the Bohemian neighbourhood, but down here in the darkness. The darkness where he waits and crouches.'

'Is that why you brought a gun?' I asked. I was unable to keep a trace of sarcastic nervousness from my voice. All of this talk, this incessant obsession with Jack the Ripper, got on my nerves.

'We may need the gun,' said Sir Guy, gravely. 'After all, tonight is the appointed night.'

I sighed. We wandered on through the foggy, deserted streets. Here and there a dim light burned above a doorway. Otherwise, all was darkness and shadow. Deep, gaping alleyways loomed as we proceeded down a slanting side street.

We crawled through that fog, alone and silent, like two tiny maggots floundering within a shroud.

When that thought hit me, I winced. The atmosphere was beginning to get *me*, too. If I didn't watch my step I'd go as loony as Sir Guy.

'Can't you see there's not a soul around these streets?' I said, tugging at his coat impatiently.

'He's bound to come,' said Sir Guy. 'He'll be drawn here. This is what I've been looking for. A *genius loci*. An evil spot that attracts evil. Always, when he slays, it's in the slums.

'You see, that must be one of his weaknesses. He has a fascination for squalor. Besides, the women he needs for sacrifice are more easily found in the dives and stewpots of a great city.'

I smiled. 'Well, let's go into one of the dives or stewpots,' I suggested. 'I'm cold. Need a drink. This fog gets into your bones. You Britishers can stand it, but I like warmth and dry heat.'

We emerged from our side street and stood upon the threshold of an alley.

Through the white clouds of mist ahead, I discerned a dim blue light, a naked bulb dangling from a beer sign above an alley tavern.

'Let's take a chance,' I said. 'I'm beginning to shiver.'

'Lead the way,' said Sir Guy. I led him down the alley passage. We halted before the door of the dive.

'What are you waiting for?' he asked.

'Just looking in,' I told him. 'This is a tough neighbourhood, Sir Guy. Never know what you're liable to run into. And I'd prefer we didn't get into the wrong company.'

'Good idea, John.'

I finished my inspection through the doorway. 'Looks deserted,' I murmured. 'Let's try it.'

We entered a dingy bar. A feeble light flickered above the counter and railing, but failed to penetrate the farther gloom of the back booths.

A gigantic Negro lolled across the bar. He scarcely stirred as we came in, but his eyes flickered open quite suddenly and I knew he noted our presence and was judging us.

'Evening,' I said.

He took his time before replying. Still sizing us up. Then he grinned.

'Evening, gents. What's your pleasure?'

'Gin,' I said. 'Two gins. It's a cold night.'

'That's right, gents.'

He poured. I paid, and took the glasses over to one of the booths. We wasted no time in emptying them. The fiery liquor warmed.

I went over to the bar and got the bottle. Sir Guy and I poured ourselves another drink. The big Negro went back into his doze, with one wary eye half-open against any sudden activity.

The clock over the bar ticked on. The wind was rising outside, tearing the shroud of fog to ragged shreds. Sir Guy and I sat in the warm booth and drank our gin.

He began to talk, and the shadows crept up about us to listen.

He rambled a great deal. He went over everything he'd said in the office when I met him, just as though I hadn't heard it before. The poor devils with obsessions are like that.

I listened very patiently. I poured Sir Guy another drink. And another.

But the liquor only made him more talkative. How he did run on! About ritual killings and prolonging life unnaturally – the whole fantastic tale came out again. And, of course, he maintained his unyielding conviction that the Ripper was abroad tonight.

I suppose I was guilty of goading him.

'Very well,' I said, unable to keep the impatience from my voice. 'Let us say that your theory is correct – even though we must overlook every natural law and swallow a lot of superstition to give it any credence.

'But let us say, for the sake of argument, that you are right. Jack the Ripper was a man who discovered how to prolong his own life through making human sacrifices. He did travel around the world as you believe. He is in Chicago now and he is planning to kill. In other words, let us suppose that everything you claim is gospel truth. So what?'

'What do you mean, "so what"?' said Sir Guy.

'I mean – so what?' I answered. 'If all this is true, it still doesn't prove that by sitting down in a dingy gin-mill on the South Side, Jack the Ripper is going to walk in here and let you kill him, or turn him over to the police. And come to think of it, I don't even know now just what you intend to *do* with him if you ever did find him.'

Sir Guy gulped his gin. 'I'd capture the bloody swine,' he said. 'Capture him and turn him over to the government, together with all the papers and documentary evidence I've collected against him over a period of many years. I've spent a fortune investigating this affair, I tell you, a fortune! His capture will mean the solution of hundreds of unsolved crimes, of that I am convinced.

'I tell you, a mad beast is loose on this world! An ageless, eternal beast, sacrificing to Hecate and the dark gods!'

In vino veritas. Or was all this babbling the result of too much gin? It didn't matter. Sir Guy Hollis had another. I sat there and wondered what to do with him. The man was rapidly working up to a climax of hysterical drunkenness.

'One other point,' I said, more for the sake of conversation than in any hopes of obtaining information. 'You still don't explain how it is that you hope to just blunder into the Ripper.'

'He'll be around,' said Sir Guy. 'I'm psychic. I know.'

Sir Guy wasn't psychic. He was maudlin.

The whole business was beginning to infuriate me. We'd been sitting here an hour, and during all this time I'd been forced to play nursemaid and audience to a babbling idiot. After all, he wasn't a regular patient of mine.

'That's enough,' I said, putting out my hand as Sir Guy reached for the half-emptied bottle again. 'You've had plenty. Now I've got a suggestion to make. Let's call a cab and get out of here. It's getting late and it doesn't look as though your elusive friend is going to put in his appearance. Tomorrow, if I were you, I'd plan to turn all those papers and documents over to the FBI. If you're so convinced of the truth of your wild theory, they are competent to make a very thorough investigation and find your man.

'But let's get out of here anyway,' I said, glancing at my watch. 'It's past midnight.'

He sighed, shrugged, and rose unsteadily. As he started for the door, he tugged the gun free from his pocket.

'Here, give me that!' I whispered. 'You can't walk around the street brandishing that thing.'

I took the gun and slipped it inside my coat. Then I got hold of his right arm and steered him out of the door. The Negro didn't look up as we departed.

We stood shivering in the alleyway. The fog had increased. I couldn't see either end of the alley from where we stood. It was cold. Damp. Dark. Fog or no fog, a little wind was whispering secrets to the shadows at our backs.

The fresh air hit Sir Guy just as I had expected it would. Fog and gin fumes don't mingle very well. He lurched as I guided him slowly through the mist.

Sir Guy, despite his incapacity, still stared apprehensively at the alley, as though he expected to see a figure approaching.

Disgust got the better of me.

'Childish foolishness,' I snorted. 'Jack the Ripper, indeed! I call this carrying a hobby too far.'

'Hobby?' He faced me. Through the fog I could see his distorted face. 'You call this a hobby?'

'Well, what is it?' I grumbled. 'Just why else are you so interested in tracking down this mythical killer?'

My arm held him. But his stare held me.

'In London,' he whispered. 'In 1888 . . . one of those women the Ripper slew . . . was my mother.'

'What?'

'My father and I swore to give our lives to find the Ripper. My father was the first to search. He died in Hollywood in 1926 – on the trail of the Ripper. They said he was stabbed by an unknown assailant in a brawl. But I know who that assailant was.

'So I've taken up his work, do you see, John? I've carried on. And I will carry on until I do find him and kill him with my own hands.

'He took my mother's life and the lives of hundreds to keep his own hellish being alive. Like a vampire, he battens on blood. Like a ghoul, he is nourished by death. Like a fiend, he stalks the world to kill. He is cunning, devilishly cunning. But I'll never rest until I find him. Never!'

I believed him then. He wouldn't give up. He wasn't just a drunken babbler any more. He was as fanatical, as determined, as relentless as the Ripper himself.

Tomorrow he'd be sober. He'd continue the search. Perhaps he'd turn those papers over to the FBI. Sooner or later, with such persistence – and with his motive – he'd be successful. I'd always known he had a motive.

'Let's go,' I said, steering him down the alley.

'Wait a minute,' said Sir Guy. 'Give me back my gun.' He lurched a little. 'I'd feel better with the gun on me.'

He pressed me into the dark shadows of a little recess.

I tried to shrug him off, but he was insistent.

'Let me carry the gun now, John,' he mumbled.

'All right,' I said.

I reached into my coat, brought my hand out.

'But that's not a gun,' he protested. 'That's a knife.'

'I know.'

I bore down on him swiftly.

'John!' he screamed.

'Never mind the "John",' I whispered, raising the knife. 'Just call me . . . Jack.'

The Brown Hand

SIR ARTHUR CONAN DOYLE

EVERYONE KNOWS THAT Sir Dominick Holden, the famous Indian surgeon, made me his heir, and that his death changed me in an hour from a hard-working and impecunious medical man to a well-to-do landed proprietor. Many know also that there were at least five people between the inheritance and me, and that Sir Dominick's selection appeared to be altogether arbitrary and whimsical. I can assure them, however, that they are quite mistaken, and that, although I only knew Sir Dominick in the closing years of his life, there were, none the less, very real reasons why he should show his goodwill towards me. As a matter of fact, though I say it myself, no man ever did more for another than I did for my Indian uncle. I cannot expect the story to be believed, but it is so singular that I should feel that it was a breach of duty if I did not put it upon record – so here it is, and your belief or incredulity is your own affair.

Sir Dominick Holden, CB, KCSI, and I don't know what besides, was the most distinguished Indian surgeon of his day. In the Army originally, he afterwards settled down into civil practice in Bombay, and visited, as a consultant, every part of India. His name is best remembered in connection with the Oriental Hospital which he founded and supported. The time came, however, when his iron constitution began to show signs of the long strain to which he had subjected it, and his brother practitioners (who were not, perhaps, entirely disinterested upon the point) were unanimous in recommending him to return to England. He held on so long as he could, but at last he developed nervous symptoms of a very pronounced character, and so came back, a broken man, to his native county of Wiltshire. He bought a considerable estate with an ancient manor-house upon the edge of Salisbury Plain, and devoted his old age to the study of Comparative Pathology, which had been his learned hobby all his life, and in which he was a foremost authority.

We of the family were, as may be imagined, much excited by the news of the return of this rich and childless uncle to England. On his part, although by no means exuberant in his hospitality, he showed some sense of his duty to his relations, and each of us in turn had an invitation to visit him. From the accounts of my cousins it appeared to be a melancholy business, and it was with mixed feelings that I at last received my own summons to appear at Rodenhurst. My wife was so carefully excluded in the invitation that my first impulse was to refuse it, but the interests of the children had to be considered, and so, with her consent, I set out one October afternoon upon my visit to Wiltshire, with little thought of what that visit was to entail.

My uncle's estate was situated where the arable land of the plains begins to swell upwards into the rounded chalk hills which are characteristic of the county. As I drove from Dinton Station in the waning light of that autumn day, I was impressed by the weird nature of the scenery. The few scattered cottages of the peasants were so dwarfed by the huge evidences of prehistoric life, that the present appeared to be a dream and the past to be the obtrusive and masterful reality. The road wound through the valleys, formed by a succession of grassy hills, and the summit of each was cut and carved into the most elaborate fortifications, some circular, and some square, but all on a scale which has defied the winds and the rains of many centuries. Some call them Roman and some British, but their true origin and the reason for this particular tract of country being so interlaced with entrenchments have never been finally made clear. Here and there on the long, smooth, olive-coloured slopes there rose small, rounded barrows or tumuli. Beneath them lie the cremated ashes of the race which cut so deeply into the hills, but their graves tell us nothing save that a jar full of dust represents the man who once laboured under the sun.

It was through this weird country that I approached my uncle's residence of Rodenhurst, and the house was, as I found, in due keeping with its surroundings. Two broken and weather-stained pillars, each surmounted by a mutilated heraldic emblem, flanked the entrance to a neglected drive. A cold wind whistled through the elms which lined it, and the air was full of the drifting leaves. At the far end, under the gloomy arch of trees, a single yellow lamp burned steadily. In the dim half-light of the coming night I saw a long, low building stretching out two irregular wings, with deep eaves, a sloping gambrel roof, and walls which were criss-crossed with timber balks in the fashion of the Tudors. The cheery light of a fire in the broad, latticed window to the left of the low-porched door, and this, as it proved, marked the study of my uncle, for it was thither that I was led by his butler in order to make my host's acquaintance.

He was cowering over his fire, for the moist chill of an English autumn had set him shivering. His lamp was unlit, and I only saw the red glow of the embers beating upon a huge, craggy face, with a Red Indian nose and cheek, and deep furrows and seams from eye to chin, the sinister marks of hidden volcanic fires. He sprang up at my entrance with something of an old-world courtesy and welcomed me warmly to Rodenhurst. At the same time I was conscious, as the lamp was carried in, that it was a very critical pair of light-blue eyes which looked out at me from under shaggy eyebrows, like scouts beneath a bush, and that this outlandish uncle of mine was carefully reading off my character with all the ease of a practised observer and an experienced man of the world.

For my part I looked at him, and looked again, for I had never seen a man whose appearance was more fitted to hold one's attention. His figure was the framework of a giant, but he had fallen away until his coat dangled straight down in a shocking fashion from a pair of broad and bony shoulders. All his limbs were huge and yet emaciated, and I could not take my gaze from his knobby wrists, and long, gnarled hands. But his eyes – those peering, light-blue eyes – they were the most arrestive of any of his peculiarities. It was not their colour alone, nor was it the ambush of hair in which they lurked; but it was the expression which I read in them. For the appearance and bearing of the man were masterful, and one expected a certain corresponding arrogance in his eyes, but instead of that I read the look which tells of a spirit cowed and crushed, the furtive, expectant look of the dog whose master has taken the whip from the rack. I formed my own medical diagnosis upon one glance at those critical and yet appealing eyes. I believed that he was stricken with some mortal ailment, that he knew himself to be exposed to sudden death, and that he lived in terror of it. Such was my judgement – a false one, as the event showed; but I mention it that it may help you to realize the look which I read in his eyes.

My uncle's welcome was, as I have said, a courteous one, and in an hour or so I found myself seated between him and his wife at a comfortable dinner, with curious, pungent delicacies upon the table, and a stealthy, quick-eyed Oriental waiter behind his chair. The old couple had come round to that tragic imitation of the dawn of life when husband and wife, having lost or scattered all those who were their intimates, find themselves face to face and alone once more, their work done, and the end nearing fast. Those who have reached that stage in sweetness and love, who can change their winter into a gentle, Indian summer, have come as victors through the ordeal of life. Lady Holden was a small, alert woman with a kindly eye, and her expression as she glanced at him was a certificate of character to her husband. And yet, though I read a mutual love in their glances, I read also mutual horror, and recognized in her face some reflection of that stealthy fear which I had detected in his. Their talk was sometimes merry and sometimes sad, but there was a forced note in their merriment and a naturalness in their sadness which told me that a heavy heart beat upon either side of me.

We were sitting over our first glass of wine, and the servants had left the room, when the conversation took a turn which produced a remarkable effect upon my host and hostess. I cannot recall what it was which started the topic of the supernatural, but it ended in my showing them that the abnormal in psychical experiences was a subject to which, I had, like many neurologists, devoted a great deal of attention. I concluded by narrating my experiences when, as a member of the Psychical Research Society, I had formed one of a committee of three who spent the night in a haunted house. Our adventures were neither exciting nor convincing, but, such as it was, the story appeared to interest my auditors in a remarkable degree. They listened with an eager silence, and I caught a look of intelligence between them which I could not understand. Lady Holden immediately afterwards rose and left the room.

Sir Dominick pushed the cigar-box over to me, and we smoked for some little time in silence. That huge, bony hand of his was twitching as he raised it with his cheroot to his lips, and I felt that the man's nerves were vibrating like fiddle-strings. My instincts told me that he was on the verge of some intimate confidence, and I feared to speak lest I should interrupt it. At last he turned towards me with a spasmodic gesture like a man who throws his last scruple to the winds.

'From the little that I have seen of you it appears to me, Dr. Hardacre,' said he, 'that you are the very man I have wanted to meet.'

'I am delighted to hear it, sir.'

'Your head seems to be cool and steady. You will acquit me of any desire to flatter you, for the circumstances are too serious to permit of insincerities. You have some special knowledge upon these subjects, and you evidently view them from that philosophical standpoint which robs them of all vulgar terror. I presume that the sight of an apparition would not seriously discompose you?'

'I think not, sir.'

'Would even interest you, perhaps?'

'Most intensely.'

'As a psychical observer, you would probably investigate it in as impersonal a fashion as an astronomer investigates a wandering comet?'

'Precisely.'

He gave a heavy sigh.

'Believe me, Dr. Hardacre, there was a time when I could have spoken as you do now. My nerve was a byword in India. Even the Mutiny never shook it for an instant. And yet you see what I am reduced to – the most timorous man, perhaps, in all this county of Wiltshire. Do not speak too bravely upon this subject, or you may find yourself subjected to as long-drawn a test as I am – a test which can only end in the madhouse or the grave.'

311

I waited patiently until he should see fit to go farther in his confidence. His preamble, had, I need not say, filled me with interest and expectation.

'For some years, Dr. Hardacre,' he continued, 'my life and that of my wife have been made miserable by a cause which is so grotesque that it borders upon the ludicrous. And yet familiarity has never made it more easy to bear – on the contrary, as time passes my nerves became more worn and shattered by the constant attrition. If you have no physical fears, Dr. Hardacre, I should very much value your opinion upon this phenomenon which troubles us so.'

'For what it is worth my opinion is entirely at your service. May I ask the nature of the phenomenon?'

'I think that your experiences will have a higher evidential value if you are not told in advance what you may expect to encounter. You are yourself aware of the quibbles of unconscious cerebration and subjective impressions with which a scientific sceptic may throw a doubt upon your statement. It would be as well to guard against them in advance.'

'What shall I do, then?'

'I will tell you. Would you mind following me this way?' He led me out of the dining-room and down a long passage until we came to a terminal door. Inside there was a large bare room fitted as a laboratory, with numerous scientific instruments and bottles. A shelf ran along one side, upon which there stood a long line of glass jars containing pathological and anatomical specimens.

'You see that I still dabble in some of my old studies,' said Sir Dominick. 'These jars are the remains of what was once a most excellent collection, but unfortunately I lost the greater part of them when my house was burned down in Bombay in '92. It was a most unfortunate affair for me – in more ways than one. I had examples of many rare conditions, and my splenic collection was probably unique. These are the survivors.'

I glanced over them, and saw that they really were of a very great value and rarity from a pathological point of view: bloated organs, gaping cysts, distorted bones, odious parasites – a singular exhibition of the products of India.

'There is, as you see, a small settee here,' said my host. 'It was far from our intention to offer a guest so meagre an accommodation, but since affairs have taken this turn, it would be a great kindness upon your part if you would consent to spend the night in this apartment. I beg that you will not hesitate to let me know if the idea should be at all repugnant to you.'

'On the contrary,' I said, 'it is most acceptable.'

'My own room is the second on the left, so that if you should feel that you are in need of company a call would always bring me to your side.'

'I trust that I shall not be compelled to disturb you.'

'It is unlikely that I shall be asleep. I do not sleep much. Do not hesitate to summon me.'

And so with this agreement we joined Lady Holden in the drawing room and talked of lighter things.

It was no affection upon my part to say that the prospect of my night's adventure was an agreeable one. I have no pretence to greater physical courage than my neighbours, but familiarity with a subject robs it of those vague and undefined terrors which are the most appalling to the imaginative mind. The human brain is capable of only one strong emotion at a time, and if it be filled with curiosity or scientific enthusiasm, there is no room for fear. It is true that I had my uncle's assurance that he had himself originally taken this point of view, but I reflected that the breakdown of his nervous system might be due to his forty years in India as much as to any physical experiences which had befallen him. I at least was sound in nerve and brain, and it was with something of the pleasurable thrill of anticipation with which the sportsman takes his position beside the haunt of his game that I shut the laboratory door behind me, and partially undressing, lay down upon the rug-covered settee.

It was not an ideal atmosphere for a bedroom. The air was heavy with many chemical odours, that of methylated spirit predominating. Nor were the decorations of my chamber very sedative. The odious line of glass jars with their relics of disease and suffering stretched in front of my very eyes. There was no blind to the window, and a three-quarter moon streamed its white light into the room, tracing a silver square with filigree lattices upon the opposite wall. When I had extinguished my candle this one bright patch in the midst of the general gloom had certainly an eerie and discomposing aspect. A rigid and absolute silence reigned throughout the old house, so that the low swish of the branches in the garden came softly and smoothly to my ears. It may have been the hypnotic lullaby of this gentle susurrus, or it may have been the result of my tiring day, but after many dozings and many efforts to regain my clearness of perception, I fell at last into a deep and dreamless sleep.

I was awakened by some sound in the room, and I instantly raised myself upon my elbow on the couch. Some hours had passed, for the square patch upon the wall had slid downwards and sideways until it lay obliquely at the end of my bed. The rest of the room was in a deep shadow. At first I could see nothing. Presently, as my eyes became accustomed to the faint light, I was aware, with a thrill which all my scientific absorption could not entirely prevent, that something was moving slowly along the line of the wall. A gentle, shuffling sound, as of soft slippers, came to my ears, and I dimly discerned a human figure walking stealthily from the direction of the door. As it emerged into the patch of moonlight I saw very clearly what it was and how it was employed. It was a man, short and squat, dressed in some sort of dark-

313

grey gown, which hung straight from his shoulders to his feet. The moon shone upon the side of his face, and I saw that it was a chocolate-brown in colour, with a ball of black hair like a woman's at the back of his head. He walked slowly, and his eyes were cast upwards towards the line of bottles which contained those gruesome remnants of humanity. He seemed to examine each jar with attention, and then to pass on to the next. When he had come to the end of the line, immediately opposite my bed, he stopped, faced me, threw up his hands with a gesture of despair, and vanished from my sight.

I have said that he threw up his hands, but I should have said his arms, for as he assumed that attitude of despair I observed a singular peculiarity about his appearance. He had only one hand! As the sleeves dropped down from the upflung arms I saw the left plainly, but the right ended in a knobby and unsightly stump. In every other way his appearance was so natural, and I had both seen and heard him so clearly, that I could easily have believed that he was an Indian servant of Sir Dominick's who had come into my room in search of something. It was only his sudden disappearance which suggested anything more sinister to me. As it was I sprang from my couch, lit a candle, and examined the whole room carefully. There were no signs of my visitor, and I was forced to conclude that there had really been something outside the normal laws of Nature in his appearance. I lay awake for the remainder of the night, but nothing else occurred to disturb me.

I am an early riser, but my uncle was an even earlier one, for I found him pacing up and down the lawn at the side of the house. He ran towards me in his eagerness when he saw me come out from the door.

'Well, well!' he cried. 'Did you see him?'

'An Indian with one hand?'

'Precisely.'

'Yes, I saw him' – and I told him all that occurred. When I had finished, he led the way into his study.

'We have a little time before breakfast,' said he. 'It will suffice to give you an explanation of this extraordinary affair – so far as I can explain that which is essentially inexplicable. In the first place, when I tell you that for four years I have never passed one single night, either in Bombay, aboard ship, or here in England without my sleep being broken by this fellow, you will understand why it is that I am a wreck of my former self. His programme is always the same. He appears by my bedside, shakes me roughly by the shoulder, passes from my room into the laboratory, walks slowly along the line of my bottles, and then vanishes. For more than a thousand times he has gone through the same routine.

'What does he want?'

'He wants his hand.'

'His hand?'

'Yes, it came about in this way. I was summoned to Peshawar for a consultation some ten years ago, and while there I was asked to look at the hand of a native who was passing through with an Afghan caravan. The fellow came from some mountain tribe living away at the back of beyond somewhere on the other side of Kaffiristan. He talked a bastard Pushtoo, and it was all I could do to understand him. He was suffering from a soft sarcomatous swelling of one of the metacarpal joints, and I made him realize that it was only by losing his hand that he could hope to save his life. After much persuasion he consented to the operation, and he asked me, when it was over, what fee I demanded. The poor fellow was almost a beggar, so that the idea of a fee was absurd, but I answered in jest that my fee should be his hand, and that I proposed to add it to my pathological collection.

'To my surprise he demurred very much to the suggestion, and he explained that according to his religion it was an all-important matter that the body should be reunited after death, and so make a perfect dwelling for the spirit. The belief is, of course, an old one, and the mummies of the Egyptians arose from an analogous superstition. I answered him that his hand was already off, and asked him how he intended to preserve it. He replied that he would pickle it in salt and carry it about with him. I suggested that it might be safer in my keeping than his, and that I had better means than salt for preserving it. On realizing that I really intended to carefully keep it, his opposition vanished instantly. 'But remember, sahib,' said he, 'I shall want it back when I am dead.' I laughed at the remark, and so the matter ended. I returned to my practice, and he no doubt in the course of time was able to continue his journey to Afghanistan.

'Well, as I told you last night, I had a bad fire in my house at Bombay. Half of it was burned down, and, among other things, my pathological collection was largely destroyed. What you see are the poor remains of it. The hand of the hillman went with the rest, but I gave the matter no particular thought at the time. That was six years ago.

'Four years ago – two years after the fire – I was awakened one night by a furious tugging at my sleeve. I sat up under the impression that my favourite mastiff was trying to arouse me. Instead of this, I saw my Indian patient of long ago, dressed in the long, grey gown which was the badge of his people. He was holding up his stump and looking reproach-fully at me. He then went over to my bottles, which at that time I kept in my room, and he examined them carefully, after which he gave a gesture of anger and vanished. I realized that he had just died, and that he had come to claim my promise that I should keep his limb in safety for him.

'Well, there you have it all, Dr. Hardacre. Every night at the same hour for four years this performance has been repeated. It is a simple thing in itself, but it has worn me out like water dropping on a stone. It has brought a vile insomnia with it, for I cannot sleep now for the expectation of his coming. It has poisoned my old age and that of my wife, who has been the sharer in this great trouble. But there is the breakfast gong, and she will be waiting impatiently to know how it fared with you last night. We are both much indebted to you for your gallantry, for it takes something from the weight of our misfortune when we share it, even for a single night, with a friend, and it reassures us to our sanity, which we are sometimes driven to question.'

This was the curious narrative which Sir Dominick confided to me – a story which to many would have appeared to be a grotesque impossibility, but which, after my experience of the night before, and my previous knowledge of such things, I was prepared to accept as an absolute fact. I thought deeply over the matter, and brought the whole range of my reading and experience to bear upon it. After breakfast, I surprised my host and hostess by announcing that I was returning to London by the next train.

'My dear doctor,' cried Sir Dominick in great distress, 'you make me feel that I have been guilty of a gross breach of hospitality in intruding this unfortunate matter upon you. I should have borne my own burden.'

'It is, indeed, that matter which is taking me to London,' I answered; 'but you are mistaken, I assure you, if you think that my experience of last night was an unpleasant one to me. On the contrary, I am about to ask your permission to return in the evening and spend one more night in your laboratory. I am very eager to see this visitor once again.'

My uncle was exceedingly anxious to know what I was about to do, but my fears of raising false hopes prevented me from telling him. I was back in my own consulting-room a little after luncheon, and was confirming my memory of a passage in a recent book upon occultism which had arrested my attention when I read it.

'In the case of earth-bound spirits,' said my authority, 'some one dominant idea obsessing them at the hour of death is sufficient to hold them in this material world. They are the amphibia of this life and of the next, capable of passing from one to the other as the turtle passes from land to water. The causes which may bind a soul so strongly to a life which its body has abandoned are any violent emotion. Avarice, revenge, anxiety, love and pity have all been known to have this effect. As a rule it springs from some unfulfilled wish, and when the wish has been fulfilled the material bond relaxes. There are many cases upon record which show the singular persistence of these visitors, and also their disappearance when their wishes have been fulfilled, or in some cases when a reasonable compromise has been effected.'

'*A reasonable compromise effected* ' – those were the words which I had brooded over all the morning, and which I now verified in the original. No actual atonement could be made here – but a reasonable compromise! I made my way as fast as a train could take me to the

Shadwell Seamen's Hospital, where my old friend Jack Hewett was house-surgeon. Without explaining the situation I made him understand what it was that I wanted.

'A brown man's hand!' said he, in amazement. 'What in the world do you want that for?'

'Never mind, I'll tell you some day. I know that your wards are full of Indians.'

'I should think so. But a hand—' He thought a little and then struck a bell.

'Travers,' said he to a student-dresser, 'what became of the hands of the Lascar which we took off yesterday? I mean the fellow from the East India Dock who got caught in the steam winch.'

'They are in the *post-mortem* room, sir.'

'Just pack one of them in antiseptics and give it to Dr. Hardacre.'

And so I found myself back at Rodenhurst before dinner with this curious outcome of my day in town. I still said nothing to Sir Dominick, but I slept that night in the laboratory, and I placed the Lascar's hand in one of the glass jars at the end of my couch.

So interested was I in the result of my experiment that sleep was out of the question. I sat with a shaded lamp beside me and waited patiently for my visitor. This time I saw him clearly from the first. He appeared beside the door, nebulous for an instant, and then hardening into as distinct an outline as any living man. The slippers beneath his grey gown were red and heelless, which accounted for the low, shuffling sound which he made as he walked. As on the previous night he passed slowly along the line of bottles until he paused before that which contained the hand. He reached up to it, his whole figure quivering with expectation, took it down, examined it eagerly, and then, with a face which was convulsed with fury and disappointment, he hurled it down on the floor. There was a crash which resounded through the house, and when I looked up the mutilated Indian had disappeared. A moment later my door flew open and Sir Dominick rushed in.

'You are not hurt?' he cried.

'No – but deeply disappointed.'

He looked in astonishment at the splinters of glass, and the brown hand lying upon the floor.

'Good God!' he cried, 'What is this?'

I told him my idea and its wretched sequel. He listened intently, but shook his head.

'It is well thought of,' said he, 'but I fear that there is no such easy end to my sufferings. But one thing I now insist upon. It is that you shall never again upon any pretext occupy this room. My fears that something might have happened to you – when I heard that crash – have been the most acute of all the agonies which I have undergone. I will not expose myself to a repetition of it.'

He allowed me, however, to spend the remainder of that night where I was, and I lay there worrying over the problem and lamenting my own failure. With the first light of morning there was the Lascar's hand still lying upon the floor to remind me of my fiasco. I lay looking at it – and as I lay suddenly an idea flew like a bullet through my head and brought me quivering with excitement out of my couch. I raised the grim relic from where it had fallen. Yes, it was indeed so. The hand was the *left* hand of the Lascar.

By the first train I was on my way to town, and hurried at once to the Seamen's Hospital. I remembered that both hands of the Lascar had been amputated, but I was terrified lest the precious organ which I was in search of might have been already consumed in the crematory. My suspense was soon ended. It had still be preserved in the *post-mortem* room. And so I returned to Rodenhurst in the evening with my mission accomplished and the material for a fresh experiment.

But Sir Dominick Holden would not hear of my occupying the laboratory again. To all my entreaties he turned a deaf ear. It offended his sense of hospitality, and he could no longer permit it. I left the hand, therefore, as I had done its fellow the night before, and I occupied a comfortable bedroom in another portion of the house, some distance from the scene of my adventures.

But in spite of that my sleep was not destined to be uninterrupted. In the dead of night my host burst into my room, a lamp in his hand. His huge, gaunt figure was enveloped in a loose dressing-gown, and his whole appearance might certainly have seemed more formidable to a weak-nerved man than that of the Indian of the night before. But it was not his entrance so much as his expression which amazed me. He had turned suddenly younger by twenty years at the least. His eyes were shining, his features radiant, and he waved one hand in triumph over his head. I sat up astounded, staring sleepily at this extraordinary visitor. But his words soon drove the sleep from my eyes.

'We have done it! We have succeeded!' he shouted. 'My dear Hardacre, how can I ever in this world repay you?'

'You don't mean to say that it is all right?'

'Indeed I do. I was sure that you would not mind being awakened to hear such blessed news.'

'Mind! I should think not indeed. But is it really certain?'

'I have no doubt whatever upon the point. I owe you such a debt, my dear nephew, as I have never owed a man before, and never expected to. What can I possibly do for you that is commensurate? Providence must have sent you to my rescue. You have saved both my reason and my life, for another six months of this must have seen me either in a cell or a coffin. And my wife – it was wearing her out before my eyes. Never could I have believed that any human being could have lifted this burden off me.' He seized my hand and wrung it in his bony grip.

'It was only an experiment – a forlorn hope – but I am delighted from my heart that it has succeeded. But how do you know that it is all right? Have you seen something?'

He seated himself at the foot of my bed.

'I have seen enough,' said he. 'It satisfies me that I shall be troubled no more. What has passed is easily told. You know that at a certain hour this creature always comes to me. Tonight he arrived at the usual time, and aroused me with even more violence than is his custom. I can only surmise that his disappointment of last night increased the bitterness of his anger against me. He looked angrily at me, and then went on his usual round. But in a few minutes I saw him, for the first time since this persecution began, return to my chamber. He was smiling. I saw the gleam of his white teeth through the dim light. He stood facing me at the end of my bed, and three times he made the low, Eastern salaam which is their solemn leave-taking. And the third time that he bowed he raised his arms over his head, and I saw his *two* hands outstretched in the air. So he vanished, and, as I believe, for ever.'

So that is the curious experience which won me the affection and the gratitude of my celebrated uncle, the famous Indian surgeon. His anticipations were realized, and never again was he disturbed by the visits of the restless hillman in search of his lost member. Sir Dominick and Lady Holden spent a very happy old age, unclouded, so far as I know, by any trouble, and they finally died during the great influenza epidemic within a few weeks of each other. In his lifetime he always turned to me for advice in everything which concerned that English life of which he knew so little; and I aided him also in the purchase and development of his estates. It was no great surprise to me, therefore, that I found myself eventually promoted over the heads of five exasperated cousins, and changed in a single day from a hard-working country doctor into the head of an important Wiltshire family. I, at least, have reason to bless the memory of the man with the brown hand, and the day when I was fortunate enough to relieve Rodenhurst of his unwelcome presence.

To Be Taken With A Grain Of Salt

CHARLES DICKENS

I HAVE ALWAYS NOTICED a prevalent want of courage, even among persons of superior intelligence and culture, as to imparting their own psychological experiences when those have been of a strange sort. Almost all men are afraid that what they could relate in such wise would find no parallel or reponse in a listener's internal life, and might be suspected or laughed at. A truthful traveller who should have seen some extraordinary creature in the likeness of a sea-serpent, would have no fear of mentioning it; but the same traveller having had some singular presentiment, impulse, vagary of thought, vision (so-called), dream, or other remarkable mental impression, would hesitate considerably before he would own to it. To this reticence I attribute much of the obscurity in which such subjects are involved. We do not habitually communicate our experiences of these subjective things, as we do our experiences of objective creation. The consequence is, that the general stock of experience in this regard appears exceptional, and really is so, in respect of being miserably imperfect.

In what I am going to relate I have no intention of setting up, opposing, or supporting, any theory whatever. I know the history of the Bookseller of Berlin, I have studied the case of the wife of a late Astronomer Royal as related by Sir David Brewster, and I have followed the minutest details of a much more remarkable case of Spectral Illusion occurring within my private circle of friends. It may be necessary to state as to this last that the sufferer (a lady) was in no degree, however distant, related to me. A mistaken assumption on that head, might suggest an explanation of a part of my own case – but only a part – which would be wholly without foundation. It cannot be referred to my inheritance of any developed peculiarity, nor had I ever before any at all similar experience, nor have I ever had any at all similar experience since.

It does not signify how many years ago, or how few, a certain Murder was committed in England, which attracted great attention. We hear more than enough of Murderers as they rise in succession to their atrocious eminence, and I would bury the memory of this particular brute, if I could, as his body was buried, in Newgate Jail. I purposely abstain from giving any direct clue to the criminal's individuality.

When the murder was first discovered, no suspicion fell – or I ought rather to say, for I cannot be too precise in my facts, it was nowhere publicly hinted that any suspicion fell – on the man who was afterwards brought to trial. As no reference was at that time made to him in the newspapers, it is obviously impossible that any description of him can at that time have been given in the newspapers. It is essential that this fact be remembered.

Unfolding at breakfast my morning paper, containing the account of that first discovery, I found it to be deeply interesting, and I read it with close attention. I read it twice, if not three times. The discovery had been made in a bedroom, and, when I laid down the paper, I was aware of a flash – rush – flow – I do not know what to call it – no word I can find is satisfactorily descriptive – in which I seemed to see that bedroom passing through my room, like a picture impossibly painted on a running river. Though almost instantaneous in its passing, it was perfectly clear; so clear that I distinctly, and with a sense of relief, observed the absence of the dead body from the bed.

It was in no romantic place that I had this curious sensation, but in chambers in Piccadilly, very near to the corner of Saint James's-street. It was entirely new to me. I was in my easy-chair at the moment, and the sensation was accompanied with a peculiar shiver which started the chair from its position. (But it is to be noted that the chair ran easily on castors.) I went to one of the windows (there are two in the room, and the room is on the second floor) to refresh my eyes with the moving objects down in Piccadilly. It was a bright autumn morning, and the street was sparkling and cheerful. The wind was high. As I looked out, it brought down from the Park a quantity of fallen leaves, which a gust took, and whirled into a spiral pillar. As the pillar fell and the leaves dispersed, I saw two men on the opposite side of the way, going from West to East. They were one behind the other. The foremost man often looked back over his shoulder. The second man followed him, at a distance of some thirty paces, with his right hand menacingly raised. First, the singularity and steadiness of his threatening gesture in so public a thoroughfare, attracted my attention; and next, the more remarkable circumstance that nobody heeded it. Both men threaded their way among the other passengers, with a smoothness hardly consistent even with the action of walking on a pavement, and no single creature that I could see, gave them place, touched them, or looked after them. In passing before my windows, they both stared up at me. I saw their two faces very distinctly, and I knew that I could recognize them anywhere. Not that I had consciously noticed anything very remarkable in either face, except that the man who went first had an unusually lowering appearance, and that the face of the man who followed him was of the colour of impure wax.

I am a bachelor, and my valet and his wife constitute my whole establishment. My occupation is in a certain Branch Bank, and I wish that my duties as head of a Department were as light as they are popularly supposed to be. They kept me in town that autumn, when I stood in need of a change. I was not ill, but I was not well. My reader is to make the most that can be reasonably made of my feeling jaded, having a depressing sense upon me of a monotonous life, and being 'slightly dyspeptic'. I am assured by my renowned doctor that my real state of health at that time justifies no stronger description, and I quote his own from his written answer to my request for it.

As the circumstances of the Murder, gradually unravelling, took stronger and stronger possession of the public mind, I kept them away from mine, by knowing as little about them as was possible in the midst of the universal excitement. But I knew that a verdict of Wilful Murder had been found against the suspected Murderer, and that he had been committed to Newgate for trial. I also knew that his trial had been postponed over one Sessions of the Central Criminal Court, on the ground of general prejudice and want of time for the preparation of the defence. I may further have known, but I believe I did not, when, or about when, the Sessions to which his trial stood postponed would come on.

My sitting-room, bedroom, and dressing-room, are all on one floor. With the last, there is no communication but through the bedroom. True, there is a door in it, once communicating with the staircase; but a part of the fitting of my bath has been – and had then been for some years – fixed across it. At the same period, and as a part of the same arrangement, the door had been nailed up and canvased over.

I was standing in my bedroom late one night, giving some directions to my servant before he went to bed. My face was towards the only available door of communication with the dressing-room, and it was closed. My servant's back was towards that door. While I was speaking to him I saw it open, and a man look in, who very earnestly and mysteriously beckoned to me. That man was the man who had gone second of the two along Piccadilly, and whose face was of the colour of impure wax.

The figure, having beckoned, drew back and closed the door. With no longer pause than was made by my crossing the bedroom, I opened the dressing-room door, and looked in. I had a lighted candle already in my hand. I felt no inward expectation of seeing the figure in the dressing-room, and I did not see it there.

Conscious that my servant stood amazed, I turned round to him, and said: 'Derrick, could you believe that in my cool senses I fancied I saw a —' As I there laid my hand upon his breast, with a sudden start he trembled violently, and said, 'O Lord yes sir! A dead man beckoning!'

Now, I do not believe that this John Derrick, my trusty and attached servant for more than twenty years, had any impression whatever of having seen any such figure, until I touched him. The change in him was so startling when I touched him, that I fully believe he derived his impression in some occult manner from me at that instant.

I bade John Derrick bring some brandy, and I gave him a dram, and was glad to take one myself. Of what had preceded that night's phenomenon, I told him not a single word. Reflecting on it, I was absolutely certain that I had never seen that face before, except on the one occasion in Piccadilly. Comparing its expression when beckoning at the door, with its expression when it had stared up at me as I stood at my window, I came to the conclusion that on the first occasion it had sought to fasten itself upon my memory, and that on the second occasion it had made sure of being immediately remembered.

I was not very comfortable that night, though I felt a certainty, difficult to explain, that the figure would not return. At daylight, I fell into a heavy sleep, from which I was awakened by John Derrick's coming to my bedside with a paper in his hand.

This paper, it appeared, had been the subject of an altercation at the door between its bearer and my servant. It was a summons to me to serve upon a Jury at the forthcoming Sessions of the Central Criminal Court at the Old Bailey. I had never before been summoned on such a Jury, as John Derrick well knew. He believed – I am not certain at this hour whether with reason or otherwise – that that class of Jurors were customarily chosen on a lower qualification than mine, and he had at first refused to accept the summons. The man who served it had taken the matter very coolly. He had said that my attendance or non-attendance was nothing to him; there the summons was; and I should deal with it at my own peril, and not at his.

For a day or two I was undecided whether to respond to this call, or take no notice of it. I was not conscious of the slightest mysterious bias, influence, or attraction, one way or other. Of that I am as strictly sure as of every other statement that I make here. Ultimately I decided, as a break in the monotony of my life, that I would go.

The appointed morning was a raw morning in the month of November. There was a dense brown fog in Piccadilly, and it became positively black and in the last degree oppressive East of Temple Bar. I found the passages and staircases of the Court House flaringly lighted with gas, and the Court itself similarly illuminated. I *think* that until I was conducted by officers into the old Court and saw its crowded state, I did not know that the Murderer was to be tried that day. I *think* that until I was so helped into the Old Court with considerable difficulty, I did not know into which of the two Courts sitting, my summons would take me. But this must not be received as a positive assertion, for I am not completely satisfied in my mind on either point.

I took my seat in the place appropriated to Jurors in waiting, and I looked about the Court as well as I could through the cloud of fog and breath that was heavy in it. I noticed the black vapour hanging like a murky curtain outside the great windows, and I noticed the stifled sound of wheels on the straw or tan that was littered in the street; also, the hum of the people gathered there, which a shrill whistle, or a louder song or hail than the rest, occasionally pierced. Soon afterwards the Judges, two in number, entered and took their seats. The buzz in the Court was awfully hushed. The direction was given to put the Murderer to the bar. He appeared there. And in that same instant I recognized in him, the first of the two men who had gone down Piccadilly.

If my name had been called then, I doubt if I could have answered to it audibly. But it was called about sixth or eighth in the panel, and I was by that time able to say 'Here!' Now, observe. As I stepped into the box, the prisoner, who had been looking on attentively but with no sign of concern, became violently agitated, and beckoned to his attorney. The prisoner's wish to challenge me was so manifest, that it occasioned a pause, during which the attorney, with his hand upon the dock, whispered with his client, and shook his head. I afterwards had it from that gentleman, that the prisoner's first affrighted words to him were, '*At all hazards challenge that man!*' But, that as he would give no reason for it, and admitted that he had not even known my name until he heard it called and I appeared, it was not done.

Both on the ground already explained, that I wish to avoid reviving the unwholesome memory of that Murderer, and also because a detailed account of his long trial is by no means indispensable to my narrative, I shall confine myself closely to such incidents in the ten days and nights during which we, the Jury, were kept together, as directly bear on my own curious personal experience. It is in that, and not in the Murderer, that I seek to interest my reader. It is to that, and not to a page of the Newgate Calendar, that I beg attention.

I was chosen Foreman of the Jury. On the second morning of the trial, after evidence had been taken for two hours (I heard the church clocks strike), happening to cast my eyes over my brother-jurymen, I found an inexplicable difficulty in counting them. I counted them several times, yet always with the same difficulty. In short, I made them one too many.

I touched the brother-juryman whose place was next to me, and I whispered to him, 'Oblige me by counting us.' He looked surprised by the request, but turned his head and counted. 'Why,' says he, suddenly, 'we are Thirt—; but no, it's not possible. No we are twelve.'

According to my counting that day, we were always right in detail, but in the gross we were always one too many. There was no appearance – no figure – to account for it; but I had now an inward foreshadowing of the figure that was surely coming.

The Jury were housed at the London Tavern. We all slept in one large room on separate tables, and we were constantly in the charge and under the eye of the officer sworn to hold us in safe-keeping. I see no reason for suppressing the real name of that officer. He was intelligent, highly polite, and obliging, and (I was glad to hear) much respected in the City. He had an agreeable presence, good eyes, enviable black whiskers, and a fine sonorous voice. His name was Mr. Harker.

When we turned into our twelve beds at night, Mr. Harker's bed was drawn across the door. On the night of the second day, not being disposed to lie down, and seeing Mr. Harker sitting on his bed, I went and sat beside him, and offered him a pinch of snuff. As Mr. Harker's hand touched mine in taking it from my box, a peculiar shiver crossed him, and he said: 'Who is this!'

Following Mr. Harker's eyes and looking along the room, I saw again the figure I expected – the second of the two men who had gone down Piccadilly. I rose, and advanced a few steps; then stopped, and looked round at Mr. Harker. He was quite unconcerned, laughed, and said in a pleasant way, 'I thought for a moment we had a thirteenth juryman, without a bed. But I see it is the moonlight.'

Making no revelation to Mr. Harker, but inviting him to take a walk with me to the end of the room, I watched what the figure did. It stood for a few moments by the bedside of each of my eleven brother-jurymen, close to the pillow. It always went to the right-hand side of the bed, and always passed out crossing the foot of the next bed. It seemed from the action of the head, merely to look down pensively at each recumbent figure. It took no notice of me, or of my bed, which was that nearest to Mr. Harker's. It seemed to go out where the moonlight came in, through a high window, as by an aerial flight of stairs.

Next morning at breakfast, it appeared that everybody present had dreamed of the murdered man last night, except myself and Mr. Harker.

I now felt as convinced that the second man who had gone down Piccadilly was the murdered man (so to speak), as if it had been borne into my comprehension by his immediate testimony. But even this took place, and in a manner for which I was not at all prepared.

On the fifth day of the trial, when the case for the prosecution was drawing to a close, a miniature of the murdered man, missing from his bedroom upon the discovery of the deed, and afterwards found in a hiding-place where the Murderer had been seen digging, was put in evidence. Having been identified by the witness under examination, it was handed up to the Bench, and thence handed down to be inspected by the Jury. As an officer in a black gown was making his way with it across to me, the figure of the second man who had gone down Piccadilly, impetuously started from the crowd, caught the miniature from the officer, and gave it to me with its own hands, at the same time saying in a low and hollow tone – before I saw the miniature, which was in a locket – '*I was younger then, and my face was not then drained of blood.*' It also came between me and the brother-juryman to whom I would have given the miniature, and between him and the brother-juryman to whom he would have given it, and so passed it on through the whole of our number, and back into my possession. Not one of them, however, detected this.

At table, and generally when we were shut up together in Mr. Harker's custody, we had from the first naturally discussed the day's proceedings a good deal. On that fifth day, the case for the prosecution being closed, and we having that side of the question in a completed shape before us, our discussion was more animated and serious. Among our number was a vestryman – the densest idiot I have ever seen at large – who met the plainest evidence with the most preposterous objections, and who was sided with by two flabby parochial parasites; all the three empanelled from a district so delivered over to Fever that they ought to have been upon their own trial, for five hundred Murders. When these mischievous blockheads were at their loudest, which was towards midnight while some of us were already preparing for bed, I again saw the murdered man. He stood grimly behind them, beckoning to me. On my going towards them and striking into the conversation, he immediately retired. This was the beginning of a separate series of appearances, confined to that long room in which *we* were confined. Whenever a knot of my brother jurymen laid their heads together, I saw the head of the murdered man among theirs. Whenever their comparison of notes was going against him, he would solemnly and irresistibly beckon to me.

It will be borne in mind that down to the production of the miniature on the fifth day of the trial, I had never seen the Appearance in Court. Three changes occurred, now that we entered on the case for the defence. Two of them I will mention together, first. The figure was now in Court continually, and it never there addressed itself to me, but always to the person who was speaking at the time. For instance. The throat of the murdered man had been cut straight across. In the opening speech for the defence, it was suggested that the deceased might have cut his own throat. At that very moment, the figure with its throat in the dreadful condition referred to (this it had concealed before) stood at the speaker's elbow, motioning across and across its windpipe, now with the right hand, now with the left, vigorously suggesting to the speaker himself, the impossibility of such a wound having been self-inflicted by either hand. For another instance. A witness to character, a woman, deposed to the prisoner's being the most amiable of mankind. The figure at that instant stood on the floor before her, looking her full in the face, and pointing out the prisoner's evil countenance with an extended arm and an outstretched finger.

The third change now to be added, impressed me strongly, as the most marked and striking of all. I do not theorize upon it; I accurately state it, and there leave it. Although the Appearance was not itself perceived by those whom it addressed, its coming close to such persons was invariably attended by some trepidation or disturbance on their part. It seemed to me as if it were prevented by laws to which I was not amenable, from fully revealing itself to others, and yet as if it could, invisibly, dumbly and darkly, overshadow their minds. When the leading counsel for the defence suggested that hypothesis of suicide and the figure stood at the learned gentleman's elbow, frightfully sawing at its severed throat, it is undeniable that the counsel faltered in his speech, lost for a few seconds the thread of his ingenious discourse, wiped his forehead with his handkerchief, and turned extremely pale. When the witness to character was confronted by the Appearance, her eyes most certainly did follow the direction of its pointed finger, and rest in great hesitation and trouble upon the prisoner's face. Two additional illustrations will suffice. On the eighth day of the trial, after the pause which was every day made early in the afternoon for a few minutes' rest and refreshment, I came back into Court with the rest of the Jury, some little time before the return of the Judges. Standing up in the box and looking about me, I thought the figure was not there, until, chancing to raise my eyes to the gallery, I saw it bending forward and leaning over a very decent woman, as if to assure itself whether the Judges had resumed their seats or not. Immediately afterwards, that woman screamed, fainted, and was carried out. So with the venerable, sagacious, and patient Judge who conducted the trial. When the case was over, and he settled himself and his papers to sum up, the murdered man entering by the Judges' door, advanced to his Lordship's desk, and looked eagerly over his shoulder at the pages of his notes which he was turning. A change came over his Lordship's face; his hand stopped; the peculiar shiver that I knew so well, passed over him; he faltered, 'Excuse me gentlemen, for a few moments. I am somewhat oppressed by the vitiated air;' and did not recover until he had drunk a glass of water.

Through all the monotony of six of those interminable ten days – the same Judges and others on the bench, the same Murderer in the dock, the same lawyers at the table, the same tones of question and answer rising to the roof of the court, the same scratching of the Judge's pen, the same ushers going in and out, the same lights kindled at the same hour when there had been any natural light of day, the same foggy curtain outside the great windows when it was foggy, the same rain pattering and dripping when it was rainy, the same footmarks of turnkeys and prisoner day after day on the same sawdust, the same keys locking and unlocking the same heavy doors – through all the wearisome monotony which made me feel as if I had been Foreman of the Jury for a vast period of time, and Piccadilly had flourished coevally with Babylon, the murdered man never lost one trace of his distinctness in my eyes, nor was he any any moment less distinct than anybody else. I must not omit, as a matter of fact, that I never once saw the Appearance which I call by the name of the murdered man, look at the Murderer. Again and again I wondered, 'Why does he not?' But he never did.

Nor did he look at me, after the production of the miniature, until the last closing minutes of the trial arrived. We retired to consider, at seven minutes before ten at night. The idiotic vestryman and his two parochial parasites gave us so much trouble, that we twice returned into Court, to beg to have certain extracts from the Judge's notes re-read. Nine of us had not the smallest doubt about those passages, neither, I believe, had any one in Court; the dunder-headed triumvirate however, having no idea but obstruction, disputed them for that very reason. At length we prevailed, and finally the Jury returned into Court at ten minutes past twelve.

The murdered man at that time stood directly opposite the Jury-box, on the other side of the Court. As I took my place, his eyes rested on me, with great attention; he seemed satisfied, and slowly shook a great grey veil, which he carried on his arm for the first time, over his head and whole form. As I gave in our verdict 'Guilty', the veil collapsed, all was gone, and his place was empty.

The Murderer being asked by the Judge, according to usage, where he had anything to say before sentence of Death should be passed upon him, indistinctly muttered something which was described in the leading newspapers of the following day as 'a few rambling, incoherent, and half-audible words, in which he was understood to complain that he had not had a fair trial, because the Foreman of the Jury was prepossessed against him'. The remarkable declaration that he really made, was this: 'My Lord, I knew I was a doomed man when the Foreman of my Jury came into the box. My Lord, I knew he would never let me off, because, before I was taken, he somehow got to my bedside in the night, woke me, and put a rope round my neck.'

The Story of The Siren
E. M. FORSTER

FEW THINGS COULD HAVE been more beautiful than my notebook on the Deist Controversy as it fell downward through the waters of the Mediterranean. It dived, like a piece of black slate, but opened soon, disclosing leaves of pale green, which quivered into blue. Now it had vanished, now it was a piece of magical india-rubber stretching out to infinity, now it was a book again, but bigger than the book of all knowledge. It grew more fantastic as it reached the bottom, where a puff of sand welcomed it and obscured it from view. But it reappeared, quite sane though a little tremulous, lying decently open on its back, while unseen fingers fidgeted among its leaves.

'It is such pity,' said my aunt, 'that you will not finish your work in the hotel. Then you would be free to enjoy yourself and this would never have happened.'

'Nothing of it but will change into something rich and strange,' warbled the chaplain, while his sister said, 'Why, it's gone in the water!' As for the boatmen, one of them laughed, while the other, without a word of warning, stood up and began to take his clothes off.

'Holy Moses!' cried the Colonel. 'Is the fellow mad?'

'Yes, thank him, dear,' said my aunt: 'that is to say, tell him he is very kind, but perhaps another time.'

'All the same I do want my book back,' I complained. 'It's for my Fellowship Dissertation. There won't be much of it left by another time.'

'I have an idea,' said some woman or other through her parasol. 'Let us leave this child of nature to dive for the book while we go on to the other grotto. We can land him either on this rock or on the ledge inside, and he will be ready when we return.'

The idea seemed good; and I improved it by saying I would be left behind too, to lighten the boat. So the two of us were deposited outside the little grotto on a great sunlit rock that guarded the harmonies within. Let us call them blue, though they suggest rather the spirit of what is clean – cleanliness passed from the domestic to the sublime, the cleanliness of all the sea gathered together and radiating light. The Blue Grotto at Capri contains only more blue water, not bluer water. That colour and that spirit is the heritage of every cave in the Mediterranean into which the sun can shine and the sea flow.

As soon as the boat left I realized how imprudent I had been to trust myself on a sloping rock with an unknown Sicilian. With a jerk he became alive, seizing my arm and saying, 'Go to the end of the grotto, and I will show you something beautiful.'

He made me jump off the rock on to the ledge over a dazzling crack of sea; he drew me away from the light till I was standing on the tiny beach of sand which emerged like powdered turquoise at the farther end. There he left me with his clothes, and returned swiftly to the summit of the entrance rock. For a moment he stood naked in the brilliant sun, looking down at the spot where the book lay. Then he crossed himself, raised his hands above his head, and dived.

If the book was wonderful, the man is past all description. His effect was that of a silver statue, alive beneath the sea, through whom life throbbed in blue and green. Something infinitely happy, infinitely wise – but it was impossible that it should emerge from the depths sunburned and dripping, holding the notebook on the Deist Controversy between its teeth.

A gratuity is generally expected by those who bathe. Whatever I offered, he was sure to want more, and I was disinclined for an argument in a place so beautiful and also so solitary. It was a relief that he should say in conversational tones, 'In a place like this one might see the Siren.'

I was delighted with him for thus falling into the key of his surroundings. We had been left together in a magic world, apart from all the commonplaces that are called reality, a world of blue whose floor was the sea and whose walls and roof of rock trembled with the sea's reflections. Here only the fantastic would be tolerable, and it was in that spirit I echoed his words, 'One might easily see the Siren.'

He watched me curiously while he dressed. I was parting the sticky leaves of the notebook as I sat on the sand.

'Ah,' he said at last. 'You may have read the little book that was printed last year. Who would have thought that our Siren would have given the foreigners pleasure!'

(I read it afterward. Its account is, not unnaturally, incomplete, in spite of there being a woodcut of the young person, and the words of her song.)

'She comes out of this blue water, doesn't she,' I suggested, 'and sits on the rock at the entrance, combing her hair.'

I wanted to draw him out, for I was interested in his sudden gravity, and there was a suggestion of irony in his last remark that puzzled me.

'Have you ever seen her?' he asked.

'Often and often.'

'I, never.'

'But have you heard her sing?'

He put on his coat and said impatiently, 'How can she sing under the water? Who could? She sometimes tries, but nothing comes from her but great bubbles.'

'She could climb on to the rock.'

'How can she?' he cried again, quite angry. 'The priests have blessed the air, so she cannot breathe it, and blessed the rocks, so that she cannot sit on them. But the sea no man can bless, because it is too big and always changing. So she lives in the sea.'

I was silent.

At this his face took on a gentler expression. He looked at me as though something was on his mind, and going out to the entrance rock gazed at the external blue. Then returning into our twilight he said, 'As a rule only good people see the Siren.'

I made no comment. There was a pause, and he continued. 'That is a very strange thing, and the priests do not know how to account for it; for she of course is wicked. Not only those who fast and go to Mass are in danger, but even those who are merely good in daily life. No one in the village had seen her for two generations. I am not surprised. We all cross ourselves before we enter the water, but it is unnecessary. Giuseppe, we thought, was safer than most. We loved him, and many of us he loved: but that is a different thing from being good.'

I asked who Giuseppe was.

'That day – I was seventeen and my brother was twenty and a great deal stronger than I was, and it was the year when the visitors, who have brought such prosperity and so many alterations into the village, first began to come. One English lady in particular, of very high birth, came, and has written a book about the place, and it was through her that the Improvement Syndicate was formed, which is about to connect the hotels with the station by a funicular railway.'

'Don't tell me about that lady in here,' I observed.

'That day we took her and her friends to see the grottoes. As we rowed close under the cliffs I put out my hand, as one does, and caught a little crab, and having pulled off its claws offered it as a curiosity. The ladies groaned, but a gentleman was pleased, and held out money. Being inexperienced, I refused it, saying that his pleasure was sufficient reward! Giuseppe, who was rowing behind, was very angry with me and reached out his hand and hit me on the side of the mouth, so that a tooth cut my lip, and I bled. I tried to hit him back, but he always was too quick for me, and as I stretched round he kicked me under the armpit, so that for a moment I could not even row. There was a great noise among the ladies, and I heard afterwards that they were planning to take me away from my brother and train me as a waiter. That, at all events, never came to pass.

'When we reached the grotto – not here, but a larger one – the gentleman was very anxious that one of us should dive for money, and the ladies consented, as they sometimes do. Giuseppe, who had discovered how much pleasure it gives foreigners to see us in the water, refused to dive for anything but silver, and the gentleman threw in a two-lira piece.

'Just before my brother sprang off he caught sight of me holding my bruise, and crying, for I could not help it. He laughed and said, "This time, at all events, I shall not see the Siren!" and went into the water without crossing himself. But he saw her.'

He broke off and accepted a cigarette. I watched the golden entrance rock and the quivering walls and the magic water through which great bubbles constantly rose.

At last he dropped his hot ash into the ripples and turned his head away, and said, 'He came up without the coin. We pulled him into the boat, and he was so large that he seemed to fill it, and so wet that we could not dress him. I have never seen a man so wet. I and the gentleman rowed back, and we covered Giuseppe with sacking and propped him up in the stern.'

'He was drowned, then?' I murmured, supposing that to be the point.

'He was not,' he cried angrily. 'He saw the Siren. I told you.'

I was silenced again.

'We put him to bed, though he was not ill. The doctor came, and took money, and the priest came and spattered him with holy water. But it was no good. He was too big – like a piece of the sea. He kissed the thumb-bones of San Biagio and they never dried till evening.'

'What did he look like?' I ventured.

'Like any one who has seen the Siren. If you have seen her "often and often" how is it you do not know? Unhappy, unhappy because he knew everything. Every living thing made him unhappy because he knew it would die. And all he cared to do was sleep.'

I bent over my notebook.

'He did no work, he forgot to eat, he forgot whether he had his clothes on. All the work fell on me, and my sister had to go out to service. We tried to make him into a beggar, but he was too robust to inspire pity, and as for an idiot, he had not the right look in his eyes. He would stand in the street looking at people, and the more he looked at them the more unhappy he became. When a child was born he would cover his face with his hands. If any one was married – he was terrible then, and would frighten them when they came out of church. Who would have believed he would marry himself! I caused that, I. I was reading out of the paper

how a girl at Ragusa had "gone mad through bathing in the sea."
Giuseppe got up, and in a week he and that girl came in.

'He never told me anything, but it seems that he went straight to her
house, broke into her room, and carried her off. She was the daughter
of a rich mineowner, so you may imagine our peril. Her father came
down, with a clever lawyer, but they could do no more than I. They
argued and they threatened, but at last they had to go back and we lost
nothing – that is to say, no money. We took Giuseppe and Maria to the
church and had them married. Ugh! that wedding! The priest made no
jokes afterwards, and coming out the children threw stones. . . . I think
I would have died to make her happy; but as always happens, one could
do nothing.'

'Were they unhappy together, then?'

'They loved each other, but love is not happiness. We can all get love.
Love is nothing. I had two people to work for now, for she was like him
in everything – one never knew which of them was speaking. I had to
sell our own boat and work under the bad old man you have to-day.
Worst of all, people began to hate us. The children first – everything
begins with them – and then the women, and last of all, the men. For
the cause of every misfortune was – you will not betray me?'

I promised good faith, and immediately he burst into the frantic
blasphemy of one who has escaped from supervision, cursing the priests,
who had ruined his life, he said. 'Thus are we tricked!' was his cry, and
he stood up and kicked at the azure ripples with his feet, till he had
obscured them with a cloud of sand.

I, too, was moved. The story of Giuseppe, for all its absurdity and
superstition, came nearer to reality than anything I had known before.
I don't know why, but it filled me with desire to help others – the greatest
of all desires, I suppose, and the most fruitless. The desire soon passed.

'She was about to have a child. That was the end of everything. People
said to me, "When will your charming nephew be born? What a cheerful,
attractive child he will be, with such a father and mother!" I kept my
face steady and replied, "I think he may be. Out of sadness shall come
gladness" – it is one of our proverbs. And my answer frightened them
very much, and they told the priests, who were frightened too. Then the
whisper started that the child would be Anti-christ. You need not be
afraid: he was never born.'

'An old witch began to prophesy, and no one stopped her. Giuseppe
and the girl, she said, had silent devils, who could do little harm. But the
child would always be speaking and laughing and perverting, and last
of all he would go into the sea and fetch up the Siren into the air and
all the world would see her and hear her sing. As soon as she sang, the
Seven Vials would be opened, and the Pope would die and Mongibello
flame, and the veil of Santa Agata would be burned. Then the boy and

the Siren would marry, and together they would rule the world, for ever and ever.'

'The whole village was in tumult, and the hotel-keepers became alarmed, for the tourist season was just beginning. They met together and decided that Giuseppe and the girl must be sent inland until the child was born, and they subscribed the money. The night before they were to start there was a full moon and wind from the east, and all along the coast the sea shot up over the cliffs in silver clouds. It is a wonderful sight, and Maria said she must see it once more.

' "Do not go," I said. "I saw the priest go by, and someone with him. And the hotel-keepers do not like you to be seen, and if we displease them also we shall starve."

' "I want to go," she replied. "The sea is stormy, and I may never feel it again."

' "No, he is right," said Giuseppe. "Do not go— or let one of us go with you."

' "I want to go alone," she said; and she went alone.

'I tied up their luggage in a piece of cloth, and then I was so unhappy at thinking I should lose them that I went and sat down by my brother and put my arm round his neck, and he put his arm round me, which he had not done for more than a year, and we remained thus I don't remember how long.

'Suddenly the door flew open and moonlight and wind came in together, and a child's voice said laughing, "They have pushed her over the cliffs into the sea."

'I stepped to the drawer where I keep my knives.

' "Sit down again," said Giuseppe – Giuseppe of all people! "If she is dead, why should others die, too?"

' "I guess who it is," I cried, "and I will kill him."

'I was almost out of the door, and he tripped me up, and kneeling upon me, took hold of both my hands and sprained my wrists; first my right one, then my left. No one but Giuseppe would have thought of such a thing. It hurt more than you would suppose, and I fainted. When I woke up, he was gone, and I never saw him again.'

But Giuseppe disgusted me.

'I told you he was wicked,' he said. 'No one would have expected him to see the Siren.'

'How do you know he did see her?'

'Because he did not see her "often and often," but once.'

'Why do you love him if he is wicked?'

He laughed for the first time. That was his only reply.

'Is that the end?' I asked.

'I never killed her murderer, for by the time my wrists were well he was in America; and one cannot kill a priest. As for Giuseppe, he went all over the world, too, looking for someone who had seen the Siren –

either a man or, better still, a woman, for then the child might still have been born. At last he came to Liverpool – is the district probable? – and there he began to cough, and spat blood until he died.

'I do not suppose there is any one living now who has seen her. There has seldom been more than one in a generation, and never in my life will there be both a man and a woman from whom that child can be born, who will fetch up the Siren from the sea, and destroy silence, and save the world!'

'Save the world?' I cried. 'Did the prophecy end like that?'

He leaned back against the rock, breathing deep. Through all the blue-green reflections I saw him colour. I heard him say: 'Silence and loneliness cannot last for ever. It may be a hundred or a thousand years, but the sea lasts longer, and she shall come out of it and sing.' I would have asked him more, but at that moment the whole cave darkened, and there rode in through its narrow entrance the returning boat.

The Doll
ALGERNON BLACKWOOD

SOME NIGHTS ARE MERELY dark, others are dark in a suggestive way as though something ominous, mysterious, is going to happen. In certain remote outlying suburbs, at anyrate, this seems true, where great spaces between the lamps go dead at night, where little happens, where a ring at the door is a summons almost, and people cry 'Let's go to town!' In the villa gardens the mangy cedars sigh in the wind, but the hedges stiffen, there is a muffling of spontaneous activity.

On this particular November night a moist breeze barely stirred the silver pine in the narrow drive leading to the 'Laurels' where Colonel Masters lived, Colonel Hymber Masters, late of an Indian regiment, with many distinguished letters after his name. The housemaid in the limited staff being out, it was the cook who answered the bell when it rang with a sudden, sharp clang soon after ten o'clock – and gave an audible gasp half of surprise, half of fear. The bell's sudden clangour was an unpleasant and unwelcome sound. Monica, the Colonel's adored yet rather neglected child, was asleep upstairs, but the cook was not frightened lest Monica be disturbed, nor because it seemed a bit late for the bell to ring so violently; she was frightened because when she opened the door to let the fine rain drive in she saw a black man standing on the steps. There, in the wind and the rain, stood a tall, slim nigger holding a parcel.

Dark-skinned, at any rate, he was, she reflected afterwards, whether negro, Hindu or Arab; the word 'nigger' describing any man not really white. Wearing a stained yellow mackintosh and dirty slouch hat, and 'looking like a devil, so help me, God', he shoved a little parcel at her out of the gloom, the light from the hall flaring red into his gleaming eyes. 'For Colonel Masters', he whispered rapidly, 'and very special into his own personal touch and no one else.' And he melted away into the night with his 'strange foreign accent, his eyes of fire, and his nasty hissing voice.'

He was gone, swallowed up in the wind and rain.

'But I saw his eyes,' swore the cook the next morning to the housemaid, 'his fiery eyes, and his nasty look, and his black hands and long thin fingers, and his nails all shiny pink, and he looked to me – if you know wot I mean – he looked like – death . . .'

Thus the cook, so far as she was intelligently articulate next day, but standing now against the closed door with the small brown paper parcel in her hands, impressed by the orders that it was to be given into his personal touch, she was relieved by the fact that Colonel Masters never returned till after midnight and that she need not act at once. The reflection brought a certain comfort that restored her equanimity a little, though she still stood there, holding the parcel gingerly in her grimy hands, reluctant, hesitating, uneasy. A parcel, even brought by a mysterious dark stranger, was not in itself frightening, yet frightened she certainly felt. Instinct and superstition worked perhaps; the wind, the rain, the fact of being alone in the house, the unexpected black man, these also contributed to her discomfort. A vague sense of horror touched her, her Irish blood stirred ancient dreams, so that she began to shake a little, as though the parcel contained something alive, explosive, poisonous, unholy almost, as though it moved, and, her fingers loosening their hold, the parcel – dropped. It fell on the tiled floor with a queer, sharp clack, but it lay motionless. She eyed it closely, cautiously, but, thank God, it did not move, an inert, brown-paper parcel. Brought by an errand boy in daylight, it might have been groceries, tobacco, even a mended shirt. She peeped and tinkered, that sharp clack puzzled her. Then, after a few minutes, remembering her duty, she picked it up gingerly even while she shivered. It was to be handed into the Colonel's 'personal touch'. She compromised, deciding to place it on his desk and to tell him about it in the morning; only Colonel Masters, with those mysterious years in the East behind him, his temper and his tyrannical orders, was not easy of direct approach at the best of times, in the morning least of all.

The cook left it at that – that is, she left it on the desk in his study, but left out all explanations about its arrival. She had decided to be vague about such unimportant details, for Mrs. O'Reilly was afraid of Colonel Masters, and only his professed love of Monica made her believe that he was quite human. He paid her well, oh yes, and sometimes he smiled, and he was a handsome man, if a bit too dark for her fancy, yet he also paid her an occasional compliment about her curry, and that soothed her for the moment. They suited one another, at any rate, and she stayed, robbing him comfortably, if cautiously.

'It ain't no good,' she assured the housemaid next day, 'wot with that "personal touch into his hands, and no one else", and that black man's eyes and that crack when it came away in my hands and fell on the floor. It ain't no good, not to us nor anybody. No man as black as he was means lucky stars to anybody. A parcel indeed – with those devil's eyes—'

'What did you do with it?' enquired the housemaid.

The cook looked her up and down. 'Put it in the fire o'course,' she replied. 'On the stove if you want to know exact.'

It was the housemaid's turn to look the cook up and down.

'I don't think,' she remarked.

The cook reflected, probably because she found no immediate answer.

'Well,' she puffed out presently, 'D'you know wot *I* think? You don't. So I'll tell you. It was something the master's afraid of, that's wot it was. He's afraid of something – ever since I been here I've known that. And that's wot it was. He done somebody wrong in India long ago and that lanky nigger brought wot's coming to him, and that's why I say I put it on the stove – see?' She dropped her voice. 'It was a bloody idol,' she whispered, 'that's wot it was, that Parcel, and he – why, he's a bloody secret worshipper.' And she crossed herself. 'That's why I said I put it on the stove – see?'

The housemaid stared and gasped.

'And you mark my words, young Jane!' added the cook, turning to her dough.

And there the matter rested for a period, for the cook, being Irish, had more laughter in her than tears, and beyond admitting to the scared housemaid that she had not really burnt the parcel but had left it on the study table, she almost forgot the incident. It was not her job, in any case, to answer the front door. She had 'delivered' the parcel. Her conscience was quite clear.

Thus, nobody 'marked her words' apparently, for nothing untoward happened, as the way is in remote Suburbia, and Monica in her lonely play was happy, and Colonel Masters as tyrannical and grim as ever. The moist wintry wind blew through the silver pine, the rain beat against the bow window and no one called. For a week this lasted, a longish time in uneventful Suburbia.

But suddenly one morning Colonel Masters rang his study bell and, the housemaid being upstairs, it was the cook who answered. He held a brown paper parcel in his hands, half opened, the string dangling.

'I found this on my desk. I haven't been in my room for a week. Who brought it? And when did it come?' His face, yellow as usual, held a fiery tinge.

Mrs. O'Reilly replied, post-dating the arrival vaguely.

'I asked *who* brought it?' he insisted sharply.

'A stranger,' she fumbled. 'Not any one,' she added nervously, 'from hereabouts. No one I ever seen before. It was a man.'

'What did he look like?' The question came like a bullet.

Mrs. O'Reilly was rather taken by surprise. 'D-darkish,' she stumbled. 'Very darkish,' she added, 'if I saw him right. Only he came and went so quick I didn't get his face proper like, and . . .'

'Any message?' the Colonel cut her short.

She hesitated. 'There was no answer,' she began, remembering former occasions.

'Any *message*, I asked you!' he thundered.

'No message, sir, none at all. And he was gone before I could get his name and address, sir, but I think it was a sort of black man, or it may have been the darkness of the night – I couldn't reely say, sir . . .'

In another minute she would have burst into tears or dropped to the floor in a faint, such was her terror of her employer especially when she was lying blind. The Colonel, however, saved her both disasters by abruptly holding out the half opened parcel towards her. He neither cross-examined nor cursed her as she had expected. He spoke with the curtness that betrayed anger and anxiety, almost, it occurred to her, distress.

'Take it away and burn it,' he ordered in his army voice, passing it into her outstretched hands. 'Burn it,' he repeated it, 'or chuck the damned thing away.' He almost flung it at her as though he did not want to touch it. 'If the man comes back,' he ordered in a voice of steel, 'tell him it's been destroyed – and say it *didn't reach me*', laying tremendous emphasis on the final words. 'You understand?' He almost chucked it at her.

'Yes, sir. Exactly, sir,' and she turned and stumbled out, holding the parcel gingerly in her arms rather than in her hands and fingers, as though it contained something that might bite or sting.

Yet her fear had somehow lessened, for if he, Colonel Masters, could treat the parcel so contemptuously, why should she feel afraid of it? And, once alone in her kitchen among her household goods, she opened it. Turning back the thick paper wrappings, she started, and to her rather disappointed amazement, she found herself staring at nothing but a fair, waxen, faced doll that could be bought in any toy-shop for one shilling and sixpence. A commonplace little cheap doll! Its face was pallid, white, expressionless, its flaxen hair was dirty, its tiny ill-shaped hands and fingers lay motionless by its side, its mouth was closed, though somehow grinning, no teeth visible, its eyelashes ridiculously like a worn tooth brush, its entire presentment in its flimsy skirt, contemptible, harmless, even ugly.

A doll! She giggled to herself, all fear evaporated.

'Gawd!' she thought. 'The master must have a conscience like the floor of a parrot's cage! And worse than that!' She was too afraid of him to despise him, her feeling was probably more like pity. 'At any rate,' she reflected, 'he had the wind up pretty bad. It was something else he expected – not a two penny halfpenny doll!' Her warm heart felt amost sorry for him.

Instead of 'chucking the damned thing away or burning it,' however, – for it was quite a nice looking dool, she presented it to Monica, and Monica, having few new toys, instantly adored it, promising faithfully, as gravely warned by Mrs. O'Reilly, that she would never *never* let her father know she had it.

Her father, Colonel Hymber Masters, was, it seems, what's called a 'disappointed' man, a man whose fate forced him to live in surroundings he detested, disappointed in his career probably, possibly in love as well, Monica a love-child doubtless, and limited by his pension to face daily conditions that he loathed.

He was a silent, bitter sort of fellow, no more than that, and not so much disliked in the neighbourhood, as misunderstood. A sombre man they reckoned him, with his dark, furrowed face and silent ways. Yet 'dark' in the suburbs meant mysterious, and 'silent' invited female fantasy to fill the vacuum. It's the frank, corn-haired man who invites sympathy and generous comment. He enjoyed his Bridge, however, and was accepted as a first-class player. Thus, he went out nightly, and rarely came back before midnight. He was welcome among the gamblers evidently, while the fact that he had an adored child at home softened the picture of this 'mysterious' man. Monica, though rarely seen, appealed to the women of the neighbourhood, and 'whatever her origin' said the gossips, 'he loves her'.

To Monica, meanwhile, in her rather play-less, toy-less life, the doll, her new treasure, was a spot of gold. The fact that it was a 'secret' present from her father, added to its value. Many other presents had come to her like that; she thought nothing of it; only, he had never given her a doll before, and it spelt rapture. Never, never, would she betray her pleasure and delight; it should remain her secret and his; and that made her love it all the more. She loved her father too, his taciturn silence was something she vaguely respected and adored. 'That's just like father,' she always said, when a strange new present came, and she knew instinctively that she must never say *Thank you* for it, for that was part of the lovely game between them. But this doll was exceptionally marvellous.

'It's much more real and alive than my Teddy bears,' she told the cook, after examining it critically. 'What ever made him think of it? Why, it even talks to me!' and she cuddled and fondled the half misshapen toy. 'It's my baby,' she cried, taking it against her cheek.

For no Teddy bear could really be a child; cuddly bears were not offspring, whereas a doll was a potential baby. It brought sweetness, as both cook and governess realized, into a rather grim house, hope and tenderness, a maternal flavour almost, something anyhow that no young bear could possibly bring. A child, a human baby! And yet both cook and governess – for both were present at the actual delivery – recalled later that Monica opened the parcel and recognised the doll with a yell of wild delight that seemed almost a scream of pain. There was this too high note of delirious exultation as though some instinctive horror of revulsion were instantly smothered and obliterated in a whirl of overmastering joy. It was Madame Jodzka who recalled – long afterwards – this singular contradiction.

'I did think she shrieked at it a bit, now you ask me,' admitted Mrs. O'Reilly later, though at the actual moment all she said was 'Oh, lovely, darling, ain't it a pet!' While all Madame Jodzka said was a cautionary 'If you squash its mouth like that, Monica, it won't be able to breathe!'

While Monica, paying no attention to either of them, fell to cuddling the doll with ecstasy.

A cheap little flaxen-haired, waxen-faced doll.

That so strange a case should come to us at second hand is, admittedly, a pity; that so much of the information should reach us largely through a cook and housemaid and through a foreigner of questionable validity, is equally unfortunate. Where precisely the reported facts creep across the feathery frontier into the incredible and thence into the fantastic would need the spider's thread of the big telescopes to define. With the eye to the telescope, the thread of that New Zealand spider seems thick as rope; but with the eye examining second-hand reports the thread becomes elusive gossamer.

The Polish governess, Madame Jodzka, left the house rather abruptly. Though adored by Monica and accepted by Colonel Masters, she left not long after the arrival of the doll. She was a comely, youngish widow of birth and breeding, tactful, discreet, understanding. She adored Monica, and Monica was happy with her; she feared her employer, yet perhaps secretly admired him as the strong, silent, dominating Englishman. He gave her great freedom, she never took liberties, everything went smoothly. The pay was good and she needed it. Then, suddenly she left. In the suddenness of her departure, as in the odd reason she gave for leaving, lie doubtless the first hints of this remarkable affair, creeping across that 'feathery frontier' into the incredible and fantastic. An understandable reason she gave for leaving was that she was too frightened to stay in the house another night. She left at twenty-four hours' notice. Her reason was absurd, even if understandable, because any woman might find herself so frightened in a certain building that it has become intolerable to her nerves. Foolish or otherwise, this is understandable. An *idée fixe*, an obsession, once lodged in the mind of a superstitious, therefore hysterically-favoured woman, cannot be dislodged by argument. It may be absurd, yet it is 'understandable'.

The story behind the reason for Madame Jodzka's sudden terror is another matter, and it is best given quite simply. It relates to the doll. She swears by all her gods that she saw the doll 'walking by itself'. It was walking in a disjointed, hoppity, hideous fashion across the bed in which Monica lay sleeping.

In the gleam of the night-light, Madame Jodzka swears she saw this happen. She was half inside the opened door, peeping in, as her habit, and duty decreed, to see if all was well with the child before going up to bed herself. The light, if faint, was clear. A jerky movement on the counterpane first caught her attention, for a smallish object seemed blundering awkwardly across its slippery silken surface. Something rolling, possibly, some object Monica had left outside on falling asleep rolling mechanically as the child shifted or turned over.

After staring for some seconds, she then saw that it was not merely an 'object', since it had a living outline, nor was it rolling mechanically, or sliding, as she had first imagined. It was horribly taking steps, small but quite deliberate steps as though alive. It had a tiny, dreadful face, it had an expressionless tiny face, and the face had eyes – small, brightly shining eyes, and the eyes looked straight at Madame Jodzka.

She watched for a few seconds thunderstruck, and she suddenly realised with a shock of utter horror that this small, purposive monster was the doll, Monica's doll! And this doll was moving towards her across the tumbled surface of the counterpane. It was coming in her direction – straight at her.

Madame Jodzka gripped herself, physically and mentally, making a great effort, it seems, to deny the abnormal, the incredible. She denied the ice in her veins and down her spine. She prayed. She thought frantically of her priest in Warsaw. Making no audible sound, she screamed in her mind. But the doll, quickening its pace, came hobbling straight towards her, its glassy eyes fixed hard upon her own.

Then Madame Jodzka fainted.

That she was, in some ways, a remarkable woman, with a sense of values, is clear from the fact that she realised this story 'wouldn't wash', for she confided it only to the cook in cautious whispers, while giving her employer some more 'washable' tale about a family death that obliged her to hurry home to Warsaw. Nor was there the slightest attempt at embroidery, for on recovering consciousness she had recovered her courage, too – and done a remarkable thing: she had compelled herself to investigate. Aided and fortified by her religion, she compelled herself to make an examination. She had tiptoed further into the room, had made sure that Monica was sleeping peacefully, and that the doll lay – motionless – half way down the counterpane. She gave it a long, concentrated look. Its lidless eyes, fringed by hideously ridiculous black lashes, were fixed on space. Its expression was not so much innocent, as blankly stupid, idiotic, a mask of death that aped cheaply a pretence of life, where life could never be. Not ugly merely, it was revolting.

Madame Jodzka, however, did more than study this visage with concentration, for with admirable pluck she forced herself to touch the little horror. She actually picked it up. Her faith, her deep religious conviction, denied the former evidence of her senses. She had *not* seen movement. It was incredible, impossible. The fault lay somewhere in herself. This persuasion, at any rate, lasted long enough to enable her to touch the repulsive little toy, to pick it up, to lift it. She placed it steadily on the table near the bed between the bowl of flowers and the nightlight, where it lay on its back helpless, innocent, yet horrible, and only then on shaking legs did she leave the room and go up to her own bed. That her fingers remained ice-cold until eventually she fell asleep can be explained, of course, too easily and naturally to claim examination.

Whether imagined or actual, it must have been, none the less, a horrifying spectacle – a mechanical outline from a commercial factory walking like a living thing with a purpose. It holds the nightmare touch. To Madame Jodzka, protected since youth within cast-iron tenets, it came as a shock. And a shock dislocates. The sight smashed everything she knew as possible and real. The flow of her blood was interrupted, it froze, there came icy terror into her heart, her normal mechanism failed for a moment, she fainted. And fainting seemed a natural result. Yet it was the shock of the incredible masquerade that gave her the courage to act. She loved Monica, apart from any consideration of paid duty. The sight of this tiny monstrosity strutting across the counterpane not far from the child's sleeping face and folded hands – it was this that enabled her to pick it up with naked fingers and set it out of reach . . .

For hours, before falling asleep, she reviewed the incredible thing, alternately denying the facts, then accepting them, yet taking into sleep finally the assured conviction that her senses had not deceived her. There seems little, indeed, that in a court of law could have been advanced against her character for reliability, for sincerity, for the logic of her detailed account.

'I'm sorry,' said Colonel Masters quietly, referring to her bereavement. He looked searchingly at her. 'And Monica will miss you,' he added with one of his rare smiles. 'She needs you.' Then just as she turned away, he suddenly extended his hand. 'If perhaps later you can come back – do let me know. Your influence is – so helpful – and good.'

She mumbled some phrase with a promise in it, yet she left with a queer, deep impression that it was not merely, not chiefly perhaps, Monica who needed her. She wished he had not used quite those words. A sense of shame lay in her, almost as though she were running away from duty, or at least from a chance to help that God had put in her way. 'Your influence is – so good.'

Already in the train and on the boat conscience attacked her, biting, scratching, gnawing. She had deserted a child she loved, a child who needed her, because she was scared out of her wits. No, that was a one-sided statement. She had left a house because the Devil had come into it. No, that was only partially true. When a hysterical temperament, engrained since early childhood in fixed dogmas, beings to sift facts and analyse reactions, logic and common sense themselves become confused. Thought led one way, emotion another, and no honest conculsion dawned on her mind.

She hurried on to Warsaw, to a stepfather, a retired General whose gay life had no place for her and who would not welcome her return. It was a derogatory prospect for this youngish widow who had taken a job in order to escape from his vulgar activities to return now empty-handed. Yet it was easier, perhaps, to face a step-father's selfish anger than to go and tell Colonel Masters her real reason for leaving his service. Her conscience, too, troubled her on another score as thoughts and memories travelled backwards and half-forgotten details emerged.

Those spots of blood, for instance, mentioned by Mrs. O'Reilly, the superstitious Irish cook. She had made it a rule to ignore Mrs. O'Reilly's silly fairy tales, yet now she recalled suddenly those ridiculous discussions about the laundry list and the foolish remarks that the cook and housemaid had let fall.

'But there ain't no paint in a doll, I tell you. It's all sawdust and wax and muck,' from the housemaid. 'I know red paint when I see it, and that ain't paint, it's blood.' And from Mrs. O'Reilly later: 'Mother o'God! Another red blob! She's biting her finger-nails – and that's not *my* job . . .!'

The red stains on sheets and pillow cases were puzzling certainly, but Madame Jodzka, hearing these remarks by chance as it were, had paid no particular attention to them at the moment. The laundry lists were hardly her affair. These ridiculous servants anyhow . . .! And yet, now in the train, those spots of red, be they paint or blood, crept back to trouble her.

Another thing, oddly enough, also troubled her – the ill-defined feeling that she was deserting a man who needed help, help that she could give. It was too vague to put into words. Was it based on his remark that her influence was 'good' perhaps? She could not say. It was an intuition, and few intuitions bear analysis. Supporting it, however, was a conviction she had felt since first she entered the service of Colonel Masters, the conviction, namely, that he had a past that frightened him. There was something he had done, something he regretted and was probably ashamed of, something at any rate, for which he feared retribution. A retribution, moreover, he expected; a punishment that would come like a thief in the night and seize him by the throat.

It was against this dreaded vengeance that her influence was 'good', a protective influence possibly that her religion supplied, something on the side of the angels, in any case, that her personality provided.

Her mind worked thus, it seems; and whether a concealed admiration for this sombre and mysterious man, an admiration and protective instinct never admitted even to her inmost self, existed below the surface, hidden yet urgent, remains the secret of her own heart.

It was naturally and according to human nature, at any rate, that after a few weeks of her step-father's outrageous behaviour in the house, his cruelty too, she decided to return. She prayed to her gods incessantly, also she found oppressive her sense of neglected duty and failure of self-respect. She returned to the soulless suburban villa. It was understandable; the welcome from Monica was also understandable, the relief and pleasure of Colonel Masters still more so. It was expressed, this latter, in a courteous message only, tactfully worded, as though she had merely left for brief necessity, for it was some days before she actually saw him to speak to. From cook and housemaid the welcome was voluble and – disquieting. There were no more inexplicable 'spots of red', but there were other unaccountable happenings even more distressing.

'She's missed you something terrible,' said Mrs. O'Reilly, 'though she's found something else to keep her quite – if you like to put it that way.' And she made the sign of the cross.

'The doll?' asked Madame Jodzka with a start of shocked horror, forcing herself to come straight to the point and forcing herself also to speak lightly, casually.

'That's it, Madame. The bleeding doll.'

The governess had heard the strange adjective many times already, but did not know whether to take it figuratively or not. She chose the latter.

'Blood?' she asked in a lowered voice.

The cook's body gave an odd jerk. 'Well', she explained. 'I meant more the way it goes on. Like a thing of flesh and blood, if you get me. And the way *she* treats it and plays with it,' and her voice, while loud, had a hush of fear in it somewhere. She held her arms before her in a protective, shielding way, as though to ward of aggression.

'Scratches ain't proof of nothing,' interjected the housemaid scornfully.

'You mean,' asked Madame Jodzka gravely, 'there's a question of – of injury – to someone?' She suppressed an involuntary gasp, but paid no attention to the maid's interruption otherwise.

Mrs. O'Reilly seemed to mismanage her breath for a moment.

'It ain't Miss Monica it's after,' she announced in a defiant whisper as soon as she recovered herself, 'it's someone else. *That's* what I mean. And no man as black as he was,' she let herself go, 'ever brought no good into a house, not since I was born.'

'Someone else—?' repeated Madame Jodzka almost to herself, seizing the vital words.

'You and yer black man!' interjected the housemaid. 'Get along with yer! Thank God I ain't a Christian or anything like that! But I did 'ear them sort of jerky shuffling footsteps one night, I admit, and the doll did look bigger – swollen like – when I peeked in an looked—'

'Stop it!' cried Mrs. O'Reilly, 'for you ain't saying what's true or what you reely know.'

She turned to the governess.

'There's more talk what means nothing about this doll,' she said by way of apology, 'that all the fairy tales I was brought up with as a child in Mayo, and I – I wouldn't be believing anything of it.'

Turning her back contemptuously on the chattering housemaid, she came close to Madame Jodzka.

'There's no harm coming to Miss Monica, Madame,' she whispered vehemently, 'you can be quite sure about *her*. Any trouble there may be is for someone else.' And again she crossed herself.

Madame Jodzka, in the privacy of her room, reflected between her prayers. She felt a deep, a dreadful uneasiness.

A doll! A cheap, tawdry little toy made in factories by the hundred, by the thousand, a manufactured article of commerce for children to play with . . . But . . .

'The way she treats it and plays with it . . .' rang on in her disturbed mind.

A doll! But for the maternal suggestion, a doll was a pathetic, even horrible plaything, yet to watch a child busy with it involved deep reflections, since here the future mother prophesied. The child fondles and caresses here doll with passionate love, cares for it, seeks its welfare, yet stuffs it down into the perambulator, its head and neck twisted, its limbs broken and contorted, leaving it atrociously upside down so that blood and breathing cannot possibly function, while she runs to the window to see if the rain has stopped or the sun has come out. A blind and hideous automatism dictated by the race, provided nothing of more immediate interest interferes, yet a herd-instinct that overcomes all obstacles, its vitality insuperable. The maternity instinct defies, even denies death. The doll, whether left upside down on the floor with broken teeth and ruined eyes, or lovingly arranged to be overlaid in the night, squashed, tortured, mutilated, survives all cruelties and disasters, and asserts finally its immortal qualities. It is unkillable. It is beyond death.

A child with her doll, reflected Madame Jodzka, is an epitome of nature's remorseless and unconquerable passion, of her dominant purpouse—the survival of the race . . .

Such thoughts, influenced perhaps by her bitter subconscious grievance against nature for depriving her of a child of her own, were unable to hold that level for long; they soon dropped back to the concrete case that perplexed and frightened her—Monica and her flaxen haired, sightless, idiotic doll. In the middle of her prayers, falling asleep incontinently, she did not even dream of it, and she woke refreshed and vigorous, facing the fact that sooner or later, sooner probably, she would have to speak to her employer.

She watched and listened. She watched Monica; she watched the doll. All seemed as normal as in a thousand other homes. Her mind reviewed the position, and where mind and superstition clashed, the former held its own easily. During her evening off she enjoyed the local cinema, leaving the heated building with the conviction that coloured fantasy benumbed the faculties, and that ordinary life was in itself prosaic. Yet before she had covered the half-mile to the house, her deep, unaccountable uneasiness returned with overmastering power.

Mrs. O'Reilly had seen Monica to bed for her, and it was Mrs. O'Reilly who let her in. Her face was like the dead.

'It's been talking,' whispered the cook, even before she closed the door. She was white about the gills.

'Talking! *Who's* been talking? What do you mean?'

Mrs. O'Reilly closed the door softly. 'Both,' she stated with dramatic emphasis, then sat down and wiped her face. She looked distraught with fear.

Madame took command, if only a command based on dreadful insecurity.

'Both?' she repeated, in a voice deliberately loud so as to counteract the other's whisper. 'What are you talking about?'

'They've *both* been talking – talking together,' stated the cook.

The governess kept silent for a moment, fighting to deny a shrinking heart.

'You've heard them talking together, you mean?' she asked presently in a shaking voice that tried to be ordinary.

Mrs. O'Reilly nodded, looking over her shoulder as she did so. Her nerves were, obviously, in rags. 'I thought you'd *never* come back,' she whimpered. 'I could hardly stay in the house.'

Madame looked intently into her frightened eyes.

'You *heard* . . .?' she asked quietly.

'I listened at the door. There were two voices. Different voices.'

Madame Jodzka did not insist or cross-examine, as though acute fear helped her to a greater wisdom.

'You mean, Mrs. O'Reilly,' she said in flat, quiet tones, 'that you heard Miss Monica talking to her doll as she always does, and herself inventing the doll's answers in a changed voice? Isn't that what you mean you heard?'

But Mrs. O'Reilly was not to be shaken. By way of answer she crossed herself and shook her head.

'She spoke in a low whisper. 'Come up now and listen with me, Madame, and judge for yourself.'

Thus, soon after midnight, and Monica long since asleep, these two, the cook and governess in a suburban villa, took up their places in the dark corridor outside a child's bedroom door. It was a quiet windless night; Colonel Masters, whom they both feared, doubtless long since gone to his room in another corner of the ungainly villa. It must have been a long dreary wait before sounds in the child's bedroom first became audible – the low quiet sound of voices talking audibly – two voices. A hushed, secretive, unpleasant sound in the room where Monica slept peacefully with her beloved doll beside her. Yet two voices assuredly, it was.

Both women sat erect, both crossed themselves involuntarily, exchanging glances. Both were bewildered, terrified. Both sat aghast.

What lay in Mrs. O'Reilly's superstitious mind, only the gods of 'ould Oireland' can tell, but what the Polish woman's contained was clear as a bell; it was not two voices talking, it was only one. Her ear was pressed against the crack in the door. She listened intently; shaking to the bone, she listened. Voices in sleep-talking, she remembered, changed oddly.

'The child's talking to herself in sleep,' she whispered firmly, 'and that's all it is, Mrs. O'Reilly. She's just talking in her sleep,' she repeated with emphasis to the woman crowding against her shoulder as though in need of support. 'Can't you hear it,' she added loudly, half angrily, 'isn't it the same voice always? Listen carefully and you'll see I'm right.'

She listened herself more closely than before.

'Listen! Hark . . .!' she repeated in a breathless whisper, concentrating her mind upon the curious sound, 'isn't that the same voice – answering itself?'

Yet, as she listened, another sound disturbed her concentration, and this time it seemed a sound behind her – a faint, rustling, shuffling sound rather like footsteps hurrying away on tiptoe. She turned her head sharply and found that she had been whispering to no one. There was no one beside her. She was alone in the darkened corridor. Mrs. O'Reilly was gone. From the well of the house below a voice came up in a smothered cry beneath the darkened stairs: 'Mother o'God and all the Saints . . .' and more besides.

A gasp of surprise and alarm escaped her, doubtless at finding herself deserted and alone but in the same instant, exactly as in the story books, came another sound that caught her breath still more aghast – the rattle of a key in the front door below. Colonel Masters, after all, had not yet come in and gone to bed as expected: he was coming in now. Would Mrs. O'Reilly have time to slip across the hall before he caught her? More – and worse – would he come up and peep into Monica's bedroom on his way up to bed, as he rarely did? Madame Jodzka listened, her nerves in rags. She heard him fling down his coat. He was a man quick in such actions. The stick or umbrella was banged down noisily, hastily. The same instant his step sounded on the stairs. He was coming up. Another minute and he would start into the passage where she crouched against Monica's door.

He was mounting rapidly, two stairs at a time.

She, too, was quick in action and decision. She thought in a flash. To be caught crouching outside the door was ludicrous, but to be caught inside the door would be natural and explicable. She acted at once.

With a palpitating heart, she opened the bedroom door and stepped inside. A second later she heard Colonel Masters' tread, as he stumped along the corridor up to bed. He passed the door. He went on. She heard this with intense relief.

Now, inside the room, the door closed behind her, she saw the picture clearly.

Monica, sound asleep, was playing with her beloved doll, but in her sleep. She was indubitably in deep slumber. Her fingers, however were roughing the doll this way and that, as though some dream perplexed her. The child was mumbling in her sleep, though no words were distinguishable. Muffled sighs and groans issued from her lips. Yet another sound there certainly was, though it could not have issued from the child's mouth. Whence, then, did it come?

Madame Jodzka paused, holding her breath, her heart panting. She watched and listened intently. She heard squeaks and grunts, but a moment's examination convinced her whence these noises came. They did not come from Monica's lips. They issued indubitably from the doll she clutched and twisted in her dream. The joints, as Monica twisted them emitted these odd sounds, as though the sawdust in knees and elbows wheezed and squeaked against the unnatural rubbing. Monica obviously was wholly unconscious of these noises. As the doll's neck screwed round, the material – wax, thread, sawdust – produced 'his curious grating sound that was almost like syllables of a word or words.

Madame Jodzka stared and listened. She felt icy cold. Seeking for a natural explanation she found none. Prayer and terror raced in her helter-skelter. Her skin began to sweat.

Then, suddenly Monica, her expression peaceful and composed, turned over in her sleep, and the dreadful doll, released from the dream-clutch, fell to one side on the bed and lay apparently lifeless and inert. In which moment, to Madame Jodzka's unbelieving yet horrified ears, it continued to squeak and utter. It went on mouthing by itself. Worse than that, the next instant it stood abruptly upright, rising on its twisted legs. It started moving. It began to move, walking crookedly, across the counterpane. Its glassy, sightless eyes, seemed to look straight at her. It presented an inhuman and appaling picture, a picture of the utterly incredible. With a queer, hoppity motion of its broken legs and joints, it came fumbling and tumbling across the rough unevenness of the slippery counterpane towards her. Its appearance was deliberate and aggressive. The sounds, as of syllables, came with it – strange, meaningless syllables that yet managed to convey anger. It stumbled towards her like a living thing. Its whole presentment conveyed attack.

Once again, this effect of a mere child's toy, aping the life of some awful monstrosity with purpose and passion in its hideous tiny outline, brought collapse to the plucky Polish governess. The rush of blood without control drained her heart, and a moment of unconsciousness supervened so that everything, as it were, turned black.

This time, however, the moment of dark unconsciousness passed instantly: it came and went, almost like a moment of forgetfulness in passion. Passionate it certainly was, for the reaction came upon her like a storm. With recovered consciousness a sudden rage rushed into her woman's heart – perhaps a coward's rage, an exaggerated fury against her own weakness? It rushed, in any case, to help her. She staggered, caught her breath, clutched violently at the cupboard next to her, and – recovered her self-control. A fury of resentment blazed through her, fury against this utterly incredible exhibition of a wax doll walking and squawking as though it were something intelligently alive that could utter syllables. Syllables, she felt convinced, in a language she did not know.

If the monstrous can paralyse, it also can affront. The sight and sound of this cheap factory toy behaving with a will and heart of its own stung her into an act of violence that became imperative. For it was more than she could stand. Irresistibly, she rushed forward. She hurled herself against it, her only available weapon the high-heeled shoe her foot kicked loose on the instant, determined to smash down the frightful apparition into fragments and annihilate it. Hysterical, no doubt, she was at the moment, and yet logical: the godless horror must be blotted out of visible existence. This one thing obsessed her – to destroy beyond all possibility of survival. It must be smashed into fragments, into dust.

They stood close, face to face, the glassy eyes staring into her own, her hand held high for the destruction she craved – but the hand did not fall. A stinging pain, sharp as a serpent's bite, darted suddenly through her fingers, wrist and arm, her grip was broken, the shoe spun sideways across the room, and in the flickering light of the candle, it seemed to her, the whole room quivered. Paralysed and helpless, she stood utterly aghast. What gods or saints could come to aid her? None. Her own will alone could help her. Some effort, at any rate, she made, trembling, on the edge of collapse: 'My God!' she heard her half whispering, strangled voice cry out. 'It is not true! You are a lie! My God denies you! I call upon my God . . .!'

Whereupon, to her added horror, the dreadful little doll, waving a broken arm, squawked back at her, as though in definite answer, the strange disjointed syllables she could not understand, syllables as though in another tongue. The same instant it collapsed abruptly on the counterpane like a toy balloon that had been pricked. It shrank down in a mutilated mess before her eyes, while Monica – added touch of horror – stirred uneasily in her sleep, turning over and stretching out her hands as though feeling blindly for something that she missed. And this sight of the innocently sleeping child fumbling instinctively towards an incomprehensibly evil and dangerous something that attracted her proved again too strong for the Polish woman to control.

The blackness intervened a second time.

It was undoubtedly a blur in memory that followed, emotion and superstition proving too much for common-sense to deal with. She just remembers violent, unreasoned action on her part before she came back to clearer consciousness in her own room, praying volubly on her knees against her own bed. The interval of transit down the corridor and upstairs remained a blank. Yet her shoe was with her, clutched tightly in her hand. And she remembered also having clutched an inert, waxen doll with frantic fingers, clutched and crushed and crumpled its awful little frame till the sawdust came spurting from its broken joints and its tiny body was mutilated beyond recognition, if not annihilated . . . then stuffing it down ruthlessly on a table far out of Monica's reach – Monica lying peacefully in deepest sleep. She remembered that. She also saw the clear picture of the small monster lying upside down, grossly untidy, an obscene attitude in the disorder of its flimsy dress and exposed limbs, lying motionless, its eyes crookedly aglint, motionless, yet alive still, alive moreover with intense and malignant purpose.

No duration or intensity of prayer could obliterate the picture.

She knew now that a plain, face to face talk with her employer was essential; her conscience, her peace of mind, her sanity, her sense of duty all demanded this. Deliberately, and she was sure, rightly, she had never once risked a word with the child herself. Danger lay that way, the danger of emphasizing something in the child's mind that was best left ignored. But with Colonel Masters, who paid her for her services, believed in her integrity, trusted her, with him there must be an immediate explanation.

An interview was absurdly difficult; in the first place because he loathed and avoided such occasions; secondly because he was so exceedingly impervious to approach, being so rarely even visible at all. At night he came home late, in the mornings no one dared go near him. He expected the little household, its routine established, to run itself. The only inmate who dared beard him was Mrs. O'Reilly, who periodically, once every six months, walked straight into his study, gave notice, received an addition to her wages, and then left him alone for another six months.

Madame Jodzka, knowing his habits, waylaid him in the hall next morning while Monica was lying down before lunch, as usual. He was on his way out and she had been watching from the upper landing. She had hardly set eyes on him since her return from Warsaw. His lean, upright figure, his dark, emotionless face, she thought magnificent. He was the perfect expression of the soldier. Her heart fluttered as she raced downstairs. Her carefully prepared sentences, however, evaporated when he stopped and looked at her, a jumble of wild words pouring from her in confused English instead. He cut her rigmarole short, though he listened politely enough at first.

'I'm so glad you were able to come back to us, as I told you. Monica missed you very much—'

'She has something now she plays with—'

'The very thing,' he interrupted. 'No doubt the kind of toy she needs ... Your excellent judgment ... Please tell me if there's anything else you think ...' and he half turned as though to move away.

'But I didn't get it. It's a horrible – *horrible*—'

Colonel Masters uttered one of his rare laughs. 'Of course, all children's toys are horrible, but if she's pleased with it ... I haven't seen it, I'm no judge ... If you can buy something better—' and he shrugged his shoulders.

'I didn't buy it,' she cried desperately. 'It was brought. It makes sounds by itself – syllables. I've seen it move – move by itself. It's a doll.'

He turned from the front door which he had just reached as though he had been shot; the skin held a sudden pallor beneath the flush and something contradicted the blazing eyes, something that seemed to shrink.

'A doll,' he repeated in a very quiet voice. 'You said – a doll?'

But his eyes and face disconcerted her, so that she merely gave a fumbling account of a parcel that had been brought. His question about a parcel he had ordered strictly to be destroyed added to her confusion.

'Wasn't it?' he asked in a rasping whisper, as though a disobeyed order seemed incredible.

'It was thrown away, I believe,' she prevaricated, unable to meet his eyes, anxious to protect the cook as well. 'I think Monica – perhaps found it.' She despised her lack of courage, but his intensity scattered her wits; she was conscious, moreover, of a strange desire not to give him pain, as though his safety and happiness, not Monica's, were at stake. 'It – talks! – as well as *moves*,' she cried desperately, forcing herself at last to look at him.

Colonel Masters seemed to stiffen; his breath caught oddly.

'You say Monica has it? Plays with it? You've seen movement and heard sounds like syllables?' He asked the questions in a low voice, almost as though talking to himself. 'You've – listened?' he whispered.

Unable to find convincing words, she bowed her head, while some terror in him came across to her like a blast of icy wind. The man was afraid in his heart. Instead, however, of some explosive reply by way of blame or criticism, he spoke quietly, even calmly: 'You did right to come and tell me this – quite right,' adding then in so low a tone that she barely caught the ominous words, 'for I have been expecting something of the sort ... sooner or later ... it was bound to come ...' the voice dying away into the handkerchief he put to his face.

And abruptly then, as though aware of an appeal for sympathy, an emotional reaction swept her fear away. Stepping closer, she looked her employer straight in the eyes.

'See the child for yourself,' she said with sudden firmness. 'Come and listen with me. Come into the bedroom.'

She saw him stagger. For a moment he said nothing.

'Who,' he then asked, the low voice unsteady, 'who brought that parcel?'

'A man, I believe.'

There was a pause that seemed like minutes before his next question.

'White,' he asked, 'or – black?'

'Dark,' she told him, 'very dark.'

He was shaking like a leaf, the skin of his face blanched; he leaned against the door, wilted, limp; unless she somehow took command there threatened a collapse she did not wish to witness.

'You shall come with me tonight,' she said firmly, 'and we shall listen together. Wait till I return now. I go for brandy,' and a minute later as she came back breathless and watched him gulp down half a tumbler full, she knew that she had done right in telling him. His obedience proved it, though it seemed strange that cowardice should borrow from its like to produce courage.

'Tonight,' she repeated, 'tonight after your Bridge. We meet in the corridor outside the bedroom. At half-past twelve.'

He pulled himself into an upright position, staring at her fixedly, making a movement of his head, half bow, half nod.

'Twelve thirty,' he muttered, 'in the passage outside the bedroom door,' and using his stick rather heavily, he opened the door and passed out into the drive. She watched him go, aware that her fear had changed to pity, aware also that she watched the stumbling gait of a man too conscience-stricken to know a moment's peace, too frightened even to think of God.

Madame Jodzka kept the appointment; she had eaten no supper, but had stayed in her room – praying. She had first put Monica to bed.

'My doll,' the child pleaded, good as gold, after being tucked up. 'I must have my doll or else I'll never get to sleep,' and Madame Jodzka had brought it with reluctant fingers, placing it on the night-table beside the bed.

'She'll sleep quite comfortably here, Monica, darling. Why not leave her outside the sheets?' It had been carefully mended, she noticed, patched together with pins and stitches.

The child grabbed at it. 'I want her in bed beside me, close against me,' she said with a happy smile. 'We tell each other stories. If she's too far away I can't hear what she says.' And she seized it with a cuddling pleasure that made the woman's heart turn cold.

'Of course, darling – if it helps you to fall asleep quickly, you shall have it,' and Monica did not see the trembling fingers, nor notice the horror in the face and voice. Indeed, hardly was the doll against the cheek on the pillow, her fingers half stroking the flaxen hair and pink wax cheeks, than her eyes closed, a sigh of deep content breathed out, and Monica was asleep.

Madame Jodzka, fearful of looking behind her, tiptoed to the door, and left the room. In the passage she wiped a cold sweat from her forehead. 'God bless her and protect her,' her heart murmured, 'and may God forgive me if I've sinned.'

She kept the appointment; she knew Colonel Masters would keep it, too.

It had been a long wait from eight o'clock till after midnight. With great determination she had kept away from the bedroom door, fearful lest she might hear a sound that would necessitate action on her part: she went to her room and stayed there. But praying exhausted itself, for it both excited and betrayed her. If her God could help, a brief request alone was needed. To go on praying for help hour by hour was not only an insult to her deity, but it also wore her out physically. She stopped, therefore, and read some pages of a Polish saint which she did not understand. Later she fell into a state of horrified nervous drowse. In due course, she slept . . .

A noise awoke her – steps going softly past her door. A glance at her watch showed eleven o'clock. The steps, though stealthy, were familiar. Mrs. O'Reilly was waddling up to bed. The sounds died away. Madame Jodzka, a trifle ashamed, though she hardly knew why, returned to her Polish saint, yet determined to keep her ears open. Then slept again . . .

What woke her a second time she could not tell. She was startled. She listened. The night was unpleasantly still, the house quiet as the grave. No casual traffic passed. No wind stirred the gloomy evergreens in the drive. The world outside was silent. And then, as she saw by her watch that it was some minutes after midnight, a sharp click became audible that acted like a pistol shot to her keyed-up nerves. It was the front door closing softly. Steps followed across the hall below, then up the stairs, unsteadily a little. Colonel Masters had come in. He was coming up slowly, unwillingly she felt, to keep the appointment. Madame Jodzka started from her chair, looked in the glass, mumbled a quick confused prayer, and opened her door into the dark passage.

She stiffened, physically and mentally. 'Now, he'll hear and perhaps see – for himself,' she thought. 'And God help him!'

She marched along the passage and reached the door of Monica's bedroom, listening with such intentness that she seemed to hear only the confused running murmur of her own blood. Having reached the appointed spot, she stood stock still and waited while his steps approached. A moment later his bulk blocked the passage, shown up as a dark shadow by the light in the hall below. This bulk came nearer, came right up to her. She believed she said 'Good evening', and that he mumbled something about 'I said I'd come . . . damned nonsense . . .' or words to that effect, whereupon the couple stood side by side in the darkened silence of the corridor, remote from the rest of the house, and waited without further words. They stood shoulder to shoulder outside the door of Monica's bedroom. Her heart was knocking against her side.

She heard his breathing, there came a whiff of spirits, of stale tobacco smoke, his outline seemed to shift against the wall unsteadily, he moved his feet; and a sudden, extraordinary wave of emotion swept over her, half of protective maternal yearning, half almost of sexual desire, so that for a passing instant she burned to take him in her arms and kiss him savagely, and at the same time shield him from some appalling danger his blunt ignorance laid him open to. With revulsion, pity, and a sense of sin and passion, she acknowledged this odd sudden weakness in herself, but the face of the Warsaw priest flashed across her fuddled mind the next instant. There was evil in the air. This meant the Devil. She felt herself trembling dreadfully, shaking in her shoes, losing her balance, her whole body leaning over, but leaning in his direction. A moment more and she must have fallen towards him, dropped into his arms.

A sound broke the silence, and she drew up just in time. It came from beyond the door, from inside the bedroom.

'Hark!' she whispered, her hand upon his arm, and while he made no movement, spoke no word, she saw his head and shoulders bend down toward the panel of the closed door. There was a noise, upon the other side, there were noises, Monica's voice distinctly recognisable, another slighter, shriller sound accompanying it, breaking in upon it, answering it. Two voices.

'Listen,' she repeated in a whisper scarcely audible, and felt his warm hand grip her own so fiercely that it hurt her.

No words were distinguishable at first, just these odd broken sounds of two separate voices in that dark corridor of the silent house – the voice of a child, and the other a strange, faint, hardly human sound, while yet a voice.

'*Que le bon Dieu—*' she began, than faltered, breath failing her, for she saw Colonel Masters stoop down suddenly and do the last thing that would have occurred to her as likely: he put his eye to the key-hole and kept it there steadily, for the best part of a minute, his hand still gripping her own firmly. He knelt on one knee to keep his balance.

The sounds had ceased, no movement now stirred inside the room. The night-light, she knew, would show him clearly the pillows of the bed, Monica's head, the doll in her arms. Colonel Masters must see clearly anything there was to see, and he yet gave no sign that he saw anything. She experienced a queer sensation for a few seconds – almost as though she had perhaps imagined everything and proved herself a consummate, idiotic, hysterical fool. For a few seconds this ghastly thought flashed over her, the odd silence emphasising it. Had she been, after all, just a crazy lunatic? Had her senses all deceived her? Why should he see nothing, make no sign? Why had the voice, the voices, ceased? Not a murmur of any sort was audible in the room.

Then Colonel Masters, suddenly releasing his grip of her hand, shuffled on to both feet and stood up straight, while in the same instant she herself stiffened, trying to prepare for the angry scorn, the contemptuous abuse he was about to pour upon her. Protecting herself against this attack, expecting it, she was the more amazed at what she did hear:

'I saw it,' came in a strangled whisper. 'I saw it walk!'

She stood paralysed.

'It's watching me,' he added, scarcely audible. '*Me!*'

The revulsion of feeling at first left her speechless; it was the sheer terror in his strangled whisper that restored a measure of self possession to her. Yet it was he who found words first, awful whispered words, words spoken to himself, it seemed, more than to her.

'It's what I've always feared – I knew it must come some day – yet not like this. Not this way.'

Then immediately the voice in the room became audible, and it was a sweet and gentle voice, sincere and natural, with feeling in it – Monica's childish voice, pleading:

'Don't go, don't leave me! Come back into bed – please.'

An incomprehensible sound followed, as though by way of answer. There were syllables in that faint, creaky tone Madame Jodzka recognised, but syllables she could not comprehend. They seemed to enter her like points of ice. She froze. And facing her stood the motionless, inanimate bulk of him, his outline, then leaned over towards her, his lips so close to her own face that, as he spoke, she felt the breath upon her cheek.

'*Buth laga* . . .' she heard him repeat the syllables to himself again and again. '*Revenge* . . . in Hindustani . . .!' He drew a long, anguished breath. The sounds sank into her like drops of poison, the syllables she had heard several times already but had not understood. At last she understood their meaning. Revenge!

'I must go in, go in,' he was mumbling to himself. 'I must go in and face it.' Her intuition was justified: the danger was not for Monica but for himself. Her sudden protective maternal instinct found its explanation too. The lethal power concentrated in that hideous puppet was aimed at *him*. He began to edge impetuously past her.

'No!' she cried. 'I'll go! Let me go in!' pushing him aside with all her strength. But his hand was already on the knob and the next instant the door was open and he was inside the room. On the threshold they stood still a second, side by side, though she was slightly behind, struggling to shove past him and stand protectively in front.

She stared across his shoulder, her eyes so wide open that the intense strain to note everything at once threatened to defeat its own end. Sight, none the less, worked normally; she saw all there was to see, and that was – nothing; nothing unusual that is, nothing abnormal, nothing terrifying, so that this second time the threat of anti-climax rose to her mind. Had she worked herself up to this peak of horror merely to behold Monica lying sound asleep in a safe and quiet room? The flickering night-light revealed no more than a child in natural slumber without a toy of any sort against her pillow. There stood the glass of water beside the flowers in their saucer, the picture-book on the sill of the window within reach, the window opened a little at the bottom, and there also lay the calm face of Monica with eyes tight shut upon the pillow. Her breathing was deep and regular, no sign of disquiet anywhere, no hint of disturbance that might have accompanied that pleading sentence of two minutes ago, exept that the bedclothes were perhaps somwhat tumbled. The counterpane humped itself in folds towards the foot of the bed, she noticed, as though Monica, finding it too warm, had tossed it away in sleep. No more than that.

In that first moment Colonel Masters and the governess took in this whole pretty picture complete. The room was so still that the child's breathing was distinctly audible. Their eyes roved all over. Nothing was anywhere in movement. Yet the same instant Madame Jodzka became aware that there *was* movement. Something stirred. The report came, perhaps, through her skin, for no sense announced it. It was undeniable; in that still, silent room there was movement somewhere, and with that unreported movement there was danger.

Certain, rightly or wrongly, that she herself was safe, also that the quietly sleeping child was safe, she was equally certain that Colonel Masters was the one in danger. She knew that in her very bones.

'Wait here by the door,' she said almost peremptorily, as she felt him pushing past her further into the quiet room. 'You saw it watching you. It's somewhere! – Take care!'

She clutched at him, but he was already beyond her.

'Damned nonsense,' he muttered and strode forward.

Never before in her whole life had she admired a man more than in this instant when she saw him moving towards what she knew to be physical and spiritual danger – never before, and never again, was such a hideous and dreadful sight to be repeatable in a woman's life. Pity and horror drowned her in a sea of passionate, futile longing. A man going to meet his fate, it flashed over her, was something none, without power to help, should witness. No human power can stay the course of the stars.

Her eye rested, as it were by chance, on the crumpled ridges and hollows of the discarded counterpane. These lay by the foot of the bed in shadow, confused a little in their contours and their masses. Had Monica not moved, they must have lain thus till morning. But Monica did move. At this particular moment she turned over in her sleep. She stretched her little legs before settling down in the new position, and this stretching squeezed and twisted the contours of the heavy counterpane at the foot of the bed. The tiny landscape altered thus a fraction, its immediate detail shifted. And an outline – a very small outline – emerged. Hitherto, it had lain concealed among the shadows. It emerged now with disconcerting rapidity, as though a spring released it. Out of its nest of darkness it seemed almost to leap forward. Fast it came, supernaturally fast, its velocity actually shocking, for a shock came with it. It was exceedingly small, it was exceedingly dreadful, its head erect and venomous and the movement of its legs and arms, as of its bitter, glittering eyes, aping humanity. Malignant evil, personified and aggressive, shaped itself in this otherwise ridiculous outline.

It was the doll.

Racing with incredible security across the slippery surface of the crumpled silk counterpane, it dived and climbed and shot forward with an appearance of complete control and deliberate purpose. That it had a definite aim was overwhelmingly obvious. Its fixed, glassy eyes were concentrated upon a point beyond and behind the terrified governess, the point precisely where Colonel Masters, her employer, stood against her shoulder.

A frantic, half protective movement on her part, seemed lost in the air. . .

She turned instinctively, putting an arm about his shoulders, which he instantly flung off.

'Let the bloody thing come,' he cried. 'I'll deal with it . . .!' He thrust her violently aside.

The doll came at him. The hinges of its diminutive broken arms and its jointed legs emitted a thin, creaking sound as it came darting – the syllables Madame Jodzka had already heard more than once. Syllables she had heard without understanding – '*buth laga*' – but syllables now packed with awful meaning: *Revenge*.

The sounds hissed and squeaked, yet clear as a bell as the beast advanced at this miraculous speed.

Before Colonel Masters could move an inch backwards or forwards in self protection, before he could command himself to any sort of action, or contrive the smallest measure of self defence, it was off the bed and at him. It settled. Savagely, its little jaws of tiny make-believe were bitten deep into Colonel Masters' throat, fastened tightly.

In a flash this happened, in a flash it was over. In Madame Jodzka's memory it remained like the impression of a lightning flash, simultaneously etched in black and white. It had happened in the present as though it had no past. It came and was gone again. Her faculties, as after a vivid lightning, were momentarily paralysed, without past or present. She had witnessed these awful things, but had not realised them. It was this lack of realisation that struck her motionless and dumb.

Colonel Masters, on the other hand, stood beside her quietly as though nothing unusual had happened, wholly master of himself, calm, collected. At the moment of attack no sound had left his lips, there had been no gesture even of defence. Whatever had come, he had apparently accepted. The words that now fell from his lips were, thus, all the more dreadful in their appalling common-placeness.

'Hadn't you better put that counterpane straight a bit ... perhaps?'

Common sense, as always, enables the gas of hysteria to escape. Madame Jodzka gasped, but she obeyed. Automatically she moved across to do his bidding, yet aware, even as she thus moved, that he flicked something from his neck, as though a wasp, a mosquito, or some poisonous insect, had tried to sting him. She remembered no more than that, for he, in his calmness, had contributed nothing else.

Fumbling with the folds of slippery counterpane she tried to straighten out, she was startled to find that Monica was sitting up in bed, awake.

'Oh, Doska – you here!' the child exclaimed innocently, straight out of sleep and using the affectionate nickname. 'And Daddy too! Oh, my goodness . . .!'

'Sm-moothing your bed, darling,' she stammered, hardly aware of what she said. 'You ought to be asleep. I just looked in to see . . .' She mumbled a few other automatic words.

'And Daddy with you!' repeated the child excitedly, sleep still about her, wondering what it all meant. 'Ooh! Ooh!' holding out her arms.

This brief exchange of spoken words, though it takes a minute to describe, occurred simultaneously with the action – perhaps ten seconds all told, for while the governess fumbled with the counterpane, Colonel Masters was in the act of brushing something from his neck. Nothing else was audible, nothing but his quick gasp and sudden intake of breath: but something else – she swears it on her Warsaw priest – was visible. Madame Jodzka maintains by all her gods she saw this other thing.

In moments of paralysing stress it is not the senses that act less speedily nor with less precision; their action, on the contrary, is intensified and speeded up: what takes longer is the registration of their reports. The numbed brain causes the apparent delay; realisation is slowed down.

Madame Jodzka thus only realised a fraction of a second later what her eyes had indubitably witnessed; a dark-skinned arm slanting in through the open window by the bed and snatching at a small object that lay on the floor after dropping from Colonel Masters' throat, then withdrawing again at lightning speed into the darkness of the night outside.

No one but herself, apparently, had seen this – it was almost super-naturally swift.

'And now you'll be asleep again in two minutes, lucky Monica,' Colonel Masters was whispering over by the bed. 'I just peeped in to see that you were all right . . .' His voice was thin, dreadfully soundless.

Madame Jodzka, against the door, frozen, terrified, looked on and listened. 'Are you quite well, Daddy? Sure? I had a dream, but it's gone now.'

'Splendid. Never better in my life. But better still if I saw you sound asleep. Come now, I'll blow out this silly night-light, for that's what woke you up, I'll be bound.'

He blew it out, he and the child blew it out together, the latter with sleepy laughter that then hushed. And Colonel Masters tiptoed to join Madame Jodzka at the door. 'A lot of damned fuss about nothing,' she heard him muttering in that same thin dreadful voice, and then, as they closed the door and stood a moment in the darkened passage, he did suddenly an unexpected thing. He took the Polish woman in his arms, held her fiercely to him for a second, kissed her vehemently, and flung her away.

'Bless you and thank you,' he said in a low, angry voice. 'You did your best. You made a great fight. But I got what I deserved. I've been waiting years for it.' And he was off down the stairs to his own quarters. Half way down he stopped and looked up to where she stood against the rails. 'Tell the doctor,' he whispered hoarsely, 'that I took a sleeping draught – an overdose.' And he was gone.

And this was, roughly, what she did tell the doctor next morning when a hurried telephone summons brought him to the bed whereon a dead man lay with a swollen, blackened tongue. She told the same tale at the inquest too and an emptied bottle of a powerful sleeping-draught supported her . . .

And Monica, too young to realise grief beyond its trumpery meaning of a selfishly felt loss, never once – oddly enough – referred to the absence of the lovely doll that had comforted so many hours, proved such an intimate companion day and night in a life that held no other playmates. It seemed forgotten, expunged utterly from her memory, as though it had never existed at all. She stared blankly, stupidly, when a doll was mentioned: she preferred her worn-out Teddy bears. The slate of memory, in this particular, was wiped clean.

'They're so warm and comfy,' she described her bears, 'and they cuddle without tickling. Besides,' she added innocently, 'they don't squeak and try to slip away . . .'

Thus in the suburbs, where great spaces between the lamps go dead at night, where the moist wind comes whispering through the mournful branches of the silver-pines, where nothing happens and people cry 'Let's go to town!' there are occasional stirrings among the dead dry bones that hide behind respectable villa walls . . .

She Walks on Dry Land
R. CHETWYND-HAYES

IF ECCENTRICITY IS a sign of greatness, then verily must I, Charles Edward Devereux, Fourth Earl of Montcalm, be among the greatest in the three kingdoms. During the length of a long life I have always been prone to follow that line of conduct that is least amendable to convention and thus brought down upon my unbowed head the unmerited disapproval of my contemporaries. But I have never understood why wealth and position should stop any man doing that which pleased him, so long as his conduct did not result in harm or discomfit to his fellow beings.

In the year of our Lord 1812, being tired of the excesses practised at the regency court, I early on the morning of October 5th, ordered my body servant Patrick to saddle two horses, and after informing my people I would be absent for an unspecified period, departed for an unknown destination.

I travelled north, leaving London by way of the Strand, then proceeded into the county of Essex, determined to follow the coastline until a whim prompted me to do otherwise. Calling myself Charles Beverley (this being my mother's maiden name) I put up at various inns and places of entertainment and on the fifth day after my departure from London arrived at the small fishing village I will call Denham.

This was nothing more than a row of small cottages that seemed to be an extension of the old grey-stoned church, plus one inn that bore the sign 'The Limping Sailor' on a creaking board over its main doorway. I ordered Patrick to take charge of the horses and entered this establishment, half determined to spend a few days in this retreat, for I was much taken by its brooding atmosphere of isolation, the thudding music of restless waves and the sad dirge of wheeling gulls.

There was one saloon, if the single room furnished only by a long bar and a few crude benches can be so designated, and several men – mainly hard of feature and sombre of mien – greeted my entrance with the undisguised curiosity of their kind. A large, red-faced man who I assumed to be the landlord, knuckled his forehead (for even plainly dressed I could never be mistaken for other than a person of quality) and asked:

'What be your pleasure, sir?'

I slapped a gold coin down upon the bar and smiled benignly.

'A tankard of sack. Also let any present who would partake of my hospitality be served with what pleases them best.'

Instantly there was much movement of feet, a mass surge towards the bar and I became the centre of flattering attention, for the way to reach your yokel's heart is through his gullet. When all were supplied with their needs and I had half-drained my pewter tankard, I broached the matter of accommodation.

'Could you put me up for a day or so?' I asked the landlord. 'Two rooms and simple fare is all that will be required.'

To my surprise the fellow shook his head and an abrupt silence stilled tongues that had been loosened by my largesse.

'This is a small house, sir and I have no means of entertaining such a gentleman as yourself. Few travellers pass this way, you understand.'

Although when making my enquiry I was of two minds if I really wanted to stay in this miserable hovel, a direct refusal had the immediate result of arousing my ire. Neither was I appeased when those who had been partaking of my liberality withdrew and began muttering among themselves. I raised my voice and again addressed the landlord.

'I would remind you that this is a place of public entertainment and you are compelled by law to provide accommodation for any traveller who requests it.'

The fellow rubbed his hands, then spread them wide in a gesture of apparent helplessness, even while I detected a gleam of fear in his small, deep-set eyes.

'I have no vacant room, sir. Ipswich is but a few miles inland . . .'

'I have no mind to ride a few miles inland at this advanced hour. There must be at least two upper rooms. I will settle for one and my fellow can sleep on the floor.'

I watched the heavy face assume a sullen expression and my rage rose to a level that was out of all proportion to the ridiculous situation, but I am not accustomed to having my will thwarted. When he spoke again his voice was no longer respectful.

'There's no room and that's final. Be gone and ride where you will. But you do not stay here.'

I struck him with my riding crop and he fell back, clutching a mighty gash on his forehead; but before the others could reach me I was covering them with my horse pistol, nigh choking with rage. The door flew open and there was Patrick, a towering figure with a blunderbuss clasped firmly in his great hands – and they slunk back like rats confronted by two savage dogs. My anger is a flame that burns fiercely for a short space of time, but soon fades when opposition to my will is overcome. When next I spoke my voice was gentle.

'Come, my friends, there is no reason for us to quarrel. Some nefarious activity doubtless makes you resent the presence of strangers. Smuggling perhaps. Do not worry on my account, for I can be both blind and deaf when I so wish. But understand this, I am determined to stay in this place for so long as the fancy takes me and it will ill-become any man to say otherwise. Now, I care not if I spend the night in this inn or another, more accommodating abode, but some roof will provide shelter. I am prepared to be a generous guest, but a ferocious outcast. So – who is ready to be my host?'

An old man with stooped shoulders ventured to advance a few steps and after saluting me, proceeded to speak.

'Sir, I am Josiah Woodward, the elder of this law-abiding community and humbly crave your indulgence when I say you do wrong to commit violence when no man's hand was raised against you. Fear for your safety, sir, forces us to be inhospitable, not evil doing. Come nightfall, it bodes ill for any stranger found within the confines of this village and I implore you to ride from hence and give thanks to Almighty God that you do so with body and soul intact.'

I laughed softly for now I realised that here was one of those isolated communities where superstition bemused the minds of its inhabitants, although I was impressed by their mien and mode of speech, which would have done justice to many a Whitehall gallant. I lowered my pistol and said gently:

'Now I understand. You are trying to frighten me with some bogey that moans beyond tightly closed windows, or a demon horseman who comes galloping across the moonlit moor. Have no fear for my safety, my good fellow, I am more than a match for any adversary, be he from this world or the next.'

Their voices rose up and created a chorus of horrified rebuke and the landlord, who had by now somewhat recovered from my admonishing blow, crossed himself vigorously. The old man shook his head.

'It ill becomes you, sir, to treat with levity advice given by those who speak from bitter experience. We who live here have nothing to fear and if so inclined could take pleasure from watching your sinful pride crumble before the wind of abject terror. A year or so ago there came one like unto yourself, who refused to heed our well-intentioned warning, and now his bones lie rotting in the churchyard. Ask not why, sir, but get you gone with our blessing.'

I experienced a thrill of excitement for here was a situation to guarantee some diversion, even though it more than probably had a mundane explanation. An ancient folk tale, embellished by imagination and retelling round winter fires, based perhaps on some actual event, the origins of which were now lost in the mists of time. I chuckled and said:

'But I insist on knowing why, old man. You cannot expect a person of my standing to flee from a shadow I have yet to see, to say nothing of unsatisfied curiosity that would pester me for the rest of my life. What dreadful fate strikes down the stranger, but leaves the inhabitants unscathed?'

The old fellow positively glared at me.

'It is doubtful if words of mine will do more than evoke scorn, but if so be your wish, I will tell you what I know, which is little, for there is no man living who can do more than repeat what his father told him, as indeed did his father before him. But you must accept that long ago, perhaps during the reign of him they now call Charles the martyr, there lived in this place a maiden called Elizabeth Coldwell. 'Tis said she was possessed of great beauty, with black hair and white skin and a face to tempt a man to sin.

'A stranger came to these shores. One of noble birth, in a ship that anchored off Needles Point and he did what no fisherman, be he master of his own vessel or a humble caster of nets, had ever hoped to do. He enslaved her heart with fine promises and fulsome words. No one knew what took place on the sleek white ship. Maybe after satisfying his own lust, he gave her to the crew, or again perhaps she stumbled across some secret that threatened his safety and so was murdered. But one fact is certain. After his ship had sailed, her body was washed up on to the beach yonder, so mutilated, no man could look upon it unmoved.'

The old man paused, whether to regain his breath or reinforce his imagination, I could not determine, but I nodded and said:

'Very sad. But I wager some variation of that tale is related in every inn along this coast. And now I suppose you will tell me her unhappy shade comes drifting over the rocks on a moonlit night and he who sees it will die within a year and a day.'

The old man shook his head sadly.

'No, sir. We never see her from one year's end to the next. But let a stranger spend one night within the boundaries of this village, then, sir – she comes up from the sea and walks on dry land.'

'For what purpose?' I enquired.

'To show him her face, sir. No man can look upon it without going mad – a singular madness, for he'll run screaming down to the sea and drown himself.'

I called back over one shoulder.

'Patrick, are you willing to risk your sanity for a sight of this lady? I'm thinking she'll have her hands full with the two of us.'

Patrick shrugged and spoke with the familiarity that had come into being over the years.

'If you had any sense you'd do what they say and ride out of here. But if stay you must, then so will I. And I can't see how any wraith can steal our sanity, seeing there's not a spoonful between us.'

I straightened up and put away my pistol.

'So, that's settled. Now in which house do I spend the night?'

The landlord growled like a wounded hound and pointed a shaking forefinger in my direction.

'We wash our hands of you and that black-visaged minion and may Elizabeth Coldwell drive you both to her sea-girt grave. But no man here will give you succour. There's an empty cottage at the far end of the street. Take that and hark you – no one will pay heed to your screams, save maybe to pray for your damned souls.'

'And food?' I asked. 'Surely you will not let us go mad on an empty stomach.'

He nodded, albeit reluctantly.

'Aye, there's victuals for the payment.'

The cottage was unfurnished and had clearly not been lived in for some time, thereby confirming my suspicion that the village was dying. In another ten years the entire place would be merely a collection of deserted houses, breeding dens for any number of wailing ghosts. Patrick had managed to acquire four blankets, how I did not enquire, and these he laid out on the floor, so that I at least could enjoy a modicum of comfort. The landlord had supplied two loaves, a slab of strong cheese and two bottles of wine (at an exorbitant price) and this sparse fare blunted the edge of our appetites while we waited for something to happen.

'Well, Patrick,' I asked, 'do you think we'll pass a peaceful night, or will our inhospitable friends put on a show for our benefit?'

He laid the barrel of his blunderbuss over the sill of the open window and smiled grimly.

'There'll be a few more ghosts around if they try it on. But I'm thinking your lordship's as cracked as an old jug to play a game like this. You were flashing your gold around in there and that's enough reason for us to be quickly dispatched and our bodies thrown to the fishes. And I doubt if your pistol and old Betsy here would do more than account for a few.'

I reflected on his words and shook my head.

'No. They're law-abiding enough, just warped by superstitious fear. And this adventure is one after my own heart, for who can say if there may not be a basis of truth to the old fellow's story. Violent death may leave scars on the road of time.'

'Surely your lordship isn't really expecting a moaning ghost to come up from the sea?'

I pointed to the scene laid out before us.

'From such a setting one must expect anything – or nothing.'

A rough road separated the row of cottages from the beach; from then on there was nothing more than a mass of jutting rocks, over which the incoming tide rolled and retreated, the waves tinted with silver moonlight, while on both sides towering cliffs curved gently inwards to form a vast bay. To our right a long wooden pier had been erected and to this several fishing boats were moored, each one jogging up and down as the waves lapped their black hulls. The scene was bleak, but at the same time not without an element of wild beauty and I pondered on the possibility of building a small retreat on this isolated coast, a place to which I could escape when the mood so took me.

Then a black, seething cloud bank came drifting high up over the east cliff and veiled the face of the moon. I went back to my couch of blankets and yawned.

'Maybe we shall have to content ourselves with hearing the lady, not seeing her.'

Patrick lit a tall tallow candle and cast an uneasy glance at the open window.

'I'd be just as pleased if we did neither. If your lordship cares to sleep, I'll keep watch and maybe take a little walk outside. I'm mindful there's a back entrance to this place and I'd not put it past those spaleens to send their ghost in through the back door.'

I uncorked a bottle and poured a generous measure into a tankard.

'Do what you please. But call out if you catch a glimpse of the vengeful lady. That's not a sight you must keep to yourself.'

I did not intend to sleep, but we had ridden far that day and the wine, though distasteful to the palate, was strong and not conducive to relentless vigilance. How long I slept I have no idea, but I was abruptly hurled back into complete consciousness by the hoarse scream of a man, surely one of the most terrifying sounds on earth. For a moment I sat perfectly still and stared blankly round the bare room, that now seemed to be filled with grotesque leaping shadows, that were trying to put the candle out.

Then my head jerked round and there was the open window, a black square that refused to admit so much as a spark of light and I *knew* – knew with unquestioning certainty – that something – someone – was standing just beyond that splodge of darkness, looking in. And all the while that hoarse scream went on and on, gradually receding, accompanied by the crunch-crunch of pounding feet, until both sounds finally merged with the endless murmur of waves surging over rocks.

But I was wrapped in a mantle of fear that drained the last vestige of warmth from my body and I could only stare at the black screen that was the window, sick to my very soul, knowing that the mere sight of whatever was watching me would shatter my sanity and send me, like poor Patrick, screaming down to the beach to seek oblivion in the restless sea.

The candle flickered and the shadows leapt up the walls, did a mad dance over the ceiling, then froze into terrifying immobility when the wind died and the world seemed to be holding its breath. I caught a suggestion of movement in the window-frame, before I closed my eyes and prayed that I might have the strength of will not to open them again until the danger had passed – if it ever did.

Then – she was there. A few feet to my left; an unseen presence that was as real as the floorboards beneath my trembling legs, the dim candlelight that filtered through my closed eyelids and the fear that held me in its icy grip. But even in the midst of my terror, I realised in some inexplicable way, that that which stood looking down at me was only a part of the being that had perished so long ago – the worst part. A personality fragment that derived some kind of obscene life from undying hate. The arrival of a stranger (or strangers), a disturbing pattern of fresh thought waves, was sufficient to energize something that was neither flesh nor spirit, but possibly formed from the essence of both.

There was a nigh overwhelming urge to open my eyes and satisfy an illogical curiosity. Like a man poised on the top of a high building, who says: 'Let me jump: it's the quickest way down,' so I toyed with the mad notion that to *see* would put an end to horrific conjecture. Might it not be better to go mad suddenly, than to sit for another eight or nine hours of darkness, knowing that something so dreadful, it had sent poor, unimaginative Patrick shrieking down to the sea, was standing a bare two feet to my left, looking down at me.

For let me make one point clear – I knew its exact location, a rough idea of its shape and size and even the manner of its attire. I sensed the likeness of a young woman, some five feet six inches high, with long black hair and dressed in a torn, white gown. Only the face and eyes escaped me, but I realised that here was the crux of the matter. Poor Patrick had seen the face, maybe looked into the eyes – and in an instant became a screaming madman.

After a while I managed to move an arm and felt strangely disappointed when no cold hand tried to restrain me. I digested a tiny scap of knowledge. Quite possibly if I got up and walked it would just follow me – or retreat in front of me – but always careful to keep the face turned towards mine. Walk! Walk out of this room, out of the cottage and not stop until I had reached the confines of the village!

Then surely I would be beyond her jurisdiction. Once I had stepped over the village boundary, I might as well be in London or the wilds of Africa. But I would have to walk with closed eyes, knowing that stark horror accompanied me, and that a stumble or a moment's distraction could result in my seeing the indescribable.

I got up – very, very slowly – and for one moment sensed the face was at a level with my own, then lurched across the room, not daring to put my arms out, lest my hands touch something it was best not to think about. I blundered into a wall, edged my way along it until an open space told me I had reached the doorway, then stumbled out into the narrow passage.

Sound returned when I came to the front door. The sighing wind, the menacing murmur of waves breaking on the rock-girt shore, the distant hoot of an owl. I turned right and, determined now to retain full control of my senses, carefully lowered one foot before raising the other. But – oh, merciful God! – it knew what I was about, for could I not sense it in front, the face all but pressed against my own and once – once – there was the faint suggestion of a cold kiss on my lips, and the merest hint of hands being laid on my shoulders.

Then did I Charles Edward Devereux, Earl of Montcalm, who had often boasted that he feared neither man nor devil, scream out my terror and run with all speed that labouring heart and gasping lungs would permit; eyes tight shut, mouth gaping, unmindful of the brambles that tore at my hands and clothes, the rock that tripped, the low wall that had to be surmounted, for I had the ridiculous notion that my very soul was in peril.

And she – she not it – whimpered like a frustrated child, clutched at my closed eyes with insubstantial hands and finally sent out a long, despairing cry.

Then I collapsed, rolled into a ditch and surrendered to the burning need to open my eyes, at that moment not caring if a dozen sanity-murdering faces were looking down at me, so long as I was permitted one last glimpse of the night sky. My head was below ground level and I could indeed see the sky where clouds were moving away, leaving the moon free to illuminate the surrounding countryside and turn the grey waves to sparkling silver.

After a while I found the courage to stand up and look back towards the row of cottages, and then to the rock-studded beach, and was just in time to see a white figure drift down to the shoreline, before dispersing into a cloud of fast retreating mist.

By luck – or God's mercy – I had stumbled across the village boundary and cheated Elizabeth Coldwell of her second victim.

I returned to the village next morning and was greeted (if that is the right word) by its inhabitants who appeared to view my continued existence as a major miracle. The old man laid a shaking hand on my arm as though to make sure I was still intact then asked in a tremulous voice:

'How did you escape her, sir? Your man was discovered cold and stiff, but an hour since.'

'I closed my eyes,' I answered briefly. 'That which cannot be seen, can be endured. Just. Where have you put my servant?'

I was taken to an outhouse at the back of the inn and looked down upon all that remained of my friend and servant. His face was a mask of frozen terror. I gave the old man two gold coins.

'See that he gets a Christian burial.'

'That we will, sir. Within the hour, lest tonight he too walks on dry land.'

I collected the two horses and rode away, sadder and wiser than when I came, and determined never again to venture forth into isolated places.

But it is an indisputable fact that even to this day, I cannot close my eyes without feeling there is something standing a few feet to my left – watching me.

The Black Cat

EDGAR ALLAN POE

FOR THE MOST WILD, yet most homely narrative which I am about to
pen, I neither expect nor solicit belief. Mad indeed would I be to expect
it, in a case where my very senses reject their own evidence. Yet, mad am
I not – and very surely do I not dream. But to-morrow I die, and to-day
I would unburden my soul. My immediate purpose is to place before the
world, plainly, succinctly, and without comment, a series of mere household events. In their consequences, these events have terrified – have
tortured – have destroyed me. Yet I will not attempt to expound them.
To me, they have presented little but horror – to many they will seem
less terrible than *baroques*. Hereafter, perhaps, some intellect may be
found which will reduce my phantasm to the commonplace – some
intellect more calm, more logical, and far less excitable than my own,
which will perceive, in the circumstances I detail with awe, nothing more
than an ordinary succession of very natural causes and effects.

From my infancy I was noted for the docility and humanity of my
disposition. My tenderness of heart was even so conspicuous as to make
me the jest of my companions. I was especially fond of animals, and was
indulged by my parents with a great variety of pets. With these I spent
most of my time, and never was so happy as when feeding and caressing
them. This peculiarity of character grew with my growth, and, in my
manhood, I derived from it one of my principal sources of pleasure. To
those who have cherished an affection for a faithful and sagacious dog,
I need hardly be at the trouble of explaining the nature or the intensity
of the gratification thus derivable. There is something in the unselfish
and self-sacrificing love of a brute, which goes directly to the heart of
him who has had frequent occasion to test the paltry friendship and
gossamer fidelity of mere *Man*.

I married early, and was happy to find in my wife a disposition not uncongenial with my own. Observing my partiality for domestic pets, she lost no opportunity of procuring those of the most agreeable kind. We had birds, gold-fish, a fine dog, rabbits, a small monkey, and *a cat.*

This latter was a remarkably large and beautiful animal, entirely black, and sagacious to an astonishing degree. In speaking of his intelligence, my wife, who at heart was not a little tinctured with superstition, made frequent allusion to the ancient popular notion, which regarded all black cats as witches in disguise. Not that she was ever *serious* upon this point – and I mention the matter at all for no better reason than that it happens, just now, to be remembered.

Pluto – this was the cat's name – was my favourite pet and playmate. I alone fed him, and he attended me wherever I went about the house. It was even with difficulty that I could prevent him from following me through the streets.

Our friendship lasted, in this manner, for several years, during which my general temperament and character – through the instrumentality of the fiend Intemperance – had (I blush to confess it) experienced a radical alteration for the worse. I grew, day by day, more moody, more irritable, more regardless of the feelings of others. I suffered myself to use intemperate language to my wife. At length, I even offered her personal violence. My pets, of course, were made to feel the change in my disposition. I not only neglected, but ill-used them. For Pluto, however, I still retained sufficient regard to restrain me from maltreating him, as I made no scruple of maltreating the rabbits, the monkey, or even the dog, when by accident, or through affection, they came in my way. But my disease grew upon me – for what disease is like alcohol? – and at length even Pluto, who was now becoming old, and consequently somewhat peevish – even Pluto began to experience the effects of my ill-temper.

One night, returning home, much intoxicated, from one of my haunts about town, I fancied that the cat avoided my presence. I seized him; when, in his fright at my violence, he inflicted a slight wound upon my hand with his teeth. The fury of a demon instantly possessed me. I knew myself no longer. My original soul seemed, at once, to take its flight from my body; and a more than fiendish malevolence, gin-nurtured, thrilled every fibre of my frame. I took from my waistcoat pocket a pen-knife, opened it, grasped the poor beast by the throat, and deliberately cut one of its eyes from the socket! I blush, I burn, I shudder, while I pen the damnable atrocity.

When reason returned with the morning – when I had slept off the fumes of the night's debauch – I experienced a sentiment half of horror, half of remorse, for the crime of which I had been guilty; but it was, at best, a feeble and equivocal feeling, and the soul remained untouched. I again plunged into excess, and soon drowned in wine all memory of the deed.

In the meantime the cat slowly recovered. The socket of the lost eye presented, it is true, a frightful appearance, but he no longer appeared to suffer any pain. He went about the house as usual, but, as might be expected, fled in extreme terror at my approach. I had so much of my old heart left, as to be at first grieved by this evident dislike on the part of a creature which had once so loved me. But this feeling soon gave place to irritation. And then came, as if to my final and irrevocable overthrow, the spirit of PERVERSENESS. Of this spirit philosophy takes no account. Yet I am not more sure that my soul lives, than I am that perverseness is one of the primitive impulses of the human heart – one of the indivisible primary faculties, or sentiments, which give direction to the character of man. Who has not, a hundred times, found himself committing a vile or silly action, for no other reason than because he knows he should *not*? Have we not a perpetual inclination, in the teeth of our best judgment, to violate that which is *Law*, merely because we understand it to be such? This spirit of perverseness, I say, came to my final overthrow. It was this unfathomable longing of the soul *to vex itself* – to offer violence to its own nature – to do wrong for the wrong's sake only – that urged me to continue and finally to consummate the injury I had inflicted upon the unoffending brute. One morning, in cool blood, I slipped a noose about its neck and hung it to the limb of a tree – hung it with the tears streaming from my eyes, and with the bitterest remorse at my heart – hung it *because* I knew that it had loved me, and *because* I felt it had given me no reason of offence – hung it *because* I knew that in so doing I was committing a sin – a deadly sin that would so jeopardise my immortal soul as to place it – if such a thing were possible – even beyond the reach of the infinite mercy of the Most Merciful and Most Terrible God.

On the night of the day on which this cruel deed was done, I was aroused from sleep by the cry of 'Fire!' The curtains of my bed were in flames. The whole house was blazing. It was with great difficulty that my wife, a servant, and myself, made our escape from the conflagration. The destruction was complete. My entire worldly wealth was swallowed up, and I resigned myself thenceforward to despair.

I am above the weakness of seeking to establish a sequence of cause and effect between the disaster and the atrocity. But I am detailing a chain of facts, and wish not to leave even a possible link imperfect. On the day succeeding the fire, I visited the ruins. The walls, with one exception, had fallen in. This exception was found in a compartment wall, not very thick, which stood about the middle of the house, and against which had rested the head of my bed. The plastering had here, in great measure, resisted the action of the fire – a fact which I attributed to its having been recently spread. About this wall a dense crowd were collected, and many persons seemed to be examining a particular portion of it with very minute and eager attention. The words 'strange!' 'singular!' and other similar expressions, excited my curiosity. I approached and saw, as if graven in bas-relief upon the white surface, the figure of a gigantic *cat*. The impression was given with an accuracy truly marvellous. There was a rope about the animal's neck.

When I first beheld this apparition – for I could scarcely regard it as less – my wonder and my terror were extreme. But at length reflection came to my aid. The cat, I remembered, had been hung in a garden adjacent to the house. Upon the alarm of fire, this garden had been immediately filled by the crowd – by some one of whom the animal must have been cut from the tree and thrown, through an open window, into my chamber. This had probably been done with the view of arousing me from sleep. The falling of other walls had compressed the victim of my cruelty into the substance of the freshly-spread plaster; the lime of which, with the flames and the *ammonia* from the carcass, had then accomplished the portraiture as I saw it.

Although I thus readily accounted to my reason, if not altogether to my conscience, for the startling fact just detailed, it did not the less fail to make a deep impression upon my fancy. For months I could not rid myself of the phantasm of the cat; and, during this period, there came back into my spirit a half-sentiment that seemed, but was not, remorse. I went so far as to regret the loss of the animal, and to look about me, among the vile-haunts which I now habitually frequented, for another pet of the same species, and of somewhat similar appearance, with which to supply its place.

One night as I sat, half-stupefied, in a den of more than infamy, my attention was suddenly drawn to some black object, reposing upon the head of one of the immense hogsheads of gin, or of rum, which constituted the chief furniture of the apartment. I had been looking steadily at the top of this hogshead for some minutes, and what now caused me surprise was the fact that I had not sooner perceived the object thereupon. I approached it, and touched it with my hand. It was a black cat – a very large one – fully as large as Pluto, and closely resembling him in every respect but one. Pluto had not a white hair upon any portion of his body; but this cat had a large, although indefinite, splotch of white, covering nearly the whole region of the breast.

Upon my touching him, he immediately arose, purred loudly, rubbed against my hand, and appeared delighted with my notice. This, then, was the very creature of which I was in search. I at once offered to purchase it of the landlord; but this person made no claim to it – knew nothing of it – had never seen it before.

I continued my caresses, and when I prepared to go home, the animal evinced a disposition to accompany me. I permitted it to do so; occasionally stooping and patting it as I proceeded. When it reached the house it domesticated itself at once, and became immediately a great favourite with my wife.

For my own part, I soon found a dislike to it arising within me. This was just the reverse of what I had anticipated; but – I know not how or why it was – its evident fondness for myself rather disgusted and annoyed me. By slow degrees, these feelings of disgust and annoyance rose into the bitterness of hatred. I avoided the creature; a certain sense of shame, and the remembrance of my former deed of cruelty, preventing me from physically abusing it. I did not, for some weeks, strike, or otherwise violently ill-use it; but gradually – very gradually – I came to look upon it with unutterable loathing, and to flee silently from its odious presence, as from the breath of a pestilence.

What added, no doubt, to my hatred of the beast, was the discovery, on the morning after I brought it home, that, like Pluto, it also had been deprived of one of its eyes. This circumstance, however, only endeared it to my wife, who, as I have already said, possessed, in a high degree, that humanity of feeling which had once been my distinguishing trait, and the source of many of my simplest and purest pleasures.

With my aversion to this cat, however, its partiality for myself seemed to increase. It followed my footsteps with a pertinacity which it would be difficult to make the reader comprehend. Whenever I sat, it would crouch beneath my chair, or spring upon my knees, covering me with its loathsome caresses. If I arose to walk, it would get between my feet, and thus nearly throw me down, or, fastening its long and sharp claws in my dress, clamber, in this manner, to my breast. At such times, although I longed to destroy it with a blow, I was yet withheld from so doing, partly by a memory of my former crime, but chiefly – let me confess it at once – by absolute *dread* of the beast.

This dread was not exactly a dread of physical evil – and yet I should be at a loss how otherwise to define it. I am almost ashamed to own – yes, even in this felon's cell, I am almost ashamed to own – that the terror and horror with which the animal inspired me, had been heightened by one of the merest chimeras it would be possible to conceive. My wife had called my attention, more than once, to the character of the mark of white hair, of which I have spoken, and which constituted the sole visible difference between the strange beast and the one I had destroyed. The reader will remember that this mark, although large, had been originally very indefinite; but, by slow degrees – degrees nearly imperceptible, and which for a long time my reason struggled to reject as fanciful – it had, at length, assumed a rigorous distinctness of outline. It was now the representation of an object that I shudder to name – and for this, above all, I loathed, and dreaded, and would have rid myself of the monster *had I dared* – it was now, I say, the image of a hideous – of a ghastly thing – of the GALLOWS! – oh, mournful and terrible engine of horror and of crime – of agony and of death!

374

And now was I indeed wretched beyond the wretchedness of mere humanity. And *a brute beast* – whose fellow I had contemptuously destroyed – *a brute beast* to work out for *me* – for me, a man, fashioned in the image of the High God – so much of insufferable woe! Alas! neither by day nor by night knew I the blessing of rest any more! During the former the creature left me no moment alone; and, in the latter, I started, hourly, from dreams of unutterable fear, to find the hot breath of *the thing* upon my face, and its vast weight – an incarnate nightmare that I had no power to shake off – incumbent eternally upon my *heart*!

Beneath the pressure of torments such as these, the feeble remnant of the good within me succumbed. Evil thoughts became my sole intimates – the darkest and most evil of thoughts. The moodiness of my usual temper increased to hatred of all things and of all mankind; while, from the sudden, frequent, and ungovernable outbursts of a fury to which I now blindly abandoned myself, my uncomplaining wife, alas! was the most usual and the most patient of sufferers.

One day she accompanied me, upon some household errand, into the cellar of the old building which our poverty compelled us to inhabit. The cat followed me down the steep stairs, and, nearly throwing me headlong, exasperated me to madness. Uplifting an axe, and forgetting, in my wrath, the childish dread which had hitherto stayed my hand, I aimed a blow at the animal which, of course, would have proved instantly fatal had it descended as I wished. But this blow was arrested by the hand of my wife. Goaded, by the interference, into a rage more than demoniacal, I withdrew my arm from her grasp, and buried the axe in her brain. She fell dead upon the spot, without a groan.

This hideous murder accomplished, I set myself forthwith, and with entire deliberation, to the task of concealing the body. I knew that I could not remove it from the house, either by day or by night, without the risk of being observed by the neighbours. Many projects entered my mind. At one period I thought of cutting the corpse into minute fragments and destroying them by fire. At another, I resolved to dig a grave for it in the floor of the cellar. Again, I deliberated about casting it into the well in the yard – about packing it in a box, as if merchandise, with the usual arrangements, and so getting a porter to take it from the house. Finally I hit upon what I considered a far better expedient than either of these. I determined to wall it up in the cellar – as the monks of the Middle Ages are recorded to have walled up their victims.

For a purpose such as this the cellar was well adapted. Its walls were loosely constructed, and had lately been plastered throughout with a rough plaster, which the dampness of the atmosphere had prevented from hardening. Moreover, in one of the walls was a projection, caused by a false chimney, or fire-place, that had been filled up and made to resemble the rest of the cellar. I made no doubt that I could readily displace the bricks at this point, insert the corpse, and wall the whole up as before, so that no eye could detect anything suspicious.

And in this calculation I was not deceived. By means of a crowbar I easily dislodged the bricks, and, having carefully deposited the body against the inner wall, I propped it in that position, while, with little trouble, I relaid the whole structure as it originally stood. Having procured mortar, sand, and hair, with every possible precaution, I prepared a plaster which could not be distinguished from the old, and with this I very carefully went over the new brickwork. When I had finished, I felt satisfied that all was right. The wall did not present the slightest appearance of having been disturbed. The rubbish on the floor was picked up with the minutest care. I looked around trimphantly, and said to myself, 'Here at least, then, my labour has not been in vain.'

My next step was to look for the beast which had been the cause of so much wretchedness; for I had, at length, firmly resolved to put it to death. Had I been able to meet with it at the moment, there could have been no doubt of its fate; but it appeared that the crafty animal had been alarmed at the violence of my previous anger, and forbore to present itself in my present mood. It is impossible to describe, or to imagine, the deep, the blissful sense of relief which the absence of the detested creature occasioned in my bosom. It did not make its appearance during the night – and thus for one night at least, since its introduction into the house, I soundly and tranquilly slept; aye, *slept* even with the burden of murder upon my soul!

The second and third day passed, and still my tormentor came not. Once again I breathed as a free man. The monster, in terror, had fled the premises for ever! I should behold it no more! My happiness was supreme! The guilt of my dark deed disturbed me but little. Some few inquiries had been made, but these had been readily answered. Even a search had been instituted – but of course nothing was to be discovered. I looked upon my future felicity as secured.

Upon the fourth day of the assassination, a party of the police came, very unexpectedly, into the house, and proceeded again to make rigorous investigation of the premises. Secure, however, in the inscrutability of my place of concealment, I felt no embarrassment whatever. The officers bade me accompany them in their search. They left no nook or corner unexplored. At length, for the third or fourth time, they descended into the cellar. I quivered not in a muscle. My heart beat calmly as that of one who slumbers in innocence. I walked the cellar from end to end. I folded my arms upon my bosom, and roamed easily to and fro. The police were thoroughly satisfied, and prepared to depart. The glee at my heart was too strong to be restrained. I burned to say if but one word, by way of triumph, and to render doubly sure their assurance of my guiltlessness.

'Gentlemen,' I said at last, as the party ascended the steps, 'I delight to have allayed your suspicions. I wish you all health, and a little more courtesy. By-the-bye, gentlemen, this – this is a very well-constructed house.' (In the rabid desire to say something easily, I scarcely knew what I uttered at all.) 'I may say an *excellently* well-constructed house. These walls – are you going, gentlemen? – these walls are solidly put together'; and here, through the mere frenzy of bravado, I rapped heavily, with a cane which I held in my hand, upon that very portion of the brickwork behind which stood the corpse of the wife of my bosom.

But may God shield and deliver me from the fangs of the Arch-Fiend! No sooner had the reverberation of my blows sunk into silence, than I was answered by a voice from within the tomb! – by a cry, at first muffled and broken, like the sobbing of a child, and then quickly swelling into one long, loud, and continuous scream, utterly anomalous and inhuman – a howl – a wailing shriek, half of horror and half of triumph, such as might have arisen only out of hell, conjointly from the throats of the damned in their agony and of the demons that exult in the damnation.

Of my own thoughts it is folly to speak. Swooning, I staggered to the opposite wall. For one instant the party upon the stairs remained motionless, through extremity of terror and of awe. In the next, a dozen stout arms were toiling at the wall. It fell bodily. The corpse, already greatly decayed and clotted with gore, stood erect before the eyes of the spectators. Upon its head, with red extended mouth and solitary eye of fire, sat the hideous beast whose craft had seduced me into murder, and whose informing voice had consigned me to the hangman. I had walled the monster up within the tomb!

Acknowledgments

The Publishers gratefully acknowledge permission granted by the following to reprint the copyright material included in this volume:

The Shout by Robert Graves. Reprinted by permission of the Author and A. P. Watt Ltd.

Mrs Amworth by E. F. Benson. Reprinted by permission of the Estate of the late E. F. Benson and A. P. Watt Ltd.

The Night the Ghost Got In by James Thurber. From 'My Life and Hard Times', published in Great Britain by Hamish Hamilton Ltd., © the Collection copyright 1963; published in the United States by Harper & Row Inc., copr., © 1933, 1961 James Thurber. Reprinted by permission of the Publishers and Mrs James Thurber.

Io by Oliver Onions. Reprinted by permission of the Estate of the late George Oliver and A. P. Watt Ltd.

Fever Dream by Ray Bradbury. Copyright © 1948 by Weird Tales, © renewed 1975 by Ray Bradbury. Reprinted by permission of the Harold Matson Company, Inc.

The Inexperienced Ghost by H. G. Wells. Reprinted by permission of the Estate of the late H. G. Wells and A. P. Watt Ltd.

The Mirror of Galadriel by J. R. R. Tolkien. From 'The Fellowship of the Ring', published in Great Britain by George Allen & Unwin (Publishers) Ltd.; published in the United States by Houghton Mifflin Company, copyright © 1965 by J. R. R. Tolkien. Reprinted by permission of the Publishers.

Lost Hearts by M. R. James. From 'The Collected Short Stories of M. R. James', published by Edward Arnold (Publishers) Ltd. Reprinted by permission of the Publishers.

The Overcoat by Nikolai Gogol. From Gogol: 'Diary of a Madman and Other Stories', trans. Ronald Wilks (Penguin Classics, 1972) pp. 71–108; this translation copyright © Ronald Wilks, 1972. Reprinted by permission of Penguin Books Ltd.